I packed my bag that night, and in the morning Gracie held onto my leg, her arms wrapped like an anchor, and I had to prise her free.

My mum was in the kitchen, Dad had already gone to work.

"Bye," I said, and as Mum looked up she seemed to blink something out of her yees before whispering, astonished and afraid, "Who are you?"

"I'm Hope's friend," I answered. "I was just staying the night."

Silence.

My mum, frozen in the kitchen door, broken egg shell oozing clear juice between her fingers.

"Who's Hope?"

"Goodbye," I said, and let myself out into the morning.

Praise for

THE NOVELS OF CLAIRE NORTH

The Sudden Appearance of Hope

"North...has established a reputation for tense, dense, science fiction/fantasy-inflected thrillers that defy facile expectations.... Simultaneously a tense conspiracy caper, a haunting meditation on loneliness and a brutally cynical examination of modern media.... Well-paced, brilliant and balanced."

—*New York Times*

"Beautifully written, with a protagonist who is both tragic and heroic, the novel is remarkably powerful and deeply memorable, the latest in a string of terrific books from this newly emerged star in the genre-blending universe."

—*Booklist* (Starred Review)

"This is an inquiry into modern human existence. Philosophical questions are threaded through the electrifying plot. Even the protagonist's darkness alias is 'why.' Reminiscent of William Gibson's best work, North leads us into a brilliant world of elite but mindless humans, and shines a sharp light on what a rare gift it is to be able to think for oneself and what the consequences of it are."

—*RT Book Reviews*

"Claire North's *The Sudden Appearance of Hope* is a novel with an argument to make about smartphone apps and online identity....North isn't here to lecture you or rehash tired debates. Instead, she's produced something that feels at the same time absent and necessary: Smart, compelling fiction about this future that asks us to outsource ever-larger chunks of our selves to the cloud."

—*Tech Insider*

"Claire North novels are...progressive and introspective—as chilling, invariably, as they are thrilling—and *The Sudden Appearance of Hope* is no exception." —Tor.com

"To me, the thing that's perhaps the most sinister about Perfection isn't that it offers you plastic surgery. But rather the way that the app decides what Perfection actually is. Instead of finding out what you want, and helping you achieve it, Perfection decides what you should want." —*Flash Forward*

"It's intricate, but somehow, once again Claire North makes it all work.... A fantastic read featuring a unique protagonist with a unique problem...definitely worth remembering."

—*Kirkus*

Touch

"*Touch* is a brilliantly balanced knife's edge of a book—fast-paced and thrilling, it's somehow also languorous, thoughtful, intelligently intimate. Kepler is a thoroughly absorbing and sympathetic anti-hero, trying to minimize harm while striving for survival....I am left staggered into an awed slow-clap at everything North has accomplished here. *Touch* is touching, horrifying, magnificent; step into it, and it will step into you."

—*NPR Books*

"The high stakes and breakneck pace of the plot will draw readers in, and the meditations on what it means to be human and to be loved will linger long after the last shot is fired."

—*Kirkus*

"As masterful as her debut...[A] fast-paced, imaginative novel.... There is plenty of conspiracy and intrigue in this deftly paced novel, but North also poses subtle questions about identity and love." —*Washington Post*

"This novel is utterly engaging, addictive, and thought-provoking. The characters are superbly drawn, their interactions realistic and engaging."

—*Civilian Reader*

"Another thrilling leap into the unknown."

—*Toronto Sunday Star*

"Little short of a masterpiece."

—*Independent* (UK)

The First Fifteen Lives of Harry August

"I don't say this lightly but *The First Fifteen Lives of Harry August* is one of the top ten books I've ever read."

—James Dashner, *New York Times* and *USA Today* bestselling author of *The Maze Runner*

"An astonishing re-invention of the time travel narrative. Bold, magical and masterful."

—M. R. Carey

"A thoughtful and considered time-travel novel, shocking twists and, most important of all, a beautiful character. Harry August will break your heart fifteen times."

—Jared Shurin

"A subtle study of friendship, love and the complexity of existence."

—Eric Brown, *Guardian*

"Fantastic."

—*io9*

"Wonderful novel...held together by a compelling mystery involving nothing less than the end of the world itself. Beautifully written and structured...a remarkable book."

—*Booklist* (Starred Review)

"A tremendously entertaining ride...You're sure to enjoy the trip."

—*Toronto Sunday Star*

THE SUDDEN APPEARANCE OF HOPE

By Claire North

The First Fifteen Lives of Harry August

Touch

The Sudden Appearance of Hope

The End of the Day

THE GAMESHOUSE NOVELLAS

The Serpent (e-only)

The Thief (e-only)

The Master (e-only)

MATTHEW SWIFT NOVELS

(writing as Kate Griffin)

A Madness of Angels

The Midnight Mayor

The Neon Court

The Minority Council

MAGICALS ANONYMOUS NOVELS

(writing as Kate Griffin)

Stray Souls

The Glass God

THE SUDDEN APPEARANCE OF HOPE

CLAIRE NORTH

www.redhookbooks.com

Cover design by Duncan Spilling – LBBG
Cover illustration by Plainpicture/Mohamad Itani

Redhook Books/Orbit
Hachette Book Group
1290 Avenue of the Americas
New York, NY 10104
hachettebookgroup.com

Originally published in Great Britain and in the U.S. by Orbit in 2016
First Trade Paperback Edition: January 2017

Redhook is an imprint of Orbit, a division of Hachette Book Group.
The Redhook name and logo are trademarks of Hachette Book Group, Inc.

Additional copyright/credits information is on page 469.

Library of Congress Control Number: 2016932294 (hardcover)

ISBNs: 978-0-316-33599-7 (hardcover), 978-0-316-33596-6 (trade paperback), 978-0-316-33597-3 (ebook)

Printed in the United States of America

LSC-C

10 9 8 7 6 5 4 3 2 1

Chapter 1

They said, when they died, that all they could hear was the screaming.

I run ink across the page, watch the world through the windows of the train, grey clouds over Scotland, and though the screaming continues still, it does not bother me. Not any more.

I write this to be remembered. Will you judge me, in reading this? Who are you? Liar, cheat, lover, thief, husband, wife, mother, daughter, friend, enemy, policeman, doctor, teacher, child, killer, priest? I find myself almost more excited by you than I am by myself, whoever you might be.

Whoever you are: these are my words.

This is my truth.

Listen, and remember me.

Chapter 2

The world began to forget me when I was sixteen years old.

A slow declining, one piece at a time.

My dad, forgetting to drive me to school.

My mum, setting the table for three, not four. "Oh," she said, when I walked in. "I must have thought you were out."

A teacher, Miss Tomas, the only one in the school who cared, full of faith in her pupils, hope for their futures, forgets to chase the missing homework, to ask the questions, to listen to the answers, until, finally, I didn't bother to put up my hand.

Friends, five who were the heart of my life, who I always sat with, and who one day sat at another table, not dramatically, not with "fuck you" flair, but because they looked straight through me and saw a stranger.

A disassociation between name and face as the register is called. My name is remembered, but the link is broken; what is Hope Arden? A scrawl of ink without a past; no more.

First you forget my face, then my voice, and at last, slowly, you forget my consequences. I slapped Alan, my best mate, the day he forgot me. He ran from the room, horrified, and I ran after him, red with guilt. By the time I found him, he was sitting in the corridor of the science block, cheek flushed, rubbing at his face.

"You okay?" I asked.

"Yeah," he replied. "Face hurts a bit."

"I'm sorry."

"It's okay; not like you did nothing."

He looked at me like a stranger, but there were tears in his eyes when he spoke. What did he remember then? Not me, not Hope Arden, the girl he'd grown up with. Not my palm across his face, not my screaming until the spit flew, *remember me, remember me.* His pain was diminishing, taking with it memory. He experienced sorrow, rage, fear, these emotions glimmered in his eyes, but where were they from? He no longer knew, and the memory of me crumbled like sand castles before the sea.

Chapter 3

This is not a story of being forgotten.

As memory of me faded, so did a part of myself. Whoever that Hope Arden is who laughs with her friends, smiles with her family, flirts with her lover, resents her boss, triumphs with her colleagues – she ceased to exist, and it has been surprising for me to discover just how little of me is left behind, when all that is stripped away.

If words on the page are the only part of me that can be remembered, and I am to write something which will survive when I am gone, it should matter.

A story of Perfection, then.

For you, it begins in Venice. That was certainly the first time the world became aware of what it was. But for me, and the part I was to play in it, the story began earlier, in Dubai, the day Reina bint Badr al Mustakfi killed herself in her hotel room on the seventh floor of the Burj al Arab Jumeirah.

Because the room cost £830 a night, and because it was clearly a suicide and thus a social faux pas, the body was rushed out of the service door within hours of discovery. A Nepalese cleaning lady was sent in to scrub at the worst of the stains, but Reina had been helpful in slitting her femoral artery in a hot bath, and thus only a few towels and the bath mat needed to be burned.

I found out she was dead because her cousin, Leena, kept on screaming. Not crying – just screaming. In later tellings of these events, she would not say the words, "My cousin Reina killed herself, and this is why" but instead, "My cousin Reina killed herself, and I've never recovered from the blow."

I didn't like Leena much. It made it a lot easier to steal from her.

I liked Reina. She didn't know that we were friends, but that's okay – I don't mind these things.

I broke into the morgue where they'd taken Reina's body, a false name on the tag around her toe, skin as grey as the steel bed she lay on. I riffled through the clothes they'd stripped from her, flicked through a notebook of curious ideas and comments on passers-by, found myself in the descriptions there: *Woman, skin like milk in coffee, deep, diluted. Pink headscarf, very close-trimmed nails, stands tall, bag in her left hand, looks at everyone without shame, doesn't care that people stare.*

I took the notebook, pressed it against my heart, then put it in my pocket, a thing to cherish and keep safe.

Her phone was in a clear plastic bag by her shoes, and the unlock code was easy to guess by the oily stain her fingers had left as she swiped across the screen. I took it, and sat on the steps of the morgue in the burning shade, flicking through messages and emails, looking for something cruel or a cry of pain to explain why Reina was now cold in the quiet building at my back.

I only found Perfection because it flashed a notification at me.

> It's been forty-eight hours since you last hit the gym – that body won't become perfect by wishing!

An app, running in the background on her phone.

> Careful what you buy today – that last shop took you over your recommended saturated fat levels for the day! Do you know that saturated fat is a leading cause of cardiac problems?

What the hell kinda app was this?

I opened it, curious.

> Make the perfect you.

The interface was simple, streamlined. There would be no accessorising, no customisation.

> Perfection is real. Perfection is now.

A policeman came up to me, asked me if I was lost. I closed the mobile phone, put it in my pocket, smiled and said no, sorry, just came over dizzy.

He said, gently and calm, "Every human grief you will ever experience has been experienced by humans living and humans yet to come. There is no readiness for it, nor no easing of the pain, but ma'am, for what it's worth, I think you should know that all of humanity that was, is and will be is with you now, by your side."

I smiled and thanked him and ran away before he could see me start to cry.

That night, lying on my belly in the hotel, sea below, dust above, I signed up for Perfection.

I gave it a fake name, a dead email address knocked together in a café.

By joining, I automatically earned five hundred points; enough for $5 off a vitamin drink from an endorsed brand. It pinged my location off the wireless, had my position within five metres, found a health-food drink store within half a mile that would accept my voucher.

> Advance faster – link your life.

It asked for a photo of me. I supplied a photo of a stranger, lifted from Facebook.

From this, it informed me that I had a wonderful body, but it could be made perfect.

> Consider switching your diet – here are some tips.
>
> Find the perfect exercise for you!

A questionnaire. I filled it out, and was informed that the perfect exercise for me was medium-distance athletics. A list of suitable trainers was supplied, along with the points value that I would win by signing up with any one of these Perfection-certified clubs.

> Link your life, it reminded me. Make the perfect you.

It asked me for my bank details.

> By giving this application access to your financial records and spending, Perfection can see the true you. Make your career and lifestyle habits perfect, with customised advice for you.

I refused to input the data, and when I checked again the next morning, I'd lost two hundred points.

> Perfection is hard, it said. The power is within you.

I closed the app and restricted its access to my phone.

Chapter 4

Things that are difficult, when the world forgets you:

- Dating
- Getting a job
- Receiving consistent medical attention
- Getting a loan
- Certificated education
- Getting a reference
- Getting service at restaurants

Things that are easy, when the world forgets you:

- Assassination
- Theft
- Espionage

- Casual cruelty
- Angst-free one-night stands (w/condoms)
- Not tipping

For a while after I'd been forgotten, I toyed with becoming a hitman. I pictured myself in leather jump suits, taking down my targets with a sniper rifle, my dark hair billowing in the wind. No cop could catch me; no one would know my name. I was sixteen years old, and had peculiar ideas about "cool".

Then I did some research, and found that a contract killing can be bought for €5,000, and the majority of people who worked in the field were brutal men in nylon tracksuits. There were almost certainly no glamorous women slipping a vial of something into the villain's drink; no cocktail parties where spies exchanged cryptic understandings, no goddess of death, no woman of mystery. Only a flash of brutality in the dark, and the smell of tyres on tar.

Later, as I hunkered down in my sleeping bag beneath the library stairs, I closed my eyes and wondered how I had come to the conclusion that murder was acceptable. In my predicament, deprived of family and hope, I already knew that crime was how I would survive, but did that mean human life had lost its sanctity? I pictured killing a stranger, and found it was easier than killing a friend. Then I slept, and in my dreams men beat me, and I tried to hit them back, and couldn't, my arm frozen in the air, my body powerless.

Do it, do it, do it, screamed my slumbering mind. *Do it! Do it! DO IT!*

And still I didn't move, and when I woke in the morning, I found someone had pissed on the end of my sleeping bag.

Chapter 5

Have you got Perfection?

Memories – do I need to explain what went before, to explain myself? Perhaps. There is a word Reina sometimes used – pilgrimage.

Pilgrimage: a journey made for exalted reasons.

A holy act.

And then again, Google search: *Pilgrimage is*

- ➔ *out of date*
- ➔ *a waste of time and money*
- ➔ *still important*

Have you got Perfection, she asked, and where was this?

Dubai, a few days before Reina died. A hotel on an artificial island; the Burj al Arab Jumeirah. When I walked in, a man offered me a chilled hand towel, a woman offered me dates in a golden plate, the receptionist asked if I'd be wanting one of the hotel's Bentleys. £650 bought you the cheapest room for a night, but for so little, your private butler might be a touch rude, and you didn't get access to the VIP lounge. Is this where it begins? I think it is.

"Have you got Perfection?" Leena asked, and behind her, Reina sighed. "The CEO is coming to Dubai. We've got a thriving investment market here; you wouldn't think companies like that needed investment, but something like Perfection, it's going to go global, it's going to go mega, I know, it's changed my life! I'm going to get treatments!"

Five women on couches in the spa, the sea blue as the morning sky, the midday sky white as the midnight moon, filling the windows all around. Drinks in multicoloured layers brought in by Bangladeshi women with bright smiles, bowed heads. Of the five of us being served, only two were from Dubai, a princess something-something-of-somewhere with flawless English and her cousin Reina, who perhaps wasn't a princess but it was hard to tell, who blogged about social reform and women's rights and was, according to Leena:

"Wonderful, isn't she just wonderful, but I do wish she was a little more . . . well, you know . . . "

A gesture, taking in the silent figure of Reina, who unlike the rest of us is wearing a swimsuit, not a bikini, and lies on her couch with laptop open, brows tight against the top of her nose.

"Treatments destroy your soul," replied Reina quietly from her laptop, not looking up. "Treatments destroy who you are."

"Darling," exclaimed Leena, "some of us see that as a good thing."

Now Reina's gaze snapped up, met her cousin's, held, turned away. "I just want to be myself," she murmured.

"But is that good enough?" Leena mused, "Or is it just selfish?' I went to sit by Reina's side, asked what she was working on while the others relaxed around her.

"This is my jihad," replied Reina, not looking up from her laptop. "This is my pilgrimage."

Jihad: to struggle. To strive in the way of God.

I've always liked knowledge. It makes me feel like I'm real, part of something after all.

"Yesterday the police arrested a fourteen-year-old girl accused of sex outside marriage with an ice-cream vendor," Reina mused, speaking to the computer, having learned long ago that no one else would listen to her. "He raped her, and will be deported. She is going to prison for adultery. I cannot accept that the rights of women are culturally relative."

"You see!" exclaimed Leena, rolling on her couch so that the Filipino woman applying her platinum-metal body tattoo could reach the back of her neck. "Reina's just so . . . so . . . well isn't she just!"

*

"Have you got Perfection?"

An American woman, Suzy or Sandy or Sophie or something of that sort, who lay, back bare, chin down as thin pieces of gold foil were delicately brushed onto her skin, creating swirls and curves of thousand-dollar colour that followed the contours of her perfectly scrubbed, perfectly tanned, perfectly toned, perfect flesh.

I leant over from my couch to see what she was talking about.

"It's an app," she explained, turning for me to look. "A life-coaching tool, a way to make a better you. You sign up, give it access to your data, and it helps you get better!"

"What kind of data?" I asked.

"Oh, everything, really. Loyalty cards, air miles, online shopping, bank accounts. The more information it has, the better it can help you. Like, when I first signed up, I took a picture of myself and it was able to tell me my height, weight, shoe size, the lot – it's clever, just so clever. And I was overweight then, I mean – well, I won't tell you! – but it found better menus for me, good trainers, because that's what matters, isn't it? And every time you reach a goal, like, getting to your perfect weight or buying the perfect shoes from an in-app retailer, you get points, and after a number of points you get a subscription-linked experience!"

"What kind of experience?"

"Oh, just amazing, amazing. At five thousand I got a free haircut at Pike and Ion, it was sensational, they just understand hair. At ten thousand I got three hundred dollars of spending money to use at the SpringYou outlet at the mall, *three hundred*! I couldn't believe it, but of course, the app knew what I bought, and just by buying the right clothes I got an automatic five-hundred-point bonus. I'm at fifty-two thousand points now, and can't wait to see what the next unlock is."

I smiled and said it sounded wonderful, amazing, how I could use something like that in my life.

"You should get it!" she exclaimed. "You're so pretty already, with just a bit of work you could be perfect too!"

I smiled. This was my third day in the company of these women, and the first time they'd ever met me. I was good at being obliging.

And that evening,

"Do you have Perfection?" I asked Reina, as we ran together in the women-only gym, headscarves discarded, sweat clumping in our hair.

"Yes," she mused. "I do. It's something my family might invest in."

"Is it as good as people say it is?"

"I . . . suppose it could be."

"You don't sound convinced."

"It . . . Leena made me sign up, she told me I was . . . do you know how sometimes people say words and they should be terrible, but because you know the people and the way they say it, they aren't? Only of course," she added, "they are really."

"What words?" I asked.

"Oh, the usual. Fat. Frumpy. Boring. Unattractive to men. Dull at parties. Frigid. Of course it shouldn't matter, those are her things, not mine."

> Hi – are you sure this is the right restaurant for you? Here's our list of recommended, Perfection-guaranteed suppliers!

We kept running. Then she said, "I used to think that it was okay just to be liked for being me."

I nearly laughed, but there was such sadness in her eyes, and I was out of breath, so I didn't. Instead, "People who see who you are like you for you, I'm sure of it."

She smiled, and looked away, and we didn't talk again that night.

Chapter 6

Why had I come to Dubai?

Specifically: to rob the royal family. My target was the Chrysalis diamond, the centrepiece of a necklace created in 1912 for Afise Lakerba, wife of Mehmed VI, the last Ottoman Sultan. When the monarchy was abolished, the jewels went on a romp through the auction houses of the world, owned at various stages by petrochemical giants, Hollywood starlets and the wife of the President of Colombia before, made infinitely more valuable by its history, returning to the Middle East via Leena's aunt, Shamma bint Bandar, one of nearly four thousand royal scions of the House of Saudi.

Why those diamonds?

Because three separate teams had all made passes at them in the last five years, and failed. Their failure meant two things: a challenge and a buyer.

It's easy, in my position, to be amateurish about these things. I find the buzz is greater when the puzzle fits together. On a whim, I once stole the President of Paraguay's wrist-watch, but it only fetched $250 and the buzz was nothing compared to the day I stole £98,000 in a casino heist that went off flawlessly, the most perfect execution of a beautiful plan, months in the making. You make your own highs in my line of work.

Shamma bint Bandar was coming to Dubai to party and celebrate with the makers of Perfection, and with her came the Chrysalis.

Leena was my way in, but as I circled round her, I found Reina ever more distracting.

"We haven't met yet," I told Reina, the fourth time we went running together. "My name is Rachel Donovan."

And again, "We haven't met yet," I said, as we sat down

together to listen to a recital of Syrian folk music in a bar beneath the hotel. "But I'm so very pleased to meet you."

"I am part of an important family, in a way," she explained with a sigh, as we shared mango served on a bed of crushed ice. "But in this place that doesn't mean anything. I'm trying to be better."

"Better at what?"

"At everything. Better at talking to people. Better at learning, understanding, at expressing myself and understanding others. Better looking, better thinking, just . . . better. It is a good thing to strive for, no?"

> Have you considered buying any of these life-changing magazines? Read inspirational stories of women who found their Perfect Lives!

"Yes. I think it is."

"I keep a blog."

"I think I've read it."

"Have you? Not many have – I should cherish you. Too many voices all at once on the internet, screaming, just all the time screaming, sometimes it's hard to be heard. Sometimes I think that the world is full of screaming."

I said . . . something. Something flat, trying to find better words, good words like the woman eating mango with Reina bint Badr al Mustakfi should have said, but somehow, in the course of our talking, I'd slipped out of character, and only Hope Arden remained, and she had very little to say for herself.

"I thought for a while that I would fight to find my place," mused Reina, staring at nothing much. "Now I just want to be happy where I am."

The next day she was dead.

I copied her emails onto my computer; threw her mobile phone into the sea.

Emails from her parents, worrying about her. From a couple of friends, hoping she was well, pictures of happy families, children growing up, isn't it wonderful?

From activist groups campaigning for civil rights, immigrant rights, environmental responsibility, legal reform, etc.

From Perfection itself, an automatically generated reminder.

> We see that you've been falling behind on your beauty and retail regime, it said. You have lost 400 points in the last week. Remember: perfection is in the mind as well as the body. Only you can chose to be perfect. Here are some inspirational stories of perfect people from the 106, to help encourage you to get back on track.

A link – pictures, men, women. Beautiful – all of them beautiful. Teeth, hair, lips, smiles, chests, breasts.

Antonyms of frigid: amicable, lovable, responsive, hot, amorous.

I read through to the end of her little handwritten notebook.

Leena is happy, she wrote. *She is incredibly happy. She is stupid, and lazy, and spoilt, and dull, and perhaps at some time knew it, and then found a way to forget that she knew anything at all. I thought maybe her confidence was just a screen, a shield to protect herself from her own sorrow, but now I see that the surface is the truth, the depths are the surfaces.*

I ate a meal yesterday by myself, but when I looked at the bill I saw there were two meals ordered, and I hadn't paid.

Today, Perfection sent me pictures of a model at a wedding, to remind me of what I could be. When she fucks a guy, does he scream in ecstasy when he comes? Does she? I think I am meant to think that she does.

The screaming is loud tonight. It's so very loud.

Those were her last words. I sat by the sea and watched the waves for an hour, then two. I wondered if she would be pleased, knowing that someone was thinking of her. I wondered if she'd be happy, given what I intended to do. I hoped she would be, and after much thought, I burned her notebook, and scattered the ashes into the sea.

Chapter 7

Types of theft: mugging, pickpocketing, smash-and-grab, auto-theft, burglary, the long con, the quick graft, forgery, identity theft, shoplifting, fencing, embezzlement, larceny, looting, stealing, filching.

Actus reus: guilty act.

Mens reus: guilty mind.

An innocent woman may perform actus reus when she picks up another woman's handbag by mistake. A guilty woman has mens reus when she does so deliberately. One may be a civil liability; only with both does the matter come before a criminal court.

I didn't want to be a thief.

My dad was a copper; he met me a few times down the station. Most people were there for things done while drunk, high or desperate. One, a drug dealer, grinned as they took his fingerprints, and laughed at the sergeant and called him "mate" and said, "It won't go nowhere, you'll see!" and he was right, and waved as he left the station, "Better luck next time, mate," gold link necklace around his throat, grubby sneakers on his feet.

The only thief I saw was seventeen years old, and even though I was just fourteen, he looked young to me. He was pale as a pillow, skinny as a stick, and he swung between inaction and violence like a weathervane in a tornado.

Now: still, shoulders down, knees bent, feet turned inwards.

Now: struggling, kicking, twisting, dropping onto the floor, trying to bash his own head out against the counter.

And now: still, silent.

And now: screaming, screaming, fucking, fucking, screaming, no words just fucking, fucking, screaming.

And now: utterly calm. Utterly silent. Staring at a locked door.

That day, my dad was supposed to take me to see a film, but he had to go back in to help apply restraints to the kid in the cell. They left him wrapped up like a carpet for twenty minutes, released him to avoid risk of suffocation, and Dad finally took me to the cinema, but the film had already begun, and the next night the kid was taken to hospital after smashing his skull on the cell wall.

"Sometimes people say it's easy," mused my dad, as he drove me home from our failed outing, a desultory, apologetic pile of half-eaten chips on my lap. "Easier to steal than to work; easier to lie, to get away with it. Sometimes they're right. Sometimes – too much – the system just isn't geared for the ones who have nothing better. The dropouts and the addicts; the ones with nowhere to go. Sometimes it's easier to cheat, because life is hard. But you gotta have your mates and your family and people around you who love you and give a damn, and you gotta have hope, big hopes for the future, ideas about what you want, because if you've got all of that, then living becomes easier - not easy, just a bit easier - and you can see that cheating is desperate, and desperate is hard."

I said nothing, still fuming at my dad for having again been a victim of too much work, too many broken promises.

He didn't say anything else for the rest of the drive, and didn't turn the radio on.

Chapter 8

The day after Reina died, Princess Shamma bint Bandar arrived in Dubai, bearing the Chrysalis diamond. I watched, bags already packed, as Leena met her aunty and her entourage outside the hotel.

"Darling, you look beautiful!" exclaimed her aunt, and *squeak*, so much to tell you, oh my God, it's been amazing, replied Leena.

No one mentioned Reina.

I stood awhile in the sun, ignoring the taxi the porter had called to take me to the airport.

"Ma'am?" he said, and when I didn't answer, "Ma'am? Do you still want the cab?"

"No, thank you," I replied, and was surprised by the certainty in my voice. "I think perhaps I'm not yet done here."

So saying, I picked my suitcase up, and walked back into the hotel.

I gathered tools for my crime.

Security can spot a scout a mile off, but security never remembered me long enough to care. I stalked queens and princes, shook hands with diplomats and spies, and no one looked twice. No one ever looks twice at me.

The plastic explosive I acquired from an ex-demolitions expert who'd been sacked from his job in Qatar after eight workers died on his shift.

"People die out there all the time," he explained, as he handed over the goods in a drawstring bag. "People are cheaper than steel. Why does it matter? Scapegoat, they made me. Hypocrisy; the death of the middle man."

Shutting down the electricity on cue was harder, but far from impossible. The virus for the job I purchased from a supplier called BarbieDestroyedTheMoon. She – I hoped she was a she – had no issues selling to me over the darknet since, as she pointed out, *Cop, thief, spy or fool, you ain't never tracing me.*

And what exactly, I asked, was it I was purchasing for my bitcoins?

It's ripped off a CIA design, she explained. *They went and used it on Iran to shut down its nuclear program, but it went public on their asses. CIA are fucking pussies. NSA are the ones you gotta respect.*

I set a timecode, and implanted the virus on the laptop of a junior engineer going through an unhappy and, it turned out, entirely irrational romantic trauma.

"My wife is sleeping with another man!" he wailed, as we shared sushi and green tea at a Japanese café whose walls were coated with images of pink, wide-eyed could-be cats. "She denies it, and I tell her I'd forgive her if she admits it, but she won't, and so I will never forgive her, never, not until the day she dies."

I smiled, skimming sushi over soy. Never over-dip sushi; a chef once screamed at me for this sin, but the waitress apologised on his behalf, explaining that his favourite newt had died that morning, and he was a very passionate man. I quite understand, I'd replied. It can be devastating, losing a newt you love.

"Of course I can't find any proof of her treachery," sighed my almost-certainly-not-cuckolded junior engineer. "But that just proves how well she's covering it up!"

I implanted the virus into his laptop while he was having a piss, and the following day he, unwitting, uploaded it to the sub-station computers where he worked along with his timesheets and a series of home-penned poems about the passions of despised love.

Chapter 9

Criminal professionalism; it is more than good practice.

Never steal in anger, and yet Reina was dead, and the Chrysalis had come to Dubai and so . . .

Breathe in. Count every breath. One – in – one – out.

Count to ten.

Heart rate: 76 BMP.

Blood pressure: 118/76. Systolic/diastolic. In 1615 a doctor called William Harvey published *Exercitatio Anatomica de Motu Cordis et Sanguinis in Animalibus – On the Movement of the Heart and Blood in Animals.* The Chinese and Indians had arguably got there first, but it wasn't until 1818 that Samuel Siegfried Karl Ritter von Basch invented the sphygmomanometer.

Knowledge is power.

Knowledge is freedom.

Knowledge is all I have.

There is nothing in this world which can master me, save me myself.

Days of pursuit in the Burj al Arab Jumeirah.

On a Monday I was a stranger Leena met by the poolside. On a Tuesday I was a stranger in the spa. On Wednesday I was a stranger who approached her over dinner. I stole Leena's mobile phone, copying all its information and linking its SIM card to mine. She was at 634,000 points in Perfection.

> By now you will be feeling the joy that can only come from knowing that you are approaching the pinnacle of potential. Your goals are not dreams – they are truths that you can, will and shall obtain to become the perfect, true you!

A text message on her phone:

> Can't believe Reina did this to us! Why would she be so stupid?

After twenty minutes of being separated from her phone, Leena began to panic. I handed it back to one of her security men, who suspected me of being someone nefarious, but I was already gone and he forgot.

It is not invisibility that I possess; more a steady blinking of the mind.

"We've all got Perfection!" whispered Suzy-Sandy-Sophie-Something in my ear as we sat in the aromatherapy room. "Even the princesses! I'm from Ogema, Wisconsin, and my pa used to sell second-hand kitchen appliances from the garage, but now I'm here and I have dinner with royalty and you just mustn't let it get to your head, because they're all just people, really, even though they're Muslim!"

I smiled and said, "You're a very foolish woman, aren't you?" and when her mouth dropped in anguish and rage, I walked out of the aromatherapy room and straight into the cold pool, where I stayed, head pounding with the change of temperature as I counted to fifty, then surfaced and breathed, then sank down again, counting back to zero.

Why had I said those words?

A lapse in professionalism; unforgivable on a job. I watched my skin prickle with icy water, felt pressure build at the back of my nose, and chided myself.

I mastered myself, always, no matter what. Discipline in all things.

When I went back to the aromatherapy room, Suzy-Sandy was still there, lying on a white towel. She opened one eye as I entered, saw no threat, closed it again.

"Hi," I said, sitting on the bench opposite her. "I'm Rachel; I'm new here. What's your name?"

*

In the evening, I met Leena for the very first time, for the sixteenth night running, and having had the practice I went straight in with, "I love your dress."

Previous approaches: *I'm interested in this amazing city. I work in finance. I'm interested in Perfection. I'm writing an article about women in Dubai. I knew Reina, sorry for your loss.*

None had worked, though the mention of Perfection had got me closest. Sometimes the truth is that the trivial route is the most successful, and thus:

"I love your dress."

"Do you, it is amazing, isn't it?"

"Is it Vera Wang?"

"It is! And you're . . . ?"

"Dior."

"I just adore Dior."

"Who doesn't?"

Empty words.

I am my smile.

I am my lips.

I lower my head as I speak to her, so that my eyes have to look up, seeming wider, rounder, more appealing. Animals reading animals. My jewels, my dress, my body, they speak for me, a woman with skin almost as dark as my mother's, wearing the perfect perfume for the perfect night by the sea. First impressions matter, when they are all you have to live by.

I am the delighted crinkle in the corner of my eyes. I am the woman she wants me to be. "I just love fashion," I said through my polished lips. "You're the most stylish woman here by a year."

Information, drifting:

Vera Wang: fashion designer, former figure skater.

Al Maktoum, royal family of Dubai, descendants of the Al Falasi of the coalition of Bani Yas tribes.

"You're wonderful," exclaimed Leena. "You're just the kind of person I like to meet."

*

Once you have your prey, keep it in sight. It's only when people no longer see me that they forget.

I stuck close to Leena, flowed with her entourage, laughed at her jokes, shared my views on fashion, celebrity, travel. "The perfect people, the perfect clothes, the perfect words, the perfect holidays!" she exclaimed, and all around her people laughed.

"I'm with Prometheus," explained a man in a white and gold Nehru suit, iced cocktail in one hand. "We really want Perfection to be good for people, to help them live better lives. With the right help, anyone can be perfect!"

I smiled and laughed, and thought of another kind of righteousness, expounded by a long-dead Indian prince. Right view, right wisdom, right speech, right conduct, right livelihood, right effort, right mindfulness, right concentration. The eightfold path. *Samyanc* in Sanskrit; rightness as denotes completion, togetherness, coherence. (Can also be used to express the notion of perfection.)

Leena and I circled together through a room latticed with gold, marble floor, fresh flowers – orchids, lilacs flecked with white. A party in full swing, barely a headscarf in sight, men and women mixing freely, a banner on one wall – *The Future Is Perfect*. The waiters were Indian and Bangladeshi, drawn from the labour camps hidden in the desert. Expats everywhere.

I used to specialise in government bonds, but now I've moved into global futures . . .

. . . the thing about insurance is . . .

Why do they call it "tax haven"? I mean, don't they realise how the press react to words like that?

. . . oil is too short-term. Sure, there's big bucks now, but I want my kids to get into digital rights.

The United Arab Emirates has a population of somewhere between 75 and 85 per cent expats. What do so many foreigners do to a society? Volvos in Abu Dhabi, McDonald's a good night out? Or does culture bite back by extolling ancient virtues: the poems of Dhu al Rummah, the music of Umm Kulthum, the words of the Hadith, the traditions of the peoples of the sands?

A bit of both, perhaps. Umm Kulthum's songs reinterpreted in the style of Beyoncé.

I counted gold watches.

I counted mobile phones.

I counted steps to the door.

I looked, and I saw the necklace I had come all this way to steal, no longer in its pressure-sensitive, motion-sensitive, heat-sensitive security case, but being worn around the neck of Shamma bint Bandar, who even now kisses a man in a smart black suit on the cheek, congratulating him on his hard work. Here, tonight, the Chrysalis was being put to its proper use; vanity makes people vulnerable.

"I've just started my treatments," exclaimed a woman in six-inch heels, the backs of her ankles incredibly thin, calves faintly etched with a translucent silver line where the surgeon had cut, visible only when it caught the light. "It's incredible, just incredible, it's changed the way I see the world."

She wore a dress that plunged at the front, the back, the sides, leaving little more than some tactically placed straps across her shoulders. The man she spoke to wore a white headdress held in place with gold, white robes, a black beard cut to a perfect V round his chin, and a ceremonial dagger decorated in rubies. They looked like they should struggle to communicate, but he exclaimed, "My first treatment was astonishing. My driver came up after, and for the first time I saw *him*. Not just him, but *him*."

I moved on. Circled, counting.

Stealing jewels from a human is easier for me than stealing from a vault. CCTV will remember my face, the vault will need experts to crack, the motion sensors will require tools to deceive. I cannot execute the long con, but must wait for opportunity to strike, alone, unaided, taking risks that anyone who feared their face being known would never take.

I turn, turn, turn in the room.

Count the security men in overt black – eleven – and the more discreet security men blending with the crowd – four that I can see.

I count Jordanian sheikhs in white robes, Saudi princes in smart silk suits, American embassy men with sweat patches seeping into the shirts under their arms, Chinese investors taking selfies against the background of the ballroom's internal waterfall, smiling to the camera on the end of its stick.

I count women who would rather not be there, their lips smiling where their eyes do not. I count wristwatches that cost more than the yearly salary of the waiters who envy them, and the number of times I hear the word "equity" said out loud. (Thirty-nine.)

I count security cameras.

I count steps to Princess Shamma, and the $2.2 million dollars' worth of jewellery round her neck. My interest in Leena is gone, now she's got me in the party, and she's already quite drunk. Her aunt is not.

Are you ready?

I count seconds, place myself in the perfect position for my move, loosen my feet inside their ridiculous high-heeled shoes, which will only be an encumbrance when the moment comes.

"Excuse me?"

The woman speaks English with a faint American accent that is pure international school: stateless, bright. I stare at her in surprise, taking in her high-collared dress in a Chinese style, adorned with silver dragons on a black background; her black hair done up high with a messiness that could only have cost a great deal of money; her silver bracelet and earrings, her black mascara, her cautious smile. The darkness round her eyes make them seem deeper than they are; the earrings hanging down make her neck seem long. After a night of drinking, she would be a pale, starling-sized creature, but now, in this place, she is moonlight in heels.

"Are you alone?" she asked. "Do you know anyone?"

Instant thought: is this woman security? Why else would anyone watch me for long enough to discover my loneliness, without forgetting my being? But she remains at the precise physical distance required to be audible, without intrusion, keeps smiling politely, head slightly on one side.

"I . . . no," I mumbled. "I don't know anyone."

"Are you British?"

"Yes."

"Here for work?"

"Yes – with the British Council."

A lie, quick and easy. I am here to promote Britishness. I spread the word of Shakespeare, the history of cricket, the memories of colonialism and the taste of fish and chips to the world. I am a symptom of goodwill. I am an adjunct to national arrogance. Who knows?

The woman, still smiling, said nothing.

"What do you do?" I blurted, to fill the space.

"I'm in research."

"What does that mean?"

"I study the human brain."

"That sounds . . . big."

For the first time, a twitch in the corner of her mouth that could be a smile wanting to become real. "All of thought is feedback and association. Faced with mounting social stress, the body responds as it would to any alarm. Capillaries constrict; heart rate elevates, breathing accelerates, skin becomes hot, muscles tight. Charm falters in the face of hypertension. From this moment of social rejection, pathways are reinforced in the brain to strengthen a link between socialising and anxiety. A series of assumptions develop which leads to a perception of social systems as threatening, triggering an anxiety response. All thought is feedback: sometimes that feedback can become too loud. Are you with the 106?"

"I don't know what that means."

A flicker of surprise, then: "Do you have Perfection?"

"What? I . . . no."

"Don't tell my brother."

"Is your brother . . . "

"He's looking to do a version that promotes Islamic values. Fifty thousand points for going on hajj; five hundred points for every direct debit made to charity and so on. I said that I wasn't sure God worked that way, through reward algorithms and shopping vouchers, but here we are ... " A gentle raising of her hands, palm up, as if she would lift the room from its foundations to be examined. "And it would appear that everything is going ... very well."

She thought she knew what "very well" meant once, but by the look in her eye, this present time is redefining it.

I opened my mouth to say oh, really, that's fascinating – but there isn't time. The virus implanted nine days ago at an electrical substation goes live right on cue, and takes out some 30 per cent of the electricity of Dubai.

A flickering, as the bulbs dim, followed by a recovery as the hotel's emergency generator picks up the load. The sound of music dips, then revives, voices oscillating quiet, then loud again in the brief lull. The woman's eyes flick to the ceiling, then out to the windows, looking across the water to where a pattern of lights have gone out across the shore.

Thirty, twenty-nine, twenty-eight, twenty-seven ...

"Sub-station," she mused. "Probably just a trip."

"My friend had Perfection," I said, and was surprised to hear my voice, see her eyes turn to me. "At the time, I didn't think she was unhappy."

"I'm sorry," the woman said. "What was her name?"

"Reina."

... nineteen, eighteen, seventeen, sixteen ...

I opened my mouth to say something more, something banal, and instead found myself offering my hand, which she took. "I'm Hope."

"Filipa," she replied. "You're much more interesting than you pretend."

"And you more than people think?"

She pulled in her bottom lip, eyes up to the ceiling, as if seeking out a bright thread of silk from a tangle of cobweb. "Exactly that, I think. Exactly that."

... six, five, four ...

Seven paces to Leena's aunt, the clasp around her neck is easy, I practised with my eyes shut on the same fitting for three hours the other night. Three people are between me and my target, now four, the turning of the room disadvantaging me.

I open my mouth to say something that matters; but in the mess of service corridors and not-so-secure locked doors beneath the hotel, my nugget of Semtex finally explodes.

The blast didn't shake the building; there was barely enough firepower to punch through the cables to which it was attached. There was instant darkness, like hands round the throat. It will be a matter of moments before someone suspects foul play, a matter of minutes before engineers have found the problem. The generators, when I inspected them on one of my nightly rounds in a cleaner's uniform, are designed to survive earthquakes and hurricanes. Repairing will not be hard.

A lack of reaction in the room – a few sighs, a little gasp, but no screaming or panic. Power cuts happen; it's just the way of things.

I turn, hands in front as my eyes adjust to the dim, feel my way between silk and velvet, past lace and pearls, counting steps, five, six, seven, not rushed, until I feel the brush of a waist against my hand and hear the little intake of breath of a stranger in front of me.

"Princess Shamma?" I ask in Arabic, inflected with my mother's accent.

"Yes?" the lady replies.

I put one hand on her wrist, hold it tight, and with the other pluck the necklace from around her throat. Easy; practised. She is surprised, but only by the unexpected contact on her arm. The eye will always follow the larger motion; the body will always respond to the bigger feeling – every magician knows that.

I pulled the diamonds away, released her wrist, and walked away.

It was all of forty-seven seconds before Leena's aunt began to scream.

Chapter 10

I was not always what I am now.

Once, I was remembered.

I had friends and family, teachers and homework.

I did badly at school and that was fine.

You'll never amount to much with your attitude, said the geography teacher.

It's not your subject, is it? said maths.

Just write it out!

One day in English, we were told we had to talk for a minute on a random subject. The girl before me, Emma Accrington, pulled the words "open-plan offices" from the hat on the teacher's desk.

"I don't know what this is," she explained, twisting painfully before the staring class. "I guess it's like an office but, you know, in the open air and that. Like, maybe everyone goes outside and like, there's animals, yeah? Like, chickens and cows and that?"

The class laughed, and she laughed too, recognising the absurdity of it all, and when the teacher told me to speak next, I was still laughing, and couldn't say a word about my subject – dog walking – for the tears running down my face.

Do you think you're funny? asked my teacher as she gave me detention. *Do you think you'll ever do anything of worth?*

Worth: the quality that renders something desirable or valuable.

Worthy: having the qualities that deserve action or regard.

Characterised by good intent, but lacking in humour.

A person notable in a particular sphere.

Synonyms: virtuous, good, ethical, high-principled, right-thinking, noble, righteous, venerable, conscientious, trustworthy, dependable, exemplary.

Antonyms: disreputable, unworthy. Nobody.

I was fifteen years old, and as I walked home through the grey winter, I knew that I was worthy of nothing at all.

When my school report came, Dad was silent. I waited for him to shout at me, but he wouldn't. My mum shouted until she wept. Her skin was dark as burnt mahogany, her hair was already grey at the temples, cut to a perfect scalp around her skull. She wore a carrots and cauliflowers apron when she cooked, which she did five nights a week unless Dad was on night shifts, in which case he cooked before going out. When I was ten she said, "You will now learn how to cook!" and I sensed that this was not a matter on which there would be any arguing. Nyaring Ayun-Arden, my mum, co-ordinated customer service at the council-housing office and was a good cook, even though she loved sardines more than anything else.

"It's just wonderful!" she exclaimed. "It's fish, in a tin, for 16p!"

My dad said he'd met my mother at a community event.

My mum laughed and said, "You call it that!"

I ignored this as a silly adult joke, until one day my aunt Carol whispered, "Your mum walked across Sudan and up through Egypt, walked until she got to Istanbul, came to this country in the back of a truck and got work sorting laundry for the hotels, but ended up begging after they said they couldn't pay immigrants minimum wage. Your dad picked her up, put her in the cells for a night, gave her a cuppa tea and a microwaved meal. Three years later she was running the reception desk at the big council office in the centre of town, and he'd just made sergeant. Your dad had forgotten her, but she didn't forget, not your mum, and that was lucky for him."

The year I was born, my mother's sister, left behind in Sudan, also gave birth and called her child Sorrow. My mother, unaware of this, or even that her sister was alive, called me Hope. Her family were Neur, but to advance their lot in life, my grandfather had insisted they all learned Arabic, in the hope his children would one day enter the civil service. The civil service would not have them, but my mother sang to me in Arabic in my crib, and cursed in Arabic, and paced up and down the room berating me in Arabic, with the words, first in one language, then another, "You will speak many languages and have the opportunities I did not!"

As a child, I heard these words as condemnation. She had not had opportunities, and so now was forcing me, her daughter, to live the life she could not. It took until after I had lost my family for me to understand what she was trying to say.

"For a copper to marry an immigrant, particularly at that time," mused my aunt, "it says a lot about their love. But then, your dad always was a good man first, and a copper second; it's why his career's been so slow. And your mum . . . she's always believed in people. That's why she called you Hope."

Chapter 11

Walking barefoot away from a robbery in Dubai.

I don't exit the hotel directly, not yet. If I do, someone with a lot of patience could pull camera footage, assess who was there when the power went, who was not there when it came back on. The comparison would yield my face.

Most police forces don't have the time, and time is money. But the Dubai police is commanded by prince someone who is a relative of prince someone, and while a petty theft, a little assault, a touch of domestic or sexual abuse might slide for want of time and energy, no one lays a finger on a member of the royal family.

So I waited.

I put the diamonds in a plastic bag in the cistern of the third toilet along in the ground-floor ladies. In Hollywood crime capers, a bumbling fool and their winsome child will stumble on my stolen goods; japes ensue, love is found and I end up as villain, femme fatale perhaps, for it is narratively impossible for me to be anything other than a sexual predator, as well as a criminal mastermind.

As it is, the police, when they arrive, immediately set to interrogating the hotel staff, pulling grown men around by the scruff of the neck, hollering in the faces of the Filipino maids, while the expats and dignitaries mingle together in shock and excitement, for this is just the most thrilling thing that has happened for a long while and they will dine out on it for years to come.

A man in the lobby, screaming down his phone. The woman dressed all in black stands behind him, watching without expression.

"At my fucking party!" he screams. "At my fucking party stole her fucking jewels do you know what this fucking does for us, do you know how much we've just fucking lost . . . ?!"

The elevator doors close, cutting him off from my view.

In my bedroom I lie down, back straight, arms on my chest.

Breathe.

Once.

Twice.

Watch the reflection of the water on the ceiling.

Discipline.

Every day: some form of exercise.

Every day: some form of social interaction.

Discipline.

I close my eyes, and breathe.

Chapter 12

I was forgotten when I was sixteen.

Why then?

My parents loved me, there was no doubt. But when my sister was born, she needed almost constant attention. Little Gracie, who at four years old caught measles off a kid in nursery whose mother thought the MMR jab was poison.

"See?" she hollered, as my sister was rushed to A&E with a fever of 41°C. "She had the jab and what good has it done her?"

I thought Mum was going to slap her, and when Dad drove me home, Mum still sat in the ICU, he almost hit a cyclist, and we had to wait in the bus lane for ten minutes while he got his breath back.

Doctors are taught the three Cs for diagnosing measles: cough, conjunctivitis and coryza (blocked nose to you and me). You could also add a K – Koplik's spots. Clustered white lesions on the buccal mucosa. They appear as little white marks, like grains of salt, around the inner lining of the cheek where it joins with the molars. Early detection can lead to a quick diagnosis before full infectiousness is achieved. We did not detect them early; we didn't know to look.

At 42°C organs start taking damage. I was allowed to miss school, and wished for the first time that I wasn't, as the rash spread across Gracie's body.

It was fifteen days before my sister was allowed home. After nine months, it was obvious that she had suffered brain damage. The mother of the unvaccinated child came over three days after we took Grace out of nursery. She stood in the door, a small woman with a rainbow scarf, and talked low to my mum, and at the end she was crying, and so was Mum, though neither raised their voices, and I never saw her again.

I think it began then, in the months and years that followed the measles.

Slowly, a piece at a time, I began to diminish, and the world began to forget.

Chapter 13

Thirteen hours after I planted the diamonds in the women's toilets, I reclaimed them, and checked out of the hotel.

The Dubai–Muscat bus was a sleek, air-conditioned cruiser that drove at unchanging, ponderous speed down the middle of the giant, sparse highway for six and a half hours, two of which were spent in a maze of border crossings. Emirati officials glanced at my American passport and weren't interested. The Indians and Pakistanis heading to Oman were subjected to several hours of speculation.

"It happens every time," said the woman next to me, chewing busily on sunflower seeds as we sat on our bags outside the customs shed. She spat the kernels to one side, and grinned a broad-toothed grin. "You're lucky; your country is rich. No one cares what rich people do. Hey, want to hear something funny?"

Sure, why not.

She grinned a dental-disaster of a grin and in heavily accented English intoned, "Do dolphins ever do anything by accident? No! They do it on porpoise!" and laughed until the tears rolled down her face.

The bus zig-zagged through the mountains, a nowhere land of empty roads before the Omani border, where we presented our luggage for search. No one bothered to open the pot of sun lotion in which the diamonds were carefully stashed; the drug dogs found nothing interesting as they snuffled along the line. Omani immigration was housed in a faux-Arabian palace, which owed more of its architecture to Disney than Sinan Pasha.

"You alone?" asked the inspector.

"Yes."

"Married?"

"No."

"You got someone to stay with?"

"Yes."

"But you're not married?"

"No."

His lips puckered a little in distaste, but though I was a single woman, I was travelling on a public bus and thus, finding no satisfactory diplomatic reason to reject me, he gave me the visa.

On the road everything was yellow.

For a while I counted cars; then I counted shrubs, then there was neither of either to count and I stared at dust and wondered how many grains of sand blew into the sea every year, and whether you could build a pyramid from them. The coast of Oman had been dug and sown with hardy dark green trees and thin, drooping beige fields, but the dust crept across every porch of every nowhere town that hugged the road.

Words, when I think of Muscat:

- Welcoming – racks of meat, smiles at every door, the words "you must meet my mother" are spoken in genuine joy.
- Hot – the sea breeze seems to bounce off the land, the dry blast from the desert scorching your back.
- Divided – not so much a city as a series of towns, joined together by clogged roads over sharp hills.
- Unified – every street must conform to a certain style, every office obey strict architectural laws.
- Old and new – ancient tapestries below; air conditioning above. Bare feet, covered head. Arabesque windows, domed roofs, a place both charming and absurd.

Street names in Muscat were almost non-existent. The hotel I checked into gave its address as "4th building after the statue of the ship on the left-hand side facing the sea", before swelling into broader strokes of area and district.

I sat on a balcony looking out across the ocean, and drank Turkish coffee, the heavy grains rubbing against my teeth. It wasn't my first choice of hotel, but this wasn't Dubai; not all places would accept an unmarried woman, travelling by herself.

In this bubble of quiet sheltered from the world, I turned on the TV and watched the news. The robbery in Dubai ran only as a background story on a few channels, the police confident of speedy success in their investigations. Details were sparse; even the internet seemed to be hushed on the matter. Only one snippet was of any interest – an interview with a man by the name of Rafe Pereyra-Conroy (Prometheus CEO), who turned direct to camera and said: "We personally feel this assault upon our friends and generous hosts, and will do everything in our power to help bring the perpetrator to justice."

I studied his face, and saw nothing remarkable in it. Turned the TV off.

In the bathroom sink, I washed sun cream off the diamonds, then laid them out on a white sheet, wrote the date and time on a piece of paper next to them, took a photo of the whole, and went about selling my stolen goods.

In an internet café in Muscat, I plugged my laptop into the Ethernet connection in the wall, loaded the photo of diamonds onto my computer, and posted the image onto an ad run through Tor.

For sale: Chrysalis diamonds, est. value $2.2 million. All offers in excess of $450,000 considered.

I signed myself _why, and this job done, closed my laptop again, slipped it in my bag, and went in search of company.

Chapter 14

Fencing a stolen object is more important than the theft.

DVD players, watches, phones, family heirlooms, odd bits of gold and silver – a pawnbroker will handle it, at a poor rate. In Florida, a judge ruled that pawnshops need not return stolen goods without having a chance to be heard in civil suit. Crime rose, so did the number of pawnshops.

"Is there a link between poverty, crime and pawnshops?" asked a journalist from Miami, sent to cover the story as part of a series on declining America.

"Ma'am," replied the local sheriff, "do you shit when you eat?"

In the UK, such a remark would have been a sackable offence. Speaking your mind in public, let alone speaking with reference to bodily functions, is not a thing done by the Ruling Classes. In the US, such brisk imagery is reassuring; almost as reassuring as seeing a sheriff with an AK-47 driving through your neighbourhood. Assuming, of course, that your neighbourhood is middle class and white.

"Do you shit when you eat?" chuckled an NYU professor who I bribed with chow mein and a night of Elgar in exchange for his knowledge of criminology. "Is shit made of complex biocarbons? Is nature a wonder, is the human body understood? Is society? Are people? Are gross over-simplifications of entrenched socio-economic problems exactly what's wrong with this polarised country? Hell yes!" He cackled gleefully at this revelation, and scooped up another load of noodles. "You know why the experts don't have an easy answer? Because a fucking expert's the guy who knows how complicated the fucking questions are."

Later – when he'd sobered up – I asked him the things I really wanted to know. Organised crime. Interpol. Law and digital footprints; everything a budding criminology student might want to ask. And why not tell me? He knew my face; no criminal would have dared been so bold.

How do you sell stolen diamonds?

"You hand it off to the courier," explained an ex-Croatian safebreaker-turned-lawman, his expertise hired out to police forces, universities and, so he whispered as we sat by the Adriatic Sea, "some of the spies, but never the Russians or the Jews, *never*, I swear on my mother's life".

I had bought his knowledge for €5,000 and a bottle of champagne, and now he threw the drink back as the sun set at our backs and the humid sky filled with diffused pink. "I wouldn't want to be the courier. He never knows what he's walking into – the cops aren't the problem, it's the guys on the other end of the deal, I mean, they could be anyone, anyone; but it's the courier who takes that risk, thank God, you hear stories. Show me a nice guy, and put a ten-carat diamond in front of him and I'll show you a monster, like that." A snap of his fingers, a gulp of champagne, sunlight through the glass. "You know what the difference is between a professional thief and an amateur one?"

No. I did not.

"A pro knows when to walk away. The deal's too good; the safe's too tough; the pigs too loud. Fine. Cut your losses. It's only fucking money, you know what I mean?"

And if the deal goes through?

"You get paid. Maybe 5 to 10 per cent if you're lucky. Best I ever got: 20 per cent of the diamond's value, and that was unique, a one-off, never happens. But the guy who's got it now, the fence, he's gotta shift the product. So he sends it to India, or Africa, maybe. Mozambique; maybe Zimbabwe? They have this thing down there, this Kimberley process, it's supposed to protect people who mine diamonds and that shit, but what it does is it produces paperwork. So you cut the diamonds, once, twice, maybe ten, twenty times, depending on what you're going for. And you get a nice new certificate while you're out there saying that this stone is authenticated shiny and clean, and you ship it off to America or China or Brazil, and you sell it on, worth less than it was before but you know, that's the cost of doing business."

So it's a business run on trust?

"Sure, sure. Gotta trust the courier, who's gotta trust the buyer, who's gotta trust the guys he's selling to. Everything's about trust, and why wouldn't it be? If you break trust, you end up in prison or dead or both, so you trust to survive and everyone's okay."

I smiled and poured him another glass of champagne.

Trust: belief that someone is reliable, honest, truthful, good.

Such beliefs are formed by time, and no one in the world remembered me long enough to trust me. So I did everything myself, and I did it alone.

Chapter 15

Muscat, looking at the sea.

I wanted to sell diamonds, knew that there were buyers out there, a market just waiting to buy.

I went into the darknet.

There were eighty-seven different replies to my ad, when I checked into the forum.

Of these, fifty-one were time-wasting nonsense, ranging from the insulting through to the patently false. That left thirty-six contacts that were suitable for consideration.

I dismissed the bottom ten and the top ten offers at once. One offer, for two million dollars, stank of idiot insurance company or security service, and the next best, at $1.8 million, came with the words: *You can trust us to protect your anonymity.*

I trusted no one, and no one worth my time would assume anything else from me.

I turned my attention to more convincing offers, ranging from $650,000 to $900,000 in various currencies. Two offered payment in bitcoin, which held some appeal, but one required me to ship the diamonds to South Africa; a risk I was unwilling to take.

Of the offers remaining on the table, I chose the four most likely: one offering bitcoin, one offering exchange in whichever city I desired, one which requested delivery to India, and a last asking me if I was interested in payment through a casino in Macau.

Macau fell out of the running when the buyer asked for a preliminary meeting on a private yacht off the coast of Tunisia. The bitcoin buyer dropped out when I pushed for logistic details. Between India and wherever-you-wanted, I went for the lazier option.

These goods have historical value, wrote wherever-you-wanted, running by the handle of mugurski71. *I am employed by a collector. Where would you like to meet?*

Two days scouting in Muscat.

The ideal location: somewhere public, to minimise the odds of being robbed. Somewhere discreet, so we could inspect each other's goods in privacy. Somewhere away from CCTV, but with access to transport and escape. I chose the Muttrah souk. Once, it could have been a place of piss-stinking alleys and thieves, of blackened corners and dead ends, tumbling goods and smoke; of fantastical dreams that played on the minds of poets and painters from the West, filling their senses with incense. Now it was a tourist trap for shoppers who still mistook "shiny" for "antique"; carefully cleaned floors and concrete. Where were the exotic baths of naked ladies who haunted the works of Ingres and Matisse, where the djinn of *Arabian Nights*, the mystic otherworldliness of *Al Aaraaf*? Why, they were priced out by the housing market, and though the stalls were sagging with goods, bartering could barely scrape you a 10 per cent discount, even if you were American and the starting price was exorbitant.

I drifted through stalls hanging with silk and cashmere, some more genuine than others. I inspected necklaces of gold, and necklaces of nearly gold, and fat bangles of not-gold-at-all laid out in gleaming brightness, trays packed so tightly together in the stall that the vendor had to stand stick-straight in the tiny gap between his wares. I idled between great brown sacks of saffron and turmeric, cloves and cinnamon; trays of dates, baths of olives, ceilings hung with glass lamps whose shells were pricked out with stars and moons. I clattered between copper cooking pans and shimmied round mannequins decked out in abayas of black and blue. One vendor held out a curved knife sheathed in a case embedded with jewels and hollered in English, "You, you, pretty lady, American, yes, the best, the best, I sell the best!"

Another caught me looking at a little orange teapot on a table of bric-a-brac everythings and exclaimed, "For your husband!" while across the tight passage, an old man with a white beard said nothing as I examined a chess set carved from veined soapstone, until at last he raised his head before my contemplation and declared softly, "You should only buy if you play."

"You're right," I replied. "Of course."

I choose my spot, plenty of people, plenty of cover, no security cameras in sight; a café selling shisha and tea, where you could duck behind the privacy of damask sheets and lattice frames of rosewood, nefarious deals to make.

I returned to the hotel room. Proof of funds from mugurski71 was waiting on my computer.

So was a new message.

```
Byron14: Why did you attack Prometheus?
```

Under usual circumstances, a message from a stranger is something I ignore. Loneliness has led to many mistakes in my life. I closed the computer and ignored it.

Two hours later, checking to see if mugurski71 had offered anything more:

`Byron14: I know you are making a deal with mugurski71.`

I considered the message for a while, walked round the room, opened the window to listen to the sea, then went back to the keyboard.

`_why: I don't discuss business matters.`

`Byron14: Why did you attack Prometheus?`

`_why: I don't know what you mean.`

`Byron14: You stole the Chrysalis from Shamma bint Bandar at the launch of Prometheus' new product in Dubai. You humiliated Pereyra-Conroy; you embarrassed his company.`

`_why: Who are Prometheus?`

`Byron14: They are Perfection. Mugurski71 works for Prometheus.`

I walked away from the computer again, idled round my room, drank cold water, grabbed my toes and stretched until my ears buzzed, sat down again.

Byron14 was waiting, patient on the other end of the line.

`_why: What's your interest?`

`Byron14: In stealing the Chrysalis from their event, you humiliated Prometheus.`

They are assisting the UAE in their investigations.

_why: That doesn't answer my question.

Byron14: Have you agreed a meet with mugurski71?

_why: What do you want?

Byron14: send a dummy. Contact me when it's done.

That was all.

Chapter 16

Lying awake in the hot darkness of a Muscat summer.

Sleeping not a wink.

Thieves are prone to paranoia. The car in the night, the footfall in the shadow; trust. Who do you trust? In most petty crime, hate is as good a word as honour. Hate the cops, hate the law, hate the world. For this reason, your average two-bit mugger banged up for three years in Pentonville isn't going to rat on his mates, because, for all they're backstabbing bastards, they're not the cops, the pig, the filth, and even if they're not friends, they're still your mates.

Up the crime, up the stakes, up the reasons for betrayal.

A night run through Muscat, and three men in white call out, *Hey, pretty lady, you hot, you sweet, you hot?*

These men might be married, might beat another man to death for even looking at their wives, their sisters, their children, but when a lone Western woman walks through the streets of Oman, that's fair game, because Western women are like that, aren't they? They must be, to walk the way they walk, talk the way they talk.

You sweet, you hot?

Briefly, I feel the fear of being a woman in a strange land.

I am the queen of taster classes: self-defence, half a dozen different forms of martial art; fired a pistol on a range in Nebraska, a rifle in Kentucky. I carry a flashlight in my bag which may, with very little effort, be turned into a blunt impact weapon in an emergency, and I am prepared to hurt someone, to really hurt them, if my safety is threatened.

I carry on running, and count steps as I do, twenty-seven until the men are completely out of sight.

I have been caught by cops three times in my career.

The first time, I was seventeen years old, and I was nabbed red-handed shoplifting from a department store in Birmingham. The security guard who tackled me held onto my arm until the police arrived. They took my name (false), my address (false), and when they discovered the lie, the sergeant looked me in the eye and said, "It's a shame, luv, cos we gotta put you through the system."

They put me in the back of the police car and drove slowly to the station. I hunkered down low, silent, listening to the cops in front chatting about the game, what their missus had said, how one wished he had more time to see the kids, the other was worried about his dad. When they got to the station one said, "Cuppa?"

"Lovely-jubbly," replied the other brightly, and so saying, they got out of the car without checking the rear seat, slammed the doors shut and went in search of their tea break, leaving me sat in the back, forgotten, wondering what I was going to do now.

In the end, a constable found me, and called the drivers of the car, and asked them what the hell was going on. They had no idea; they recalled being summoned to a shoplifting, but there hadn't been anyone there to arrest.

"Then what the hell is she doing here?" demanded their superintendent. "Who is she?"

I said, "These guys just grabbed me off the street, they grabbed me and said they were going to do things and I don't know why, they were just saying stuff like I thought maybe they were drunk!"

Then I cried, which, given the situation, wasn't very hard, and the cops let me go, and asked me not to sue.

The second time I was caught, they got me through the darknet.

I was twenty-four years old, and had come to Milan for the food and the fashion. First impressions – my life is about making a good first impression. When one attempt fails, I will go away, and reinvent myself, and return to try again. Though first impressions may be the only thing I have, at least I get to practise until they're right.

Milan during fashion week is full of strange crowds at unlikely venues. Turn a corner and there they are, the young and old, dressed in incredible shoes and ridiculous hats, waiting to see someone-who-knows-someone-who-is-someone's-friend walk up the red carpet. Models abound, but are surprisingly hard to spot in the streets without their make-up and pout, the glamour gone, walking with legs, not hips. It is an exercise in transformation, one I was determined to study.

Getting into the Dolce & Gabbana after-party was easy. You walk in as a waitress, and once inside you change into a gown. That year, collars were high, skirts were short, and the look was paisley meets *Star Trek*. I noted every woman of power, every model climbing that greasy pole, and copied their smiles and walks, one foot in front of the other, a perfect straight line, toe to heel.

It was a spiteful whim that led me to rob Salvatore Rizzo, sixty-nine years old and the king of beauty.

"A shame, a shame," he said, looking at me. "You could be someone, but you're not someone, you don't have the face, the eyes, the lips; and if you were going to be someone, you'd be someone by now."

I thought about speaking my mind, and didn't. I was twenty-four years old, and I was learning professionalism.

"These," he said, running his fingers down first the gold-and-sapphire choker around a model's throat, then the line of her collarbone, then the slope of her arm, "are the Tsarina's Tears. They were worn by Alexandra of Russia the day the Winter Palace fell. Do you know what they're worth?"

Approximately six million dollars, I thought. "Oh no," I replied. "How much?"

"To ordinary people – money. To me – the human soul. The girl who wears this isn't just beautiful, she is extraordinary, she is an icon, an icon of what women should be. Women should be beautiful, they should be diamonds, we should worship them, we should want them, we should need to be wanted by them, we should keep them safe and polished and perfect, that is what I believe in, that is what I fight for, I am a feminist you see, it is the only thing that is important in life. Women. And beauty. And the soul."

I smiled and wondered if any of the on-site security personnel carried guns.

At the bar, a model from Riga, seventeen years old, whispered, "They told me I should sleep with him, but my friend let him do things to her last month and then got sent home without her pay, so I'm just going to keep working, stay in control, get to the top the hard way."

"Why do you do what you do?" I asked.

"Cash," she answered. "If I can keep this up, I can pay for university, but it's hard – it's a hard life, you have to change everything you do, how you eat, how you speak, how you exercise, how you sleep, how you walk; everything. But sometimes, when I walk down the catwalk, and everyone stares at me, I feel it."

"Feel what?"

"I feel like . . . yeah. Fuck you. I am fucking amazing. I am fucking strong. That's what the clothes mean, you see. When they're good, I feel more like me, and I'm unbeatable."

That's what the smile means too, I thought, lips locked in place. I smile, and I do not speak my mind, because when I am restrained in my actions, I am more than myself: I am unstoppable.

"What do you want to study?" I asked.

"Urban redevelopment."

"Not fashion?"

She shrugged. "I know about fashion already. But I don't know enough about mass transit links."

For a moment, the smile becomes genuine. "You should study," I said. "I think it sounds like an excellent idea."

Three hours later, I found her passed out behind the bar. Someone had slipped something into her drink, and her pants were torn. The hospital said there was no sign of penetration, but the management let her go, just in case. Two hours later, the Tsarina's Tears vanished from Salvatore Rizzo's room, taken by a woman whose face no one could remember.

Usual pattern of behaviour.

I offered the stolen jewels for sale, agreed an exchange in a café in Vienna, arrived, ordered sachertorte, and within five minutes was staring at an arrest warrant and a small man with the beginning of a premature bald spot who said, "Did you have a coat?"

So stunned was I by the situation, by the policemen swarming around me and the small crowd of tourists staring at me through the café window as the handcuffs were clamped on, that I didn't register the question at first.

"What?"

"A coat," he repeated patiently. "It's very cold outside."

"By the door; the blue one."

"This coat?"

"Yes."

He patted it down quickly, found nothing of interest, draped it over my shoulders. "All right then."

He sat next to me on the drive to the police station, and was applauded by the Viennese officers as he led me inside. They took my fingerprints – a problem. Computers remembered me. I'd have to be more careful after this.

In the interview room I asked, "Why did they clap when you came in?"

His German was laced with an accent I couldn't place; neither the precise snap of Berlin nor the low scuffle of Vienna. "I've been looking for a jewel thief for three years," he replied. "Catching you is a big break. Would you like tea, coffee?"

"You're not with the local police?"

"Interpol."

"I thought Interpol was just something people talked about in movies."

"In movies, there's less paperwork," he replied with a sigh. "Writing emails and sorting spreadsheets doesn't sell cinema tickets, though I have some very exciting databases."

To my surprise, I smiled, examining this policeman anew. He was an inch shorter than me, long-armed and squat-necked, with a tight constellation of three small, flat moles by his left ear. His fingernails were trimmed painfully short; had he chewed them as a child?

Onychophagia: an oral compulsive habit, nail biting. Apply a chemical lacquer to the nails to prevent chewing. Denatonium benzoate: the most bitter taste known to man.

"What's your name?" I asked, surprised to hear myself speak.

"I am Inspector Evard."

"Interpol has inspectors?"

"We are policemen as well as pen-pushers."

He spoke gently, shoulders curved, hook-nosed and narrow-eyed, intent through his aura of polite absent-mindedness. My fear at being arrested was beginning to diminish in the face of more rational thought. The odds of escape seemed high. This was only a slight setback, surely? Then again, he had my fingerprints, and now a photograph too.

He watched me, watching him, and said at last, "Your German has an accent."

"So does yours."

"We can speak in another language?"

"I prefer Spanish."

"My Spanish isn't very good."

"Then German's okay."

"Did you want a drink?"

"Coffee, please."

He uncuffed me, and left the room. I was alone.

The walls were beige. There was no two-way mirror, but a CCTV camera watched my table. The door was heavy blue metal, locked. I stood up, walked until I was standing directly beneath the CCTV camera, and began to count.

Sixty seconds: my face would begin to fade.

One hundred seconds: Inspector Evard would begin to wonder why he was holding two coffees.

Two hundred seconds, and the cops who applauded Inspector Evard on making his arrest would already have forgotten why they clapped. Perhaps they applauded him for recovering the Tsarina's Tears, waiting to be returned to their unrighteous owner. Perhaps already their minds were spinning a story, the diamonds recovered but the courier fled, a half victory for now.

I waited, back pressed against the wall, CCTV camera above my head.

I waited an hour, then two, then four, not moving, not making a sound, out of the line of sight of the camera.

I waited until eleven p.m., when at last I hammered on the cell door and barked in my best German, "Let me out of here! Idiots, where is my client?"

After a few minutes of banging, someone came running, and the interview room door was unlocked. An astonished officer stared at me, and before he could speak I exclaimed, "Where is my client? I have been waiting here for an hour!"

Confusion, doubt: what was this woman, dressed in smart

clothes, doing locked in an interview room? "Where is your senior officer?" I added, pushing past towards the reception desk. "Tell him I wish to lodge a complaint – oh, the bathroom!"

I lunged for the toilet door before the copper could say anything, and he, foolish he, did not follow. Inside the bathroom I waited another five minutes, then washed my face, straightened my shirt, pushed my hair back and marched out of the police station, past the receiving desk, back straight, head held high.

No one followed.

The next day, newspaper headlines reported the recovery of the Tsarina's Tears, but that, regrettably, the thief had evaded capture. Two days later, I followed Inspector Evard from the station to the hotel where he was staying, a square, grey thing in Donaustadt, and when he went out to find supper, I pulled on my coat and my winter boots, and followed him through the night.

Snow fell, four inches on the ground, a boot-clinging crispness that soaked up trousers and turned your knees blue. It hushed the trams, emptied the pavements, made the yellow lights behind every window seem hot, far away. I shoved my gloved hands under my armpits and followed, and sometimes Evard saw me, and sometimes he turned away, only to see me again for the very first time.

Now.

And now.

But never *again*.

He walked to a Gasthaus of minimal merit, a low-ceilinged room slotted beneath a concrete apartment, where they served Czech spirits that smelt of aniseed and tasted like cough mixture, and German beers each in their own special glass, and boiled sausage and boiled vegetables and breaded chicken and various flavours on a theme of cabbage. He settled into a corner and to the waiter's disgust ordered only a half-pint of unremarkable beer, and schnitzel with chips. When he had finished his beer, I sat down opposite him and said, "Excuse me, are you Inspector Evard?"

"Yes, but I . . . "

"I'm Joy," I said, hand out in greeting. A hand which is offered, most people will instinctively take; rejection requires conscious decision-making. "We met in Milan, do you remember? I'm a freelance press photographer, I saw you and thought . . . ?"

He didn't remember, but the mind will fill in gaps. He had been in Milan, certainly, tracking the thief behind the Tsarina's Tears. Sometimes he met journalists. His eyebrows creased, how had he forgotten me? Well – who remembers the photographer?

I let the thoughts play out behind his eyes then said, "Congratulations on recovering the Tsarina's Tears, I read about it in the papers."

"Thank you. It would have been better if we'd arrested her, but . . . thank you."

"Her? The thief's a woman?"

"We have her face on CCTV from a dozen different robberies. She's been lazy – fingerprints, DNA."

"May I buy you a drink?"

"I was going back to the hotel, an early flight . . . "

"Of course; not to worry."

"Miss . . . Joy, did you say?"

"Joy, yes."

"I'm surprised I don't remember you."

"We only met briefly, in Milan, and there were a lot of people that day."

"Well," he murmured, "well. I hope I see you again soon."

So saying, he rose, and I followed him at twenty yards distance back through the night and the falling snow, and stood outside his hotel until I saw the light go out in his room, and I was happy, giddy even, like the new girl at school who has finally made a friend.

Chapter 17

Some few years later, I sat by a pool of shallow running water in the shade of the Sultan Qaboos Grand Mosque, my head covered, my feet bare, and thought of nothing much, and everything in particular. Even in the shade, the stones were still hot from the midday sun, but the burning was good against my skin.

Sun goddesses:

- Amaterasu, who split from her moon-god brother, Tsukuyomi, after he slaughtered Uke Mochi.
- Bast, lion goddess of the sunset.
- Shapash, judge of the gods who refused to shine until Baal was resurrected again.
- Bridgit, Celtic goddess of the heart who, when her child died, wept and sang all at once and was later acquired by the Catholic Church as a saint whose powers lay in burning hearths and holy wells.

I felt no need to pray, and wondered if any goddess of the sun would watch out for me regardless.

I thought about Byron14, and mugurski71.

I thought about the Chrysalis diamonds, hidden back in my hotel room. Why had I stolen them? At first it had been part of a plan, a challenge, a thing to do. But Reina had died and I had been prepared to walk away until someone had said . . .

Perfection.

And Princess Shamma bint Bandar had been perfect, and so had Leena, and Reina had not been and she had died and perhaps . . .

. . . with the wisdom of hindsight . . .

. . . I had let a little bit of spite infect my professionalism.

Spite: malicious ill will. The urge to hurt or humiliate.

Byron14 had an agenda. That didn't necessarily make Byron14 wrong.

I sat in thought for an hour and a half, until the motion of the sun pushed the shade away from my face and my skin began to burn. Then I went into a hall of white stone and crystal chandeliers, and wondered if this simple opulence, this elegant extravagance was what the Prophet had really had in mind when he preached, and listened to a lecture in English on the interpretation of the Hadith, and closed my eyes as the mullah talked, and thought some more.

Chapter 18

There's a lot of crap talked about the darknet.

Encrypted data, hard (but not, please note, not impossible) to trace. It lurks beneath the internet, that public stewing ground of tracked data and tweets, like the submarine beneath the cruise ship. There, political dissidents post videos of their kin being slaughtered by the powers that be; here, the factory workers in Yunan driven to despair, their final moments shown as they throw themselves from the highest windows. Their deaths are filmed on a smartphone and smuggled through the Great Firewall of China; the man who died that day made your computer, and it was cheap – will you, knowing his suffering, buy elsewhere? (But it was cheap! So wonderfully cheap!) Governments use the darknet to negotiate and communicate away from prying eyes. The US Navy invented it, and through it treaties are salvaged, truths revealed.

Anonymous don their Guy Fawkes mask and take down government servers and giant corporations, fight for petty feuds and noble causes. Today a DDOS attack against the Russian government in retaliation for the death of a journalist who spoke out over Ukraine. Tomorrow a police server is wiped in Scotland Yard, erasing records of one of their kind and, incidentally, securing the freedom of two aggravated assaulters, three burglars and a rapist.

Causes are sometimes blind, they say. Sometimes people are hurt in the fight for freedom.

Free to look at child pornography.

My website has over 40,000 positive reviews and over 3,000 images!!

Or perhaps:

Heroin, uncut, 2kg slab direct from Afghanistan. This is the highest quality, carefully packaged and delivered. Please place your offers with the subject line, "Auction bid".

There is no act too degrading, no violence which cannot be indulged on the darknet. Pay in USD, euros, bitcoins or yen, someone, somewhere, will make your dreams come true.

On the day I was to exchange $2.2 million worth of diamonds with an anonymous user by the name of mugurski71 in a café in Oman, I took a gamble on Byron14, and sent a decoy in my place.

Her name was Tola, and she had been trafficked from Thailand four years ago into domestic service. Her passport was taken by the agency who'd arranged her transit, her salary was held back for "security requirements" and after three weeks in the house where she was labouring, the fifty-four-year-old father-of-nine attempted to rape her. She bit his ear hard enough for him to need stitches, and she was arrested. Once he was out of hospital, the man didn't press charges, but the agency which had trafficked Tola gave him compensation for his trouble and had Tola in a brothel in the desert before the cheque had cleared.

"I'm nice," she said, when I phoned. "I have good French."

I told her to meet me in the souk, and left a mobile phone on the table in the café where the transfer was to take place.

Through the mobile phone's camera, I watched her face bob in and out of focus. She didn't pick up the phone, didn't examine it, expressed no curiosity about anything. Just sat and waited, her features stuck in tiny motion, like a piece of degraded film on a loop.

From my phone a few shops away, I sent her location to mugurski71 and waited.

They arrived in seventeen minutes, and the moment they did it was obviously a trap. The man who went into the café was respectable enough: a cream linen suit, sunglasses, hair receding from his high forehead and a silk handkerchief folded in his jacket pocket. The seven armed men who positioned themselves around the little shop and nearby pathways didn't even bother to hide their weapons; one, an idiot who deserved to lose both his testicles in the inevitable slipped-trigger, had a gun lodged in his trouser belt.

All this I saw as I walked between them, examining the sights of the market like a good tourist. In my ear I could hear a conversation unfolding in the café that I was happy not to be a part of.

Where are the goods?

Good. Good good.

Where are they?

You know place near here? I know place near here.

Do you understand what I'm talking about?

Good good. Yes, of course, very good.

Tola leaning across the table, one hand reaching out to caress the buyer's thigh. A slap; he pushed it away, she recoiled, animal hurt now on her features.

I dialled the mobile phone in the café.

mugurski71 answered.

"Yes?"

"Too many guns in the room," I said. "Diamonds say bye-bye!"

He tried to speak, but I hung up, pulled out my battery and SIM card, and threw them in the rubbish on my way out.

I left Oman that night, stealing a ticket from a passenger on a cruise liner heading for the Red Sea. I couldn't use the passenger's cabin; she had shouted her way back on board, and a search was quickly underway for the stowaway. But I could sit by the bar, ordering a series of desultorily alcohol-free concoctions and waiting for security to give up, declare "Maybe you lost it, ma'am," before we pulled out of port. I could bring no luggage that would attract attention, so walked round with my stolen goods, and stayed awake until 3 a.m., when I finally managed to snooze during a screening of a bad romantic comedy in the ship's all-night cinema lounge.

By day I slumbered on a balcony overlooking the sea, as the engines roared above and grumbled below. I bought a bikini from the over-priced on-board shop, changed in the toilets, swam in the cruiser's outdoor pool, washed myself in the fountains that spurted up either side of the deck, dried in the sun, met a preacher and his wife, a retired commander of the RAF, a former tap-dance teacher and her four abhorrent children, a man who reported himself to be in "commodities" and who I suspected of being an arms dealer, and a group of student actors who every day put on the "happy matinee show for the kiddies!" (*The Big Friendly Giant*) and then in the evening, on the same stage, performed the "grown-up show for culture" (*Richard III*).

"I play King Richard," whispered one conspiratorially. "It's a big part, I mean, a big deal, and like, an amazing role, just so amazing, but between you and me, I'm happier being a talking broccoli in the matinee."

"I didn't realise there were any talking broccoli in *The Big Friendly Giant*."

"Me neither! But the director's inspired like that."

A couple in the first-class dining room, I didn't think I'd seen such beauty before. His radiance, rather than obscuring hers, seemed to set it off, and the whole room turned to look at their entrance. Waiters scurried to fulfil their wishes – which was for a bland vegetarian option and an obscure protein drink – and all the while she rested her chin on the back of her hand and laughed at his jokes with the high sound of silver tapping on a crystal glass, and didn't look at his face, but scanned the room, like an animal wary of predators in the grass.

I approached them out of curiosity, told them I was a producer with the BBC, and forgive me intruding, but had I seen them on the TV?

"Not yet," replied the man with a dazzling smile.

"Oh a producer, how wonderful!" exclaimed the woman, and a few short sentences later and a couple of references to my friend the director general and how exciting it was to meet new talent, I was at their table.

"I'd just love to be on the TV," she exclaimed. "Not for the fame, you understand, but just because I think there's so many important things I could say."

Her partner joined in when I mentioned *Top Gear*, wondered if I'd met the boys, driven the cars.

"They're darlings, such darlings – that chemistry you see on screen, it's real, all of it, it's just so real," I lied. "Are you interested in cars . . . ?"

Why yes, yes he was, he'd just bought his first Jaguar . . .

"He wanted a Ferrari," exclaimed the missus, "but I won't let him do anything so silly."

I listened to them a while, dropping in occasional total lies and abject flatteries, until at last the woman leant over and said, "Have you got Perfection?"

"Why yes, of course. Though I haven't used it for a while."

"Changed. Our. Lives," she intoned.

"Changed our lives," he concurred.

"This trip – elite access, VIP upgrade to first class. It said 'you need a break' and you know, it was right, I mean, of course it was, it had GPS on me, knew I spent far too much time at work . . ."

"Far too much . . . " sang along the mister.

" . . . 'The perfect holiday for the perfect you,' it said and, well, isn't it? I mean, isn't it just?"

"You don't feel like you've just been sold a package?" I enquired.

"Of course we've been sold a package," he replied, bristling at the notion that any thought might occur in this world which had not first occurred to him. "All these cruise companies and holiday companies, they all have tie-ins with Perfection, of course they do. But then, it *is* the perfect holiday . . . "

" . . . the perfect holiday!"

" . . . isn't it?"

I smiled, and looked at this couple again, and imagined the hours they'd spent in dentists' chairs, the wash of the general anaesthetic before plastic surgery, the days lost to shopping trips, the friends abandoned for lack of social graces.

"The perfect holiday, for the perfect couple," I murmured, and stole their room key, and while they were finishing their dinner I used their shower, stole his watch, their currency and her make-up bag.

Chapter 19

Choices for the lonely: to seek human company in all its forms, or to be content with the fact that you have no company at all.

I switch between the two.

I made it fifteen days by myself in a cabin in the forests of Canada before breaking. In the end, paralysed and sobbing, I had to phone the police to come and rescue me.

A woman in a brown hat picked me up, and when she arrived I clung onto her arm, and said I was sorry, I was so sorry, I don't know what came over me, but I couldn't move, my legs couldn't move, I tried walking and my legs wouldn't lift me, I'd crawled on my belly to the phone and there were shadows in the windows, sounds in the dark, and I thought I'd be okay and I hadn't been, I hadn't been at all.

She held me tight, this perfect stranger, and said, "It's okay, it's okay, you'll be okay. The forest gets to people sometimes. You're not the first one to call, and won't be the last I reckon. It's okay."

In any other place, she might have charged me with wasting police time, but here, where her beat was nine hundred square miles of forest, where she knew the name of every person that lived within, she wasn't about to stand on ceremony. She drove me fifty kilometres into town, invited me into her home, made coffee, turned on the TV and said, "My kids will be home soon. You wanna stay and watch a film?"

We watched *Bedknobs and Broomsticks*, a lesser-known Disney romp involving con men, Nazis, soccer-obsessed lions, rabbits and magic.

"When I grow up," said the youngest child, and I waited for her to proclaim her intention to be a witch, a knight, a soldier, "I want to own a museum."

When the light was out and the kids asleep, I thanked the sheriff calmly, and said I didn't know what had come over me.

"Some folk just ain't built for living solo, I guess," she replied. "There's nothing to be ashamed of, if that way ain't for you."

In the months that followed, I travelled across North America. I met psychologists and attended conferences, studied journals and newspapers. I talked with scholars and monks, men and women who'd been held in solitary confinement for years on end.

You find the happiness you can, one said. *Sometimes it's hard, sometimes you gotta dig deep, but it's there, the thing inside that you can be content.*

I asked what happened when he'd been freed from his prison cell after seven years in isolation.

I went to the hotel and met my wife. She was crying, holding me, but I didn't say anything. All my feelings were cold. It had been seven years since I'd last had to speak, I didn't think I knew how.

A prisoner from a supermax in Florida, sat on the end of the hospital bed.

I'm lucid now, he said, *but I been in the hospital for eleven days. They had me in administrative segregation before. That's where they segregate you from the population, so as you can't do no harm to another.*

"Did you do harm?" I asked.

I killed a man, he replied with a shrug. *He was gonna kill me.*

"You sure of that?"

Sure I'm sure. I seen the way he were looking at me, like he knew I were gonna die. I had to get there first, is all.

"And why are you in the hospital now?"

Tried to strangle myself with my own bedding. This is the third time I try to kill myself, and I feel okay now, now that the doctor seen me, but I guess when they send me back I'll try again until I get it right.

Calmly, so calmly, sat with his chin in his hands, three-time killer by twenty-two, segregated for life.

I used to dream when I were in solitary, he explains, staring through his hands. *Now I don't dream so much. I'm just waiting.*

"Waiting for what?"

Dunno. Just waiting.

I do not fear loneliness – not any more.

Discipline.

I am the queen of internet dating; I am a one-click wonder. People forget me, but my digital profile remains, enshrined in binary code, remembered by the internet, so much more reliable than the human mind. The web is designed for the short-term; see something you like? Bookmark it. Like what you see, right now? Call me. I'm right here; I'm waiting.

"You don't look anything like your profile picture!" people exclaim when I introduce myself to them at our pre-arranged meeting.

I look exactly like my profile picture, but my face is easier to forget than a date and time you've saved onto your smartphone. People usually have to blurt something out, to cover the embarrassment of not having remembered me, or recognised my face.

"I mean, you look really good," the gentlemen will add. "Like . . . much better in reality."

Toilet breaks are the destruction of a good date. Men who, after a mere twenty minutes, need to empty their bladders are no use to me. In the three minutes they spend in the gents, their memories fade, and by the time they emerge, even the most ardent of lovers will have forgotten my features, and the vast majority will have forgotten they were even on a date.

Equally, men who are tedious are easily got rid of. Three minutes in the ladies, and by the time I emerge the gentleman will probably be paying the bill and texting his mates.

Hi, he says, *in town having a quiet drink by myself. You guys around?*

The mind fills in gaps, invents excuses.

"I'm a good man," said Inspector Luca Evard, the day he found out. "I don't forget the people I've slept with; that's not who I am."

Just because you have forgotten me, does that mean I am not real?

Now.

You forget.

Now.

I am real.

Reality: the conjectured state of things as they actually exist.

I breathe, and in the time the air takes to leave my lungs, I vanish from the minds of men, and cease to exist for anyone except myself.

Chapter 20

The cruise ship docked at Sharm el-Sheikh just before dawn, edging towards the quay as the sun came up. I put on make-up to hide the tiredness round my eyes and crossed the border on my Australian passport, hid amongst the tourists. Egyptian Arabic is very different from the standard and Sudanese dialects I spoke, and though I could pick up a fair amount, replying with fluency proved difficult. Even had I been able to speak, the locals weren't very interested in conversation.

"You want see pyramids? I take you! You want buy icon? I have all the icon you ever want, ancient goods, good goods, you come, you see! You want taxi? You want restaurant? You want see Nile? You want tour? I know best, very very best!"

Only one local woman in the resort seemed willing to engage with me, switching to Syrian Arabic in response to my accent and saying, "You're not a tourist?"

"Social worker," I replied, "with Médecins Sans Frontières."

"Ah! You working in Egypt?"

"Sudan."

"Terrible place; you are a good woman to go out there."

"It's not that bad."

"Terrible place – the people! – just terrible."

"Egypt isn't without its problems."

"Sure, but at least here your problem is only the government."

"Can I buy you a coffee?" I asked. "I'd like to hear more about that."

"I'd love to," she replied, "but someone might think you are a journalist."

Rebuffed, I tried talking to the tourists, focusing on anyone travelling alone. Sharm is hotels, palm trees, swimming pools and restaurants, each more expensive than the next. Once, the crystal blue waters and salt lagoon attracted Americans and Germans. In recent years the clients were changing, and the surface of the water shimmered with a slick of suntan oil. I watched a Russian father throw his weeping son into the sea, shouting, "Swim, swim, swim!" while the boy bobbed and gurgled and half drowned in his desperation to please. I saw Brazilian daughters sniff at the food served to them on crystal platters and exclaim, "No good, too many calories!" sending it back to the kitchen.

"Liquid foods only," explained a Portuguese princess. "I have to watch my weight."

I slept during the worst of the heat, recovering from my stowaway time on the ship, and at sunset went looking for company. Crossing the town in British weather would have taken less than an hour. In the Egyptian boil, I had to stop every ten minutes to cower in shade. Even my hair felt hot to the touch.

At night I log into the darknet, looking for Byron14.

Byron14 is not there.

Another day spent pacing the town, bored now, bored with the sun, bored with indolence, bored with being on the run.

"I lost five stone through Perfection!" said a British woman I swam with in the salt lagoon. "I'm at seven hundred and fifty thousand points, and it automated my online shop because I was buying too many fatty foods, put me on a seasonal diet of greens and nuts, isn't it wonderful?"

I looked at her, a perfect body, the perfect shape, the perfect curves, the perfect teeth, the perfect hair, the perfect smile, and realised I hated everything about her, and everything about me, and everything about this place, and snapped, "When was the last time you fucking thought for yourself?" and swam away from her as fast as I could, and dived underwater to hide the shame of my imperfect self, and stayed down until I could no longer hold my breath.

In an ice-cream parlour at night, I logged into the darknet, waiting for Byron14 to call. When he appeared, it was one in the morning, and the party was still going strong in the nightclub next door.

```
Byron14: Are you safe?

_why: How did you know about mugurski71?
```

Byron14: I know his work.

A photo, the man in the café in Muscat, taken another time, another place. He looked old in this picture, his shoulders down, head turned to one side, like a man who'd forgotten where he put his wallet – not like the stranger with a gun who'd come to claim my prize.

_why: That's him. Who is he?

Byron14: Security for Prometheus.

_why: Why is he after me?

Byron14: His employer feels that you humiliated him by stealing from his guests. Your actions compromised a deal; he somewhat hastily pledged to find you, and return the diamonds, as proof of his company's strength.

_why: How do you know this?

Byron14: I monitor Prometheus.

_why: Why?

Byron14: That is my business. How did you get access to the 106?

_why: Who are the 106?

Byron14: My questions mean you no harm.

_why: I simply don't understand them. I was after diamonds; that's all.

Byron14: Was it?

I licked melting pistachio ice cream from the back of a spoon, watched the beautiful and the wealthy ambling by.

_why: A woman died. She was my friend. She wanted to be perfect, and being perfect disgusted her. It pleased me to make perfect people afraid. I liked taking what they had.

Then, Do you want to buy some diamonds? Cut price, for favours given.

Byron14: Perhaps. Do you have Perfection?

A moment.

I sit back, and find to my surprise that I am already counting, looking out of the window. I count sports cars (three) and cars whose weight on their wheels suggest reinforced bodies and bullet-proof glass (two). I count beautiful young things in shoes ladder-high, and handbags with a value of more than two hundred British pounds. I count leaves on the carefully planted palm trees, and the number of street lamps I can see. An immaculate white four-wheel-drive passes by, briefly pulling my attention. At its back, on a trailer, is a large white yacht, its hull and cabin adorned with stickers proclaiming, “Free Palestine”. I realise I am laughing, and people are watching me, and so I stop, and return to the keyboard. Byron14 is waiting.

_why: No. I despise everything I have seen of Perfection. Is this relevant?

Byron14: To potential employment.

_why: You want to hire me?

Byron14: We should resume this conversation another time.

_why: Why?

Byron14: mugurski71 is looking for you, and the darknet is not immune to attack.

_why: He won't find me.

Byron14: You are in Egypt, probably a coastal area, likely the Red Sea, probably a tourist resort.

I count.
My breaths.
My world.
I type slowly, carefully.

_why: Why'd you think that?

Byron14: I tracked mugurski71. He was in Oman five days ago. Logically you would flee after a failed exchange. Unlikely you would risk returning to Dubai; the border with Saudi Arabia is closed, and it is risky to cross into Yemen. The only options remaining are air travel or sea. Four days ago, a passenger on a cruise ship registered a complaint that her ticket had been stolen on a vessel headed for Egypt. That vessel arrived this morning, and according to customs, one passenger more than was registered on the vessel disembarked. These things are not so difficult to check. As I said: we could perhaps both benefit from suspending this conversation.

A moment, to consider all this. I could find nothing in it to pick apart.

I wrote, and was surprised to see that I had written it:

_why: What if we worked together? What then?

Byron14: Could you gain access to the 106 club?

_why: I can get into anything.

Byron14: I am not interested in boasts.

_why: I have the goods from Dubai.

Nothing.

I ran my fingers between the keys on the keyboard, the lightest of touches, feeling their shape.

When learning to lockpick, roll grains of salt between your fingertips to increase sensitivity.

I half closed my eyes, felt the tiny irregularities in the keys, dirt stuck to the sides, the raised bump of the letters.

I waited for Byron14 to reply, and wondered if he too was counting his breath.

Byron14: So you do at that. Would you care to resume this conversation in three days' time?

_why: With pleasure. Thanks for your help.

```
Byron14: Good luck.
```

Byron14 was gone.

Chapter 21

Back to the hotel; a hasty pack, a premature checking-out. Has the time come to risk a plane? I look up Sharm el-Sheikh airport; not impossible to smuggle diamonds out, but what if mugurski71 is watching?

What if, what if, what if; the perpetual mantra of the thief on the run.

I count my breaths, looking for that fine line between sensible caution and unwise terror. It is perfectly possible for a man to hold a picture of my face in his hand, and look on my features, and know that the two are the same. In the future, he will remember only holding the picture, not my face, but it is the present tense we need worry about.

Standing in the hotel foyer, I ask the receptionist to call me a taxi.

"Where to?"

Nowhere to go, except the airport.

"I'm catching a cruise ship," I lied. "I'm going to sail up the Suez."

Doesn't matter if she believes me or not; she'll forget the lie as easily as the truth. The important thing to disguise is digital records. Let any calls recorded to a taxi company hear only reference to the sea.

"Ten minutes," she said.

I smiled, and walked out into the smiting sun, to find a cab for myself.

*

The smell of air freshener, the sound of Arab pop, undulations and the tapping of the drum, a mat of wooden beads down the backs of the seats, the high scrape of the violin and twang of electric keys.

Where to? asked the driver.

The airport, I replied.

A nowhere building in the sand. Mountains behind, dust-yellow all around. They were thinking of adding another terminal, extending the runway, as people flocked to the sea. اهلا وسهلا! Bienvenue! 欢迎! Добро пожаловать!

I bought a ticket to Istanbul, waited in the departures lounge, watching people, watching security, waiting.

Quietly terrifying, going through customs.

I was tempted just to wear the necklace, but no; still too many images of the stolen jewels floating about. Ridiculous plans floated through my mind; a diamond in my shoe, swallowed diamonds in my stomach, in my pockets, in my coat, in the back of my mobile phone where a battery should be . . . but no. Once a customs inspector finds one diamond, they'll start looking for them all. Best to just brave it out, and rely on memory failure should I need to run.

Nearly every courier and mule caught crossing a border, is caught because they look afraid.

I stand in the lady's bathroom and paint a picture of who I want to be. Eyeshadow the colour of the desert at sunset; a smile to charm – weary from travel, wry at the thought of distances yet to be covered, but happy to be going home, relieved and relaxed, a body warmed in the Egyptian sun.

I am not Hope Arden.

I am not afraid.

(My parents would be ashamed of me, if they could see me now.)

I straighten my back, and head towards the border.

Chapter 22

I think I have met someone like me.

I say this with some hesitation, since I can't remember the experience.

A collection of documents: letters, photos, a snowglobe with the Empire State Building inside, a ticket stub for a show on Broadway. I remember the show, I remember the Empire State, I remember a cold night in November, the snow beginning to fall – but I do not remember having company for any of it.

And yet, in a small lock-up in Newark, there is a plastic box, carefully sealed, which contains within it a photo taken of me and a man, a stranger to my memory, smiling together outside the theatre. Another picture, a face I can't recall, on Fifth Avenue, waving, a woollen hat with ear flaps pulled down across his head, two green and white bobbles bouncing around his neck. He looks ridiculous. Maybe early thirties? A letter in an unknown hand says he's thirty-two. If I look at his photograph I can say that he is probably five foot eight, with mousy blond hair, grey eyes, and a mole on his chin. He looks as if he should be overweight, but that is a trick of his features, of eyes too wide for the face that holds them, skin soft, a neck a little too short for the body on which it sits, for look – the camera pulls back and for a moment beneath the winter coat and winter boots he's a kid, a skinny child who hasn't yet reached his destiny as a portly old man.

Now I close my eyes.

Now.

And now I cannot remember his features at all, though I saw his photo not a minute ago. I remember writing them, and can write them still – hair, eyes, height – but these are just words, abstract concepts, not an individual. This must be how it is for Luca Evard.

I open a box full of recorded memories, and meet someone who was like myself.

A letter, from myself, to myself, written when I was twenty-four years old. A photograph of me writing, then another of a stranger in the same place, 53rd Street Station, waiting for the train to Queens. I remember writing; I don't remember exactly what I wrote, but I'm sure there wasn't anyone with me – no photographer. Why did I write the letter? Because I was bored, maybe, and waiting for the train. Why was I going to Queens? Curiosity. Nothing else. These are the memories I have, and yet I hold a letter which says, in my handwriting:

Tonight I met someone who is like me. Like us. I say "us", even though I am writing this to myself, for the me who reads this will not be able to recall the events that I remember now, and through forgetting will, in a way, be a different person from who I am now, in this moment. We are the same, I am you, you are me, but we will have experienced the moment of now, this moment in which I write, in an entirely different way, when now becomes then, and then is now.

~~Tonight I met someone~~ – no, that's not right. I think we have met each other many times before, but only tonight, only when we saw the photo, did we get it.

We met at drop-in for the St Sebastian Nursing Home in Harlem. You should remember sitting with men and women at the dining table, everyone always delighted to meet someone new, asking about my life, about the outside world. They don't care that they've never met me; they're always happy to meet someone new, for the very first time. You will remember other volunteers, too, ranging from the charitable to the dispassionate, the vivacious to the inept. Goodwill, I think, is no substitute for training in how to handle patients with dementia; but this is not about that.

What should also be within your mind is the memory last week of the ninety-first birthday of Rose Daniels. A photo was taken of everyone in the dining room, young and old. I enclose the photograph here. See if you can spot the anomaly.

A moment – let's look at the photograph. In the very centre, beaming from her wheelchair, Rose Daniels, who in the 1970s had been beaten and imprisoned by the NYPD for being an African-American woman who dared to kiss a white man in Central Park, and who in the 1990s, already advanced into her old age, was told by her doctor that she shouldn't make a fuss about the lump in her breast, because black women always got frightened at the smallest little thing. After the cancer had grown to the point where she had to have a double mastectomy, she attempted to sue the offending physician, and was awarded five thousand US dollars out of court and a curt letter telling her to go away.

"My husband said that God is waiting for these people in the next life with fire and judgement and righteous retribution," she'd say. "But I think it's only proper to give them a taste of what they're making in this life too."

Surrounding her, the other inmates of the home. Some smiling; some confused; some with food around their mouths; some dressed so smart they could be going to a wedding. Behind them, the underpaid carers, arms folded across their chests, smiles pinned onto their lips like a tail to the donkey. Lastly, the volunteers. Bobby from 10th Avenue, who lived next to the railway sidings and above the billiard hall and made his living attending focus groups. "My job is to be real," he explained. "I'm a professional real person." Maxine from the Bronx, whose mum had died in this home not five months since, and who "Didn't want to leave the ladies alone, even more now that Mom has left us." Big B from Morris Heights, who said almost nothing at all and who I thought was cold and thoughtless, until the day I found him holding Mrs Watroba when she started crying, just crying, for no reason at all.

And at the back, in the middle of it all, me, smiling to camera, my hands at my sides, and him next to me, a pale-faced, grinning stranger, one hand resting on my shoulder.

Who was he?

Who *is* he?

I stare at the photo, and I can't recall.

His hand is on my shoulder; surely I would remember that?

I close my eyes to remember the moment of the camera flash, and cannot recall skin touching mine.

Answers in a letter – I read on.

Can you see it? I ask. *Can you see him?*

The photo was put up on a noticeboard three days after it was taken, to remind people of the party. I must have stood looking at it for ten, fifteen minutes, trying to figure it out. I couldn't. In the end I stole it from the board, and went round the room, trying to spot the man in the picture. Of course, he wasn't there – the universe is not so neat – but after lunch, as I was on my way out, there he was, coming in. I didn't recognise him, of course, but I still had the photo and the very fact that I didn't remember him, made me wonder. I compared his face to the face in the photo, saw they were the same, went up to him, said my name, said we hadn't met yet, and he said, "No, I'm new here."

Then I showed him the photo.

At first I think he thought I was some sort of security. He picked up his coat, like he would go, but I caught his arm before he could and said, "No, listen. You don't get it. I don't remember you – can you remember me?"

Now he looked at me.

Now he looked at the photo.

Now he looked at me again.

Now he began to understand.

We left together at that moment, we didn't need to say the words. We went to a diner round the corner, not daring to let each other out of sight, until at last he said, "I have to test this." His accent is American, East Coast – he says he's from Maine.

So, he left himself a note – "You know this woman, she is like you" – and put it on top of his coat. I left myself a note too – "The man who sits next to you is like you, he is someone you will forget, talk to him, look at the picture, remember, REMEMBER." Then he went to the bathroom, and I stared at the photo until my eyes hurt. When he came back, he'd forgotten, but as he went to pick up his coat, he saw the note he'd left himself, and he saw me.

Another item, a note, scrawled in my handwriting, on the back of a napkin from Morris's Grill and Diner.

Remember, REMEMBER.

"Hi," he said, holding out his hand. "My name's Parker – the one and only Parker of New York. Except Spider-Man, who's a jackass."

"Hope," I replied. "It looks like we've met before."

"You're British? Jesus – I guess I must have already asked you that."

"I don't remember you asking, though it might be we've had this conversation dozens of times."

"I forgot you."

"And I forgot you."

I think he laughed then; I know I did. The absurdity of it – totally daft. But when I laughed, I also wanted to cry, though I wasn't sad. What would he be like, this mirror image of myself? How did he live? Could we create a thing between us that had meaning?

He grabbed my hand, held it hard, and I let him, because I needed to cling to him too. "We don't leave each other's side," he said. "Not yet; not today."

We went round the city together. All day, we've moved from café to café, place to place, like tourists. The movement is good; as strangers we find new sights, new places, find our voices through walking together, being together. We went to Central Park, had hot chocolate and whisky; went to the top of the Empire State Building; had dinner on Broadway. We don't leave each other's side, don't dare take our eyes off each other's faces. He proposes scientific tests, says we can time how long it takes for us to be apart before we forget, see if we can remember by touch, with our eyes shut, by sound; he says, this is an opportunity, an amazing opportunity, but even as he says it, I can see the doubt. I stand outside the cubicle in the bathroom and sing when he needs to pee, and he's shaking with fear as he locks the door, in case he forgets me, and I'm scared also. Remember, I say, remember.

I am interested to know how much you – I, that is, the I that will be you, when I have forgotten – remember of all this. Soon I shall be you experiencing this letter, and what then? Will I remember the Empire State, will I remember chocolate and vanilla cheesecake, the Guggenheim and the way he slid down the plastic seats of the express as we rode through Manhattan? What do you see?

I see the Empire State, New York spread beneath me. I remember the way the cheesecake clung to my fork, sticky, white and dark chocolate marbled together. I remember riding the express train, but no one slid along the plastic seats, and no one was by my side.

Do you remember feeling? Do you remember laughter? Do you remember joy, hope, fear?

I remember . . . I remember laughing in the Guggenheim, though now I cannot remember what I was laughing at.

I am frightened now. I am frightened that when he fades from my memory, a piece of me will die too. The feelings, the things I have learned, the ideas I have had today, so many ideas, so many feelings, they will die with my memory. I fear that loss. But more, a terror that I must share with my future self. I fear what this means for me. If you forget the joy of this day, then what joy you give to others will also be forgotten, and your life has no consequence, no meaning, no worth. I am a shadow, blasted away by the sun, a meaningless occlusion of light that fades with the day.

Remember. God, please God, please, remember. Remember him. Remember me.

I will put my pen down now.

He will walk away.

He is going.

He is going.

Remember.

There the letter stopped, and he was gone.

Chapter 23

Many years later, I walked up to the customs post at Sharm el-Sheikh airport, stood in a queue of nine people, counted my steps, concentrated on my toes until I could feel each individual end, could define the shape of every part of my feet. They didn't pat me down as I went through security, and they didn't bother to check my luggage. In duty-free territory, I bought bad international coffee and a bad international magazine, and waited for my gate to be called.

Colourful pictures, words on a page.

Revealed!! Celebrities without their make-up!

How was Daring Duncan's first night as a stripper? The full story!

Roisin and Abby's Feud: Now It's Personal.

I flicked through without paying much attention, eyes still circling the hall.

This season's must-haves: get the A-list look.

"She says she loves me, but why's she so frigid in bed?"

Perfection 106: the insider report.

I stop. Flick back a few pages. Look more closely.

A series of pictures: beautiful people in beautiful clothes. Not a gram of fat between them, no grey hair, no wrinkles, only perfect, cosmetic smiles. Champagne from glasses with twisting spines; gold at the women's necks, gold in the cufflinks of the tuxedos.

The world's all the rage for Perfection, the new life-enhancing, you-enhancing app from Prometheus. But only a very few ever earn enough points to be invited to join the 1×106 club. We meet the exclusive few who've made their lives truly perfect . . .

A bewildering tapestry of names and faces. She used to be a PA, but now she's head of her own media firm. He used to work in the invoicing department of a stationery shop, but now he's a management consultant, and fabulous. He used to weigh twenty-two stone and was scared of meeting new people, but having earned 1×106 points through Perfection his life has been transformed and he's just got engaged to the runner-up of Miss Colombia 2009.

She loves her yacht.

He loves his house.

He met his wife through Perfection, the perfect woman, he hadn't known what perfect meant until he saw her.

"I thought my life was going to waste," she explains, "but now I realise that I can be perfect too."

I lay the magazine down as my flight is called, walk to the gate, diamonds temporarily forgotten, the worst of the job done. From here, things should be easy.

A premium-class seat near the door; not quite first, not quite economy. Padding and iced water in a plastic cup. The air stewardess who directs me to my chair wears stunningly red lipstick.

Standard uniform requirements for female cabin crew:

- 5'2" to 6'1" in height, with body weight that is proportional to this height.
- Regulation skirt, not trousers.

- Hair in one of fourteen regulation styles. If worn in French plait, end of plait not to exceed 1.3 inches.
- Powder and lipstick to be worn as a minimum requirement for make-up.
- Handbag must be carried over the right shoulder.
- Hat to be worn at all times, over the right eye.

The seat next to mine is empty. I pull on my seatbelt, tugging it a little too tight around my middle, lean back in my chair.

The door closes, a clunk as we're sealed from the outside world.

I half close my eyes.

A man sits next to me.

He wears a linen suit, a white cotton shirt, glasses balanced on the top of his head. His watch has a thick leather strap, but the face is constructed so you can see the gears turning beneath, a skeleton watch, £450 at a pinch, more indulgent than his shoes (£60) or his haircut (£15) – a thing that perhaps carries meaning for him. I wonder if I should steal it, but decide the strap is too wide, it won't fit, and besides I'm not in the mood.

I glance up at his face, and he is known to me, and he is mugurski71, pulling the flight magazine from the chair back in front of him, flicking through, eyebrows drawn, face crinkled, considering Black Sea holidays and resorts on the Aegean.

I look away.

Can he remember my face?

Impossible: we haven't met, he has no picture in his hand to compare against my features.

Yet equally impossible: coincidence. _why and mugurski71 do not meet by chance, not like this.

The plane begins to taxi to the runway. The cabin crew perform safety checks, seatbelts, lockers. With perfect painted smiles they indicate the emergency exit here, there, air masks, lifejackets, stay calm, save yourself, then the kids.

I pretend to read my magazine, he pretends to read his.

How has he found me?

"The money."

He spoke so calmly, eyes turned still to the pages in his lap – *Detox to perfection with our 5★ holistic getaway* – that I wasn't entirely sure he'd spoken at all.

Then he spoke again.

"I followed the money. Once we concluded you had stowed away on the cruise ship, I sent people ahead to watch the ports, see who disembarked, who checked into what. The day the ship arrived in Sharm el-Sheikh, an Australian passport cleared customs, which wasn't on the ship's manifest. We found you as you checked out, but you used the same account for both the hotel and the flight to Istanbul. I had to run to make this flight, which is undignified. My name is Gauguin."

He held out one hand, club-fingered and pale, his eyes still not rising from the magazine. I declined to shake it.

"You're talking to me?" I asked.

"Yes. I am."

"I don't know you."

"I work for Prometheus."

"I'm afraid that means nothing to me."

"The flight to Istanbul is approximately an hour and forty minutes. The magazines run dry after barely ten minutes of entertainment."

Silence.

I gave up pretending to read, sat back in my chair.

Counted backwards from ten.

"Gauguin, right?"

"That's right."

"French post-impressionist artist, died 1903, days before he was due to start serving a prison sentence for libelling the governor of the Marquesas Islands. Have you seen *Tahitian Women on a Beach*? There are two women by the sea, a pattern in the sand, as if they've been doodling, a pipe, some tobacco, not used. They have flowers in their hair."

"You know more about it than I do."

"Then why call yourself Gauguin?"

He shrugged. "It's a name. I can use something else, if you want."

"Gauguin is fine."

"And you are . . . ?"

"You can call me Why."

A push, a rise of engine, the wheels come up, heads go back; I glance out of the window to watch the dust outside give way to the sea, and there's the town, barely bigger than the airport that serves it, five streets of luxury, a nowhere place in the desert. He waited until the sound of the engine had slowed, the flight levelled off, before folding his magazine perfectly, precisely, into the pouch in front of him.

"There are some questions we'll need to ask," he said.

"What questions?"

"About the robbery. How you accessed the 106 Club in Dubai; how you got into the party. How you escaped. Why you targeted Prometheus."

"I targeted diamonds."

He smiled at nothing much and said, "My employers don't see it that way. Only a fool steals from a party, in the manner in which you did. Anyone reasonable would have targeted the safe, or while the jewels were in transit."

"I'm a better thief than I am a safe-cracker," I answered, honestly enough.

A stewardess leant down, interrupting before Gauguin could open his mouth to reply, took our cups, promised a trolley service with light refreshments still to come. Gauguin thanked her courteously; I didn't have the heart.

When she turned away, I said, "If you knew I was on this flight, why not simply wait until I reached Istanbul?"

"Pressures of time."

"You're playing catch-up."

A shrug: he's here, isn't he?

"You brought guns to our meeting in Muscat."

"You sent a prostitute."

"Guns," I repeated. "Sometimes it's not paranoia."

He shrugged, a busy man in a busy world.

"You want diamonds, right? I heard you made a deal – your guys help get the diamonds back, the UAE invests in your company?"

A flicker across his face, the tiniest twitch to his smile, and I've made a mistake, a right balls-up, and I will have to walk away soon and let him forget. But he's between me and the aisle, so I added, "I don't have the diamonds with me now. You want them, we're going to have to negotiate."

He smiled at nothing much, turned away, examined the buttons in the plastic ceiling above our heads, the fans blowing in cold air, the illuminated seatbelt light. "No," he murmured. "No, I think not."

Silence.

I waited, he waited, and the realisation began to dawn that this man could out-wait the ice age. A childish desire in me; I counted to one hundred, then counted back. Still he waited. I leaned my head back in my chair, ran my mind over my body, feeling each little ache and pain, readjusting my posture so my back was straight, feet on the ground, knees together, shoulders relaxed. Still he waited.

I permitted myself to play out a few scenarios in my mind, and they all ended badly.

I focused until my mind ached on the faint grey pattern woven into the fabric that covered the seat in front of me, and heard myself say without quite knowing from where the words came, "Perfection killed a woman I knew."

Does he react?

No audible gasp, no nod, no frown. What does he do?

He stares at nothing much, and adjusts his cuffs. I watch him do this, and wonder if he's even conscious of the act. With the index finger of his right hand he explores the inside edge of his sleeve, feeling the stiff fabric, probing for irregularities. This done, he tugs, once, twice, on the cuff, bringing it into alignment with the bone down the inside of his arm.

Radius, ulna, humerus, scapula, clavicle. *Hip bone connected to the thigh bone, thigh bone connected to the knee bone, now hear the word of the Lord . . .*

"Was that why you stole the Chrysalis?"

"No. But it made it more satisfying when I did."

He nodded, said nothing. Is he also reciting all the bones in the body to himself, is that his mechanism? Femur, patella, tibia, fibula, tarsals, metatarsals, phalanges, how does he not move, how does he not blink?

I can learn a lot from Gauguin, but now isn't the time.

Then he said: "Tell me about your relationship with Byron14."

I was less surprised than I thought I'd be. The question had been one of many that circled around my possible list of scenarios, a hovering curiosity on the edge of my mind. "Who's Byron14?" I replied.

"Byron14 is the individual who you have been in communication with for the last few days via Tor," he murmured, staring at nothing much, cufflinks rolling between his fingers. "Byron14 is a killer and a terrorist. What have you been discussing?"

"I need to go to the bathroom," I said.

"Are you sure you can't hold it?" Like a schoolteacher at an exam.

"Yeah – no."

As I tried to stand, he grabbed my wrist, face turned upwards, eyes fixed on mine. I felt something brush against my leg, thought it was my seatbelt falling away, but the pressure remained. His eyes flicked down; mine followed.

The knife was ceramic, of course, and only four or five inches long, with a blue plastic handle. Four inches are three more than enough. The angle of his arm, where he held it against my femoral artery, obscured it from all but my inspection, the curve of his fingers along the back of the blade making it look like, perhaps, at worst, he was touching the side of my leg. I sat back down slowly, and the knife followed my journey, before returning back inside Gauguin's jacket.

My heart, my breath.

I closed my eyes.

"You wouldn't risk it," I said at last. "Not on a public flight."

"I have a very slim chance of being arrested," he replied. "You'd die for sure."

"Can't help you dead."

"You aren't helping now."

"Can't do anything at thirty-five thousand feet."

"That's fine; we'll land before you know it."

My heart, too fast, breath too quick. I tried to count and the numbers were tangled, come on, *come on*!

I found I was trying to remember Parker, forcing myself to picture his face as I had seen it on the photograph. I could see the photograph in my mind's eye, but his features were flat, unreal, and I bit my lip until I tasted blood. A list of characteristics – mousy hair, pale grey eyes, a mole on the right side of his chin, large ears, small nose – these are just words, they are nothing that has meaning.

"Just relax, Why," said Gauguin, leaning back in his chair, eyes half closed like a man about to sleep. "Just stay calm. Stay calm."

My mum, walking barefoot across the desert.

I close my eyes, and feel the sand beneath my feet.

"I'm calm," I say, and it is true. "There's really nothing to worry about."

We fly north-east, towards Istanbul.

Chapter 24

Five weeks after my friends, teachers and family began to forget me, I vanished from their memories altogether.

It was a simple thing – so simple.

Coming home on a Tuesday, I found half my stuff had gone, given to charity or my baby sister.

"Why'd you throw my stuff out?" I asked Mum, not shouting, not screaming any more, but quiet – so quiet.

"I didn't touch your stuff," she replied, looking at me bewildered. "There was just a lot of junk in the spare room."

"That's my room."

"Yes, that's what I meant. In your room."

I gave up going to school.

I had lost patience after being welcomed to my French class for the seventh time – *Bonjour, comment tu t'appelle? Bienvenue à l'école* – and introduced to my oldest friends day in, day out.

For a while, being the new girl was okay, and I made the most of it. I smashed the window of Mr Steeple's little Ford Fiesta, in response to four years of quiet, institutionalised bullying I had received from this shiny-skulled teacher.

"*Dum spiro, spero*, Ms Arden?"

"What?"

"*Dum spiro, spero*, from the Latin as you will know, and its meaning . . . ?"

Empty faces staring at my vacancy, for I knew not a word of Latin and Mr Steeple knew it well, but had taken to quietly humiliating those students who he felt were not taking his mighty intellect seriously enough.

"While I hope, I live, taken from Virgil. I had thought it was apposite to your nature, Ms Arden, but clearly I was mistaken."

Dum spiro, spero. While I breathe, I hope, taken from Cicero. When he was murdered by the soldiers of the Second Triumvirate, sent by men who had formerly been his friends, he was said to have turned to them with the words, "There is nothing proper about what you are doing, soldier, but do try to kill me properly." I chatted to a woman at a charity ball about Cicero once, and she nodded wisely and said, "Was he the Roman who wrote all those fart jokes?"

Other actions. Empowered by my predicament, I punched Eddie White in the face. He was the obligatory bully who had reached the peak of his power the day he force-fed Azim pork sausages in the canteen. A religious education class the week before had given him the idea, but his true success came not from forcing the sobbing thirteen-year-old to eat meat that was haram to his faith, but in gathering unto him nearly twenty-two screaming and cheering students who stood by laughing as the boy spluttered and choked. Punching Eddie White was a pleasant fantasy fulfilled. However, within a few hours, everyone had forgotten how Eddie got his black eye, which was why, the next day, I stole Eddie's phone instead, smashed it with a hammer, and left it on top of his locker. Physical consequences last much longer than any actions where my memory is involved.

Mischief-making was only fun for a while.

The world forgot me, and I lost interest in the world.

As the exams came nearer, I considered hanging around long enough to sit my GCSEs, but what was the point? Paper, ink, my name – these seemed to last, like the diary of a dead man or a piece of frozen footage – but they would mean nothing to me. No future, no job, no life at all seemed possible for me anymore, and so I took to wandering around Derby, looking at things I couldn't afford to buy and playing games in my mind to pass the time.

Seconds in a minute: I close my eyes and count to sixty, again, and now – again, until my counting matches the passage of the seconds.

Counting: minutes in an hour.

Perhaps now the hour has gone.

Or perhaps now.

Or now.

I stared at strangers who stared back, but no sooner are their heads turned than the memory begins to fade, and so they look

now

and now

and now

and each time they see me it is for the very first time.

And turn away.

I exist in this physical world as sure as stone, but in the world of men – in that world that is collective memory, in the dream-world where people find meaning, feeling, importance – I am a ghost. Only in the present tense am I real.

Now.

And now.

And now.

Then you close your eyes.

And I am gone.

Alone in Derby, forgotten by all, I went to the cinema, watched the blockbusters, then the comedies, until I fell asleep in the back row, and had to be shooed out by the cleaner. I went to the theatre. I'd never been before, but at matinees there were enough empty seats at the back. Some of it was dull. Some made me laugh until my face hurt. Some made me cry.

We shall find peace. We shall hear angels, we shall see the sky sparkling with diamonds.

I cried a lot, at that time.

People who lead a lonely existence always have something on their minds they're eager to talk about.

I opened my mouth to speak, and found I had no one to talk to. My parents grew distant, looked at me across the table as if unsure, unknowing; who was this girl, how did she come to be here? Only Gracie remained, my baby sister, for whom every plate was thin, flexible metal; every fork was plastic, every beautiful thing that could be broken by her clumsy, grasping hands put up high, out of reach. I'd resented her for a long time, but now I'd sit in her room and tell her about the things I'd seen walking through Derby, and she'd lie with her head in my lap until she was asleep, and I didn't know if she understood, and it didn't matter, because she was warm and listened, and that was what I needed.

The day before I vanished entirely from my parents' minds, they being the very, very last to forget, I wrote my name down a thousand times.

I wrote with lipstick on the bathroom wall.

I wrote with sticks and stones in the dirt of the park.

I wrote with chalk in the street, and with ink on paper, and with blood drawn from a cut in my thumb on the window of our living room and on the back door. I wrote in flowing Arabic, which my mother had insisted I learned to write as she had not. I looked up my own name in Mandarin and Coptic, Cyrillic and Katakana. I wrote on the walls and floors, the tables and books, Hope Arden, Hope Arden, and after a while, I wrote only Hope.

Hope.

Hope.

Hope.

I wrote it on the back of receipts. I hugged Grace and cried, and she let me hug her because sometimes this was what people did and you had to be patient with people. I had a notion that monks would repeat their prayers a thousand times, and that there was something magical in this number which would draw the attention of a creator, and when I was done I went into the living room, and found my parents sitting there, silent.

"Hey, Mum, hey, Dad," I said, and they both looked at me, and then looked away, their arms wrapped round each other, as if uncertain of anything in the world save each other. There were tears on my father's face, but I didn't know why – I had never seen him cry.

"I'm going to bed now," I said to the half darkness of a TV on mute.

"All right, dear," my mum replied at last, so slow, so long. Then, "How much longer are you with us?"

I packed my bag that night, and in the morning Gracie held onto my leg, her arms wrapped like an anchor, and I had to prise her free. My mum was in the kitchen, Dad had already gone to work.

"Bye," I said, and as Mum looked up she seemed to blink something out of her eyes before whispering, astonished and afraid, "Who are you?"

"I'm Hope's friend," I answered. "I was just staying the night."

Silence.

My mum, frozen in the kitchen door, broken egg shell oozing clear juice between her fingers.

"Who's Hope?"

"Goodbye," I said, and let myself out into the morning.

Chapter 25

A thief's progress.

I began, homeless, on the streets of Derby.

First I stole food – fruit from the grocer, sandwiches, rolls wrapped in cling film – things from the local bakery and market stalls, where I thought there wouldn't be any electronic surveillance but with crowds to hide in. I stole because I was hungry, and slept at the bottom of the stairs beneath the local library, which led to a community hall where resided the taekwondo, knitting and book clubs, as well as breast-feeding club every other Friday.

On my fourth day I tried stealing from a supermarket, and was astonished when no alarms went off. On the fifth day I tried again, but this time the juice I stole was expensive, and had been tagged, and the alarm sounded, and my heart popped up through my throat like something out of Gracie's cartoons, but I'd planned for this, and I kept walking, moving quickly into the crowd, and the security guard didn't even leave his post.

"We're not supposed to chase thieves," he explained the next day, when I asked him about his job. "We might get hurt, and that could leave the store liable."

"Then what's the point?"

"You know," he replied, "I'm not sure. Maybe it's just to make people feel good."

On the sixth day, someone threw beer on me as I slept. I woke, too late to see their faces, but heard boys laughing as they ran away, and on the seventh day I stood by the railway tracks, and told myself that it was time to die, but the trains were suspended that day for a fault on the line, and I lost interest and my nerve.

By the time I saw my friends again, laughing and hanging out at our spot in Westfields, the place we always used to hang together, I'd lost track of time. I stood on the balcony above, and watched my friends below, and they had forgotten too. I leaned against the railing, imagined throwing myself down, head first, tumbling over and over like a gymnast, only no stop, no bounce at the bottom, just white tiles and blood, all over, and my mates screaming and running from my broken corpse, and found that though I could picture every part of my death, feel the wind in my face and the floor vanishing beneath my feet, yet I could not do it.

What was I living for?

I saw a dead rat, flattened on the A38 where it passed Markeaton. Whatever had hit it must have been heavy, fast, because it wasn't gross, it wasn't an explosion of organs or blood, it was just rolled down, fur still attached, legs sticking out beneath it, nose turned towards the side of the road, tail behind it, like a carpet waiting to be shaken out. I counted yellow cars. I counted lorries from Germany. I counted suppliers of frozen food. I thought about what I'd look like, flattened like that, my head thin as a pancake, and as the trucks and lorries rolled by, I thought:

Now.

Now.

This time.

Now.

Now I'll step out.

Now.

This car.

This truck.

Now.

And I didn't move.

On the twenty-third day of my loneliness, I saw my mum in the centre of town.

She was walking with Gracie in an oversized pushchair, a thing which one day my mum would have to admit should be a wheelchair for her growing child. They were shopping for new light bulbs. I hovered behind them as she made her choices, her judicious demands slowly annoying the acne-plagued boy behind the counter.

And what's its wattage? she asked, for she always cared about bills.

It seems a very cold light, she tutted. Do you have something nicer?

Grace sat patiently in the middle of the shop, watching a lava lamp. I stood next to her, and at my approach, she turned, and made a little sound, and looked away, and a few moments later I felt a brush of skin, and found that her hand was resting in mine.

"Gracie, stop that!" blurted my mum, scooping her away. "I'm so sorry," she exclaimed, "my daughter's a bit like this sometimes."

"It's okay," I replied. "It's okay."

I waited then, for what I knew had to happen. For my mum to look at me, smile an uncertain smile, say, "Do I know you?" or "Have we met?" For her to feel a strange, uncommon bond that leads her to turn to me as I stand in the door and say, "There's something about you . . . " and invite me round for tea, or ask me my name, or say, "I had a daughter who was like you . . . " or . . . some other form of fantasy.

She did not, though Gracie stared at me as Mum pulled her away.

A moment.

Standing by the railway tracks.

The train is coming, the train is coming.

Here.

Now.

Step out.

Step out now.

Out into the railway tracks.

I close my eyes and I can see

my dad walking by

my sister holding onto my leg

my mum, walking across the desert.

Strange, how that image had grown in me.

I painted a portrait of my mum, before her hair turned grey, before she cut it close to look more professional, to be taken more seriously by the men at work.

I dressed her in dusty robes, perhaps lifted in my imagination from *Star Wars*, or maybe a documentary on the BBC. I gave her a stick to lean on, a sack of water, nothing more. I made her feet bare, hardened to stone as she walked, and then I sat, as lonely as she, upon a dune some few miles off, and watched her – just watched her – walking through the desert of my mind, getting nearer, until her face was visible, and I found that it was mine.

I read a book about the desert, and the people who cross it. For some, it said, the desert is a punishment, torment, exile. The Israelites made false idols and were disrespectful to their god, and for forty years they wandered in the dust, trapped between the Nile and the Sea of Galilee. When the Ottomans killed the Armenians, they marched thousands of husbands, wives, children into the sands of Syria, and there they remain still, white particles of sand-blasted bone that roll away in the wind. Whole peoples have vanished into the desert; the desert eats the people whole.

T. E. Lawrence lost himself and found himself, crossing Sinai. Moses and Job, Confucius on a white bull heading to the west. Muhammad in a cave where a spider wove; Jesus wandered and Satan whispered, and from the sand came prophets and dreams, forty days and forty nights of solitude. Elijah walked in the

runway, no passports shown, and drove along a straight road surrounded by scrubby grass until we hit the motorway. The sky was grey-yellow, shimmering with haze. The taxi drivers were deadly, the buses were full, honking horns and grubby exhaust. We drove towards the city, then turned and began to twist through industrial sprawl, houses of unpainted breeze block, warehouses of corrugated iron. I watched it all, tracking the direction of the sun, counting miles, noting signs, landmarks.

Ads: the newest kitchen utensil for the perfect housewife, the perfect clothes, the perfect car for the perfect family, a picture of Daddy (manly driver), Mummy (holding baby) and three grinning children (all destined to be doctors and lawyers) before the sleek silver curves of their newly purchased vehicle (The Journey is Everything).

Perfect: complete and correct in every way. Without fault.

Fault: a flaw, a failing.

At fault: blameworthy. In a dilemma.

Gauguin watched me watching, then said, "Have you been to Turkey before?"

"Sure," I replied, not taking my eyes from the road. "I've eaten sheep brains."

"I've seen them served, but never tasted."

"You shouldn't be put off when they're presented to you – in this town it's customary to show you your food before you eat it. Raw meat, raw fish, raw brains. It's a practice which is unpalatable to our plastic-packaged sensibilities."

"Are you a gourmet?"

Gourmet: cultural ideal in the culinary arts; haute cuisine, meticulous preparation and presentation of food, often expensive, though that may be an economic irrelevance, often served with rare wines.

A gourmet: a person of refined taste and passion.

"I like to lick the icing sugar up from round the edge of the dessert dish," I said. "Also I lick the plate when there's good gravy." He didn't reply.

*

An industrial workshop in the middle of nowhere.

A long concrete wall surrounding an internal courtyard of yellow pressed dirt. A pile of old tyres against one corner of the yard, within which a pair of skinny kittens yawned, reluctant to leave their den.

A square, one-storey building; shutters that could be rolled back to allow a truck inside; metal doors, windows high and barred. Broken glass, weeds growing from the cracks in the bricks, extractor fans above that extracted nothing.

A tatty sofa, once adorned with the images of water lilies, yellow foam now coming through. A new purple kettle on a small stand; several chipped mugs, also adorned with images of flowers, trailing weeds dotted on one bright green pixel at a time, purple buds.

Doors that could be locked.

Gates that could be guarded.

A very unfashionable secret base for secret men.

One of them sat on a beanbag by the door; another sat outside on concrete steps, smoking a thin brown cigarillo, the stench drifting through the broken windows. Gauguin waved me to the sofa. He opened up my suitcase and prodded idly at the contents therein. I folded my arms and waited. A tube of toothpaste squeezed in the middle earned the tiniest crinkle of distaste in the corner of his mouth; my American passport was scrutinised in detail, and when he found the Australian passport at the very bottom of the case, tucked into a book on trekking in Oman, he went so far as to permit himself a smile.

Both passports and my wallet were handed off to one of his men, who took them away. I added up the value of the accounts that were about to be compromised, the identities about to be exposed. The sum was considerable. How much of my digital life would I have to destroy, when all this was done?

Then a woman with a headscarf depicting birds in flight against a cloud-skimmed sky came and took my fingerprints, a sample of my hair, a swab from the inside of my mouth, and the damage to my career worsened.

"In many ways, you are rather inept, for a thief," mused Gauguin, as the woman bottled her samples and took them away. "How have you survived all this time?"

"I have a forgettable face."

"You do yourself an injustice."

"No," I replied, crossing my legs, my arms. "I don't."

His fingers brushed the tub of sun cream, and I became aware of how defensive my body language was, how tightly my hands gripped the tops of my arms, how heavy my legs felt. I wanted to uncurl, and didn't, not while he held the diamonds.

He undid the lid, peered inside, looked up, studied my face, his head tilting a little to one side, wondering.

I met his eye, let him wonder.

His expression didn't change, his eyes didn't move, but he reached down into the tub, rummaged around inside, and without a sound, pulled Princess Shamma's necklace from within, laying it, still coated in vanilla-coloured goo, on the table between us.

He put the tub to one side.

Stood up. Walked to a stainless-steel sink against a wall, cabinets below, pipes running up the chipped sometime-green concrete to the side.

Washed his hands.

Returned to his chair.

Sat down.

Silence.

I said, "I think I would like to be arrested now."

Silence.

Gauguin shifted a little in his seat, leant forward so his elbows rested on his knees, his fingers knotted together in the gap between his legs. There was a silver pen in an inside pocket of his jacket, briefly visible as the jacket drifted forward. It seemed an ostentatious, silly thing for a practical man to carry.

I unfolded myself, one limb at a time. Feet flat on the floor, hands flat in my lap.

"I think you should call the police," I said.

Silence.

I listened to the silence, and all the words within.

Silence.

Awareness, in the silence, of sounds around. Distant traffic, the dripping of the tap, the crunching of footsteps outside the room, buzz of a fly trapped on sticky blue paper by the light. We waited, until the muezzin began to sing, out of tune through a loudspeaker, and a few minutes later, a rival, more tuneful but further off, calling the faithful to prayer.

Allah is the greatest, Allah is the greatest.

I bear witness that there is no God but Allah.

I bear witness that Muhammad is the Messenger of Allah.

Hasten to worship.

Hasten to success.

Allah is the greatest, Allah is the greatest.

There is no God but Allah.

Then Gauguin said, "Tell me about your relationship with Byron14."

I heard the words as if they were spoken through water, slowed down and deepened as they travelled to my brain, and turned my head to look at him more closely, waiting to see if he'd speak again, if there was a meaning I didn't understand within the sound.

"Did you accept any employment from Byron14?"

Louder, clearer, his head rising.

My turn to be silent. I closed my eyes and tried to assemble thoughts, weave a path through obscurity.

He interrupted. "Miss Why, wondering what you should or should not say is irrelevant at this juncture. The truth will come."

"We both have something to offer," I replied. "You want information; I want out."

"You are mistaken; there is no negotiation."

I looked round the room. Only one of Gauguin's men remained, chewing gum, seemingly uninterested in all that happened. Outside there would be more men, guarding the way, but they would be forgetting me already, just strangers lounging in the sun.

I stood, but Gauguin didn't move. I walked round the back of the sofa, turned, walked the other way. I scanned the room for weapons: a biro, a cigarette tray, a mobile phone, anything. Somewhere he still had a knife. My shoes were flat but not ideal for running in. "I'm a liar," I said at last. "I lie when scared."

"Are you afraid?"

"I'm calm," I replied. "As you can see. Can I make a suggestion?"

"If you want."

"I think you're a liar too, Mr Gauguin, mugurski, whatever we call you. I think we are dancing around each other when we should speak plainly. You're not interested in the diamonds." How wretched the jewels looked now, covered in cosmetic goo, dripping on the table between us. A proper barney for a few lumps of carbon. "Sure, you need to get them back to Dubai so your boss doesn't look like a twat, family honour, business acumen, all that. But you don't really care, do you? Not your business."

His lips narrowed, then broadened again into a tight smile. "No," he admitted softly. "Not really."

"But Byron14 is?"

"As I said – Byron14 is a killer, a terrorist. The darknet is not infallible, as you know. I know you've been in communication; now I need to know what was said. Did Byron hire you to steal the Chrysalis?"

"Why would he?"

"You tell me."

I turned on my slow amble, walked the other way, paused by my chair, didn't sit, walked to the walls, walked back to the chair, stopped. "Reina bint Badr al Mustakfi – do you know the name?"

"The young woman who died; I heard of her."

"She was a cousin of Princess Shamma bint Bandar."

"That is why I heard; her death was flagged at a briefing."

"She had Perfection."

A half shrug, Gauguin waiting for me.

"I stole the Chrysalis because it was a challenge. Then when she died, I stole it because I wanted to piss someone off, and the guys who make Perfection seemed about right."

"Why?"

"She had Perfection."

"You said, but Perfection didn't make her kill herself."

"Do you have Perfection, Gauguin?"

"No, though I am familiar of course with its system."

I paced again, a few steps, stopped again, chose my words very carefully. "I think ..." I murmured. "I think you're wrong. I think it helped her die. She was nice. I liked her. Even though she didn't remember, I felt ... affection ... for her. I think I might be prone to making these things more important than they are, but still, that's my thing, it's a side-effect of ... everything. What's the opposite of perfect?"

"Imperfect?" he suggested.

Synonyms: flawed, defective, faulty, bad.

I looked at Gauguin, and didn't see any sign that he cared or understood, so closed my mouth and kept on walking.

After a while, a little shifting, a little sigh, Gauguin tried again. "Byron ..."

"Wanted to know if I had Perfection. Why are you so interested, Mr Gauguin?"

"What did Byron want?"

"To warn me about you."

"What else?"

"That was all. I get the feeling you guys like to fuck with each other, more joy me."

"I need you to contact Byron14."

"Why?"

"To request a meeting."

"You request a meeting."

"I don't think Byron will talk to me."

"So you want me to be your stooge? I don't think there's

much honour amongst thieves, Mr Gauguin, but even by my standards that's a bit shit."

"Yes." He sounded wistful, a good man in a dirty world. "I think it might be."

I paced again, walking it through. Walking helped thinking, thoughts without words for now, but words coming, ideas growing.

I looked at Gauguin, watching me from his crooked plastic chair.

I looked at the man on the beanbag in the corner.

I said, "I need a laptop and a cup of coffee, please."

Gauguin smiled.

Chapter 27

You don't need weapons drawn to be threatening.

Fear grows in the face of unanswered questions. How far will Gauguin go, what are the tools at his disposal, will he kill me, when this is done?

They brought me a laptop and a bad cup of coffee.

They already had Tor installed; it was easy to return to the chatroom where Byron14 liked to play.

Byron14 wasn't there.

"We wait," said Gauguin, sitting on the sofa next to me. "We wait for Byron."

We waited.

An hour, then two.

Gauguin watched the screen. I said, "Does this thing come with solitaire?"

"We wait," he replied.

We waited.

I counted bricks in the wall.

Steps to the door.

Lines on my hand.

We waited.

The muezzins called from the minarets, Allah is the Greatest, Allah is the Greatest.

Sun cream dried on the diamonds; how disgraceful Leena would find it, that something so precious should be casually disregarded between the ashtray and a nine-month-old magazine about snowboarding.

I counted viable weapons in the room, things that were heavy, things that were hard, things that could puncture skin.

I counted hiding places, found only one that was any good.

After a while I said, as much to pass the time as anything else, "You and Byron – is it personal?"

Gauguin's eyes snapped to me, fast and hard, before he looked away.

I shrugged, smiled at nothing much, said, "Thought so. Your boss know you're pursuing a vendetta here?"

"My boss wants to see Byron drowned in liquid concrete," he replied, without rancour. "My views are more complicated."

"Would you have come after me if Byron hadn't got in touch?"

"Yes. You stole the diamonds, you embarrassed my employer, deliberately, it seemed. That made you my problem. It made sense for Byron to contact you, for exactly the same reasons."

"Byron's got it in for Perfection?"

"What do you think?"

I shrugged, and turned my attention back to the waiting screen.

The sun, setting, orange-pink light tracking long and thin across the ceiling.

The man on the beanbag got up and went outside to answer his phone.

I was alone with Gauguin.

I looked at him and he seemed unaware of my attention, his concentration fixed on the screen of the laptop.

I said, "Here," and reached out for the machine.

His hand lashed out, caught my wrist, held it hard. I fixed my face in an expression of wounded surprise. "I'm not going to break anything."

"What are you going to do?"

"See if Byron's in another room."

"Why didn't you mention this before?"

"Because you're a fucker with a knife?" I suggested. "What's the worst I can do?"

Slowly, Gauguin released my wrist. I picked up the machine, put it on my lap. He leaned in behind me to watch what I did. I opened a few more windows, checked a few more places, nothing untoward. How long had the guard been outside? Long enough to forget to come back? He may forget me, he might not forget his duty quite so fast.

I reached for my coffee cup, the third of the afternoon, and knocked it a little too hard. The coffee spilt across the table, soaking into the snowboard magazine, brown liquid mixing with sun cream. Gauguin's eyes flickered to it, a slight intake of irritated breath, and in that moment I hit him across the side of his skull as hard as I could with the laptop. He crumpled back, still awake, still aware, and I hit him again, slamming it onto his forehead, between his eyes, and again, the plastic case crumpling, the screen going black, and one more time for luck, having to fight the urge to scream, swallowing my own breath, swallowing the animal sounds in my throat. He fell back on the sofa, blood in his eyes, and I grabbed the laptop and ran across the room, breath ragged and fast. I opened the cupboards beneath the sink; two with shelves secured in place, but one larger where once a kitchen bucket may have been, or bottles of bleach. I curled in, head to knees, arms to shins, locking my body so tight it was a struggle to breathe, smaller than a cat, smaller than a spider, eased the door shut with my fingertips, waited in the dark.

My breath conjured hurricanes, shook sleeping grizzly bears from their beds.

My heartbeat sent earthquakes across the earth, my skin melted metal.

I closed my eyes and breathed, breathed, breathed.

The heavens turned and the mountains fell, and I breathed.

Silence in the workshop.

A door opens; how lonely the sound seemed, when I could not see the man who pushed it.

A voice cried out; footsteps on concrete.

Boss, boss, help, help!

More footsteps, more people.

A commotion of moving men, Gauguin groaning, feet moving, a rattle above, a first aid kit being pulled from its place above the disused sink, legs moving against the thin light around the cupboard door.

Boss, what happened, what happened?

Footsteps run across the floor, above me, right above me, turning on the taps.

Gauguin's voice, too faint to hear.

Civilisations are born and galaxies die, but has it been long enough?

A slow drip on my right shoulder, a leaking pipe from the sink above, I feel each drop roll down my skin like the first river across barren stones. The tap stops.

The cupboard next to mine opens, I catch my breath, wait for someone else to catch it too; but no. They are pulling out cloths, perhaps, tissues or tea towels to mop their boss's bloodied head.

"What happened?" asks the woman who took my fingerprints.

"I don't know," Gauguin replies, and then, oh blessed then, sacred words in whose breath are goddesses born, "I don't remember."

I find that there are tears in my eyes, and I am shaking. I bite down on my own wrist to muffle the sound, remember, remember, the sand beneath my feet, the sun above, lines in my skin, I am now, I am Hope, breath and hope and now and . . .

Words fly away from me.

I push my awareness into my toes.

I am my toes.

The effort makes my head ache, but the shaking recedes.

Trees grow, pyramids are built, flowers wither and die upon the vine, the widows of Ashur are loud in their wail.

I am the wood of the cupboard that presses against my back.

I am the darkness.

In the room around me, people try to make sense of the scene.

See diamonds on the table, covered in gunk.

See blood on the floor.

What lies are they building, I wonder, to justify this picture?

A suitcase on the table, women's clothes; clearly they found the thief's baggage, but not the thief. Yes, now they concentrate, they can remember meeting the plane as it landed, but the seat next to Gauguin was empty, the bird had flown. They remember driving through the city streets, searching the thief's baggage, finding the diamonds.

And now?

Someone had crept up behind Gauguin and hit him over the head, clearly, in order to rob them. Yes: that must be what happened. How did the thief get in? How did he get out? Why did the diamonds remain?

Minds strained under the effort of making sense of this scene, and confidence began to crack.

When confidence fails, routine kicks in.

Search the building, search the streets!

I am the wood.

I am darkness.

"Did you see who attacked you?" demands one man.

"No," replied Gauguin. "I didn't."

His men searched the building, but not enough, nothing to see, nothing here, just some old pipes, broken cupboards, the thief long gone.

Footsteps move across the concrete, the tap runs above my head.

I am water.

Cars come, cars go.

I get pins and needles in my feet and want to laugh; cramp in my back and want to cry.

I am my vertebrae. I do not mind the pain.

And slowly, everyone forgets.

They do not forget that Gauguin has been attacked – that is a bloody reality that cannot be shaken. Nor do they forget the diamonds on the table, the passports they have taken from me, the credit cards in my name. They might remember my fingerprints too, but perhaps in their minds they are prints lifted from my luggage, DNA sweeps from my clothes, the details blur, imagination fills in.

I think the light might be fading outside, but it could be my imagination, eyes changing in the dark. I read a study once of people who were confined in perfect, silent darkness for forty-eight hours; some took only a few minutes before they began to hallucinate.

I am goosebumps.

I am a fusion of flesh. My arms are my legs, my legs are my chest, my head is my neck, my neck is my knees. I doubt I shall ever move again.

Why do these men not find me?

Because they are not looking.

Footsteps in the workshop.

A door shutting.

A car driving away.

I wait.

I wait.

A smell intruding on the senses, so gentle as to be barely noticeable at first, a trick of the mind, a manifestation of my own inertia: burning toast.

I wait.

The smell gets stronger.

A hint of petrol.

A moment where the rational mind says that a thing cannot be so, and the more intelligent, unconscious brain replies with a bang-on retort of "fuck that shit; of course it fucking is."

Of course the fucking workshop is on fire.

I push the cupboard door open, flop out onto the floor. The smaller of the two fires has been started in the sofa, accelerated by a can of petrol, but is growing fast. The larger, more impressive threat is in the far corner of the building, fuelled by an unknown propellant, and already licking at the ceiling, smoke filling the top of the room. Squatting at the sink, I throw water over myself, soak my arms up to the shoulders, push my head beneath the tap, cover my face with my sleeve, crawl on my hands and knees along the floor beneath the pall, reach the door, push it, find it's locked.

Standing up, the smoke makes my eyes water.

I drive my shoulder into the door, throw my full weight against it, but it will not budge, and I cannot breathe.

I drop back down onto my hands and knees; haul in air. Steam rolls off my sodden clothes.

I look for another way out, but it's getting hard to see.

Fire procedures, what did I remember about tackling fire?

wet clothes, wet face

cloth across the mouth

percentage of deaths from smoke inhalation, 50–80 per cent

Cause of death

respiratory trauma

poison

thermal damage to lungs

I feel the hinges of the door, run my fingers over the lock, concentrate.

carbon monoxide poisoning

CO bonds with haemoglobin in the blood, giving it its red appearance

Two locks, one a fairly simple mortise lock that I could beat with a fork and a bit of time, the other heavy-duty, need a knife or a piece of metal, something to get leverage with

unlike O_2, CO will not separate from the haemoglobin, continues circulating

treatment for CO poisoning and smoke inhalation: hydrated oxygen

Can't see, the black smoke throws the light of the fire around
oxygen toxicity: too much oxygen in the body tissues
central nervous system damage
retinal damage
pulmonary damage, only really a problem in a hypobaric chamber
or undersea
or in
pressurised conditions
My fingers fall away from the lock.
I am
the fire
I am
my fingers
I am
crawling
Climb on a table away from the fire, window furthest from the fire, smash what's left of the glass
eyes closed
breathe
smoke running out
my face
my skin
can't open my eyes, just darkness
cold air
hot smoke
breathe
the tiny hairs in my nose are burning, I feel the air scald my throat
I am
breath
I am
fire
I am
darkness.
The darkness is me.

Chapter 28

I dream, and I dream of a fantasy that could be Parker.

It must be fantasy, since I cannot remember a thing about him. What do I actually know about this man from Maine?

The me-that-met-him wrote some impressions down, as we shared pancakes and coffee in a café off Seventh Avenue.

Parker: Who Is He?

Surprisingly funny, talkative (he talks because the alternative is silence), passionate about music to the point of obsession, kind to strangers. Today I have seen him chat to a homeless man from the Bronx for half an hour, grill a waitress about the history of her tattoo, perform coin magic for a pair of marvelling five-year-old twins on the train, entertaining them while their mum comforted a shrieking baby. A show-off. Fearsome in his hatred of the news in the US, dismissive of politics.

Flashes of melancholy, sometimes laughs too loud, too high. His opinions often flare into certainties – an insistence that the Tale of Genji was written during the Kemmu Restoration, and he sulks, proper sulks, for ten minutes when I prove him wrong. Envious of celebrity to the point of contempt, bitterness inflecting his words. "They're just people," he says, "just fucking people", and yet his knowledge of who said what and who was seen at what party is encyclopaedic.

Erudite, to the point of obsession. Am I the same? I can't help but measure myself by him, the only equivalence I have ever met. Constantly on his phone, constantly double-checking the world around him. We order pancakes; he looks up the history of maple syrup.

Nanabozho, he says. Trickster god of the first peoples, credited sometimes with the invention of maple syrup. At the Sugar Moon, first full moon of spring, the tribes of the north would celebrate the coming of warmer days by tapping the trees, collecting sap until the rising temperatures of the forest made the sugars less sweet, unpalatable.

"How many cultures," he muses, "so far apart, have gods that delight to play tricks."

More letters, memorabilia. A menu from the diner where we ate the pancakes – I remember eating a *lot* of pancakes, until my belly ached with it, which was not my normal pattern of behaviour, and now I think about it, perhaps it does make sense that some figure I can't remember was there too, encouraging gluttony.

A note, and I remember finding it in my pocket when I let myself into my downtown apartment and just standing in the hall, staring in wonder.

Today you met someone like you. You cannot remember him, but here is his picture. He has a note just like this one, and you are to meet again at 10 a.m. at the Brooklyn Botanic Garden.

I barely slept that night, and the next morning went to the Brooklyn Botanic Garden to meet someone I'd never met before. A letter, recounting that meeting, along with a mug showing cherry blossom in full pink bloom, which I thought I could remember buying but which, upon further racking of my memory, I wasn't so sure I had.

We met at 10 a.m.. He came up to me, a nervous man with mousy hair I had never seen before. He had my picture on his phone, grinning at the camera, giving it a thumbs up, his face pressed in from the side of the frame.

"Hi," he said, holding out his hand stiffly. "I got a note from myself telling me to be here to meet someone I can't remember ever meeting before."

"Hi," I replied. "I got the same thing."

His eyes widened in fear and delight, and then he's talking, just talking, non-stop for nearly an hour, maybe two. He wonders how long we've been meeting like this, if we're already the best of friends, tells me about his life – has he told me this already? – wants to know everything about me, how I live, how I eat, how I keep myself sane.

I tell him about taster classes, speed dating, card counting at the casinos, and am briefly surprised when he replies, "I go to prostitutes, so much easier. Once you've found one or two who you like, who you know will be good with you, then it's just better and so much more honest, I mean, more honest for us both, than me trying to pick up some date in a bar."

Perhaps he's right; I don't feel anything either way. Cautiously, I admit that I have sometimes done a little thieving, and steal his wallet while he's distracted by a family squabble on the other side of the rose beds. He exclaims in wonder at this, and finally admits, "I just rob people."

That's when he shows me the gun, small and dark, hidden in a holster underneath his arm. "It's okay!" he exclaims, at my expression of horror. "No one ever remembers being robbed, I mean, it's just like they dropped their wallet or something."

"Have you ever killed anyone?"

"Jesus, no! Jesus!"

And now I wonder: do I believe him?

I have no memories of him on which to construct a pattern of his truths and lies, but in much the same way that I see how it is logical to seek sex with a hooker, I can also see how someone in our predicament might find it easy to make their living with a gun. Perhaps I read too much. I must examine myself as thoroughly as I examine him, if I want to make this sort of judgement. Yet, in that I have no other resource than these words now by which to remember him, I feel I must write it down: this is the thing I feel, these are the questions I have. Remember them.

He's funny, he makes me laugh; when was the last time I actually laughed?

"You gotta laugh," he says. "It's the best thing you can do for your health."

In the evening we go to see stand-up, and after the first fifteen minutes of not being very impressed, I found that I was laughing until my face hurt.

I remembered that night. I had been alone, and wondered in retrospect quite what had prompted me to visit the club; not my usual scene, not the sort of thing I usually did. I tried to remember who sat next to me, and drew a blank. We must have held hands throughout, though, to avoid forgetting. More notes – six in total, all written in the same form.

Today you spent the day with someone you cannot remember. You have agreed to meet him again at 10.30 at the Coney Island ferry.

. . . at Grand Central Station
. . . at the Metropolitan Museum of Art
. . . at Times Square

Collections of photos and memorabilia pile up. I remember going to the theatre twice that week, once to see a show about a dysfunctional Irish family that left me bored, once to see a production of *Coriolanus* that left most of its cast variously drenched in blood, water, vegetable matter, paint and pain. The audience, when the scarlet-soaked actors bowed at the end, stood and cheered, and so did I, and did someone cheer next to me? Was there a man in the seat beside mine who whooped at this tale of ambitious mothers and vengeful generals?

Can't remember.

Photos: he and I, grinning outside the theatre. Ticket stubs, menus, napkins with doodles on them – he has a gift for caricature, there I am, my nose too big, my eyes bulging like they're going to burst, hair like candy floss exploding from my skull, tiny curving body. I have doodled a reply – a stick figure, barely human, waving in a corner. At the end of every day a letter, carefully written from the me that was to the me that is now.

Tonight we had sex. It seemed something we should do. It was fine. Now he's sitting on the bed writing a letter to himself, explaining the day that has been and everything that has happened, before we forget. It's 4 a.m., and I just want to sleep. I find it hard to gather words, and am so afraid of putting my pen down, closing my eyes, killing everything that today was.

Would we be friends, lovers, were we not what we are? Two asthmatics meet in a room, will they stay together simply because they are asthmatic? Do I like Parker? Do I like him?

An email address, a phone number. In a stranger's handwriting: just in case. In my handwriting:

The address of someone you cannot remember, in case you ever need him.

On the seventh day, a note written on hotel stationery.

Today we agreed not to see each other.

That was all it said.

And at the very bottom of the box, a letter, written in someone else's hand, which read:

Dear Hope

My name is Parker. I hope that you have letters about me already, which you have been keeping, as I have been keeping photos and letters about you. I hope that you are favourable in your report of me. I don't know you – today is the first day we have ever met – but I see from pictures and notes that we've met many times before. I think the days that went before have been wonderful, but I cannot remember you in them. I wanted to write to you, before we part, so that there is something physical of me in your hands, which you may remember when I am gone.

How stupid it must seem that I want to tell you things about yourself; I know that I have known you, and yet cannot know you. I am very frightened of what you know about me, of what you have written down. I could tell you the contents of my own letters, my accounts of everything that's passed between us . . . but they'd only be words describing words, and that doesn't feel fair.

You said a thing, when we agreed to go our ways, that I am desperate to remember. Look, I've written it here, and I've written it on my hand, and I've written it in my diary, and I'll write it on my phone – I will remember it, because it seems to me the way in which you live your life. You said that, since the past vanishes with memory, all that we can live in is now. Remembrance is an act of looking back, and we do not exist in the past, except here, in these letters and photos. Even reading these is not an act of remembrance, because I write now. I hold your image now. I re-read these words, now. I look at you, now. I close my eyes, now. I exist only now. Only my thoughts, the thoughts that I have in this present moment, they are the prism through which all else travels, and even the past, even memory, is remembered only now. We exist in the present tense, and even our futures will one day be the past, and the past will be forgotten, and so only now remains. What matters, therefore, is not hope for things to come, nor regret for things passed, but this action in this moment, these deeds, this now.

Hope – I have lived a complicated life. Can a thing which is forgotten change a man?

I hope it can. Hope, for hope, in hope, of Hope.

I don't know how to end this letter. Should I say that I love you? I don't think that would be right. I think it is inappropriate, so I will leave it,

with very best wishes,
the one and only Parker

I kept the letter, along with all the rest.

I cannot remember Parker now. I do not remember his face, his touch, his body, his words, his deeds, our days.

But I have one thought that I cling to in this present time: that at the end of that week we spent together, I had acquired a taste for comedy.

He is forgotten, but I am changed.

I have no words to express how wondrous this is.

Chapter 29

Some people fantasise about being rescued by firemen.

The fantasy perhaps involves muscular men, faces coated in a manly quantity of soot and sweat, pushing bodily through the flames that dare not touch them in their heavy boots, to sweep the invalid victim off her feet and carry her, slung across one shoulder, bosom heaving, hair flapping around her curiously untouched face, to moonlit safety.

Having been rescued by the fire services of Istanbul, I can report that this is not the case.

Smoke inhalation rendered me unconscious; I woke in pain, on a bed in an ambulance, to find a woman with a face like a rotting potato cutting my trousers away from my legs. I tried to speak, and my lungs were full of flame. I tried to move, and my arms were fallen ebony. Another woman, this one younger, brown-black lipstick, heavy shadow around her eyes, stepped forward and said, in Turkish, a language I do not speak well at all,

"Can you hear me, ma'am?"

She gave me water. The water burned, and I wanted more.

"Ma'am, can you tell me your name?"

"Hope," I said, before I could remember to lie. "My name is Hope."

The elder woman continued cutting at my clothes, oblivious to the activities around her. The doors to the ambulance were open, and I could hear fire still raging, see its light cast across the tarmac of the street, hear the sounds of men rushing, masonry crumbling. Who had called the fire engines in? Unlikely I'd ever know; a stranger without a name, who'd saved my life.

"Are you experiencing . . ." A series of words that I didn't understand in Turkish, accompanied by careful gestures on the paramedic's own body, indicating places perhaps where I should be feeling pain. I stared at her uncomprehending, tasted soot on my teeth, felt the air rush through my suddenly hollowed-out, suddenly scorched nose. I shook my head, and the young paramedic smiled awkwardly, trying to find different words, in an easier language.

With a sharp tear the elder removed the last of my severed trouser leg, ripping it up the seam. The flesh beneath seemed remarkably unburned, save for a patch around the back of my left calf, though I couldn't remember how that part had been injured.

The junior listened to my heart, my lungs, took blood pressure, put a mask over my face. I understood very little of the conversation that ensued, the junior uncertain, the elder uninterested, until at last the latter looked up and barked in strict, unyielding English, "Nausea? Blurred vision? Yes?"

"Yes."

"Hospital: we go to hospital now. You family, friends?"

"No."

"Embassy?"

"Is that necessary?"

She stared at me like I was a fish too stupid to swim, then turned away. "We go hospital," she barked, and as a final thought, "You okay. Very okay."

In the hospital they put me in a booth cordoned off by sky-blue curtains. A nurse plugged me into a heart monitor, took my blood pressure again, an EEG, put an O_2 monitor on my finger.

As she worked, a doctor appeared, and listened to my lungs, listened to the paramedics, shone a torch into my eyes, examined numbers on a screen, looked at the burn on the back of my leg, another on my left shoulder blade, another down the side of my left arm, tutted, then smiled at me and repeated the motto of the moment, "You okay! You very okay."

Then he turned to a junior doctor, a girl in a grey headscarf, a doll with a painted face, gave her orders and marched away. She turned to me and said in flawless English, "Ma'am, you have suffered some mild burns and smoke inhalation. We are going to put you on a nebuliser and keep you in overnight for monitoring. Do you have health insurance?"

"Yes," I wheezed.

"That is good; I will fill out a report for you, you will need it to make a claim."

So saying, she marched away.

I stayed in the hospital until the first dose of nebuliser ran out. No one came to check on me, except the evening porter to see if anyone needed a cup of tea. He was used to meeting strangers; my presence was no surprise.

After five hours in the hospital bed, a nurse pulled back the curtains and found me, and was surprised. She looked at my chart, looked at my face, smiled uneasily, and strode away. A few minutes later the matron appeared, and went through the same procedure, smiled as uncertainly as her colleague, turned her back on me and exclaimed, "Who signed in this patient, please?!" in a voice that rang across the floor.

I considered trying for another dose of heparin on the nebuliser, making a bigger meal of my burns, but the hospital had already forgotten me. Sometimes it's only paperwork that keeps you alive – without it, even the memorable can die of forgetting.

Clothes in tatters, stuck in a tea-stained gown, I hobbled through the slumbering corridors of the hospital until I found an in-patient ward where the night nurse was sleeping and the lights were dim. From a woman lying on one side, a bandage around her head and hands beneath her cheek like a child, I stole a pair of trousers and some slightly too large shoes. From an ancient lady with pipes taped to the end of her nose and corner of her mouth, I stole seven hundred lira in mixed notes. I changed in a toilet, and sat on the cold floor and shook for a while as waves of nausea rocked the world beneath my feet. I drank a sip of water, and it was good. I drank another sip and almost choked on it, head down in the toilet, heaving, gasping for air.

When I could stand, I washed my hair in cold water from the tap, slicked it back over my face, scrubbed with tissue paper until my eyes were red and my skin was raw, water running away grey from my cleaning. I shuffled my feet around the palaces of my shoes, pushed the door open, stepped out into the hall.

No one shouted; no one called my name.

The morning prayers sounded from the minarets.

I let the sound fill me, and carry me away.

Chapter 30

No credit card, no passport.

No reputable hotel would have me, but a cab driver had a friend in Zetinburnu who knew a place run by his mother-in-law. The house was four storeys tall, and had been in the family for seventy-two years. Now it was a refuge for the dispossessed: migrant workers who'd entered the country illegally; newly released prisoners thrown onto the street with not a hundred lira to their name, nowhere to go. Wives fleeing husbands; husbands thrown out by their screaming wives. Twenty lira bought a mattress on the floor; forty got the bottom of a three-storey bunk bed.

The matron's voice whined high as a mosquito. She clung onto my arm as she showed me my room, buzzing, buzzing all the time in heavily inflected English, "Little thing, dear thing, lost your passport, lost your friends, dear thing, I'll be nice, you'll see, very nice."

She gave me a cup of tea in a cracked tulip glass, a slice of thick brown bread with a dollop of jam on the side.

"Dear thing," she tutted, as I tried a few cautious nibbles. "So hard to be alone."

As the sun rose, I slept, and when three in the afternoon came she marched into the room and exclaimed, "Who are you? Who are you? What are you doing here?" and threw her shoe at me as I fled.

I sat on the pavement round the corner from her apartment for half an hour, then went back. She'd found her shoe and was studiously sweeping the concrete path to her door.

"Dear thing!" she exclaimed, as I enquired about a room. "Little thing, dear thing, I'll be nice, you see . . . "

She gave me back my old bed, still disturbed from the shape of my sleeping body.

In the night I woke wheezing, burning, fire in my legs, fire in my chest.

From the phone by the door, I called a taxi, and went straight to the nearest hospital.

Four hours in this hospital.

Then four hours in that.

I moved from emergency room to emergency room, and waited patiently while they diagnosed me every time – burns, smoke inhalation – and tutted and gave me more cream and another round on the nebuliser. After twenty-eight hours I could recite every procedure, list every medication by rote, and my medical Turkish had taken a leap for the better, to the point that I could stagger through a door and whisper *duman inhalayson* to every curious nurse who came my way. After thirty-two hours, the problem was beginning to become one of over-medication, and I carefully revised my reporting of what had happened to reflect the dosages I'd been receiving. In every hospital someone approached me with forms forms forms, are you ready to claim for your insurance? and I filled in a few vapid lies and waited for them to forget before folding the documents into paper aeroplanes and gliding them into the bin.

After thirty-six hours and seven different hospitals around Istanbul, I released myself into unexpected, blinding sun, and realised I didn't know where I was. I had seventy lira left, no phone, no clothes that weren't stolen, and shoes that didn't fit. I had somehow worked my way near to Zincirlikuyu Mezarligi, though I didn't remember crossing the bridge at Galata or how I'd come to be here.

So I stood, and had no sense of place or time, of memory or distance travelled.

Here.

I stood.

And that was all that there was.

I closed my eyes, counted my breaths.

Lost count at four, started again.

Five, six, seven.

The pop of a motorcycle engine jerked me from my reverie.

I found that I was shaking, and thought perhaps I should go back to the hospital, get that looked at.

I found that I was sitting on the ground, and still shaking, and didn't know where to go.

Closed my eyes, closed my eyes.

Remembered

goddesses of the sun

comedy night in New York City, someone was sat next to me all the way, even though I cannot remember

remember

a man had set fire to a warehouse in Istanbul, and a woman had nearly burnt alive

and now only I remembered

no better than a fantasy, a thing not-shared, an experience made not-real because I

was the only one who knew

Luca Evard, drinking small beer in Brazil

I opened my eyes.

Did he think of me?

He thought of someone whose actions were my own, whose face, when he looked at it, bore my features, who had walked in places where my memories were and performed deeds which had shaped who I was now.

Whether such a one could be characterised as I, myself, I wasn't sure. But it was something.

It was a start.

I went looking for help.

Chapter 31

From an internet café between the wealthy apartments and growing international hotels of Besiktas, I resurrected an untouched email address and sent a cry of help to someone I couldn't remember.

Whether Parker would reply, I didn't know, but I lived in hope.

Chapter 32

I ride the Istanbul metro, picking pockets as I go, and idly, between the faces, I think of Inspector Luca Evard.

Our relationship has not always been professional.

The first time I met him, he arrested me.

The second time, he'd come all the way to São Paulo to consult on my MO. I'd stolen $3.3 million of mixed jewels in an operation that had taken me seven months to plan, twelve minutes to execute. I'd formed relationships (which no one could remember), learned pass-codes, copied keys, corrupted security systems, it was a beautiful job, so sensational that for the first time in my career I kept a few of the lower-valued pieces for myself, simply to remind myself of how good I could be. Silly sentiment; these things are a crutch.

I should have left the country, but the heist was still on local news, and when I phoned Interpol under the guise of a harried policewoman on the case, I was informed that Inspector Evard was on the scene. A CCTV camera had caught the features of a woman who'd been identified in connection with several other cases, and so he'd come to town.

I waited outside police headquarters, a woman in huge sunglasses and a big blue hat, until Luca emerged, and trailed him to the scene of the crime, a meeting with forensics, and finally back to his hotel.

I stood next to him in the lift, and nearly giggled with excitement. I clasped my hands in front of me and wore red and wondered if he'd look my way, but he didn't, and when he got off at the seventh floor I followed him until he looked back, at which point I pretended to lose my key in my handbag and he walked on.

The next day I put my camera on a ledge by Lago das Garças, set a ten-second timer, scuttled a few feet away from it, posed in what I hoped was a distracted manner with the day's newspaper, and caught a photo of myself looking, I had to say, really quite mysterious and alluring.

I sent it to the police from a dummy email account with the words, *Hey, is this the thief you're looking for?* and managed not to dance when I heard Luca Evard tell the receptionist he'd be extending his stay. That night he ate with his colleagues in a small café round the corner from the station, a bowl of rice, fish and beans, and I trailed him through the city, watching him struggle with the unforgiving traffic, wincing every time a boy on a motorcycle bucked up onto the pavement to dodge the gridlock. He was too neat, too quiet a man to be in a city as loud as São Paulo; he missed Geneva, perhaps.

The next day, while he was out, I stole the cleaning lady's master key and broke into his bedroom. On the desk was my photo. Pages of notes, records of DNA, fingerprints, snatches of my features, here, in Milan; here, in Vienna; here, in São Paulo, lifted from scenes of crime, and around, scattered thoughts.

Not afraid of being seen?

No team; works alone?

Why does no one remember her face?

He'd written this last in thick black pen, a late-night scrawl, by a beautifully clear picture of my features from Dublin, the day I stole data on 4G phone networking for a client on the darknet. I was smiling at the camera, the name on my badge was Rachel Donovan, and the receptionist had told me about her kids and how she wanted them to live in the countryside, learn all about the real world, as she inputted my data onto the system.

In the bathroom, he'd rolled the toothpaste tube up from the bottom as he squeezed it empty. His aftershave was an old bottle from Germany, €2.50 from the pharmacy. I sniffed it, ran my finger round the edge of the plastic cup with which he rinsed his mouth, lay back on his bed, felt the indentation where his head had rested, traced the lines of disturbance across his sheets, wondered which side of his body he naturally slept on, or whether he tossed and turned the whole night through.

He had two books, perfectly aligned with the right-angle of the table by the bed. The smaller, cover faded, was called *The Lemon and the Wave*, written by a pair of initials only – R. H. On top of it was a newer, larger book, a macro-economic analysis of capitalism vs. environmentalism. The phone in his room had a number written on it; I copied it and let myself out.

*

In the afternoon I went shopping.

I bought a crisp new shirt, smart new shoes.

I bought a book on macro-economics and environmental policy.

In the 1950s, society re-geared towards a celebration of consumption. Opportunity awaited all, but how was success to be measured? Not everyone could be a Faraday or an Einstein, a Monroe or a Kennedy – but everyone could own their own television, microwave and dishwasher.

I ate frozen yoghurt from a shop full of beauty queens, felt the blast of air conditioning on the back of my neck.

In the course of the twentieth century opportunities afforded by technological advance redefined societal aspiration. Yet humanity inherently aspires to more. History is full of "celebrities" – those who are celebrated for an act – but in the last century, we celebrated consumption.

I closed the book and counted cars for a while, but the traffic was slow, so I counted bolts in the wheel hubs, and piercings in the ears of the women who walked by me.

What do we celebrate now? Is it nature? Is it simplicity? Even these words have become imbued with a cultural meaning that lends itself to excess.

I wondered where Luca Evard was, and smiled, to know that he was thinking of me.

That evening, at seven p.m. exactly, dressed in white shirt and navy jacket, I knocked on Inspector Luca Evard's door and said, in English, "Hi, my name's Bonnie. I'm with the Polícia Civil do Estado de São Paulo, I think you're expecting me?"

He looked flustered, unshaven, a crinkle in his sweat-stained shirt; in short, a man caught off-guard, who lived his entire life guarded.

"Sorry," he replied, "I didn't think . . ."

"I phoned ahead!" I explained. "Did you get my message?"

"Ah, yes, the message . . ." He remembers a message on his hotel phone, can't remember the voice, the words, or me. But a gentleman, always a gentleman is Luca. "Just . . . let me change my shirt."

He stood aside to let me in, and I waited, tactfully staring out of the window, while he changed in the bathroom. With the door shut, I kept up a running commentary, lest he forget my presence.

"How do you like it in São Paulo? It's a beautiful city, I think, so vibrant – I grew up in England, you see, but my mother's from Rio and I always thought I wanted to come back here, see where they began, and once I was here, well, I couldn't leave, could I? It's just so alive!"

The view from his window: medium-rises blocking the view of more medium-rises, skyscrapers pressed together. On the horizon, favelas, breeze-block houses with iron roofs, trees popping up behind crumbling walls, the maripa palm and bacuri tree, whose seeds were rubbed on eczema. São Paulo, Terra da Garoa – land of drizzle. One in every 74 people owned a gun; of every 74 guns, 70 were illegal. To avoid the gridlock, the rich took helicopters to work; an estimated 70,000 flights every year.

"Yes sir," I cried out, before my silence could let Luca forget. "This is the place to be."

He emerged from the bathroom, tucking the back of his shirt into his trousers as I turned. "Sorry," he mumbled. "I didn't mean to keep you waiting . . . did you say Bonnie?"

"That's right. Let me buy you a drink or something, to thank you for your time."

"I don't, thank you . . ."

"I insist, absolutely, my pleasure, it's an honour to meet someone from Interpol – did my boss tell you I was interested in applying?"

"No, he didn't."

"I think the work you do is incredible, just incredible, please, let me buy you a drink."

He was tired, frustrated, had walked into his hotel room, wanting to be alone.

I was charming, interested, fluent, friendly.

I was company.

I was everything I thought he might want me to be.

"All right," he said. "Just one drink."

I bought him a half pint of expensive German beer, myself a glass of red wine.

"We have CCTV of her face from a dozen different crime scenes," he mused, as I sat, chin resting on the palm of my hand, nodding along. "She doesn't wear a mask – that's part of her MO. She looks like a wealthy woman who you might genuinely believe is going to buy a diamond ring, up to the moment where she robs you. No guns. No team. Her victims aren't fools, someone should have noticed, should have raised the alarm, but no one did. You can show cashiers an image of themselves talking to her, sometimes for an hour at a stretch, and they deny it, while looking at the footage, they deny it, not possible, they'd have remembered her. How does she make them forget? Maybe people are just blind, maybe the world doesn't know how to pay attention. I'm sorry; this must be boring for you."

"Not at all. I'm interested in the case."

He smiled, weary, a man tired from chasing shadows.

"I'm not sure there is a case," he mused, eyes elsewhere. "Just one failure after another."

I gripped my glass.

Feelings of . . .

sympathy, a desire to comfort, a desire to say it's okay, really, it's not you, it's me . . . feelings of . . . guilt?

Is this guilt?

I look away and find it hard to look back, hard to meet his eyes.

"Tell me about her," I said. "Tell me about the thief."

He leant back in his chair with a puff, rolled the glass between his hands for a moment, drained it down, laid it on the table between us, stared into nothing much. "Cocky. Sometimes sloppy, though she's getting more professional. Takes risks, but doesn't appear to care. Whimsical. Her choice of targets aren't always the biggest hauls or the easiest grabs; spiteful, perhaps? Ambitious, maybe. Milan felt like a crime of opportunity, and she was sloppy with the hand-off in Vienna. Self-destructive, perhaps. Wanting attention. She sells mostly on the darknet. Absurd: she should have a fence, couriers, reliable contacts. When I get permission, I try to bid, lure her out. Nearly had her in Vienna, but we found only the jewels, not her. We found hot coffee and a blue coat, stolen property in a paper bag, but she had vanished. Did we miss her? Did we blink?"

I don't dare blink, in case this moment disappears for ever.

"How long have you been on the case?" I asked, barely breathing, words in my mouth, *des mots*, *das Wort*, 词字, *la palabra*, *a palavra*, كلمة, come on, *come on*!

"I think . . . three years. We don't investigate so much, but coordinate. A repeating MO across international borders, a purple notice issued, I got drawn in and it has been . . . it is . . . stagnant."

"Perhaps this time . . . "

"No," he cut me off, soft, a shaking of the head, a curl of the shoulders. "No, I don't think so."

Silence between us.

I lounged in it a while, let it soak through my skin.

"Why are you a policeman?" I asked at last.

"Why are you?" he replied, quick, smiling, deflecting hard.

"I think we make things better."

"Do you?" He bit back on laughter, then shook his head, raised his hands in an apology, sorry, sorry, of course.

"Also," I added, wry smile, head down, "my dad was a copper."

"That sounds more like it."

"And you?"

He drew in his breath slowly, rolled his lips into his mouth, then puffed them out again with a little exhalation of breath. "I dislike arrogance."

"Is that it?"

"The law is the great equaliser. All of us, we must obey the law, we must act within a certain code. To refuse that . . . it is very arrogant, don't you think?"

"I suppose so, but I would have expected . . . "

He raised his eyebrows, pressing his palms against his empty glass.

" . . . something else," I mumbled.

Silence between us, eyes looking away, apologising for things not said. Then I said, "Do you . . . think you'll ever catch the thief you're looking for?"

His eyes wandered up to the ceiling, an old question he'd asked himself many times before. "I don't know," he said at last. "Sometimes I think . . . no. Sometimes I think that. Sometimes you find yourself thinking it's okay to be a failure."

I opened my mouth to say something that Bonnie might say, something like no, it's fine, you're wonderful, don't be . . .

I was slow, the words didn't come, and by the time they were ready, it was too late.

Silence.

"Sorry," he began, an apology for honesty, embarrassment at his life, his work, himself. "Sorry."

"No – don't be."

Silence.

"When are you flying back?" I murmured, looking into my glass.

"Day after tomorrow. They wanted me to stay around a while longer, look interested."

"What do you want?"

"The case to be over. Perhaps it's worth being here. Perhaps we'll find something."

"I heard about a photo, the woman in the park . . . "

"It came from an anonymous email account. Upstanding

citizens don't send photos of international jewel thieves to us without making themselves available."

"Then do you think . . . "

"I think it was her," he replied, clear and simple. "I think she sent us the photo. It's real, no doubt. I think she wants us to look for her; that's how she gets off."

"'Gets off'?"

"Is it wrong?" he queried, eyebrows rising. "'Gets off'?"

My face, hot. I would not flush, I drank red wine, the redness of the drink brighter than the rising blood in my capillaries. "In English, it implies sexual arousal from an action."

He considered this a moment, lips narrow, eyebrows tight. "Yes," he said at last. "Yes, I think that is correct."

I am my fingers, perfectly at rest.

I am my legs, easy on the floor.

I am at ease.

"What you're describing . . . sounds pathological."

"Yes," he mused again. "I would not disagree with that."

"Do you . . . have sympathy for her?"

"Sympathy?"

"If she is . . . everything you think she is . . . do you feel sorry for her?"

"No. Of course not. She breaks the law." He hesitated then, head on one side, considering the statement further.

I am at ease.

I am at ease.

I fail to be at ease. My face is hot; what is this? Excitement, terror, happiness, dread, guilt, pride, giddiness of companionship after too long alone, what a companion, a man who knows everything about me, who knows me, the shock of it, the delight, the . . .

His features flicker in unexpected concern. I am at ease, I am at fucking ease. He mumbles, "I'm sorry, you are . . . did I say something? I'm not selling my job well, it is of course—"

"No," I cut him off, sharper than I'd meant. Then soft, smiling, I am my smile, I am my bloody fucking smile, "No, it wasn't anything you said. Sorry. It's been a long day for me too. Let's . . . talk about something else."

We talked, he and I, for another hour and a half.

Then he said, "I should . . . "

Of course, I replied, jumping to my feet. You're very . . .

It's been a pleasure . . .

. . . good luck with the . . .

. . . of course, you too.

A moment, perhaps.

But no: he looked at me, and saw a young woman, looking to him for ideas, inspiration, an example. He would set a good example.

Luca Evard was always a good man.

Good night, Inspector Evard.

Good night. Perhaps we shall meet again.

Chapter 33

Pickpocketing on the Istanbul metro. Find a crowded train, bounce, body to body, the rattle of people, motion keeping your mark preoccupied. I stank, my eyes were bruised, I wanted to sleep and couldn't believe sleep would ever come, that my mind would ever stop.

I counted supporters of Fenerbahce and Besiktas, of Barcelona and Madrid, Munich and Manchester. I saw one lone supporter of Sheffield United, and wondered if he had picked up the shirt because he liked the pattern.

I counted patent-leather shoes and flip flops.

Gold bracelets and plastic bangles.

I counted until there was only the world, the numbers, the breath, and I, my aching mind and my burned body, didn't exist. I was only eyes, counting, only fingers, reaching, only the slight pressure against the stranger's arm as I bumped against him, lifting the wallet from his pocket as he turned away. I counted buckles on bags as I pulled the mother's purse; counted the studs in a student's ears as I pilfered his phone and ID; I counted coins as I rode the funicular to Karakoy. The wallets themselves I threw away – no use to me. The face of the student on his ID tumbled into the bin. The mother's library card fell into the dark. The lawyer's credit cards vanished into the remnants of a sticky lamb kebab at the bottom of the trash can. They would be angry. They would feel violated. They would waste time and money restoring the things I had stolen. They would tell their friends that they no longer felt safe on the metro.

I didn't care.

I would *live*.

On Siraselviler I bought a bowl of spiced yoghurt and lamb served with scalding rice and ate it in great shovelling mouthfuls. From an ice-cream house, the walls decked out with pictures of cartoon characters with ice-cream cones grafted into the frame – Princess Jasmine and Aladdin sharing a couple of cones on their magic carpet, the Pink Panther licking his lips with satisfaction, a half-devoured strawberry cone in one hand – I ordered lemon and honey with extra sprinkles, and ate until my belly hurt.

From one of the dozens of mobile phone outlets that lined the street, I bought a cheap handset with a cheaper SIM card, and accessed my email.

Parker hadn't replied.

As the sun set, the lights brightened on Siraselviler, and a patter of light rain began to fall. I stood a while, letting it wet my hair, run into my skin, enjoying it like the sleep I hadn't yet had, before wandering into the nearest universal-brand of universal-store that sold the same universal-clothes that you could buy anywhere, and dressing myself like a tourist.

Chapter 34

Why counting?

A lesson learned from my dad. A common trick in the police: when you're sitting opposite the bastard who you knew did it and who won't say a word; when you show that bastard the pictures of the old woman he beat, the child he robbed, the woman he raped and his face doesn't even flicker, no surprise, no regret, just "no comment, no comment", when you think you're going to punch him in the face, shake him by the throat and scream, *Say something, you bastard, show some fucking humanity!*

at that moment, instead, let out a slow breath, and count backwards from ten.

Ten nine eight seven six five four three two one.

You can always get the fucker on forensics anyway.

Not that my dad ever swore. Not worth it, he'd say. People are just people, doing people things. Sometimes they're stupid, and sometimes they're desperate, and a lot of the time it's just bad luck. Don't get your knickers in a twist over people.

By midnight, Parker still hadn't replied. Had these been normal circumstances, I might have found a casino, somewhere to count the cards; but Istanbul had shut its casinos years ago, and I didn't have the contacts to find where the gambling was now.

Reluctantly, I went back to the bunk bed in Zetinburnu, and slept badly, and dreamed of sand.

Forty-nine hours after I'd contacted him, and thirteen stolen wallets later, Parker replied.

Dear Hope

I'm sorry to disappoint, but I don't deal in these

things any more. Should you need help, I suggest you approach an embassy or consular authority. I wish you luck,

Yours faithfully,

Parker

What did I feel?

I had no memories of this man, no face to hate.

Was he just a fantasy in my mind, a dream?

Was he real?

(Was I?)

If I had been in Newark, and had access to the box where I stored my memories of him, I would have torn them to pieces and, as they burned, I would have rejoiced in the murder of the flames.

I tore the dressings off my burns.

I walked through the street in three-quarter shorts and a strappy top so people could see my still-blazing injuries.

On the tram, I stole a wallet from a woman who'd looked at me with contempt, and fumbled the grab, and as she began to scream and cry thief, thief, thief, I slapped her across the face and ran away, until my lungs burned again and I couldn't remember where I was or how I'd got there.

No one would remember me as I stood upon this corner, gasping for breath.

There was only now.

The now in which I opened the stolen wallet, tore the contents out, ripped the money to pieces, snarled like an injured animal, sat on the pavement, remembered I was alone.

This now.

I stand up.

The now is fading.

Those who saw it, forget it.

Now it is gone.

Now I am walking.

Counting my steps.
And gone.

On my seventh day in Istanbul, I bought a laptop, loaded up Tor, and went looking for Byron14.

He was hiding, tipped off perhaps by my silence, or by my looking, or by some other action of Gauguin's. I posted up the following:

```
whatwherewhen: For sale. Perfection base
code, unencrypted. Full 106 Club database
with names and bank details. Total access
or your money back.
```

Byron14 was there in less than twenty minutes.

```
Byron14: I am interested in your product.

whatwherewhen: Hello, Byron14. I hoped you
would be.
```

On the ninth day after a man called Gauguin nearly burned me alive in a warehouse in Istanbul, I struck a deal with a stranger by the name of Byron14.

I said: I need papers, cash, clean, untraceable.

Byron replied: I want the base code of Perfection. Do I take it you do not, in fact, have this?

Not yet, I confessed. But you help me, and I will rip Perfection apart. I will tear Prometheus to pieces, I will . . .

You seem to be taking this quite personally, Byron mused.

You've got some fucked-up shit with Gauguin, haven't you? I retorted.

No answer for a while, then,

Fair enough, he said. Okay. Let's make a deal.

Byron14 was as good as his word. Within twenty-four hours of making our bargain, fifty thousand lira in mixed bills was waiting for me in a brown jiffy bag at a post box in Beyoğlu, and twelve hours after that, a forger by the name of Emine contacted me informing me her services had already been paid for and when would I be able to meet?

We met that evening on a yacht on the Sea of Marmara. The boat was called *Good Intention*, had high white sides and wooden finishes, a steering wheel with the face of a dragon carved in its centre, and a mahogany cigar-smoking Indian by the door to the bottom deck. Emine was in her mid-fifties, with an almost spherical face framed by an almost spherical burst of grey hair. The walls of the yacht were hung with watercolour paintings of Istanbul, none very good, all homemade. She wore a blue chiffon robe over a white cotton shirt, and as she led me into her workshop beneath the waterline her ankles jangled with jewellery, wooden charms and silver bangles, blue glass eyes to ward off evil. "Come, come, come!" she barked, leading me downstairs.

Her business was passport reclamation. "I'm an artist," she exclaimed, "but people don't appreciate my work, so I do this on the side. Come, come!"

She sat me down on a stool by a long bench covered in inks and glues, magnifying glasses and bits of computer cable. Opening a blue Tupperware box she started flicking through passports – Turkish, American, British, French, Russian, Indian, Japanese, Egyptian – all acquired from the foolish, the naïve or the dead.

"Are you British?"

"Yes."

"You want to still be British?"

I shrugged. There are worse passports.

"You'd make a lovely American," she exclaimed. "But no, too many people hate America, no good, no good. Iranian? No – wrong face for an Iranian. I can do you Bhutan, no one knows anything about Bhutan, and it's clean, totally clean, you can use it for eight years no problem, money-back guarantee."

"British is fine."

"British passports are tricky, tricky! Barcodes, and now they're putting in chips, I have to get my nephew to help me out with that sort of thing, he's very good, bang bang, new identity, passport programmed happy good! In the old days," she added, voice dropping with a sudden wistfulness, "it was just about making beautiful documents. But computers get everywhere now, all the old skills, dying; dying for machines."

I smiled my most beatific smile, and resisted pointing out that certain professions, including mine, had proven themselves both flexible and immune to change.

UK passport photo requirements: professionally printed, 45mm x 35mm; in colour on plain white paper, taken against a plain cream or light grey background. The frame must include your head and shoulders; your head can occupy no more than 34mm of the height of the space, and no less than 29mm. You must wear a neutral expression, with your mouth closed, looking directly at the camera, without any head covering unless it is worn for religious purposes.

I told her all this, and she looked bewildered. "Just stand still for photo!" she barked.

The passport she eventually doctored for my purposes was of a British woman who "Went to Bangladesh," she sighed, "and never came back."

I was on a flight for Tokyo the same night.

Chapter 35

It was not the first time I had been poor, but I was out of practice. I had assets, years of cash squirrelled away in the event of emergencies, documents and new IDs; but none were in Turkey and too many could be traced by Gauguin. How easily my little empire had crumbled, but strangely I didn't care. I thought I would feel regret at the loss of belongings, and yet, informing the clerk at the airport that I had no baggage to check in I felt curiously happy. My shoulders rolled back, my head drifted up, and when the plane taxied down the runway, I looked out of the window and found that I was smiling.

I had nothing in the world to call my own, but I had a passport, a destination, a bargain and a purpose.

It wasn't merely the £1.2 million that Byron promised upon completion of the job that gave me a sense of ease; it was the job itself.

I was going to Tokyo to crack open the little piece of software that seemed to obsess both Byron and Gauguin, whose name had haunted me around my travels between the Red Sea and the Mediterranean. I was going to steal Perfection, and it was good.

I'd asked:

whatwherewhen: What's your interest in Perfection?

Byron14: What's yours?

whatwherewhen: They pissed me off.

Byron14: Is that all?

whatwherewhen: Reina used it, in Dubai. Reina died.

Byron14: So? Software didn't kill her.

whatwherewhen: It told her she was broken. Every day a reminder: you're not trying hard enough, not eating, exercising, drinking, being, buying – buying your way to perfection, with Perfection. Perfection is owned by Prometheus, Prometheus flew in Princess Shamma bint Bandar, a deal to be struck, perfect things, perfect truths, perfect way to be Muslim, perfect hajj perfect zakat perfect fucking lives made fucking perfect and Reina was perfect already, she was depressed and never said it, alone and never spoke, she was good and she was fucking good she was the best one of them all and

I stopped typing, made myself a cup of tea.
Byron was waiting.

whatwherewhen: I think Gauguin would have been happy getting the diamonds back and arresting me, if you hadn't got involved.

Byron14: You may be right.

whatwherewhen: I made a mistake when I got involved in this. I stole the jewels out of spite, not professionalism, and here we are.

Byron14: Perhaps.

whatwherewhen: If it weren't for you, I could walk away.

Byron14: I doubt that.

whatwherewhen: I'm forgettable – Gauguin would forget me. He's more interested in you. He called you a killer and a terrorist.

Byron14: That's his point of view.

whatwherewhen: What gives?

No answer.

whatwherewhen: You want my help; I hate being a sucker.

Byron14: The man you call Gauguin and myself were lovers.

The answer was so simple, so easy, that I thought for a moment Byron was mocking me. But no jibes followed, no sign in our conversation that there was anything other than simple truth.

whatwherewhen: And now?

Byron14: I doubt he knows what he wants. It is good that you dislike Perfection, and good that you blame it for your friend's death. You are right, to a degree. It has no mercy for those who do not conform. But you should understand that what you regard as a mobile app is a far more potent tool. It rewards conformity with financial and social advancement. At a hundred thousand points your diet, your exercise habits, your interests begin to habitually skew towards that which the creators of Perfection have dubbed "perfect". At five hundred thousand points, your speech, your hobbies, your friends are all beginning to be turned the same way. At a million points you are invited to join the 106, where everyone is as perfect as you, and by the time you have reached this target, you are perhaps very different from who you are before. Perfection taps into every part of your life. It monitors phone calls, reads emails, accesses your bank account, tracks your internet search history, uses GPS to trace your location, rides shopping loyalty cards and mines data on your purchase habits, has access to the microphone and camera of your phone, can monitor your sleep, your waking hours, your work habits, your leisure activities. At its most basic it is a tool for marketing. The services you use – health, fitness, food, fashion – the services which make you perfect – are all paying a handsome fee to the app for their referral. At the purely theoretical end of its operation is the truth that Perfection comes with a pre-defined notion of what perfect means, and "perfect" is beautiful, confident, arrogant, rich, pampered and obscene. If there is a new Illuminati for our time, then it is the elite of Perfection, and unlike the legends of the Illuminati which went before, the only purpose of the 106 is to feast and feed. Do you want to destroy Perfection?

whatwherewhen: I think so, yes.

Byron14: Do you know why?

whatwherewhen: Reina died.

She died and it is obscene. She died and I think, if I destroy it, she would be pleased.

Byron14: Investigate Rafe Pereyra-Conroy. Visit the treatment centres, learn how they work. Find Filipa Pereyra-Conroy in Tokyo. She has seen the future.

I wondered for a moment if I was working for a madman, a fanatic.

A fanatic who had access to money and passports was still useful, regardless of his beliefs. The only reason Byron14 remembered me was because our interaction was digital, a thing recorded in words and symbols. I could back away whenever I chose, without ill-effect. If I wished to.

whatwherewhen: I am a woman.

Byron14 took longer to reply than he had on any message we had shared until that time.

Byron14: Yes.

whatwherewhen: So are you.

Silence again.

Byron14: We are in business, whatwherewhen. That is all.

So saying, she signed off, and seventy-two hours later, I looked down on the East China Sea, and wondered what it was that I had wrought.

Chapter 36

Things I know about Japan, contemplated at thirty-five thousand feet:

- The *sakura zensen,* the annual blossoming of the cherry trees, from the southern islands of Okinawa to the north of Hokkaido, is a national news event. Salarymen, the blue-suited servants of the *zaibatsu*, who work their whole youths to get the jobs that they will keep their whole lives, send their juniors out into the parks to find the perfect spot to sit beneath the trees and contemplate their blossom, perhaps composing a thoughtful haiku on the transience of life on their smartphones, to tweet later.
- The ancient Shinto shrines with their *torii* gates that separate the sacred from the mundane, are almost always some form of new. Every twenty or so years, the old buildings are taken down, and new timbers, carved the traditional way, in exactly the same form, will take their place, old and new, all at once.
- Suicide is the leading cause of death for women aged 15–34, and men aged 24–40.
- The manga market in Japan is worth more than $5.5 billion dollars. In 2010 the Tokyo Metropolitan Government attempted to limit images of extreme violence and sexuality in children's manga, prompting an outcry across the country. The government argued that depictions of children in sexual situations, of rape by both people and fantastical creatures, and the illustration of brutal mass murder was unsuitable for young readers. "It's an outrage," exclaimed one artist. "This is government restriction of the freedom of expression for both artists and readers," and of course, everyone was right, in their own way.

*

A question: why are planes always at thirty-five thousand feet, not ten and a half thousand metres? Has the sky not gone metric?

I flew into Tokyo as the sun rose.

A traditional Japanese-style hotel room. Tatami mats on the floor, mattresses in bright neon greens and pinks to be rolled out, a view of a French-style café and a computer-repair shop across the street. A sliding door to the bathroom; a toilet with a control containing twelve different buttons, of which only one was "flush". There is no international symbol to represent that function best described by the slow release of waters into the toilet bowl to disguise the sound of a woman pissing. The music the toilet could perform from a tiny speaker above the cistern was of five sorts – traditional Japanese, girl-band, boy-band, the sound of birds chirruping, or Rod Stewart.

Next to my hotel, a love hotel offered its services, pink neon signs inviting courting couples in for an illicit few hours together, no questions asked. The screen between the outside world and the receptionist was opaque, so that no one might see your features. The entrance and exit were hidden from view, but I thought I saw a couple – a man in his fifties, bespectacled, ironed shirt, shoes shined, and a girl, barely seventeen years old, long dark hair and a little pleated skirt, scuttle away with the look of good people caught in a shameful moral trespass. In recent years the government had tried to crack down on love hotels; sex and play were two words they were uncomfortable putting together.

Would it be fair to say that Japan is racist?

Perhaps fairer to say that Japan is not used to black women, and definitely not women of mixed race, even ones who carry a forged British passport and a large quantity of unfavourably converted yen. No one's really racist any more, just as no one's really sexist. They've just got their view about things, you see.

I forced myself to stay awake as long as I could, buying a few supplies, lifting the occasional wallet, searching for food that would be gentle on the stomach. Sushi was a safe start, if you ordered wisely. Stone fish, pickled plums, jellyfish, unagi – these all took a little more building up to. No point trying to walk anywhere in Tokyo, the city was too big. Take the train, find a district within which you're willing to walk, Asakusa or Ueno, where the older styles and skills still survived beneath the skyscrapers; the fish market at Tsukiji. Outside a pink bar in Shinjuku a man approached me, grinning widely, and exclaimed in English, "You hostess?"

I shook my head, and he nodded fervently, adding, "You hostess? You very beautiful."

His teeth were perfectly white, his hair was in full retreat from his forehead, though he could not have been a day over thirty. From the door of the bar, a woman with blonde hair down to her hips, a freckle-spotted tan and an Australian accent emerged, took the customer by the arm and guided him back indoors with a cry of, "So sorry, so sorry, she's just a visitor, more sake?"

He said something I couldn't hear, and she laughed dutifully, and afterwards came out for a cigarette and said, "It's a decent life really. Most of the men just want company, to talk. If you're white and interested, it's even better. It doesn't get to sex unless you want it to, and you can make them pay, but I don't need to. Champagne, gifts, tips – in four months I'll have earned enough to buy a house back home."

She offered me a cigarette, and I shook my head.

"You thinking of joining? You'd be unusual, but this is Shinjuku. You can be disgusting as a decomposing rhino and someone will want to fuck you, because you're *unusually* disgusting. But you're very beautiful, I think."

"Get many salarymen?"

"Lots. Most of them are married but, like I said, it's just talk. Lonely men who like to talk with someone . . . else."

Out of interest, I said, "Have you got Perfection?"

She laughed. "Sure. I used to. Everyone in this city wants to be perfect. I did okay too, won like, six months discounted membership at some really swanky gym downtown, the perfect gym you know, to get the perfect body. But it got access to my bank accounts or something, or maybe my loyalty cards, you know like I don't even know how it did it but I must have ticked a box or something, and at thirty thousand points it started telling me to quit smoking and drink less, and I was like, fuck that, and at forty thousand points it started sending me stuff from agencies that it said better matched my character profile than my current work – I mean, fuck? Like, a fucking app telling me what to fucking do with my life? Anyway, after that I started to lose points like a space invader. 'Perfection lies within you,' it said. I deleted the fucking thing when I got back to ten thousand points, but you know what? My friend, who fixes computers and shit, says there's still, like, stuff on my phone tracking me, I mean, like, Perfection has still got all that access because I can't like, just stop it, what the fuck."

Permissions that the Facebook Messenger app requests when downloaded to your phone:

- Allows the app to change the state of network connectivity.
- Allows the app to call phone numbers without your intervention.
- Allows the app to send SMS messages.
- Allows the app to record audio with microphone. This permission allows the app to record audio at any time without your confirmation.
- Allows the app to take pictures and videos with the camera. This permission allows the app to use the camera at any time without your confirmation.
- Allows the app to read your phone's call log, including data about incoming and outgoing calls. This permission allows apps to save your call-log data.
- Allows the app to read data about your contacts stored on your phone, including the frequency with which you've called, emailed, or communicated in other ways with specific individuals.

- Allows the app to read personal-profile information stored on your device, such as your name and contact information. This means the app can identify you and may send your profile information to others.
- Allows the app to get a list of accounts known by the phone. This may include any accounts created by applications you have installed.

Perfection had almost exactly the same permissions, with one difference:

- Allows the app to monitor internet history and keystrokes.

I considered for a moment the power of this tool, and saw bank accounts and passwords, online shops and credit cards, maps and travel patterns, blackmail and bribery roll before my eyes.

I wondered what I could do with that knowledge, being a thief.

Then I chided myself for narrow thinking, and asked instead: what could I do with that knowledge, being a god?

Chapter 37

A week of investigation.

Why had Byron14 sent me to Japan?

Prometheus, owner of Perfection. Subsidiary offices: Mumbai, Shanghai, Dubai, Johannesburg, Nairobi, Paris, Hamburg, New York, Seattle, Mexico City, Caracas, Santiago, Grenville (tax purposes?), Geneva (absolutely tax purposes) and Tokyo.

The Tokyo office was registered to a building in Yamanote.

I walked by it twice, counting twenty-eight floors to the top of its sheer glass and concrete sides, before going in search of a business suit.

Out of curiosity, I lay on my belly in my hotel room and poked on a laptop at Prometheus. Dragging data off the net was slow, but not impossible. Like a huge number of companies across the world, the majority of Prometheus' value was owned by a holding company, a multi-fingered corporation whose sole purpose was to own other things. At the top was Rafe Pereyra-Conroy. I recognised his face: he'd worn black in Dubai, and smiled at the royal family, and as I walked away from the robbery he'd been in the lobby, screaming down a mobile phone.

At my fucking party stole her fucking jewels do you know what this fucking does for us, do you know how much we've just fucking lost?!

Searching in depth for Rafe Pereyra-Conroy, you mostly found his father.

Matheus Pereyra, born in Montevideo, carried by his mother to England aged three years old, grew up in a two-bedroom bungalow in West Acton with a violent stepfather and a mother struggling to survive. Aged sixteen, Matheus left home to start work on the print floor of a Fleet Street journal, hauling reams of paper and gallons of ink into the noisy belly of the machines. There he was "Matty", and though he hated his English stepfather, he used his surname and became Matty Conroy, one of the lads. He bought a tie and a suit, and every Friday night went down the pub with the journos, learning how to swagger and smoke, until one day someone turned round and said, "Bugger me, Matty, you're wasted in the print room . . . " So began Matty Conroy's journey into the world of media.

"Work, work, work," he was quoted as saying. "Young people just want everything to drop on their plate, but I know, you have to work, and you have to believe. People tell you you're too small: you prove you're bigger than them. They say you'll never make it: you remember those words and every time you fall down, you remember, you'll make it, you'll make it, you'll make it."

As a journalist, he was a disaster; as a seller of advertising space and developer of market strategies, he was a genius. Within five years he'd quit the newspaper that first hired him, and aged twenty-six he started his own.

"You know the difference between a tabloid and a newspaper?" he asked. "A tabloid actually gives people stories they're interested in."

Aged thirty he controlled 23 per cent of the print media market in the UK; aged thirty-four he bought his first TV station. When, aged thirty-five, the Royal Ascot Racing Club declined his membership on grounds that he did not conform to their requirements, the two newspapers and four tabloids under his control ran headline stories on the subject, with tag-lines ranging from a moderate "Old-Fashioned and Out of Touch?" through to "The Bigoted Berks of Berkshire". To his surprise, the ancient white-gloved gentlemen of Ascot, rather than yield to this pressure, dug their heels in deeper.

"Mr Conroy's campaign of harassment only serves to emphasise the validity of our initial judgement in declining him membership, as is our right," explained one spokesman in a top hat.

The aristocracy of England had survived revolution, emancipation and war. Time was long, memory faded, but they never changed.

Two years later, Matty Conroy was Matheus Pereyra again, owner of a luxury cruise-ship line, a chain of chicken restaurants, a hire-car company, half a bank, and an island near Nassau. The day his value exceeded £1 billion, a rival newspaper in the UK ran an article pointing out that he paid an estimated 0.7 per cent tax on his fortune. The newspaper was sued for libel, and though the case was dropped – "for reasons of fact" as the editor put it – the lawyers' fees crippled the paper for years to come, and it ran no more such articles.

The year his daughter, Filipa, was born, a controversy broke out as one of his US TV stations chose fourteen individuals from Washington DC and tagged them as a "Sleeper Homosexual Infiltration Squad".

"I firmly believe," explained Matheus, "that the government of the United States of America is being infiltrated by units of liberals and homosexuals wishing to force their atheist agenda on the people of this nation through the top-heavy institution of centralised government."

When accused of speaking without any evidence, Matheus Pereyra added: "There is evidence – there is evidence, I have seen it. But the government's repressive bodies make it impossible to share with the world what I know."

Fifteen months later, his son was born, and Matheus Pereyra acquired American citizenship and a three-thousand-acre plot of land in Colorado from which he could "consider what next to do for the world".

What he did was buy more stuff, and fill the newspapers and airwaves with celebrity scandals, Hollywood gossip, unconfirmed rumour and domestic bigotry. His control of the airwaves surged, and when he was sixty-one years old, he was found poisoned in his home, the murderer never caught.

Aged eighteen, his son, Rafe Pereyra-Conroy, took control of a company whose net worth was estimated at approximately £3.8 billion. Groomed, confident and assured, Rafe gave a speech in public on the greatness of his father's legacy, but also the need for a new, conscientious company which strove for the betterment of mankind. His sister, Filipa, three years his senior and nearly through her first degree in biochemistry, stood behind him and a little to the left, and said nothing. I knew her face too; I had met her in Dubai.

All of thought is feedback. Charm falters in the face of hypertension. Are you with the 106? Ten years later, with the company now worth £5.09 billion, work on Perfection began, with Filipa Pereyra-Conroy at its head.

Chapter 38

Discipline.

My Japanese is pretty poor, but my hosts were charming and patient.

Discipline.

Dressed in a lilac summer dress, I started to hang out at the karaoke bar round the corner from Prometheus' Yamanote office. On the third night, having practised carefully in my room, I sang "Black is the Colour" in front of a floor of extraordinarily drunk executives, one of whom had butchered the song the night before, and who immediately bought me a bottle of champagne and invited me to join their group.

Mr Fukazawa worked in human resources for Prometheus, and after we savaged a duet of "Summertime" together, he put his head on my shoulder and with tears pricking the rims of his eyes proclaimed, "There are no women as wonderful as you in all Japan."

He passed out in a gentle alcoholic stupor before I could disillusion him of this notion, so instead I lifted the cash contents of his wallet and his security pass, and laid his head gently down on the white leather couches and snuck out before the next rendition of a Bon Jovi number could deface the walls of the bar.

Discipline.

Two doors down from the love hotel on my street, and below a restaurant specialising in grilled fish, a café dedicated entirely to arcade games lured in men and women, young and old. I played Mortal Kombat against a girl with pigtails sticking out either side of her head, and she won, and I said, "Have you got Perfection?"

"Sure!" she replied brightly, pulling her phone from her bag. "But I'm not doing very well."

"Why not?"

"When I came in here, it registered the local wireless networks and knew where I was, and perfect women don't come here."

"That doesn't seem to stop you."

She hesitated, looking for a moment guilty. "I dunno," she said at last. "In seven thousand points I get a free make-over at Peach Princess Parlour, and I just *love* their products, and I know tonight's going to set me back on points so I suppose . . . I dunno . . . I suppose I'll have to do better."

She was hoping to get an internship at Prometheus, the office in Yamanote.

"And what do they do there?"

"They design computer software, you know. I'm good at all that sorta stuff and no one is going to marry me so I gotta look out for myself, you know?"

On the screen, her avatar spat lightning from his fingertips, and my character fell down dead, the screen blaring my defeat.

"One more round?" I asked, manoeuvring my bag closer to hers, the better to steal her mobile phone.

"Okay . . . one more . . ."

Discipline.

The day Rafe Pereyra-Conroy flew into Tokyo International Airport to visit the offices of Prometheus, I had already bought a complete itinerary of his trip from a disgruntled driver in Monaco, who felt he hadn't been given his fair tip.

The guy's a billionaire, he grumbled. *Guys like that shouldn't get to pay going rate.*

I was at the airport when he arrived on his private jet, and I trailed his convoy of three cars through the streets of Tokyo to his top-floor suite in Chiyoda. At the front door of the thirty-storey building, he was met by a woman. Filipa Pereyra-Conroy, older sister, sometime scientist, now head of development on Perfection in all its technical wonder. The newspaper photos had done her no favours; she had been a slightly out-of-focus blob of pixels behind her younger brother.

All thought is feedback.

The world of the super-rich/super-powerful isn't so large. Sometimes you run into familiar faces, even if they don't remember you.

As a woman in a sharp suit with a sharp business card and a significant bribe that I presented in both hands with a bow to the manager of the building, I got a tour of the tower where the Pereyra-Conroys stayed.

"My company specialises in luxury housing projects for the developing market in the Middle East. We can learn so much from Japan," I announced, as he showed me the internal waterways that trickled busily through the atrium of the building, the palm trees growing from great pots of dirt layered over with white pebble, the dry garden on the twenty-first floor – "Mr Ko at 128 is a zen master," he explained. "He tends to these things."

"And does Mr Ko ply his trade anywhere else?"

"Of course, ma'am. He's a gynaecologist *and* a zen master."

"Is that a usual combination?"

"I don't think so. Most of the priesthood come from finance."

I counted birds taking flight, etched in silver on the walls of the twenty-third floor. If the patterns of bending reeds and lotus flowers, of cherry blossom swept away by the wind and creatures bursting from the water into the sky repeated, I could not see where.

"And how do you get an apartment here?" I asked. "I couldn't find it listed on the web . . . "

"No, ma'am! One must achieve perfection."

Was this a Buddhist aphorism I didn't fully comprehend . . . ?

"No, ma'am. Only members of the 106 Club live here."

I stopped dead in my tracks, and only when he too stopped to look at me askance did I remember to keep smiling, keep walking, be my smile, be my walk, and said casual as anything, "Of course. They are exactly the kind of clientele we cater to."

I counted doors, windows, floors.

I counted steps.

From these, I counted members of the 106 Club living in this building alone, and was briefly afraid.

A woman in the cramped tailor's shop round the corner from the apartment.

"It used to be cheap housing, good housing, for people government supports," she grumbled, examining a tear in a skirt as I leant on her counter and struggled to pull meaning out of her heavily inflected English. "Poor people, hard life. But bosses said no good, pull down, put up big apartments for important people. Much protest, many petitions, but do no good. Minister says big new apartment good: now minister lives there! Protested to police, but police commissioner live there. Say it perfect, perfect place for good people to live in."

"Where are the poor people now?" I asked.

She shrugged. "Tokyo too expensive for them. Leave city; go somewhere cheap. Hard, hard. Can't get work in cheap places. Can't live in expensive ones. No way up."

She held up the skirt with sudden triumph and declared, "What you think of this?"

I examined the offending garment – not mine – a thing of grey wool woven with a light blue chequer pattern. "It's all right," I said with a shrug.

"It skirt of club dancer! She tear it with nail while stripping! She nice girl, very nice girl, wanted to be computer scientist but didn't get grades. Now she owns club; always tips, sometimes brings sweet buns because I'm widow. Always way, yes? People say must do one thing, but world says must be another."

She cackled brightly at her wit, and I thanked her in English and Japanese, and left to the sound of her merriment.

Discipline.

A run.

A walk.

A talk.

Back straight.

Eyes forward.
Head up.
Shake hand.
Wash face.
Study target.
Prepare plan.
My life is a machine.
I am a machine, living my life.
Click click click, the gears turn, and I live.
I live.

Chapter 39

In the middle of the night, I woke, and found that I was missing Byron14.

Missing Gauguin, even.

Missing people who missed me.

I thought of Luca Evard, and found myself by my laptop, wondering what crime I could commit to bring him to Tokyo.

I went out into the streets, dressed too thinly for the cold and the dark.

Found a man in a bar.

He was tipsy, but alcohol made him sentimental, childish, an affectionate drunk.

Found a room in a love hotel, booked it for two hours, was done in twenty minutes, left him snoring in a stupor, went back to the hotel room, back to the hotel bed, could have been anywhere in the world. Electric life, electric key, electric footprint in a digital age. CO_2 emissions I have created, things I have consumed, windows broken, surfaces scratched, I am the mark my life leaves behind, I am a number in a system, I am the smell on a drunk man's lips when he wakes, naked, in the love hotel, which he washes off in the morning.

I am destruction.

I slept badly, and brief.

The third time I met Luca Evard, I went looking for him.

The job had been in Kunming; the exchange was in Hong Kong. Arriving for the swap, jewels for cash at Hung Hom Ferry Pier, I found three men instead of the expected one, and when I went to leave, a fourth stopped me, gun in hand, sunglasses and slicked-back hair, shining with gel used in so much profusion that pale blue beads clung to his temples. He seemed unperturbed by the few late-night commuters waiting for the ferry to North Point, his only concession to their presence being to gently turn his body until it was between them and us, pushing me back against the wall, hiding the gun. He signalled with a tilt of his head to his colleagues, who formed a tight pack, blocking air, light, sound, and then, in a surreal twist of camouflage, proceeded to chat loudly and cheerfully about their favourite pop group and how hard it was finding a place to live cheaply these days.

Against this babble of merry noise, my assailant leant in gently, his breath meeting mine, and whispered in flawless, private-school-precision English, "You match the description I have been given."

Words remain in people's minds, even if my face does not. Dark skinned, dark haired, hair twisted into long ropes down my back, a runner's body, a woman waiting for the ferry who is all these things – there were only so many candidates. I gave it my best stab regardless, whispering, "Not me, not me, I don't know—"

"If it's not you," he breathed, "there's no reason not to shoot."

His gun was a .22, and the sound – while noticeable – wouldn't be as great as it could be if fired directly into my belly. Even if the noise disturbed people, it is easier to dismiss a loud bang as an engine or a firecracker, rather than an act of murder happening not ten yards from where you stand. The payoff was that a .22 bullet might not kill me; but a perforated stomach or a collapsed lung had long-term implications, especially given my condition. What would happen if my surgeon needed to pee during a life-saving operation?

Blood vessels in the stomach: inferior vena cava, celiac trunk, renal veins and arteries, gondal vein and artery, common iliac vein and artery, leading to the great saphenous vein and femoral artery. Someone cut in the femoral artery can bleed out in less than two minutes; first aid requires the first-responder to stand with all their weight on the injury to prevent this.

"I'm not alone," I lied, as the man with the gun began to search me, fingers against my skin, pulling at my clothes, touching, prodding, gripping, words I didn't want to find, probing, fondling, more than just the gun a threat, more than just death. "You do this and there'll be consequences."

He shrugged; he was a crook in Hong Kong, he'd met consequences before and didn't think much of them. Men had died, women had died, and still he stood so what the hell did it matter?

His fingers wrapped round my shoulder bag, eased it down my arm. He pressed it against his own body, then pushed his body against mine, so I was squeezed further into the wall, our combined shapes supporting the bag between us. With one hand he opened the zip, rummaged within.

His fingers closed round the brown jiffy bag where I'd stashed the jewels. Emeralds, paid in tribute by the kings of Thailand to a Chinese emperor, the tribute system, buying peace, China, 中国, the Middle Kingdom, centre of the world, rivers flow from its heart, the world is the sea, the emperor, the mountain, 河, 山, the job had taken less than four minutes to complete from entering the museum grounds to exiting with my prize. A buyer on the darknet, a collector in Hong Kong, drug man, money man, trafficker, killer, but he loved all things Thai, the food, the art, the jewels, he had built temples, buying his way to heaven, good karma, should never have taken the deal.

A moment. The man with the gun could feel something in

the jiffy bag, but he wasn't sure. A glance down, his eyes briefly turned from me, checking, he needs to see, needs to verify that I haven't planted a dummy in my bag. I hit him, my right hand across his face, simultaneously my left pushing the gun to one side. I stepped to the right and his finger jerked around the trigger on automatic pilot, I heard it hit the wall behind me, felt the passage of the bullet tug at my clothes, the bag which had been supported between us fell.

The three friends, three would-be murderers, kids hoping to impress their boss with their killing, looked to their employer. One made a lunge for me, and I hit him blindly, panicked, with the side of my elbow, having no room to move, no space to get a decent punch. He looked barely seventeen years old, but put his hands up to protect himself as my arm turned. His fingers bounced back with my strike, hitting himself in the face, and as he recoiled, more bewildered than wounded, I pushed past him and ran.

The gunshots were definitely gunshots now. The idiot with the .22 shot wildly, catching the boy with the bruised jaw in the shoulder. The few passengers in the terminal began to run; not screaming, not shouting or crying for mercy, but rather as sparrows turn in the sky, a single silent consensus to move.

I didn't feel the bullet that entered my leg, but when I tried to turn a corner the turn went wrong, and I slipped on washed tiles and found myself hanging onto the low green barrier that separated pier from water. I heard feet behind, saw blackness below, and with absolute certainty, tipped myself over the side of the pier, head-first into the water.

How long does it take a stranger to forget?

A minute?

Hold your breath for a minute.

Ready?

Go.

One two three four five six seven eight nine ten eleven twelve

If you had time to inhale, your cheeks are puffed up with air, pushing against your lips from the inside out, so you can see, at the bottom of your vision, the curve of your own expanded face.

Thirty thirty-one thirty-two thirty-three thirty-four thirty-five

Your cheeks begin to ache from the pressure.

The first bubble of air breaks from your nostrils.

Your mouth deflates.

Your diaphragm rises.

Your throat tightens.

As you exhale, you feel your lungs shrinking down to wet envelopes in your chest.

Forty-nine fifty fifty-one

Trachea, collapsing.

Face, collapsing.

Chest, collapsing.

Heart, collapsing.

How long to forget?

I hold myself beneath the pier, hands pressing against it to keep me under.

I am the cold.

I am the darkness.

I am the sea.

I am the sea.

Respiration. Muscle, lungs. Amyotrophic lateral sclerosis, motor neuron disease, the body shuts down from the limbs inwards, eventually autonomic function in the lungs begins to fail, breath fails, life fails, life on a respirator, life trapped, frozen, death from suffocation, death from drowning, ice buckets and the internet, drowning for an emperor's emeralds in Hong Kong, I am the sea, I am the sea, I am . . .

My body broke the surface of the water, and I was relieved. I did not control its action, my legs kicked, my arms pulled, and I gasped down air, felt my nose explode with it, my head explode, my eyes popping from their sockets with it, and looked up.

My pursuers were gone.

*

The police were called.

Someone had fired a gun on Hung Hom Pier, so the police arrived, white cars, blue shirts, polite and organised. Someone gave me an orange blanket and a carton of sugary drink. I said, "I think I scratched my leg," and it took a while for a paramedic to cut back my trousers and reply with the calm of a professional, "I do believe you have been a little bit shot, ma'am."

Then they put me on a trolley and took me to an ambulance, and a plain-clothed police inspector asked me what I knew, how much I remembered.

"Almost nothing," I replied. "I heard shooting and felt a pain in my leg and I ran, and I guess I must have slipped and fallen because next thing I know I'm in the water and the people have gone."

"Did you see how it started?"

"No, officer, it was all very confusing."

The inspector forgot about me quickly enough; the paramedics were attentive enough to get me to hospital, and the efficiency of paperwork and queueing systems saw the bullet removed by a junior surgeon under local anaesthetic. They said I could go in a few hours, and I stole a pair of crutches, a handful of painkillers and antibiotics, and let myself out as soon as the bandage was secure.

The shooting made the evening news.

I saw a picture of my own face, captured on CCTV, as I ran away and plummeted into the water. It looked like an alien, someone fearful and unknown, and, as no body had been found and no one matching my description could be remembered, a manhunt was underway for a possible victim in the sea. There was no footage of the hold-up itself, but the suspects' faces were caught, grainy and looking the wrong way, as they fled the chaotic scene. My bag was in their hands; my work stolen.

That night, sitting in a warm painkiller glow in a hotel room overlooking the bay, I compiled a file for Luca Evard.

I gave him correspondence between myself and the buyers, detailed physical descriptions of my assailants, details of the jewels that had been stolen and the agreements surrounding the heist. Most of all, I gave him the number of my mobile phone, hidden at the bottom of my stolen bag, and hoped it wasn't too late.

Nine hours later, the man who'd held a gun on me was arrested. He'd tried to sell my phone to a second-hand store in Mong Kok, an act of greed – unforgivably stupid. The store-owner, when suddenly faced with fifteen heavily armed police on his porch, had given up the customer's details in a flash.

They found him in his underpants, joyfully wired on cocaine, watching tennis in a flat near Sham Mong Road. He lived with his mother, who tried to attack one of the arresting officers with a mop when they took her son away, before being informed of the nature of his crimes and declaring, "His father always set a bad example!" and asking if the police could help have him cut out of her will.

Within three hours, the rest of his confederates were in custody, but none were willing to give up their employer. I trawled my records, seeing if there was anything I could find which might help incriminate him, and pulled a blank.

Five hours later, Luca Evard arrived in Hong Kong, looking for the woman who'd vanished over the side of the pier.

I found him on Tsim Sha Tsui as the sun went down, sitting on a bench, watching the sea. Behind, the lights of the city were beginning to burn: Philips and Hyundai picked out in blue and red, white Hitachi and green hotels, a competition in neon and LED. I sat down on the opposite end of the bench, and started reading.

The book was called *The Lemon and the Wave* and was a mostly bizarre account of a brutal murder in northern Italy, written in a hectic, breathy style by its author, R. H. It wasn't my thing, but it had been a book by Luca Evard's bed in Brazil, and now I sat next to him on the bench as the daylight faded and the white light of the promenade took over, and leant back so he might see the cover.

He looked, and looked away, then looked again, and now looked at me, and hesitated. His head tilted down, and he thought perhaps of speaking, of asking me my name, of approaching the beautiful woman who sat by him on the bench. But that second passed, and he seemed as though he might stand so I lowered the book and said, in English, "Do you have the time?"

He did.

I closed the book, slipped it into my bag, stood up, leaning on just one crutch to support the weight of my wounded leg. He, having begun the process of standing, stood too, and looked at me again, and wanted to speak, and turned, and began to walk away. I limped after him, heading away from the pier, towards the hotels, and when his speed threatened to take him away from me I said, "Excuse me, are you American?"

He stopped, turned, smiled – no he wasn't.

"Sorry, I realised when I spoke – speaking in English, I mean, you don't look like you speak Cantonese, but you might, sorry, that's presumptuous, but I shouldn't assume, but it's . . . anyway, I didn't mean to be rude."

"You weren't rude, ma'am."

I smiled again, a last-ditch effort, urging him come on, come on, come on! He smiled back, turned to walk away.

I cursed inwardly and swore to track him to the hotel, meet him in the bar, over supper, put the damn book between us, or maybe a cutting about the Hung Hom Pier, or something, *anything*, to pull his attention.

Then he stopped, and said, "Are you able to walk, ma'am? Do you need assistance getting to a taxi or a bus?"

I leant a little more on my solitary crutch, smiled, said, "No, thank you; I had an accident at work, but I'm fine, really, it's not as bad as it looks."

"All right," he murmured, unconvinced, and again turned to go, and again stopped himself, looked back. "Forgive me, the book you're reading ... Do you ... did you find it in Hong Kong?"

"Yes," I replied. "At a second-hand place in Ho Man Tin. Have you read it?"

"Yes – many times."

"I haven't finished it yet, but it seems like a funny choice of book, I mean, if you've read it that often."

"It's not ... it's something to do with my job."

"What's your job?"

"Police inspector."

"Oh, sorry, I had no idea! In Hong Kong?"

"No. Interpol."

"Seriously? I didn't realise Interpol had inspectors. I mean, sorry, that's rude. I'm being very rude aren't I? I just ... can we try again?"

I am my smile.

I am beauty.

Luca Evard, a man who lived his life by ironed shirts and folded underpants, toothpaste squeezed from the bottom of the tube, looked at me, and looked at the sea, and perhaps in that moment thought of the thief he'd pursued halfway round the world, who'd been at Hung Hom Pier the night gunshots were fired, and wondered if she'd drowned that night, or if she lived still and was thinking of him.

And he looked at me.

And he said, "May I help you get to a cab?"

"No need – my hotel's nearby."

"Which one?"

"The Southern."

"I'm staying there too."

"Really? What a coincidence. In that case, you'd be welcome to help me get to the bar."

Chapter 40

Words to characterise my behaviour:

- Obsessive
- Needy
- Unprofessional
- Stalker-esque
- Manipulative
- Cruel

Words to characterise Luca Evard:

- Conventional
- Tidy
- Driven
- Unrewarded
- Socially inept
- Lonely
- Obsessive

He was not a man who had a drink with a strange woman in a strange city, however much she may have dressed herself for his delight. He was not a man to open up about himself, his life, his fears. That was not who he was.

Have a drink, I said. We're both strangers in a strange land, we both read the same books. I'm an injured woman; have a drink with me.

Just one, he said at last. I don't really drink in hotel bars.

On the third glass of wine I said, Are you single?

Yes, he replied, tongue loosened by good Australian wine. For the last three months.

I'm sorry, I said, feeling a flush of something that might have been . . . surprise? I hadn't considered the possibility of anything in his life except his work – except me.

We drifted apart, he said. My work, her work – you know how it is. You?

Single, I replied. It's how I like it. Tell me about this book – *The Lemon and the Wave.* Why have you read it so many times?

He smiled at nothing much, ate fried squid from a bowl, studied the room where we sat, taking in people, décor, sound, light. Every table was glass, blue lights ran beneath to cast strange shadows through the plates, lights brushing up the line of his chin and neck.

"I think it's written by a killer," he explained. "There was a spate of murders in Austria in 1989, four women and a man all killed the same way. One man came under suspicion. The police wanted to arrest him, but there wasn't enough physical evidence, and they had to let him go. He left the country three weeks later, and then in 1993 this book came out, and though the names are different, the chronology, the manner of the murder, down to the finest detail, down to where the victims were left, the knots used in the nooses that strangled them, the size and make of the blade, everything, the same. The writing takes the point of view of a policeman, but he never catches the killer, comes to admire him by the end, *becomes* a killer himself, the policeman is transformed by what he sees into a murderer. I was part of the liaison, tried to trace the writer, this R. H. – but he'd moved on, somewhere in North America. We alerted the FBI, but again, what do we have? Nothing. A work of fiction. A killer laughing at the men who cannot catch him, perhaps. A flight of fancy from a twisted mind. You can't arrest a man for fiction, can you?"

"If you can't do anything, why do you read it so much?"

Surprise; the question almost too ridiculous to be asked. "As a warning," he replied. "To remember. To remember the ones who died, whose killer we never brought to justice."

Justice: the quality of being just, righteous. The moral principle of determining just conduct.

The administering of deserved punishment or reward.

I thought through my understanding of justice, and found no place for me in it. But then again, to *do* justice: to act or treat fairly. To acquit in accordance with one's abilities or potential. It could not be denied that I was unrighteous in my life, but did I *do* justice?

Then Luca said, "I came here to find a thief."

My eyes turned back to him from another place. He was the world, the universe, so big in my attention that, for a moment, I wondered if he wasn't some fractured figment of my own imagination, a voice I had conjured for myself. But his eyes were elsewhere, his words came from some place in his soul that spoke for its own sake, not for mine.

"My superiors think she drowned. She stole from a museum. Forty years ago, the items would have been sold by the Chinese government to raise capital for tractors and shovels, but now China is reacquiring a taste for a glorious and opulent history. This is what gives the item value, more than its chemical composition."

Emerald: a compound of beryllium aluminium cyclosilicate and trace amounts of chromium, which gives it its green colour.

"I think she came to Hong Kong to sell it. There's a man, Bogyoke Dennis. He started out as a smuggler in Cambodia; now he kills his enemies with snake venom. He runs the prostitution and people-smuggling racket in the South China Sea. She should never have ... but she must have got greedy, or arrogant, or just ... stupid."

Stupid: dull. Lacking quickness.

Stupid, the quality of ...

... of being bloody stupid.

Just

stupid.

"You're ... sad, that she's dead?"

"If she's dead."

"But you're sad."

He shrugged. "I'm always sad at a loss of human life."

"Even a thief?"

"Still human."

"Is that all?"

His eyes refocused onto mine, quick now, sharp, a drawing in of his features. "What do you mean?"

"You sound like you've been looking for her for a while."

"For years. I know every detail of every crime she's committed. I know how she likes to dress, how she does her hair, what kind of car she likes to drive, what food she eats. In Munich she scammed €75,000 from a lawyer whose speciality was getting drug traffickers off by accusing the police of corruption, and I was . . . a little bit pleased, God forgive me, but I thought that the crime had humour in it. She skimmed him while he was attending a fundraiser at the opera, scanned his credit cards, cloned his phone, and after she listened to two hours and a quarter of Verdi, I saw her on the security cameras, and again, photographed by one of the journalists there to cover the fundraiser, and she looked . . . You know, I find it hard to picture her face now, the details are . . . I know every part of her, but it's so hard to find . . . She looked astonished. Held by music. I can't . . . I remember thinking that's how she seemed. I remember thinking those words. Now she's probably dead; all that for nothing."

Silence.

Then,

sorry, he said.

Sorry.

Didn't mean to talk about . . .

sorry.

Silence.

I reached across the table, my hand on his, and he did not pull away.

I felt the blood in the veins on the top of his hand.

I felt the tendons under his skin.

Was this pulse in my fingertips his heart, or mine?

He looked down, like a man ashamed, and did not pull away.

"I have a terror," he said at last. "I . . . fear."

I waited. All he needed was silence.

"I fear sometimes that ... she isn't real. That she does not exist. It is irrational, of course; we have evidence, DNA, prints, her face, her MO, we have everything we need to convict her. But everywhere we go, every crime she commits, people cannot remember her. Is she a trick, an illusion? A fabrication, a puppet show performed for our delight, a cover for a conspiracy, an experiment, a witch? Why can't people remember? I can describe her every feature to you and yet ... the description is just words, rehearsed for hours on end in briefings – hair, height, weight, colouring – just ... words. I look at you and you could be her, you fit the words, but I studied her picture, I know her face, you are not her, I would recognise her, I would know her instantly, I would *know*!"

Voice rising; pain, fear, confusion.

I pressed my hand tighter against his, my reality, his skin, my warmth, his blood.

"I received a file," he went on. "I thought perhaps it was from her. How did she know about me? Perhaps she had it ready to send, in case the exchange went wrong. Perhaps she is using me from beyond the grave, vengeance against the men who killed her."

"There'd be some justice in that, I think."

The slightest of smiles. "Yes," he conceded. "Perhaps a little."

Justice. In Chinese the symbol is 义, *yí*, a pictogram I always thought looked rather joyous, full of hope. If I were to sign my name with a symbol, I think I would want it to be 义.

"Just because no one remembers seeing her doesn't mean she died," I said, and as he smiled at nothing, I added, "It seems like an extraordinary series of events."

He looked at me again, or perhaps for the first time, and I wondered if now he was listing words that matched my features. My height, weight, skin, eyes, the slightly bulbous end of my nose, ears a little too large, high forehead, thick brows, deep black hair pulled back into a loose knot, a suggestion of freckles under my eyes. All these things could be described, annotated, he could stand in front of my photo every day and recite these qualities, and now he looked at me and perhaps, for the first time, attempted to annotate my face, categorise it and find a match. Did he see who I was?

Perhaps he did.

But he believed too much in his own rationality, and so at the very moment that his eyes widened and his lips parted in realisation, he turned his head to one side, pulled his gaze away, and informed himself perhaps that no, no – he knew the face of the thief, it was impossible to meet her now and *not* recognise her, not him, not after all this time.

And so the moment passed, leaving only him, me, now.

I said, "Do you want another drink?"

He shouldn't.

He was . . . it wasn't . . . he wasn't that kinda guy.

"I was alone last night, I'll be alone tomorrow," I replied. "How about you?"

His hand, still beneath mine.

"Okay," he said. Then, "Okay."

Chapter 41

Forget to count.

Forget to remember.

I have forgotten my age; every document with my face is a lie.

I have forgotten my friends, as they forgot me.

I have forgotten the turn of the years, for what are they to me?

The years will not remember me.

My face fades from the minds of men.

Only my deeds remain.

Chapter 42

On his seventh day in Tokyo, I followed Rafe Pereyra-Conroy to a sumo match.

Traditional arts in Japan: sumo, karate, kendo, judo, kyudo, kabuki, origami, flower arrangement.

Hierarchy. A sumo stable is organised with military discipline. At the bottom are the *jonokushi*, then *makushika* and *juryo*. Only forty-two elite *makuuchi* exist at any time, their matches broadcast on television, life expectancy at least ten years lower than the national average.

Nomi No Sukuni, Shinto god of sumo. Once upon a time, the wrestlers performed their rites on temple grounds, to ensure good harvest, and the referees still made the *dohyo* sacred with sprinkled salt.

Did Rafe care, as he took a seat in a private area of cushions and clean tatami mats right by the ring? Probably not. I watched him through a small pair of binoculars from a wooden bench high in the auditorium. He was a foreign dignitary being taken to sumo to entertain and enthral, to have an anecdote to tell his friends when he returned home. I saw a sumo match, yes, yes I did; understand it? No, of course not, but I was there, I've experienced Japan now, yes, oh yes I have.

In the reception afterwards, I listened to the chatter as I circled the room.

I was getting better at recognising those who had Perfection.

She: her perfect teeth, her perfect hair, her perfect smile, her perfect clothes, fashionably chosen, gracefully worn.

He: silk and cotton, the white of his shirt sharp as thorns, the perfect drink in his hand, the perfect woman on his arm.

Do you have Perfection?

("Oh my," said the woman with the surgery-enhanced waist. "It's changed my life.")

("It's not just about looking after myself," added the man

whose champagne I refilled. "It's about meeting people like me. The best of the best.")

A polite smattering of applause, a man dressed in full Shinto robes, oranges and yellows, a high black lacquered hat, stood on the dais and in formal, steady Japanese thanked everyone for attending.

"In the way of the gods," his translator limped through the words, "we seek to purify ourselves from unclean rituals and sins. We wash away sinful thought, unclean practice, guilty deeds, and emerge radiant at last. Every child who is born in Japan, regardless of their creed, is welcomed into the shrine and made a family child, their name given to the spirits for blessing and protection. It is in this spirit – welcoming, and purification – that I am proud to call Mr Pereyra-Conroy a friend, and say that the work he does in Japan helps men and women in their souls."

First Dubai, now Tokyo. Rafe was a busy bee.

"Perfection," he continued, after the pause, "makes people better."

Turning to walk away, and there she was, Filipa Pereyra-Conroy, dressed in black, a glass in one hand, nails trimmed short, hair tied high. She stood in my path and said, "Hello. I saw you alone. Do you know anyone here?"

Not accusatory, not angry; a woman who has seen a stranger and wonders if she needs company.

Just like Dubai.

"Hello," I replied, offering my hand. "My name is Hope."

"Filipa."

"I know; I've studied your work, Dr Pereyra."

A flicker of an eyebrow, a nervous tug at the end of her sleeve.

"Have you? I didn't think . . . What aspect of it?"

"I read your paper on cognitive reconstruction and reinforcement. Very interesting, even to an outsider."

"Are you an outsider?"

"I read, for company."

A smile, sudden, strong, that flashed away as quickly as it had come, locked down beneath manner and etiquette. "So do I."

"I understand you're working on treatments?"

Too fast, too much prodding for information, suspicion, a slight angling of her body. It's fine: if this should occur, I will walk away, do a lap of the room, return to her side, try again, build a little more trust. This is an opportunity too good to miss.

The index finger of her left hand tapped a few times against the top of her glass, and I doubted she noticed. "Do you have Perfection?" she asked at last.

"Yes."

"Are you . . ."

"With the 106 Club? Yes."

"Then you'll know about treatments already."

"Not yet; I haven't had an appointment. I've been very busy recently – family."

"Family is important."

A mantra, recited, and she does not look at her brother as she speaks, does not express her words with her body, but stands stiff, upright, watching. I move on quickly, and she is happy to be moved.

"Can I ask: where did the idea for Perfection come from?"

Her eyes, lifting a little, head up, chin out. "What can you mean?"

"I mean . . . what inspired you?"

Silence a while. Then, "My brother. He is . . . as a child, I thought he was . . . our father very much loved him, you see, and he always thought the world could benefit from something of his . . . quality."

Sadness. She smiles, she is still and straight, but these were not the flowing words of the woman I'd met in Dubai; this was hurt, and justification, and hollow gaps where truth should be. To my surprise I found myself wanting to touch her, and tightened my grip on my glass.

"All thought is feedback," I said at last, and now her eyes were fixed on me, through me, I had her full attention, so intense I wondered if she would ever forget me, if she could ever forget this moment. "Faced with mounting stress, the body enters an alarmed state. Capillaries dilate, heart beats faster, breathing increases, skin flushes, muscles tense. With each social rejection, pathways are reinforced in the brain which links social rejection with physiological anxiety. Thus reinforced, you are more likely to experience a physical reaction to even slight social discomfort, thus making you more uncomfortable, thus reinforcing the physical and so on and so on. All thought is feedback: sometimes that feedback can be too loud. That's what I think, anyway."

Silence a while.

Her body seemed to uncoil, shoulders releasing from their stiff posture, knees softening, face softening, eyes softening. For the first time she seemed to see the room, see the party, a swaying, laughing, tinkling mass of perfect people with perfect smiles.

"You aren't in the 106," she said simply.

"Why do you say that?" I asked.

"Because you're not perfect."

"What does 'perfect' mean?"

She smiled, arms folded, head to one side. "If you were in the 106, you wouldn't ask. Perfection is you, and you are perfection; that is the truth of it."

"And you don't have Perfection either," I replied. "I can see it too."

Her eyes flickered round the room, caught her brother for a moment, half bowing, shaking hands, all smiles, charm, beauty. Her gaze returned to me, and for a moment, I thought she might cry.

"Have you eaten?" she asked. "I'm starving."

We ate noodles. She ordered spicy Singapore style, I had udon in soup, and she tried a spoonful of the broth, slurping from the shallow wooden spoon.

"The party, won't your brother be . . . "

"He won't care."

"You sure?"

"It's one of the things Rafe shares with my father – a single-minded commitment to an ideology. The rest is noise."

"What ideology is that?"

"Victory."

"Is that an ideology?"

"I think so. Rafe hides it better than Dad did. Dad was always proving something, that he was better, smarter than everyone else; but Rafe has to prove that he's better than Dad."

My eyebrows must have risen, because hers did in reply, mirroring, and she asked, a little too high, "What's the matter?"

"This seems like something you wouldn't tell a stranger."

"I'm sorry, I've made you . . . I'm not very good at meeting new people, you see."

"You seem to be very good."

"No," she replied, a little sadly. "I'm not. Rafe drags me along to all his parties, his big launch events, points at me and says, 'There's the head of development, my sister' and everyone smiles at me and shakes my hand and then he keeps on talking, in case I speak."

"You spoke to me."

"You were alone. You were imperfect."

"Is that all it took?"

"You . . . know something of my field. I can talk to people at work but they don't really get it, not really, but you were alone and imperfect, and you thought about thought, about what thinking means, about minds and people and . . . Are you a journalist?" The words came fast and sudden, an almost physical jerking back of her body at the idea.

"No. I'm not. I'm writing a paper on Perfection."

Her eyebrows flickered upwards, sharp, an attention fully honed. "What body?"

"Oxford, St John's."

"You know Professor Vikkendar?"

"No. I'm in anthropology."

A little nod, her interest diverted almost instantly; humanities bore her, but I pushed on. "I'm interested in the definition of 'perfect' over time, and the construction of the self. Perfection is becoming a movement, a global redefinition—"

"No it's not. That's not the point."

I bit my bottom lip, chose my words slowly. "Maybe that's not the point for you, Dr Pereyra," I mused, "but that's what it is becoming."

"The point is thought. Patterns of behaviour, patterns of thinking, breaking boundaries, creating new pathways – I'm sorry, I thought you understood this, when you said—"

"Perhaps we should be clear – there is the science, and there is the product. I'm talking about the product."

"Oh." Her interest almost gone now, the noodles growing cold in front of her. "I don't really deal with that."

Silence, suddenly awkward, a hard fall from the place we'd begun. I looked round, my gaze briefly meeting the eyes of one of the two security men who shadowed Filipa to the restaurant. One stood by the door, one was in a booth a few rows behind, keeping a polite distance.

"What's with the . . . ?"

She dismissed them with a flick of her chopsticks, not looking up from her plate. "My brother's worried about security."

"Are you in danger?"

"Rafe's worth a lot of money; I think he's scared someone might try to kidnap me. It's ridiculous, really, but then . . . " I waited, and in time it came. "Our father was killed."

"I'm sorry to hear that."

She dismissed it with another mouthful of noodle. "It was a long time ago. Officially, no one was ever caught."

"Unofficially?"

A half shrug. This isn't something that interests her. Then sudden, fast:

"Isn't it worrying, I mean, not worrying, not an emotional response, but isn't it interesting that in a room of perfect people the two imperfect people move together at once, and two societies form – as an anthropologist this must interest you – the beautiful and the ugly, and the beautiful stand and talk and are wonderful together, and the ugly have noodles. Is this something you've observed? In your studies?"

"I . . . yes. Perfection encourages perfect people to congregate. So does the 106 Club."

"And doesn't that make you frightened?" she asked, watching my face for something only she knew to look for.

"No, not really."

"It should do. It's not my research, not at all, but the product – the thing Rafe did with it, it's brilliant of course, pure brilliance, he's like that. Growing up, I was the oldest, but Rafe was . . . You see, Dad needed to prove that he was smarter, better than the world. Rafe just needs to prove that he's better than Dad. So Perfection is an aspiration carved from socio-economic values, not ethical ones. Perfection is wealth, fashion, interest and power. It is glowing skin, pleasant laugh, easy conversation. It is . . . a thing that the world aspires to, and it is of course very dull, and hugely elitist. I'm not very interesting, you see. I'm my brother's boffin sister, in fact. 'Don't worry about her – she's into the science stuff,' he says, and everyone laughs, because it's funny. You and I are having noodles together, and this is a disaster by Perfection's standards, cheap food full of nasty chemicals – lose a thousand points – and we are the minority, and we will be looked down upon. Ugly, fat, lazy, not capable of looking after ourselves, bad habits, junk food, junk."

Frigid. A word spoken by Reina, the day before she died. *The screaming is very loud now.*

Filipa was still talking, high speed, a rata-tat-tat of words, tumbling fast. "It's easier to be perfect if you're from a certain socio-economic background. Perfection takes time, effort, and if you're poor, if you're struggling then . . . and Perfection can help with that too, find a way to make the pennies work, learn to let go of things you don't need, aesthetic lifestyle, simple lifestyle. It's made for everyone of course, but easier, so much easier, if you're already wealthy and as an anthropologist, surely you can see – Perfection as a product creates a digital aristocracy, and the imperfect of this world are little better than the serfs."

Silence a while. The security man in the booth behind Filipa ordered another glass of mineral water; the guard by the door watched the street.

Finally she said, "A woman died in Dubai. I didn't know her name. She died just before we went there for a launch – a disaster as it turned out, a humiliation, a thief got in but . . . anyway. A woman killed herself. She had severe depression but no one was treating her, I mean, no one helped, even acknowledged it, because it's not an illness, is it, it's just something you deal with, right? Anyway. She had Perfection. It didn't save her."

Silence.

"If you aren't perfect, then you are flawed," she continued, staring at nothing much, a piece of ginger pinched between the end of her chopsticks, going nowhere. "Rafe is a genius, but none of this was the point of my research."

"What was the point?" I asked, soft, in case we broke the spell.

"To make people better. Of course. To make the world a better place."

She rolled the ginger between her chopsticks, put it back down.

"I think my brother has taken something beautiful and made it obscene," she said at last. "That's why I left the party. You've studied Perfection: what do you think?"

I opened my mouth to answer, found all the easy words were now hard, said nothing.

"'*Qui tacet consentire videtur*'," she mused, with a half-empty smile.

"'He who is silent is seen to consent.'"

"You studied Latin?"

"Read it in a book somewhere."

"They made me study it at school. Latin, economics, business studies, maths, further maths, piano, singing, speech and drama, computer sciences, French, Russian, Japanese, debating, journalism . . . "

"Your school wasn't much like mine."

"We were my father's legacy. Or rather my brother was. My brother was always going to be better at that sort of thing."

"I don't know Latin – just the famous bits."

"Is that famous?"

"Thomas More, just before King Henry VIII decided to cut his head off. 'He who is silent is seen to consent' – he refused to take an oath, but neither did he speak against it. He hoped by his silence to escape the axe. Sorta noble, sorta an arsehole."

She laid the sliver of ginger carefully back down, tucked her chopsticks to one side, folded her hands, raised her head, looked me in the eye. "If I were to write the parameters for Perfection," she said, firm and steady, "I would forgive all cowards."

"If you believe so strongly that your brother has done something . . . with your work, then why do you continue working on it?" I asked.

"I work on treatments, not the software."

"What do the treatments do?"

"They make people happy."

"How?"

"They . . . help people feel happy about themselves."

"That sounds like a drug."

"It's not. It's . . . this isn't how I wanted it to work, it's not . . . not right yet, but my brother funds it. Rafe got the money and no one else would let me do the things I do, so I needed him, we had to make a bargain – he's always making bargains you see, and I have always been a coward. You believe that, don't you?"

"I don't know."

"I have. Always. It's why I chose the treatments. He's done something with it that is . . . But one day with the technology, giants on the shoulders of giants, we'll build something . . . good. Happiness for everyone. One day we'll get it right."

Happy: to be pleased, delighted or glad.

Favoured by fortune.

The experience of pleasure, or joy.

Happiness: a lie, constructed to ensure that we never find it.

"Are you happy?" I asked, and she didn't answer.

I pushed a couple of notes under our bowls, squeezed my hand tight said, "Come on. Let's go walking."

She didn't speak, but neither did she resist as I led her away.

Chapter 43

A night-time walk through Tokyo. The electric district, almost brighter than the day, manga manga everywhere; girls with huge spoon eyes waving their neon arms above the doors, tiny pale-faced creatures in school uniform on the covers of the comics in the window; men with swords and spiky hair fighting great monsters, families of blue-eyed cats, descendants of Hiroshige's red-ribboned cat as it plays with a string, picked out in bright, wet inks.

Bars with girls dressed in French waitress uniforms, cartoonish, black puffed sleeves and little white aprons. Teahouses where the matrons wore soft silk robes and bowed to the visiting guests – not a geisha house, not like the houses of Kyoto, the geisha were something else entirely, but a pleasant, tatami-matted alternative where the tea was hot and there was a corner for the visitors to charge their mobile phones.

Fish tanks in the windows of the restaurants, full of live, prowling monsters. A fugu chef demonstrating the range of knives he uses in the dissection of his poisonous dish – not the dissection process itself, which requires three years of training – but the delicate tools for pulling out liver, ovaries, slicing away strips of flesh, cleaning, grating, peeling, scrubbing.

"Poison: tetrodotoxin," and it takes a moment for me to realise that it is Filipa who is speaking, not me. "Contained mostly in the liver, ovaries and the eyes. Acts in a similar manner to sarin. No known antidote. Paralyses muscles, leaving patient conscious but asphyxiating. A thousand times more potent than cyanide. Cure—"

"Respiratory and circulatory support – artificially maintaining life – until the poison is metabolised by the body and excreted away," I concluded, and she beamed, and wrapped her arm into mine and said:

"Did you learn that in anthropology?"

"There's many cultures where people eat poisonous mushrooms, frogs, fish and herbs to achieve a heightened state. A thousand years ago, LSD would be sanctified."

She grinned, a genuine flicker of delight, and as we walked together through the hot night-time streets, her security never far behind, she said:

"'Dwell on the beauty of life. Watch the stars and see yourself running in them.'"

"'Everything we hear is an opinion, not a fact. Everything we see is a perspective, not a truth.'"

She laughed – a surprisingly childish sound, and immediately pushed her hands over her mouth to silence the unlooked-for sound. Removing them slowly, she said at last, "I was made to read the *Meditations* at school, and hated them."

"But you quote from them now?"

"Something stuck from the exam. You?"

"I read it a few years ago."

"Anthropology?"

"Long flight, I think."

"Marcus Aurelius," she mused, "born April AD 121, died . . . "

"AD 180, Vienna – Vindabona, yes?"

"Succeeded by Commodus . . . "

" . . . a disaster emperor . . . "

"Assassinated 192, maybe in the bath but the sources are dubious, the statues cast down; the senate declared him posthumously an enemy of the state . . . "

"A gladiator, loved to fight."

"The beginning of the end, Gibbon said. The bit of that book where the history got interesting," she replied, and stopped, so suddenly that I nearly stumbled over her grip on my arm, an anchor holding my body in place even as my feet tried to walk on by. "It isn't . . . *perfect* . . . to have knowledge," she stammered, the joy stripped away. "Perfect people aren't knowledgeable, they aren't . . . wise. That's what my brother says. Knowledge is for show-offs and people who don't get out of the house enough, we've got Google, Wikipedia. Knowledge is a place where sexy should be. *Clever* is sexy, the sociopath genius, the smartest man in the room, but that's clever that doesn't need to work, that's not investing in knowledge, spending time at work, that's just . . . being brilliant. Being brilliant is sexy, not working hard. Sexy sells. That's what Rafe always says: sexy sells."

The two of us, frozen in the middle of the street, arm in arm. Men stared as they walked by, heads turning though their bodies kept on moving, necks swivelling to gawp, wondering at our story. She was crying, silently, holding my arm, crying. I let her cry a while, held her close, felt her snot and tears on my shoulder, wanted to cry myself, why is that, when I hear a child cry on the train it makes me sad, see a stranger weep and feel tears come to my eyes, a weakness, perhaps, a place where emotion hasn't become accustomed to the extremities of feeling.

"Filipa," I breathed, as she pulled away, rubbing at her face with her sleeve. "What is Perfection?"

"It's the end of the world," she replied. "It's the end of everything."

I opened my mouth to say something, to ask, anything, offer, anything, but one of her security men stepped close, a tissue held in one hand, a mobile phone in the other, murmured, "Ms Pereyra, are you okay?"

His accent was American, his eyes didn't meet mine. She ignored the tissue, kept pulling at her face with her sleeve, and he said again, "You okay, ma'am?"

"Yes," she replied. "I'm fine."

"They're missing you at the party."

My eyebrows wanted to rise in scorn, but I was professional, I was a thief, and this man was an enemy entering my domain.

She nodded, sniffed, smiled at the man, sniffed again, then smiled at me. "Sorry," she mumbled. And again, "Sorry. You are . . . if it were up to me, I would . . . but my brother is very . . . I hope your paper goes well."

"Thank you."

A pause, nodding at nothing much, security waiting, phone on, connected to someone unseen. Filipa nodded again, half turned, then turned back, and pulled a bracelet from her wrist. It was silver, a thin band turned into a seamless Möbius strip. She held my right hand in her left, pushed the bracelet over my fingers, nodded with satisfaction at the shape of it around my wrist, said, "Thank you for a lovely evening."

I opened my mouth to say no, it wasn't . . . that wasn't . . . but thought again, wondered what the words were that would be best for now, and said simply, "Thank you."

She looked at me, and I looked at her, and she smiled, and let the security man lead her away.

Chapter 44

What is perfection, what does "perfect" even mean?

Perfect: as good as can possibly be.

Free from fault or defect.

Searches on the internet, trawls through books, history.

Look for the words "perfect woman" and you find bodies. Diagrams, explaining that the perfect face belongs to an actress with smoky eyes; the perfect hair comes from a princess; the perfect waist is barely narrow enough to support the generous breasts that balance on it; legs disproportionately long, smile that says "take me". Photoshopped features combining the faces of movie stars and models, pop idols and celebrities. Who is the perfect woman? According to the internet, she is a blonde white girl with bulimia; no other characteristics are specified.

And the perfect man? He has a wide range of interests, is polite and courteous at all times, handsome and sexually considerate, intelligent, preferably funny, has a high income and his own home, mortgage free.

A Möbius strip. Take a strip of paper, give it a half twist once, tape it together, creating a surface that is non-orientable, the top is always the bottom, the bottom is always the top. Discovered in 1858, but mathematically not fully defined in equation form until 2007, hard to model a thing that goes on for ever, a closed loop without end.

The silver, warmed by Filipa, now warm around my wrist. I run my fingers round it for ever.

What was Perfection?

Maybe Filipa was right. Maybe it was the end of the world.

I went looking for the 106 Club.

Surveillance is easy, when the world forgets you.

Watching the Pereyra-Conroy building from a parked hire car, I began to chart and catalogue the lives of the 106 Club members who lived inside, and no one stopped me.

A woman getting into a chauffeur-driven car to attend a party may notice the girl on the other side of the street and be surprised, but if she then forgets, surprise is as far as her feelings go.

A security guard, helping Rafe into his limousine, notices me as he closes the door, and considers me suspicious, but not yet a threat, not on the first observation. When he returns in the evening, he experiences the same thought process again, and again it is the first time he has seen me, and so again he does not raise an alarm.

I picked pockets, stole bags, broke into apartments. I cloned mobile phones, accessed email accounts, Facebook pages, Twitter feeds.

I shadowed men to work, women to parties, I stole their

names, the names of their cleaners, their tailors, their drivers, their friends.

In the morning I ran, in the evening I visited temples, bars, clubs, lectures, plays, and in the intervening hours, I studied the 106 Club.

On the seventh day of observation, armed with foreknowledge gleaned from purloined mobile phones, I followed a party of four 106 men from the apartment to an invitation-only party in Azabu.

It advertised itself as "Sugarbabes and Sugarboys", and access was determined by one of two things – by a declaration of an annual income of over $110,000 with financial documents to back up the statement, or by writing a personal application stating why you, the invitee, were so keen to meet your sugardaddy.

Hi! I wrote. *My name's Rachel Donovan, I'm 24 years old, and I love people. I love meeting people, I love caring for people, I love listening to their stories and jokes, I love learning about the jobs they have and the things they love. If I could spend my life just meeting people and seeing the world, that would be my heaven.*

With this introduction, I attached a picture of myself in a revealing red dress, smiling, all teeth, for the camera.

I want to meet wealthy men, I explained, *because they've just seen so much more than I have.*

I want to meet wealthy men and women, I mused, because theft is an art, and you are my canvas.

I work out three times a week, and am a champion 10k runner. I think my best quality is my smile; it just seems to make people happy.

The invitation came back within hours. Digital records remember me, and my name was left on the clipboard by the door.

Sounds at a party. The crowd is vastly international; English is the default language. The waitresses are dressed as geisha girls, but no geisha would wear such shiny wigs or permit a thread of polyester in their glimmering robes.

"I tried dating, but my money became a problem; women didn't know how to be around me once they found out how rich I was."

"The key to my success? I knew I'd succeed. That's all I needed."

"I have to travel by helicopter now, because it's not safe for someone like me to be in the streets."

"People are complicated; money is simple."

"This isn't prostitution. Prostitution is illegal. This is a mutual agreement between potential partners with realistic expectations."

"People – people and governments – try to punish people like us for being rich. Envy, that's all it is. Why should I give up money that I earned, so someone else can live off the state? If they can't pick themselves up, like I did, then I don't see why I should give a damn."

I move through the room, skimming a credit card here, a phone there. This is the research stage. I don't need to say very much; a hello, a goodbye, and then if I need to return to the target, hello again, goodbye again. But I want to talk, I need to talk, words silent on my tongue, so I say: "Oh my God, that's so interesting, you're so right," because that's what Rachel Donovan would say, and then I realise I hate the words, so I smile a different smile and say, "Actually, no, fuck you, fuck you and your arrogance, fuck you and your selfishness, fuck you for thinking that you deserve what you have, for thinking that because you know which little green numbers would get greener, because you knew how to play with abstract quantities and mathematical variants, you somehow deserve to rule the fucking world."

Mouths drop, people move to summon the staff, to complain, there's a woman here, there's a woman in a red dress and we thought you vetted these people before they came, we thought you were selling us demure little children who were only interested in us for our money and knew how to pretend, what the fuck is this?

But I turn away, and push through the crowd, and feel like the queen of the universe, and by the time the man has found a manager to complain to, he's forgotten what it was he was going to complain about.

Only briefly, only for a moment, do I remember that I am a thief, and that I lost the moral high ground a long time ago.

"Fuck you," I repeat to myself. "Fuck that."

Discipline in all things.

I am a machine.

I am my smile.

I am delight.

Okashi, delight, joy, enchantment. An old-fashioned word, much beloved of Sei Shōnagon, who found her delight in the little beauties of this life. A sprig of cherry blossom, delicately borne by a handsome boy. The icy cold of snow falling from a clear sky. I find all this wonderful, she wrote, and marvel that others do not.

I am *okashi*.

I stand on a balcony overlooking the street, a glass door separating me from the rest of the party. A few people have stepped outside too, away from the light nothing-music and the swirl of people in Dior, Hugo Boss, Chanel, Armani. I observe them haggle over the price, champagne flutes in hand, smiles never faltering. I count patent-leather shoes and gold wristwatches, tailored shirts and cashmere socks, and feel for a moment almost ashamed.

"I'm looking for someone who'll be there," says a man who introduces himself to me as Geoff – just Geoff. American accent, greying hair. "My work takes me places, but sometimes, when I come home, I just want to have a few days with someone who I can hang out with. We'll go to the cinema, maybe the theatre, we'll have supper together, and yes, I'd like the relationship to be sexual, but I don't demand monogamy, she can lead her own life, do her own thing, I'll put the money into her account in advance."

"It's a good deal," whispered a woman in my ear after Geoff

turned away, confused by my polite rejection. "It's better than what most men want."

A recollection of a similar system, an ancient idea. *Danna*. Patron to geisha in medieval Japan. Sometimes the relationship was sexual; sometimes artistic; sometimes an undefined, unspoken agreement between geisha and patron that it was considered uncouth to ever express. How little the world had changed.

"Do you have Perfection?" a woman asks another, their bodies turned as though they are contemplating the view, their eyes flickering constantly back to the room. I only half tune into their conversation, my eyes drifting shut, the wind cold against my skin.

"Yes, it's just wonderful. How many . . . ?"

"Two hundred and thirty-three thousand!"

"You look sensational on it."

"I am, I am, I feel sensational, it's just changed my life. You know, this is how I got into this party?"

"Seriously?"

"I hit two hundred and thirty thousand and there it was, just like that, the invitation in my inbox, a gift from Perfection – find the perfect man for the perfect woman. And so good, I mean, look at this place, so good, the men just so . . . "

"I know."

"And have you seen him? I mean, I would just for the fuck, just for that body, but he owns like, one of the biggest tyre manufacturing companies in East Asia or something."

"God, with a body like that . . . "

"Jesus!"

"Do you think he has Perfection too?"

I squeeze my eyes shut, let out a breath, count to ten, look for the three men I was meant to be tracking.

Okashi, *okashi*, I am *okashi*.

"I'm looking for the perfect woman," explained one, a Brazilian man with a gold watch the size of my fist – bespoke, engraved, nightmare to fence even if I could be bothered stealing it. "I need her to have at least eight hundred thousand points on Perfection, and be willing to work to reach a million."

"That's very precise."

He stared at me like I was an idiot. "A man can't be perfect until he has a wife," he explained. "Marriage is the union of two hearts, two bodies, two souls. Whoever she is, she has to be perfect too."

"And how do you measure that perfection?" I asked. "Will your app tell you?"

"Of course it will," he replied. "That's how I'll know."

I stole his watch.

Something of a spite had settled over my soul.

On my ninth day, I followed Mrs Goto.

Apartment 718, forty-three years old, divorcee of two years' standing, currently re-engaged to Mr Moti of apartment 261 – the perfect man, for the perfect woman. How I was learning to loathe those words.

Her driver took her towards the Meiji Royal Gardens, but she showed no interest in this royal spread of land, in its arching bridges and hanging trees, crafted so that every step changes the vista that you might behold; instead she buzzed at an anonymous white door to an anonymous white building, which closed with a pneumatic hiss behind her.

Anonymous reinforced doors always engage a thief's curiosity. At seven p.m. I stole the security pass from a guard going off-shift, and at two a.m. I broke in by climbing the rubbish chute from the rear car park, his swipe card in my pocket and internet-purchased lockpicks in my bag.

Private medicine. Easy to identify: public medicine doesn't have as many potted plants or espresso machines. Sofas are not padded leather, carpets are not thick and clean, departments are not laid out with little brass plates, no one is happy to see you.

I had imagined plastic surgery. ("So much happier with my body," whispered one man on 430,500 points who I shared sake with. "Even with exercise and good eating, I just didn't look like the way men look in the movies until I got Perfection.")

You didn't get to 1×10^6 points in Perfection without some sort of surgery, I had concluded. Even the most beautiful, even the most astoundingly naturally beautiful, had *something* tweaked, tucked or smoothed. Perfection seemed to be an inhuman quality.

Yet, walking through the treatment centre, past doors labelled with the names of professors and doctors, departments and facilities, I saw no sign of surgical operating theatres or recovery rooms. I moved at the speed of someone who shouldn't be remarked upon, and trusted to my condition to protect me from comment should I encounter any of the cleaning staff or night guards.

Counselling, coaching, detox therapy, physical therapy, dietary therapy – the doors rolled by, and I didn't understand what they were doing here, or why they mattered. At a door marked "spectrocraniotomy" I stopped, and with my stolen security pass, let myself inside.

A white room: white floors, white walls. A large red couch in the middle, stainless-steel column supporting adjustable parts. Lights, wires, inactive machines, acronyms and characters in katakana and hirogana. A skullcap attached to a central hub of machines. A pair of goggles plugged into network cabling. A server hidden behind one cupboard wall, top of the line, ninety thousand US dollars just for the basic hardware. A flick of a switch, and the goggles produced light, images flashing across the lenses too fast to follow.

A cardboard box of brochures told me more than my thin grasp of neuroscience. In English and Japanese it read:

> *Exclusive to the 106, the treatments provided by our clinic will help you find the perfect you within. Confidence, self-esteem, optimism, ambition, and dedication – if you've come this far, they all lie within you, and with our revolutionary new service we can help you find the strength to be the person you want to be.*

Pictures.

Perfect women in the chair, skullcap on their heads. Earbuds pushed in, connected to a sound I couldn't hear. Nose clips, a sensor stuck to the tongue, or perhaps not a sensor, perhaps something else, a thing creating sensations, *senses*. Clips on the fingers, a needle in the arm, drugs and electricity.

Perfect men in perfect white shirts, the sun at their backs, beaming proudly.

Perfect families playing with their perfect children on perfect beaches by sapphire seas.

Testimonials from clients.

I used to have to pretend that I was someone I wasn't, and whenever life went my way, I would think that I hadn't earned it. The treatments helped me see the world in a new way. I am worth so much more than I ever thought.

And below, a picture of a woman in a silk suit, arms folded, shoulders back, head high.

What is my life worth? asked the caption, as the city spread out beneath her through great panes of glass. *My life is perfect now, and I make the world better by simply being.*

The door to the room opened; a cleaner all in blue.

Surprise on her face, then immediately suspicion. If the world remembered me, this would be a low point, a failure, for here I am, undeniably doing wrong, and in the moment of uncertainty I feel guilt flash across my features, before I lock my smile in place. Giving my description to the police in ethnically not-so-diverse Tokyo would be easy, but I am nothing, I am the slight start in your chest which you later will put down to hiccups, I am the fear that faded as quickly as it came, I am

(worthless?)

practically forgotten already, as I push past her and run for the door.

Chapter 45

A suspicion growing, which now I acted on.

By stealing the identity of a journalist from the *San Francisco Chronicle* who looked perhaps a tiny little bit like myself, I got a meeting with a junior housing minister. He bowed as I entered, and I bowed lower, and we exchanged cards with both hands. As well as his normal card, he produced another, which transpired to be a dozen or so incredibly thin cards, each made of pressed platinum, his name engraved in gold.

"I donate them to the temples," he explained, as I turned one between my fingers, feeling the sharpness of the edge. There must have been something of the thief in my face, for he quickly pulled it back, slipping these precious objects back into their hiding place. "It is both a financial gift, and a means of ensuring my name is remembered."

I locked my smile in the attack position, and looked the minister up and down, adding up the value of his suit, his bespoke leather shoes, his watch – a beautiful piece, the face changing gently as the hands moved, the moon to conquer the retreating sun. In the 1500s, watches had been filled with symbols of Death: Death beating on the bell, creeping from his cave; Death waiting at the end of every dangerous hour. How time had changed.

My mind, wandering, again; there is a human in the room, there is company, he can see me, he can see me, focus on that.

Questions – the easy ones first, gently prepared. How long in his job? New challenges in housing? Changing demographics. Over-population in urban areas? Loss of rural communities? Planning laws. Tenant protection. Market imbalance. The 106 Apartments.

"Ah, yes, a beautiful piece of design, no?"

Beautiful indeed, and was I right in thinking that he was personally involved in the project?

"Not personally, not involved, but yes, I helped give it clearance."

But wasn't there a building standing there already?

"Unsafe building, terribly old, the residents living in unsanitary conditions, terrible, really, terrible."

Low-income families evicted from their homes, sent away from the city and—

"That is the worst way of seeing it!" he interrupted, suddenly sharp, suddenly hostile. Strange how fast the switch may happen. In a society where good manners are king, the breakdown of such formalised structures rapidly reveals a need to not only save face, but to save face by chewing off the face of your adversary.

I do not need him hostile, so I bob in my seat, smile humbly, bat my eyelids, throw out a few harmless questions – new initiatives, lessons learned, wisdom acquired – and only at the very very end, as I stand up to leave, snapping my satchel shut around my entirely redundant notes, do I ask, quiet, conspiratorial:

"Do you have Perfection?"

His eyes dart up from the leather top of the desk where they had rested, to study my face. "Seven hundred and ninety-four thousand, five hundred," I murmur, gentle as you like.

"Nine hundred and eighty-one thousand, four hundred," he breathes, eyes now fixed on my face. "It's changed my life. I thought I was worthless, now I know I can do whatever I want."

"That's how I feel."

"I am a better person, now."

"Me too."

He leant forward, and I bent in to join him, so close I could feel his breath against my neck, feel him enjoy it, the heat rising in his skin, stayed still, didn't flinch, didn't curl away. "I got two hundred and fifty thousand points the day the 106 project went through. 'You have made the perfect decision,' it said. 'You are building the perfect life.' It is the perfect home."

I smiled and nodded, and said nothing in reply.

He beamed at me, like an old friend happy to discover that time has not diminished our bond, as I walked away.

Chapter 46

A different party, another day. A gathering for the 106, for the elite, for the perfect. I stole one of the caterer's badges, wore black shoes, black skirt, black shirt and white gloves, and walked in with a tray of sashimi served with green-tea powder, just as the party was getting warm.

All the perfect people, they chatted so easily, laughed so high, spoke so fair.

Hands picked treats off the tray, made by a chef flown in specially for the night, each mouthful marked with a calorie count and vitamin breakdown.

Perfection knows what you're eating! said a card on my tray.

I let hands take food, then went to the bathroom, locked myself into a cubicle and changed. Dress by . . . someone . . . I'd stopped caring. Shoes by . . . someone else. I'd had to skim six credit cards, grab as much cash as I could before the accounts were closed, and even then fashion had nearly broken my budget.

Perfection was not for the poor.

I stepped back into the party, a beautiful woman who'd always been there. I drank champagne, ate sashimi, nodded at anecdotes about fashion, film, technology, power, and in this manner made my way towards my mark.

There she was, standing where she always stood, Filipa, just behind her brother. Her bracelet, silver, a mathematical challenge in metal form, still around my wrist. I hadn't taken it off since she gave it to me. I looked, and saw that, like me, she was imperfect. The only imperfect woman in the room, though she tried so hard to fit in. Her smile was not dazzling; her wit was not razor-edged. Her nails were not perfectly lacquered, her dress was – such a sin – the same dress she'd worn last time, and out of season. And more, something else, a thing I'd seen before.

Sorrow, in her eyes, sorrow in her lips, closed and tight, as she watched the room turning.

You cannot be sad and be perfect.

I slipped into position beside her, watched in silence the perfect people with their perfect lives turn, turn and turn again, before I spoke.

"Thought is feedback," I said, and her eyes rose to me, though her head did not turn. "Social anxiety triggers a physiological alarm. The physical reinforces the social. Through very few cycles, we may become convinced of fallacies. That we are afraid of people. That we are worthless. You and I could be perfect, if only we could tame that weakest part of ourselves – our thoughts. Do you not agree, Dr Pereyra-Conroy?"

Her eyes turned to me, and I thought I saw the glimmering of tears in them. "Yes," she said, at last. "I do."

"You do not have Perfection," I said.

She answered without hesitation, eyes still on mine, studying my face. "No."

"In the 106 Club, you may receive treatments. What do they do?"

"They make you happy."

"Perfect?"

"Better."

"Define better."

Her lips sealed, a physical pressing together, her eyes flickered to her brother, chatting idly away. "Smarter? Sharper? Wiser?" I suggested. "Confident. Ambitious. Sexy. Sensuous. *Just like they are in Hollywood.*"

Her eyes, back to my face, a slight tilt of her head. "I make the technology," she breathed at last. "My brother designed the parameters of what it should achieve."

Now I looked at him, Rafe Pereyra-Conroy, back straight, smile bright, shaking the hand of a stranger. Smooth as a millpond, hard as marble, bright as moonlight in a starless sky.

"How does it work?" I asked.

She spoke fast, blank, staring at thoughts only she could see. "High-speed reinforcement learning. Neuroplasticity is on your side. Positive values are extolled. Positive behaviours are reinforced. Dopamine released on the mimicking of positive actions. Electrical stimulation activates axon terminals. Visual and auditory aids. In early testing, we inserted electrodes into the heart of the brain. All thought is feedback, social anxiety triggers a physiological response, fear, terror, sweat glands, capillaries dilate, blood pressure, respiration—"

I put a hand on her arm, stopping her. Her eyes flashed up fast, body turned, she was short of breath. She stopped, forced herself to slow, exhaled with a shudder, half closed her eyes. Then, slower, "A new reinforcement. Ideas of success reinforced by persistent ideation. I will be successful. I am successful. I can achieve success. I am happy. I am happy. I am happy. We stick electrodes in the human brain and repeat this idea until it is true."

Silence a while, my hand still on her arm, holding her tight. She swayed a little. For a moment I thought she might fall, freed by speaking. Then she let out another breath, and said, "I designed treatments to make people better. I thought I could use it to make me brave. But people don't want to be brave, Rafe said. People want to be perfect. That's what they do now, the treatments. They erase your soul, and make you someone new."

She closed her eyes, let out a final breath, opened them again, seemed to see me for the very first time.

"It must have been hard," I said at last, "to see your idea turned into a monstrosity."

"Yes," she replied, still not turning her head to face me directly, "it is."

We stood together a while, in silence, ignored, not worth the attention of the room. Then her hand was on my arm, gripping too tight, and she'd seen the bracelet around my wrist, held so tight her fingers might bend into bone, and whispered, just in my ear, just for me, "Is it you? Are you the one we forget?"

I pulled my arm away hard, stumbled a little, shook myself free, stared now into her eyes. I saw no hostility, merely curiosity, enraptured, enthralled. "Matisse showed me CCTV footage of my meeting you, in Dubai, and again, here, eating noodles. I said I had eaten alone that night, but there you were, talking to me for hours. I thought I'd remember you, after they showed me your picture, but I don't. I held your picture and saw your face, and closed my eyes and couldn't see it any more. Rafe said I was mad but security didn't remember you either and Matisse proved it, he proved it was the truth – is it you?"

I had no words, I had no breath, I am my breath, I am breath, I am my breath

too fast though it runs.

Fascinated, and perhaps another word, as she studied my features, ran her eyes along my body, looked for some sign of what I was, how I worked, written on my skin. "They said you might come back. Is it something chemical, or electrical, that you do?"

I stepped away, turned, looking for the exit, panic

pure panic

can't control my breath

can't control my legs

my legs are not my own

my eyes are not my own

my world, as I move for the door, turn, press, push against the crowd

not my own

cannot smile

cannot be the thief

professional

I am

out of control

stumbling for the way out and it is only because fear is a physical reaction

because adrenaline heightens all sense

that I see Gauguin before it is too late.

He stands there, in a smart black suit, earpiece in his right ear, hands folded in front, surveying the crowd. He doesn't seem to have a picture of me to hand; but no – there, a phone, he checks it every minute or two, and he's not looking at text messages.

Gauguin has followed me to Japan.

I cannot control my own body.

I cannot control my mind.

I turn without direction, looking for another way out, and a man says, "Excuse me, are you all right?"

He is . . .

. . . perfect.

Of course he's fucking perfect.

Perfect teeth, perfect skin, perfect hair, perfect suit, perfect smile, perfect poise, perfect perfect perfect, and my make-up is smudged. Something more too, some sense of the familiar that passes as soon as it comes.

"Shall I call for some assistance?" he offers, American accent, dressed in black, a robe crossed right to left – cross your kimono the other way for the dead; a white boy somehow pulling off looking good in formal Japanese clothes.

"Would you like to borrow my handkerchief, your mascara appears to be a little . . . "

Perfect: to be superficial to your very core.

Bright blond hair, perfectly smooth skin, not a wrinkle in sight. I feel my hand move to slap him and physically jerk it down to the side, hard enough to catch his eye, my body contorting like a dropped puppet. I dig my nails into the palm of my hand, break the skin, feels good, focused.

Gauguin's eyes are still drifting round the room. I will not run; not while he has my picture in his hand, a square of light shining from his phone. He will look for the woman who runs.

"Thank you," a voice says, charming, rich, a cliché of English wealth, inexplicably mine. "That's very kind."

With his handkerchief I dab very gently at the rim of my eyes, a gesture which explains in its delicate motion that no, of course no, I wasn't crying, merely had something in the corner of my eye . . .

The nails dig deep in the palm of my left hand.

I am my pain.

"Did someone say . . . ?" The beginning of a chivalrous gesture, perhaps? Did someone slight my honour, is there a battle to be fought here? Manly perfection: to be in perfect accord with what society deems to be the quality of masculine.

Words associated with masculine: logic, confidence, authority, discipline, independence, responsibility.

He was watching me, head slightly on one side, letting me wriggle in his gaze, a half smile on his lips, and again, I held back the temptation to slap him and said instead, "Do you know what a Möbius strip is?"

Words, happening for words' sake, Gauguin by the door.

"Yes," he said, and I was so surprised that for a moment, my field of perception narrowed back down to his face. "Yes I do. What a curious question."

A flare of irritation; I was prepared to actively dislike this man already, and his expression of amusement was not diminishing this instinct. "Can you express its qualities mathematically?" I snapped.

Words associated with the quality of feminine: sensual, demure, nurturing, compassionate, emotive.

"... golf?"

He had been saying something banal, listing things more interesting than maths, perhaps. Sailing, sake, sumo ... golf.

I grabbed a canapé off a passing tray, allowed the motion to turn my body, angling myself so that Gauguin can only see the back of my head, and surely even he cannot identify me by that. "Golf, how interesting," I intoned, rolling the battered vegetable between my fingers before biting it in half.

At this motion, he flinched, and it took a moment for me to conclude that it was the indelicate sight of a woman eating with relish, teeth churning, lips pushing, half an eaten-thing still between her greasy fingers, that caused him so much distaste. I licked my lips, smiled deep into his concerned eyes, and very slowly, very deliberately, wiped my fingers clean on my sleeve. His eyes widened, and I wrapped my arm in his and said, staring deep into his pale grey eyes, "Have you played Cypress Point?"

A moment, in which he wavered between a medley of

thoughts. The secret to the con is always to offer the thing that the mark most desires; and every golf-loving mark desired Cypress Point. "No," he breathed. "But I know there are some here who have membership."

"I got in at nine hundred and fifty thousand points," I replied, fingers dallying in the hook of his elbow. "You haven't seen perfection until you've seen Cypress Point."

"How?!" Envy now, bringing his attention right back to me. "I've been trying to get in for years!"

"I played the game." I shrugged. "I achieved perfection."

"So have I," he replied, "but my life won't be complete until I've played that course."

"You'll see it; you can be anything you want to, now."

Still, my fingers, his arm, keeping that contact, Gauguin behind me, but I was confident now, I knew what I was doing, back in control, controlling my environment, this man, myself, hell yes, bring it, world. Fucking bring it.

Perfect: to be inhuman in your perfection.

Then he said, "My name is Parker," and for a moment, I lost my breath again, and had to catch it, pull it in deep, count backwards from ten. "You've heard of me?" he asked, when my silence stretched.

"I knew a Parker once," I replied, "in New York."

"Impossible!" he chuckled. "I'm the one and only Parker of New York."

"Except Spider-Man." Words – I remember reading them, not hearing them, but still . . . "I'm sure if we'd met, I'd remember you."

A flicker, perhaps, in the corner of his eyes, but the smile didn't waver. "I'm sure you would too."

"What do you do, Parker?" Turning him again, using him to shield me from Gauguin, manipulating his body, easier now, easy.

"Casinos. I had a lot of luck on the tables a few years back; now I own the tables where I used to win."

"And how long have you had Perfection?"

"Three years."

"How did you find the treatments?"

"I can honestly say they changed my life."

"In what way?"

"They made me who I am."

"And who is that?"

"Someone worth remembering."

My fingers still in his arm, he wanted to be physically closer. It was not me he lusted after, I decided, but rather he was aroused by himself. Seducing me gave him an outlet to express his brilliance. Easy to manipulate someone that vain. His body, a half shuffle closer, his hip bumping against mine.

I let it play, I was my smile, I was my skin, I was a woman as aroused by him as he was by himself.

Gauguin by the door, watching. I kept my back to him.

"And why are you here, the one-and-only Parker from New York?"

Who is this person who speaks?

A tinkling laugh, a little smile, practically a bob of the knees, a caress of his arm under its sleeve, who is this woman who wears my face?

She is the creature I have created, the default position I retreat to when I am under threat. She is whoever she needs to be to get the job done.

"I was presented with an opportunity. There's a club in Macau, looking to do more business. You always know you can do business with the 106, with people like us."

I looked to his face for a flicker of something, anything, which might be called doubt, humour, and saw nothing. The crowd turned and we turned with it, and there was Filipa again, her eyes elsewhere, I had already vanished from her memory, but this man, this stranger with a familiar name, watched me, enjoyed watching me and I felt . . .

My fingers tightened round his arm.

With my other hand I reached up, touched the corner of his jaw, turned his head this way and that, feeling the skin around his face. What could I remember about Parker, the man I'd met in New York? Not *him*, only a list of characteristics that I had written down, words without meaning. Mousy hair (that could be dyed), grey eyes (he had those), a mole on his chin (missing – not my Parker then, clearly not)

my fingers brushed his chin, felt the tiny change in texture, a place where a surgeon with inestimable skill had carefully excised the offending growth. I probed that spot in fascination, invisible to sight but just palpable to touch, a slight scaling of the scar tissue, and he caught my wrist, pulled it away, the smile never wavering (perfect people always smile), curiosity in his eyes.

"Your surgeon was incredible," I stammered. "Did you have anything else done?"

"A little. My nose; a few lines in my forehead, a little work elsewhere, you know how it is. I thought why not? Why not be better? Now people see who I really am," he mused. "They envy me."

"Is that a good thing?"

"Yes – of course. We set an example for how people should be."

"And do they remember you now?" I asked, and there it was again, the slightest flickering in his eyes. "Do they remember who you are?"

"Everyone remembers me," he replied softly. "I'm the one and only Parker from New York."

"And before your treatments? Before Perfection? Who were you then?"

A glib answer rises quickly to his lips, it is Perfection about to speak, about to brush off anything that might be frightening, that might threaten the mask he wears, but no.

Perhaps no.

Perhaps there is a tiny shard of hope left, for in that moment, Parker from New York stopped, and reined in his glib, charming reply, and instead looked me in the eye and held my wrist hard and said, "Who are you?"

And it was him.

Of course it was.

Of course.

I pulled my hand away, turned my back, stepped into the crowd, pushed through it fast, Gauguin's eyes rose to me but that was fine, that was absolutely fine, let him look, I just need to break his line of sight for a moment, let him forget again, turn and turn and turn, Filipa behind her brother, Gauguin by the door, Parker in the middle of the room and Parker

being perfect

Perfect: devoid of any feelings that might mean anything, any more

does not attempt to follow.

And within thirty seconds, he has forgotten.

I turn, turn again, circling the room. There are no CCTV cameras here, which is a mistake – someone on CCTV might have seen me, that's happened before, back when I was robbing casinos, the computers always spotted me before the humans did – but the 106 are too exclusive to be monitored and so I turn, and turn, and turn, and at the end I smile delightfully at Gauguin as I walk by him, and see his hand close around the mobile phone in his pocket as I go.

I do not wait for him to look for my features; I round the corner at the end of the hall, pull off my shoes and run.

Chapter 47

Total fucking fail.

Total fucking breakdown.

A woman sits in her hotel room, hugging her pillows to her chest, and cries – she cries – like a fucking six year old.

Hope Arden get your fucking act together!

No good.

Hope Arden – the woman who was Hope Arden, before Hope Arden became no more than a blip in a digital record, a carbon footprint – this woman, sits now in a grey room in a grey hotel beneath a grey sky, and cries.

I want Luca Evard here to hold me, I want Gauguin staring in surprise, I want Filipa Pereyra looking at me in wonder, I want my mum who crossed the desert, my dad who told me never to turn to crime. I want Parker from New York, the one I can't remember; Byron14, I want Reina bint Badr al Mustakfi, I want

someone

to say my name.

Gauguin didn't even remember me long enough to chase after me when I fled from his sight.

Filipa will not remember eating noodles with me.

I am dead in all but deed.

My deeds are worthless.

one two three four five six seven eight nine ten eleven twelve thirteen fourteen fifteen sixteen seventeen eighteen nineteen twenty 一二三四五六七八九十十一十二十三十四十五十六十七十八十九二十 *eins zwei drei vier fünf sechs sieben acht neun zehn elf zwölf dreizehn vierzehn fünfzehn sechszehn siebzehn achtzehn neunzehn zwanzig* twenty-one twenty-two twenty-three twenty-four twenty-five twenty-six twenty-seven twenty-eight twenty-nine . . .

I am the number one thousand four hundred and seventeen.

It is there where I stop crying.

Stand up.

Wash my face, cold water.

Wash my hands, two presses of soap on the dispenser above the sink.

Tidy my hair.

Stand up straight.

At one thousand four hundred and seventeen, I became disciplined again.

Chapter 48

I found Parker easily enough; exclusive hotel, exclusive car, exclusive . . . everything.

Exclusive: to exclude. Limiting possession or control to a single group.

Followed him, watched him laugh, smile, shake hands, bow from the hips.

He had a website-picture of himself on the front, dressed in white, one hand resting on a roulette table, mirrors behind, crystal chandeliers above. Portraits of ancient kings showed them with their hands resting on the world; the sceptre and the orb; soldiers at their backs. A roulette table beneath his fingers, Parker from New York, Perfect Parker, ruling the world, perfect in every fucking way

not angry.

I am one thousand four hundred and eighteen.

Nineteen.

Twenty.

Used to be, no one remembered me, said his personal testimonial. *Now I know what it takes to make an impression. Take a chance on perfection!*

One thousand four hundred and twenty-one.

One thousand four hundred and twenty-two.

I watched him, and he didn't remember me, but the world, it seemed, remembered him.

I contacted Byron14 the very same day.

```
wherewhatwhy: I want Perfection. I want
to tear it open and know everything about
how it works. I NEED to know how it works.

Byron14: So do I.
```

I am a thief.

A USB stick is left in a storage locker at Tokyo station.

I take it and go.

Chapter 49

Only two stops from Tokyo station to Inaricho. I ran my finger round the endless knot of Filipa's Möbius strip, knew it would be sensible to leave the bracelet behind, didn't want to take it off.

Fine: I permit myself a little indiscretion. A lapse of professionalism.

Tools of the trade. IDs stolen, security badges forged. Week after week, I built up faces, addresses, every phone stolen, every computer accessed, every face noted, wallet lifted, every name, every number. I could walk into the Tokyo offices of Prometheus right now, but Gauguin is in town, Gauguin has realised that he cannot remember my face, and so I go armed to Yamanote.

The last thing I collect is the first whose absence will be noticed – a security token, the size of my thumb, which displays six changing numbers when the correct fingerprint is pressed against it. These numbers correspond to a passcode on a door – this door stands between me and Prometheus' servers. Once I steal it, there'll be no stopping.

The man who possesses both the token and the thumbprint is Mr Kaneko. He is watched over by a security man at all times, but I have now made contact three times on three different reconnaissance missions and only once was security in my way.

Mr Kaneko is too boring for sin. But he believes in what he does, and lives by Perfection. Every Tuesday, Perfection informs him that the best thing he can do is go to the gym, so to the gym he goes. The gym is male-only, and so exclusive it doesn't need to advertise.

The security guard waits in the foyer. I gain access through the service door, using the key stolen eight days ago from a personal trainer. Mr Kaneko has a private locker, always the same number – 324 – believing that these numbers are particularly auspicious. His lucky direction is north. His blood type is A+, which means he is a warrior, creative and passionate. (He is not.) He believes all this, so I have of course studied it.

Professionalism: conduct, aim or qualities connected with skilled people.

I walk into the male changing room without pause, horrifying many of the clientele who sit, towels hanging loose from their bare, honed flesh – and let myself into his locker with the receptionist's master key.

Men shout: out, out, who are you, what are you doing? I find the secure tag I need, smile brightly at them, give a half bow, and leave them to their nudity, and by the time one of them has put on his dressing gown and sandals and waddled to reception to complain, he has already forgotten.

With the security tag in hand, I head towards Prometheus.

Preparation, preparation, preparation.

This was the sacred tenet of a jewel thief I once shared cocktails with on the coast of Croatia. He'd run with the Pink Panthers, back before the younger generation stepped in and things got sloppy. "Preparation!" he exclaimed, sucking alcoholic juices out of a slice of orange. "This new generation, they have no craft. They break into any old place, wave their guns around, grab the first thing to come to hand, maybe ten, twenty thousand dollars' worth at most, not worth it, just not worth it."

And again, lying in Luca Evard's arms that night in Hong Kong, letting his breathing push my head up and down as it lay on his chest, the happiest I think I'd ever been, the happiest I can remember ever being.

I'd asked ... something ... his skin pressing against mine. I was scared that when we stopped talking, he would sleep, and when he slept, he would forget, and this moment would be lost.

Now.

And now.

And gone.

So I'd made him talk, and he'd said: "A thief breaks the law once, something small, and it was easy, you got away with it, you feel great, this is easy, no harm done. The next time, easy again, and the next and the next and the next until it becomes habit. Just a thing you do. And then one day, you need something more – a new car, perhaps, or a new house – and someone has it, and you don't, but that's okay, because you know how to get it, and also that you deserve it, because this is not just the thing you do, it's who you are. And the next day you have a gun, and you're not going to use it, but it becomes familiar in your hand, comfortable, and when the first person dies perhaps you're scared, but perhaps you're okay, because you've been carrying a gun around for so long that it was natural. Inevitable. Who you are. It's people like that who scare me, the ones who aren't doing a job, but *becoming* the job. The ones who don't know where they'll stop."

"Don't coppers do the same thing? Become the job?"

He thought about it for a second, then gave a half laugh, a thing from the back of the throat. "Maybe they do. There is a certain pressure that comes on you when you are, for example, trying to trace a murderer. You know he's out there, ready to kill, you have the family of his latest victim downstairs and you think . . . do I have the right to go home at five p.m., knowing this? Can I really take a weekend off, when he's out there? It is sometimes hard to be a good policeman and anything else."

"What about the woman at Hung Hom? Is she a killer?"

"Who knows? Maybe one day."

Silence a while, but he was still awake, eyes white in the half light of the hotel room, mind elsewhere. I kiss his neck, keep him awake, keep this moment for ever, him, now, me, now, this remembrance, this us, a thing I had almost never said, an us together, a me and someone else who is a part of me, this present tense.

*

And a little while later, he said, “I never said Hung Hom Pier.”

“What?”

“You said the woman at Hung Hom, but I never mentioned it.”

He was wide awake, but I was getting drowsy.

“Sure you did,” I replied. “Of course you did.”

“I don’t think so.”

Silence between us. He was alert now, four thirty a.m. and the city stirring, sunrise across the sea, watching me, and the thing that had been, the moment that should have been for ever, was fading.

Now.

I felt it rush away.

Becoming memory, only my memory, only a thing for me, and somehow unreal in its solitude, as if perhaps I had imagined this whole thing, a fantasy of a night with Luca Evard, a passing dream.

And now.

Gone. Broken like a spider’s web, trailing in the breeze.

And I said, “I’m going to get a drink of water; do you want anything?”

“No.”

And I went to the bathroom, and I locked myself in, and I sat with the light off and my head in my hands for five hundred breaths, and when I let myself out again, he had forgotten, and he was asleep, and it was over.

Preparation, preparation, preparation.

I stole Mr Kaneko’s security tag from a gym, his thumbprint from a wine glass.

I stole a silk suit and a large briefcase from a department store, gutted the briefcase and put it back together again with what I needed inside.

I stole a collapsible nightstick and a can of pepper spray from the back of a police car. Fact: Japanese policemen must all study judo.

I stole a set of mini screwdrivers, a tiny electric drill, a torch, a pack of candles, a bottle of lighter fluid, a pair of safety goggles. I timed how long each candle took to burn, cut the remainder down to size.

The lockpicks I bought online. The tub of plain yoghurt was remarkably expensive, but this was Japan. My hotel handed out matches, and I took them. The firecrackers were hanging by the temple gate, but it felt like sacrilege, so I bought them from the shop across the road.

I stole codes and keys, careful now, fast towards the end – everything had to be stolen close enough to the day of the robbery that credentials wouldn't be deactivated, codes wouldn't be changed.

I gained access to the front-line computers at Prometheus' reception desk by stealing the email ID of an IT man on the eleventh floor, and sending an attachment in his name entitled, "Vital Security Upgrade" to the receptionists, who opened it, and every keystroke they made from there on in became mine.

I purchased the services of whoever coded behind the name of OsumiWasAPterodactyl and ten minutes before I walked through the front door of Prometheus, she broke into the reception desk webcams and froze the feed from ten seconds before my arrival to ten seconds after; my face never logged.

I walked in through the front door, and no one stopped me.

This was my sixth time in the offices of Prometheus.

Gauguin would be nearby. How had he come to Tokyo? Perhaps he pulled footage of the plane from Sharm el-Sheikh, trying to find me, and instead found himself, holding a knife on a woman he couldn't remember. Perhaps he hadn't been able to invent a convincing story for how he had recovered the diamonds, my luggage, my passports. A man like Gauguin struck me as an individual who took pride in his memory, and so, of course, he had come to Tokyo because Filipa had eaten with a woman she could not remember, and Tokyo was where Perfection was.

He would be watching, but that was fine. I counted security

cameras, walked fifteen steps towards the elevators, hugging the left-hand wall, took a sharp right turn on the sixteenth, counted seven steps across the hall, took a hard left, shuffled eight more steps with my back pressed into the wall, and avoided the first two cameras.

A sharp left back across the hall for eight steps, a sharp right, twenty-two paces took me to the entrance to the men's toilet. The entrance to the ladies was visible to a camera perched high and to the right; men didn't merit the same interest.

In the toilet I opened up my briefcase, and changed into a cleaner's tabard and blue slacks. I pushed my hair into a baseball cap, took a bucket on wheels from a cupboard by the sinks, put a plastic bag containing my tools and tub of yoghurt inside it, balanced the mop on top.

I walked at a cleaner's shuffle to the elevators, head down, turned a little to the left, avoiding the angle of the camera on my face, and summoned the lift.

A stolen ID badge took me to the seventeenth floor. Lights off, every desk spotless. Mr Yamada, the stern head of development, insisted on it. He also insisted that every day for ten minutes, his floor practised zazen, and he walked up and down the silent lines of meditating employees with a small bell to initiate and close proceedings. Other foibles of Mr Yamada: an obsessive if talented keeper of potted plants, a fanatical supporter of the San Francisco Giants, and a man who, in his youth, was credited with creating a whole new generation of VHS technology. The days of brilliance were gone; now he was management, and growing fat.

His office was glassed off from the rest of the open-plan floor, though he proudly pointed out the blinds across the windows were never down. But of all the people on the seventeenth floor, only Mr Yamada had access to the floor above, where the real work of Perfection was done.

He kept his pass in a safe behind a plywood cabinet door in the north-eastern corner of his office. The safe was digital; five buttons were clearly marked with the accumulation of grease from his fingerprints, two numbers even beginning to wear away. I wrote down 1, 2, 5, 7 and 9, rearranged them to 25/11/79, the birthday of his eldest son. My first attempt failed, but inverting the day/month to the American style opened the safe with ease.

I stole his passcard, foolish to keep it in such a silly place, and walked eleven steps with my shoulder pressed to the wall, then crawled fifteen paces on my hands and knees between the desks, dragging my bucket behind me, to avoid the cameras, until I reached a bin out of the camera's eye. It was sturdy metal, next to a filing cabinet. I filled it with handfuls of crunched paper, tipped it on its side, squirted lighter fluid all around, and gingerly lit my stub of candle, setting it on the edge of the pool of liquid.

I crawled away, letting the flame slither down.

The door to the eighteenth floor was two and a half inches thick, driven by pneumatic pistons. There was no avoiding the security camera here, and I couldn't disable it without being caught in the line of sight of another camera on the other side of the room, so I ignored it, and swiped myself through.

Somewhere, the act of opening the door would trigger security, absolutely, for Mr Yamada was not in the building and the door should not have opened, and doors built to withstand high explosive did not open and shut without notice. I started the stopwatch on my phone, and took the stairs two at a time, bucket held tight, no alarm sounding, lights flickering to life around me, woken by my footsteps. Mr Yamada's passcard opened the door to the floor above, and now we were in a place I hadn't yet been, an office disappointingly like every other office on the surface of the earth: chairs, desks, computers, two or three screens each, some off, some still running silently, processing a file overnight, churning through numbers while the humans slept.

Fifteen metres from the stairwell to another security door. An eight-digit numeric code, changed every three days, impossible to crack at speed but then, its strength was also its weakness, for an eight-digit code changed every three days is next to impossible for busy members of staff to remember, and it's always the human element that is most frail in these systems. I looked for the desk of Miss Sato, the only woman in the office, a brilliant coder relegated by her senior staff to a junior position by dint of being a woman, who had complained as we chatted after a Pilates class that next to her was Mr Sugiyama, who never remembered the door code and always wrote it down, a shocking security breach, just shocking, but who listened to her?

I had listened.

At Pilates, Miss Sato had worn a T-shirt bearing the image of a black bear devouring a fish. A small wooden rabbit had hung down from the zip of her rucksack. Hanging from the koi-patterned case of her mobile phone was a tiny straw sparrow, that bounced against her wrist when she made a call. Engimono: good-luck charms. Now I looked for those charms, and found a desk on which a single straw creature, perhaps a fat panda bear, perhaps merely a blob with a painted face, smiled serenely. To the left was the desk of the much-hated Mr Sugiyama, he of the poor memory, and scrawled at the very back of his leather-bound appointment book in almost indecipherably tiny writing on a pink Post-it note was an eight-digit code.

Preparation, preparation, preparation.

The eight-digit code opened the door; Mr Yamada's credentials sealed the deal.

Twenty-three seconds on the stopwatch; six breaths in, five breaths out.

More alarms would be sounding now, and that was fine. Let them come.

The room beyond was close to how I had imagined and all I had hoped for. I heaved the door shut behind me, heard it lock tight. Lines of servers, heat burning off them as fast as the fans could push cold air in, labelled and marked with letters and numbers, trails of cat5 cables bundled into intricate plaits, data highways rushing off into the void. The noise was a low rumble of moving air, a high hiss of magnetic plates and coils.

A single active computer terminal with a single screen, bright and blue in the noisy gloom. I pressed the image of Mr Kaneko's thumbprint into the grey fob I'd stolen from him, and six numbers appeared in the panel. I typed the numbers into the terminal, waited, counted my breaths, two, three, four, heard voices in the office at my back. The computer unlocked. I slipped my USB stick into the port, special delivery from Byron14, executed the file, waited.

Nine breaths, ten breaths.

My skin burns with expectation, my blood is on fire within me, I am alive, I am alive, in this moment, I am alive after all.

How long does it take to write data to a USB drive?

(USB 2.0 – 60 MB/s but in reality closer to 40 MB/s. Assuming that there's at least 16GB of data to copy across from Prometheus' server and that's what, 1,000MB – call it 1,024, think binary – ×16 that's what . . . 16,348MB to copy, divided by 40 that's 410ish seconds, divide by 60 that's just under seven minutes, no matter how fast you look at it seven minutes is six minutes too long.)

Preparation, preparation, preparation.

I leave the USB stick running, and at last hear the distant song of the fire alarm as the candle I had set downstairs finally burns down to a point where it touches the lighter fluid. The fluid ignites, the ignition sets paper burning in a bin, paper sends up smoke and heat, one or the other – probably the latter – triggering the fire alarm.

May not buy me time; may buy me a few minutes.

I stand by the shut door, pepper spray in my left hand, baton in my right. Taster classes – I am the queen of taster classes. There are fitness, language, sewing, cooking, painting and martial arts classes across the world where, for weeks at a time, I was invited not to pay for my tuition because "the first one's free". After ten weeks of attendance I'd say that I'd "done a little" and after twenty the experience would usually lose its value, as the length of time it would take a teacher to discover that I had experience would be as long as the class itself, and I could progress no further.

Intensive courses. Five hours of swimming instruction. Eight of Spanish. Four of karate. Six of "boot camp fitness and boxing" on a freezing November weekend in London Fields. Enough to get an idea of all the ways I could go wrong. Enough to know that, if I was pushed to it, I would fight.

Fifty-five seconds.

Sixty.

Whatever voices had come to the eighteenth floor had been distracted by the fire on the seventeenth, for a moment – only a moment.

One, two, three, four, five, six, seven . . .

A hundred seconds.

One hundred and twenty.

On the one hundredth and fiftieth second since I had triggered the alarm, a disgraceful response time if ever I'd met one, someone tried to open the door to the server room from the outside, and found it locked.

Voices moved, shouted, feet ran, I waited.

Codes and cards were sought, two hundred and twenty seconds, two hundred and forty.

On the three hundredth second, someone inputted a code and the door began to open.

I shot a burst of yellow pepper spray into the face that appeared in the gap, and at a man's scream, slammed the door shut again and braced against it.

Voices, high and fast, a babbling sound, then someone a great deal more aggressive and confident than his still-howling partner began to slam his full weight against the door. I pushed back, first strike, second strike, third strike, and on the fourth I moved off, and he fell shoulder-first, balance gone, through the open door and into the room. Again, a burst of pepper spray, and this time, for his enthusiasm, a smack across the side of the face with the end of my baton, teeth breaking, blood drawn, and damn right too for the man had a gun in his hand. He falls, I take his gun, and fire almost entirely at random, at the door.

Busy silence within, hard silence outside, accompanied by the ever-present hum of the computers.

Intensive courses: I thought learning how to use a gun would be hard, but in America it was forty bucks and a smile.

They waited; I waited.

There was only one way in and one way out. The man at my feet groaned, half conscious, hands pressed to his face. I nudged him with my toe. "Off you go," I said, and although he was half blind, he didn't need telling twice, fumbled his way to the door, ran away on all fours, looking for a place to dry his eyes.

Waited.

Three hundred and twenty seconds; less than another hundred and my USB stick would be done.

Then a voice, speaking English, soft and familiar, and though I was prepared, my breath came fast.

"Ms Donovan?" Gauguin. Who else but Gauguin? "Ms Donovan, are you there?"

I pulled a firecracker from my mop bucket, began to tape it round the can of pepper spray.

"Ms Donovan? Ms Donovan, can you hear me?"

No point answering, but the flash drive hasn't finished downloading and I need a little more time.

"Hello," I said. "Come in and I'll shoot things."

An over-blown sigh, but perhaps also, a slight breath of excitement? Did Gauguin do excited? "Ms Donovan, there is no way out."

Why Ms Donovan? The passports he'd found in my luggage bore a medley of names, but Rachel Donovan was an old, old alias.

"I think we've met before," he mused, through the half-open door. "It would appear we were in proximity, for a while."

"Can you describe my face?"

Silence from outside. Then, "I have your photo in my hand."

"How many times have you looked at it?" Silence, again. "Close your eyes," I suggested, "see if you can tell me what I look like."

Silence. From my mop bucket I pulled the pair of safety goggles.

"Ms Donovan," he said at last, "whatever you are, however you manage your . . . your trick, you are too remarkable for this to be your end. However, I am tasked by Mr Pereyra-Conroy to protect his interests, and protect them I will."

Four hundred and sixty seconds.

Sixty-one, sixty-two, sixty-three ...

"Please – throw the gun down and step out," he went on, reasonable – but there it was, fear, fear in his voice, fear that I had thought was excitement but no, it is fear, for I am the great unknown, a thing he cannot explain, and Gauguin isn't excited by such things, but rather, he is afraid.

Four hundred and seventy-three, seventy-four, seventy-five.

On the four hundredth and seventy-ninth second, the USB stick finished downloading the full content of Perfection's core programming from the servers. It made no sound, there was no change to the room, no computers exploded, no sparks flew. A thing which had been unique was now cloned, and I tied my smart white shirt across my nose and mouth, pulling it tight by the sleeves, as Gauguin waited.

At last he said, "I saw the footage of you speaking with Dr Pereyra-Conroy at the noodle bar."

I picked up the USB stick, taped it to my ankle, pulled my sock over the tape.

"Her security swore she ate alone, though they watched you the whole time."

Baton under one arm, the gun stolen from a fallen guard held tight, a firecracker taped to a can of pepper spray, safety goggles on my face, plastic bag containing the remains of my tools and a pot of yoghurt hooked into my elbow and really, I was starting to run out of limbs, only my legs free, ready to run.

"I saw you again on the cameras at the party in Dubai, just before the diamonds were stolen. And again, here, in Tokyo, at the 106, exploring the apartments, circling the Pereyra-Conroys. I was there, must have looked straight at you, but it would appear that the connection between the image I have on a screen and the image I see – or rather, fail to see – of your features in my mind is severed. Such a lasting disconnection implies that you have achieved something far more than merely some ...

temporary magic trick. Dr Pereyra says it is the most exciting thing she has ever heard of in her whole career."

Filipa Pereyra-Conroy is one of the most exciting people I've met in mine, I muse, but I say nothing now, for he is focusing his words, his attention all on me, lest he forget, making himself a prisoner to the awareness of me, this moment, now.

Behind me, servers begin to shut down, a slow whine of disappointment, a whimper of breaking parts. Byron14's USB stick stole a lot of data, but it only needed a few kilobytes' worth to implant a virus as it committed its crime. It won't stop them, of course, not a little pissy bit of code, but I think Byron enjoyed the gesture, as the room turns to sudden, fan-washed quiet.

Silence. I close my eyes, and picture Gauguin nodding to himself, understanding what I'm doing, perhaps caring, perhaps not.

He said, "Even being forgotten is a modus operandi of its kind."

A threat; he just threatened me. With what, precisely?

Modus operandi: from the Latin, first known use 1654, a way of doing something.

Abbreviation: MO, used by police forces across the world.

Other police abbreviations: APB, MVA, CSU, SWAT, FTA . . .

Modus operandi, a tool used by police forces to link crimes
and Luca Evard said, "I promise you won't be harmed."

Here.

Here.

Now.

This moment.

I am here.

This space.

My universe.

The whole universe.

Here.

And Luca Evard speaks.

and he says, "You don't have to be afraid."

He isn't here – the past consumed him, left him sleeping on a bed in Hong Kong. The past swallowed the words we had shared, it killed him, the past killed him as surely as it killed his words, as surely as it kills me

he can't be here. They can't have brought him to Tokyo. He sits in perfection still where I left him, waiting for me in a moment frozen in my memory

He cannot be here.

And of course, the thief that Hope Arden has become, the professional, knows that he can. Gauguin followed my money, he would have followed my MO, and who waited at the end of that trail? Who was the world expert in the woman everyone forgets, years of his life given to this single purpose?

Luca Evard, here, now.

The universe opens and the skies fall, galaxies turn and oceans dissolve away, I think perhaps this moment will last for ever, destroying everything I ever built, erasing the perfect moment in Hong Kong, because look, here we are, here he is, seeing me as a thief, knowing me as a thief, knowing perhaps that I'm something more. Does he know that he has forgotten does he understand what he has forgotten does he suspect does he hate me did he ever love me at all like I loved him

a professional thief who has my name lights the fuse in the firecracker.

Gauguin hears it, shouts a warning.

I throw the firecracker through the door.

A scurry, a scuttle.

I close my eyes.

Nebulas condense into suns; comets lose their endless battle with the force of gravity and burn through the atmosphere of massive worlds.

The firecracker pops.

The pepper spray pops with it, a cloud of yellow goo filling the room, bursting into the atmosphere. Through the shirt across my nose and mouth, it burns; no, burn is not the word for it, burn does not pull up your stomach lining, doesn't make your throat contract. It sears, it sickens, it tastes of swollen tongues spat out whole.

I step into the room beyond. A yellow, acid cloud swirls in the air, obscuring sight. Fire crackers still burst and hiss, loud enough to shake the eardrums, sparks spitting from their ends, the red stalks hopping up and down on the floor as they fire, flapping, a suffocating fish in a pan. Through the fog of chemicals and smoke, I see six of them, one already on the floor, all smartly dressed. All except Luca – he's come casually, or as casual as he can be: unironed shirt, trousers a little too short, a hint of black sock rolled up high against his calf, eyes closed tight shut, choking on the fumes in the air.

I would feel pity for him, but there's no time for that now.

The man nearest the door has a gun. My left hand pushes his elbow up, right smashes the baton down as hard as I can on his wrist. These men are blind, but someone fires anyway at the sound, until Gauguin, his hands pressed over his face, cries out no, don't shoot, you're shooting blind at us you imbecile!

His accent, when he is in pain, isn't as refined as I thought. There is a hint of something West Country in it, a change in vocabulary, his face is swollen like a pumpkin, and perhaps it *is* pity

whatever pity means

which makes me smash my baton into his knees, rather than his throat.

Could I kill him now?

In the busy way of things, it is not an entirely disquieting thought.

Neither is it very exciting.

One man, keeping his eyes forced open against the settling yellow cloud, tries to grapple with me. A flailing arm catches at my wrist; with his other he tries to punch me in the stomach, misses. He has power, which he generates by moving his body, arm never extending, but rather legs, chest, hips, coming into my space. Usually that power is devastating; today it is too much, and the momentum of his own punch throws his balance. I smash his arm as it passes me, drive the butt of my baton into his neck, kick his knees out as he begins to fall, and move on.

One man with a gun left; he doesn't even know where to point it. I take it from him without a word, without needing to break anything, throw it into the room behind me, pull my own weapon, holler, "Everyone down!"

"Do as she says," says Gauguin, wheezing, and was that a hint of Bristol in his accent? Perhaps, but he was fighting it, pulling himself together. "Do as she says," he repeated, a little more himself, pressing his chest into the ground, and they all did as I said, even Luca Evard, eyes squeezed shut, face a crinkled plastic bag.

I stood in the middle of a room at my mercy, and thought that this too was a kind of perfection. Perfect thief; perfect control.

Silence in the room, save for the groans of the injured, one man dribbling thin yellow saliva out of the corner of his mouth.

I barked, "Are you recording this?"

Silence.

"I think you are," I concluded, looking from Gauguin to Luca and back again. Neither man raised their heads. "I think you have realised that machines don't forget, even if you do. I want you to listen to the sound of my voice, when I'm gone. My name is Hope. I want you to remember my words. These words are the only part of me that exists. Do not follow. Do not try to find me. Do not forget."

I walked to the door, counted my steps, counted my breath.

Luca, the nearest to the exit, his head turned away, eyes closed tight, lips red, face swollen.

Words: a cascade of words.

I felt them on my lips, and sealed my mouth shut.

I ran.

Chapter 50

Preparation, preparation, preparation.

Police coming, no way out below, but that was fine.

Preparation, preparation, preparation.

The security office was on the sixteenth floor. I walked in at gunpoint, held three men at bay, shot out the computers, watched the screens go dark, and walked away.

Me, they forgot, though the bullets would take some explaining.

A cleaning cupboard on the eleventh floor. I chose it for the ceiling void above; especially large, to accommodate some piece of environmental apparatus they'd never got round to installing.

I broke into a vending machine and took three bottles of water, two packs of wasabi beans, and a bar of chocolate.

I lay in the ceiling void, drinking slowly, eating chocolate. I smeared yoghurt onto my face, hands, wrists, neck – anywhere which had been exposed to the fumes of tear gas. I ate the rest, waited.

An hour.

Two.

Three.

Nine hours.

A day.

Time passed, and I waited.

Police ransacked the building, and no one looked for me.

I closed my eyes, stayed on my back in the ceiling void, ate a few wasabi beans, needed to go to the toilet, counted to one hundred in the silence and the dark, and waited.

Time passed, and I waited.

Waited for memory to fade.

Wondered where Gauguin was, where Luca Evard was staying.

A cheap hotel – he always stayed in cheap hotels, even when someone else paid. Was he listening to the sound of my voice, did he have my words on repeat?

Perhaps he could cheat, write my words down a dozen times, and then a dozen more, and in doing so he would remember the act of writing, and in that way words would survive, even if the link between me speaking them and what entered his memory grew thin.

I counted to a thousand, and perhaps I slept, and when I woke, I counted to two thousand, and stayed wide awake.

And when it was done; when I reached twenty-four hours by the clock, I slipped out of the ceiling void, took the stairs down to the sub-basement, smiled at the security guard by the door. My picture, captured by CCTV, was on the wall behind him as I passed by, but his back was to it at that moment, and though he must have studied it all day, its features had faded in his mind, and he smiled at me as I walked away.

Chapter 51

My name is Hope.

I am the queen of the fucking universe.

I am the best thief ever to walk this fucking earth.

I am . . .

. . . I am fine.

I'm . . .

. . . fucking great, just, amazing, I'm . . .

. . . professional.

Disciplined.

A fucking fuck-you fuck it all fuck fucking machine.

Lines of code in a machine, in ascending order:

Least –

- Space shuttle
- Windows 3.1
- Mars Curiosity Rover
- Android operating system
- Windows 7
- Microsoft Office 2013
- Facebook
- Modern internal car software

– Most.

Data.

I sat on a bench, in a place, and stared into nothing.

I ate food.

I drank water.

I walked from a place to another.

Data only becomes information when it is translated.

I am

crying now

don't know why.

This is the thing I am doing but it is not information.

On the high-speed train out of Tokyo, how did I come to be here?

I had bought a ticket in advance, an escape route, now I seem to be using it.

I put Byron14's USB stick into my laptop, and had a look at what I had stolen.

Gobbledegook, unintelligible to anyone except an expert.

The base-code of Perfection.

Chapter 52

Parker opened a casino in Macau.

I watched the announcement on the news, saw him shake hands, smile for the cameras. He was famous now. Everyone knew his name, the one and only Parker of New York.

Rafe Pereyra-Conroy signed a deal with the royal family of Dubai, to jointly develop an Islamic version of Perfection, extolling virtues worthy of devout people

virtues such as generosity, kindness, charity, pilgrimage, duty, honour, loyalty, modesty

modesty codes

veils for the women

women not to be seen with unmarried men

no kissing in public

rape victims punishable by jail

etc.

I thought about turning round, going back to Tokyo, finding Luca Evard, telling him look, look, it's me, maybe if you arrest me everyone will see that you were right, that you've been chasing a forgettable thief, and then you'll be happy and then you'll love me, really love me, because I know you would if you could only remember me!

Sat in Kyoto airport and didn't move.

Rolled Filipa's bracelet round and round my wrist, a journey without end.

And after a while, because there didn't seem anything else to do, because nothing else that I did had any meaning whatsoever, I logged back into the darknet.

```
whatwherewhy: I have Perfection.

Byron14: Send it to me.
```

```
whatwherewhy: No. I want to meet.

Byron14: Unacceptable.

whatwherewhy: We meet, or you don't get
Perfection. I'll be in Seoul in three
days' time.

Byron14: Impossible.

whatwherewhy: I'll see you there.
```

Chapter 53

There are two exceptions to the circle of memory loss that surrounds me:

1 Animals. Perhaps it's a smell thing? Perhaps if I wore a remarkable perfume people would remember me, nasal déjà vu. Perhaps one day I'll get a dog. Maybe two.
2 The old, the ill or the mad. That's how I met Parker, in the old people's home in New York, talking to the old ladies and gents. They were used to loneliness, and smiled and put a brave face on it, and that made my condition easier, easier to smile because they did. The old folks never remembered me, save one, who had gently encroaching dementia, who always exclaimed, "It's Hope! Hope's come to visit us again!"

Then I considered becoming a care-home worker, just to be with people who remembered me, but she had no bladder control and didn't want to eat, not now, not that, that's disgusting, but I'm hungry! and so I visited her every year at Christmas and Easter instead, until she died, quietly in the night.

Walking through the streets of Manchester one day, out to rob a jeweller's. Three months' preparation, set to go in the middle of the jazz festival, the sound of sax and sousaphone to hide the very small but necessary explosive I'd primed for entry.

A voice cried out, "Hope!"

I ignored it, since it hadn't been my name for so long, but there it went again, "Hope! Stop! I want to see Hope!"

A woman's voice, young, shrill and urgent. A kerfuffle, a clatter of metal and rubber, another voice, chiding. I glanced back and there was a girl trying to rise out of her wheelchair, one arm crossed over her body, one side of her face loose from muscular fatigue, but eyes like mine, voice raised high and bright, "Hope!"

My baby sister.

I close my eyes and I count

breath

steps

cracks in the pavement

hairs on my head

stars in the sky

And there is my baby sister, Gracie, not grown-up but getting there, twelve, perhaps – no, thirteen by now, thirteen as of three weeks ago – being wheeled along in a little group of girls and boys. She is alert, awake, uncaring for her disability for what is it to her? Just life; whatever. My Grace, and she said, "Hope! Look! We're going to the station!"

Holding out one hand, summoning me, imperious, to her side. Her carer, a woman with three chins and blonde curling hair sticking out beneath a hand-knitted grey hat, apologised profusely but I said no, it's fine, I don't mind, and knelt down in front of my sister's chair.

She surveyed me, and seeing everything to her satisfaction said, "There was spaghetti for lunch, but I don't like spaghetti so I had pizza instead."

"Did you?" I asked.

"Yes. Tomorrow is Friday so there'll be curry which is all right."

"That's . . . good."

Again, a mumble from the carer, so sorry, you don't need to, it's not at all . . .

I didn't listen. Gracie's hand, shifting an inch, resting in mine. The carer stopped speaking, stared at Gracie, stared at me, her mouth hanging ajar. How often did my sister touch another person? How often was she silent with her hand resting in a stranger's hand?

I said, "She reminds me of my sister; did you say you were going to the station?"

"Yes."

"May I come with you?"

The carer looked at Gracie, her bottom lip turning uncomfortably, professional training coming up hard against the truth of this moment. "What do you think, Grace?" she asked, voice too loud, voice for someone stupid, my sister is not stupid. "Do you want this lady to come with us to the station?"

Gracie nodded, an awkward gesture, head heavy as it dropped, fast, and then slow, rolling back round and up into its erect position.

"It's not a problem," I said. "I'd like to come."

We walked to the station.

Gracie chatted briskly, told me that she liked the colour blue, but not the blue on the bedroom door, that was the wrong blue, but she liked the blue of the nurses, that was a good blue, and she wanted more things to be that blue but never purple she hated purple especially cabbage, cabbage made her sick. And she had been learning to sing she liked singing but she liked painting more I should come and see some of the things she painted at school there were beautiful things she always used blue not purple of course but that was what made beauty, everything beautiful, just like me.

And they'd been learning about science. And animals. And she liked animals, and animals liked her, and when she was grown-up, she'd keep two cats and a dog, but not a zebra, because zebras were horrid things even though they were stripy.

And the carer said, Grace was doing very well, very well indeed, and the school were very proud of how well she was doing and she knew that she'd grow up and be just fine, and that she'd been reading better recently, and her favourite books were the ones where good defeated evil, and her favourite film was *Star Wars*.

Why *Star Wars*? I asked, my hand still in Gracie's.

Because in *Star Wars*, my sister explained, everything works properly. People are good and people are bad and good people do good things and bad people do bad, and there's a good Force and a bad Force and that's how it should be.

She thought about it a moment longer, then added, and sometimes the bad become good, and that's good too, because good is better than bad, obviously.

I found I was crying, just crying, just a girl crying, and the carer asked softly, where's your sister now?

Not so far away, I replied. Not so far.

Chapter 54

Change of place, change of name, change of appearance. Plane to Incheon; air-conditioned coach to Seoul.

A hairdresser in Euljiro said, as she cut the ropes of my hair down to a fuzz above my skull, "I've never cut African hair before. It's just amazing!" and her apprentices gathered round to stare and fumble with the falling knots.

A department store at Myeongdong. I stole a T-shirt, jogging bottoms, thick padded jumper with a grey hood. I stole a smart white shirt, suit trousers, a pair of trainers, a pair of black leather shoes. On the street outside, I bought a slice of pineapple served on a stick from an icy slab, and green-tea ice cream from the doughnut shop beneath the noodle bar. From a stall pushed through the streets on two tiny, creaking wheels, I bought three mobile phones. From an international bookshop above the subway station, I bought a travel guide and a phrasebook.

My hotel was "traditional"; bed mats in bright neon yellow and green rolled out across the floor, Wi-Fi and seventy channels on the TV. By night, red neon crosses blazed from the Protestant churches that lined the railway tracks out of the city. In Itaewon I found hamburgers and American service personnel. I joined them for a meal of ribs and beer, and there was a private who looked at me with wide, terrified, lustful eyes, and he said he was afraid the continued presence of US troops on Korean soil would never allow for peace between the divided nations of the peninsula, and that socio-economic forces were now a greater source of disunity than history herself, and that was strange, because history was a powerful mother, in his opinion, ma'am.

In the morning, my face was on Interpol's most wanted, and more quietly being circulated through the darknet. From a dealer in Yeoksam, I bought three USB drives the size of a fingernail, copied the base code of Perfection onto them, and sent them to PO boxes around the world.

```
whatwherewhy: I'm heading south, towards
Namwon. Find me there.

Byron14: Regretfully, I will comply.
```

A train ride from Seoul, heading south, towards the sea.

A child cheered as the screen showing our speed surpassed 300km/h. A woman in a grey uniform got an electric shock off the door as her flat-heeled shoes rubbed static off the carpet. On the cuttings by the railway track were squeezed vegetable gardens and tiny, two-person paddies, plastic bags tangling on the fences; cars went backwards along the motorway.

A man in a sharp blue suit sat down next to me, stared at me for a long while, though I was avoiding his gaze, and at last said, "Jesus rubs you."

I met his eye, waiting to hear what Jesus might do next. He gave me a leaflet. On the front was a picture of the Saviour in a brown robe and white tunic, holding a startled-looking goose. Behind him two lambs grazed peacefully, and a rabbit nestled against his feet. The title of the piece was "How To Escape Hell And Live Free From Mental Illness".

"Jesus rubs you," repeated the man firmly, pushing the paper into my hand. "Jesus rubs everyone."

So saying, he rose from his seat, and went to spread the word of Jesus' rubbing in his more fluent native tongue.

Mokpo: an industrial city, an ugly port, wide belching roads heavy with lorries, buildings of grey, roofs of iron, a noticeable decline in the number of women on the streets.

The receptionist stared at me as I signed into the hotel, then blurted, "American?"

"Yes."

"Come here for husband?"

"No."

"Come here for lover?"

"No."

Her face crinkled up in bewilderment. "Why you come here?" she asked at last. "I think here no good for you."

At night, in a fast-food dim sum bar off a pedestrianised shopping street, I met a passport dealer whose handle was cantopopisdead. The passport she sold me was French, and I'd requested German.

"This good!" she exclaimed, shovelling pork dumplings between her lips, chewing with mouth open, eyes wide, cheeks bulging with meat, like a woman who isn't sure she will ever eat again. "French good, good work, good passport, you see!"

I considered arguing the point, and decided against it. The passport would be good for one trip and then I'd destroy it, get to the Schengen zone or into the US and pick up something better, from a more reliable source.

Outside a restaurant specialising in fried rooster feet, a waiter struck up a conversation in halting English.

"I don't get to practise very much," he explained, one word at a time. "It is so good that you are come here."

I stayed and talked with him for half an hour, until the mistress of the restaurant came out and shouted at him for neglecting his work, and he ran indoors, no saving face before this matron's wrath.

A woman with Perfection, snubbing the food her partner offered her at the café where I ordered breakfast.

A man with Perfection, updating the app on his phone, a sports bag slung over his back, arms bulked up with protein shakes, chest heaving, sweat on the back of his neck.

A teenager with Perfection, looking at the prices for the perfect haircut.

Open your eyes: it is everywhere.

At night, I sat at a laptop in the hotel, while in the background a twenty-four-hour TV channel showed a top-down view of a go board, over which hands sometimes moved, laying a counter, removing a piece, while off-shot voices "Aaahhed" and "Oooohhed" and sometimes were moved to applaud the elegance of the play.

```
Byron14: I'm in Namwon.

whatwherewhy: I'm in Mokpo.

Byron14: I do not appreciate being led a
dance.
```

```
whatwherewhy: Come to Mokpo; get a mobile
phone.
```

I lie awake, and do not sleep.

I count down from a thousand.

In my dreams Luca Evard is dead, and I killed him.

Chapter 55

The ferry port at Mokpo. Grim, single-storey buildings surrounded by empty car parks. Distant yellow cranes loading and unloading the freight ships. Tourists heavy with bags going to Dadohaehaesang national park, to its mountains and its beaches, its spa resorts bathed in the light of the setting sun.

I call the number that Byron14 has given me and tell her to come to the ferry port.

Her voice, when she answers, is refined, English, soft, and reminds me of Gauguin. I am brisk – too brisk – and something northern comes out in my voice. I sound frightened, didn't realise that was what I am.

Byron14 is easy to spot, as she waits in the terminal. She and I both stand out, but I wait on the other side of the car park with a pair of binoculars, watch the windows, call her mobile phone and say, "Now let's have the real Byron14, please."

The woman who answers is tall, blonde, her hair wrapped up high in a bun, smart suit, two-inch heels. She explains, "I am Byron."

"No you're not," I reply. "Byron was always going to send someone in her place, it was inevitable. I'd like to speak to the real Byron, please."

"I am Byron . . ." the woman tries again, then stops, listening to a sound I cannot hear, then smiles at nothing much, shakes her head, hangs up, walks away.

A moment later, my phone rings, and a different voice, inflected with a hint of something older, warmer, real, says, "Would you be the young lady watching the ferry port from the car park?"

I lower the binoculars, nod at nothing much, looking around but not seeing her. "Would you be Byron14?"

"That I would."

"I'm boarding the 14.03; would you care to join me?"

"I don't care much for these antics, whatwherewhy. We had an understanding, and this sniffs of abuse."

"The 14.03," I repeat. "I'll text it to you, just in case you forget."

I hang up. Rudeness doesn't bother me.

The boat is a catamaran. The skies are grey, the seas are rough enough that sometimes a wave breaks against the bottom of the hull, knocking us up. Every time it happens, the women scream and the men, perhaps in an effort to appear unrattled, convert their screams to great "whaaay" noises, and laugh nervously at each other as the ship settles again. The youngest women make a show of dabbing ineffectually at their sweaty brows. Femininity is fashionable; femininity is frail and prone to giggles. I watch it all, and conclude that femininity can jump into the ocean and drown.

A man approaches me three times – having forgotten that he has approached me before – and asks me my name, where I'm from, where I'm going. The first time I tell him I'm French, I'm a marine biologist, come to study the fauna in Dadohaehaesang, and he says, "Ah" and "Ooh," and sits down next to me and is very boring. I go to the back of the boat, let him forget that I existed, and return to my seat when he is gone. The second time he approaches I tell him I'm meeting my husband on the island, but that doesn't seem to deter him, so on his third pass, I speak French, and inform him I don't understand a word he's saying and finally he leaves me alone, and the journey isn't long enough for him to make a fourth pass.

Byron sits at the very back, spine pressed into her seat, a good place to be, observing all, unobserved. She stands out as much as me, but she is old, and my skin is dark, and she has mastered the art of being worthy of little attention.

I stare at her unashamedly as I walk again to the back of the ferry, and she meets my eye, and recognises me for what I am, but before the moment can linger, I walk on, and she forgets, and I repeat this pattern five or six times, and each time she looks at me for the very first time, and each time I stare rudely, and walk away, until I am confident that her face is embedded in my mind.

She is old; far older than I expected, but strength rolls from her. Her face is all small, straight lines. Little ears flat back against a square skull; a little chin that barely disrupts the box of her jaw. Thin grey lips, pressed to a straight line. Little blue eyes beneath flat, grey brows. Straight silver hair cut to a pudding-bowl across her forehead. Little straight nose to the curve of her top lip. Philtrum, the indent between lips and the base of the nose – in Jewish mythology the angel of conception, Lailah, touched her finger to that curve, and at her touch, the infant forgets all it knows. The curve of the lips, cupid's bow, vermillion border, *labium superius oris*, *labium inferior oris*, does Byron14 smile?

I look at her, and think that sometimes she does, and when she does it must be a beautiful thing to behold. Then I picture her frowning, and that too is easy, and the image is terrifying. Walls fall beneath her glower, minds turn to mush at her gaze; in modern re-imaginings of ancient myths, were there not shinobi who could kill men with their famously un-lyrical piercing-eye technique? Did I read that somewhere, or was it on the TV?

She looks, sees me, recognises me, forgets; even Byron14, even she.

Islands passing by. Hongdo, Heuksando, Baekdo. The fourth island the catamaran stopped at was named for the volcanic mountain at its heart, black rock blurred by the weight of birds nestling in its crags, and was called Yan-ri. Here, at auspicious times, young couples came to be married, the mountain above and the sea below, flowers in bridal hair, proud fathers posing next to silk-clad sons, champagne glasses and ceremonial drums. This time was not auspicious; only four of us got off the ferry, and Byron, seeing me and starting with surprise – surprise to see me, surprise that she had not seen me before – was one. Of the other two, one was a waitress, who rushed away immediately towards a timber and steel hotel upon the hill, her night-bag over her back. The other was a fisherman, his wife waiting to meet him at the end of the slippery, green-washed pier, her arms folded and a woollen hat pulled down across her ears, who exclaimed as he arrived that he wouldn't believe what had happened, and then lost interest in her words as she held him tight.

There were three cars on the island, a man chewing gum informed me in hesitant English. He knew this, for he was the owner of one of them, and the only taxi on the island to boot, and he knew all the places that people could go, and some of the places that people didn't, and he knew both hotels and which was the nicer, and the way to the restaurant by the shore.

I thanked him for his kindness but declined the lift, and looking back, saw Byron, waxy green coat, thick brown trousers, slip her arm into the strap of a grey, stained rucksack and meet my gaze. I nodded back at her, and started the twisting climb up the hill.

Byron followed.

Two hotels: one was little more than a room behind a woman's kitchen, a bedspread rolled across the floor, no curtains but a promise of soup in the morning. I was tempted, but the presence of Byron would have made such accommodation complicated.

Higher up the hill. Cloud on the top of the mountain, hugging the spines of the evergreens. A predatory bird circling overhead, eyeing up smaller birds nestling in the slate roofs below. The rumble of an engine, a great ship out to sea, sound carried on the wind. A woman in a bright skirt that hugged her knees almost too tight to let her walk nodded at me as I walked by. An old man in a grey waterproof jacket, seeing Byron, exclaimed in a mixture of Korean and Japanese that it was outrageous, shocking, marvellous, incredible that a woman of her age should be travelling alone, and called down to me to help this revered older lady, but Byron shook her head and replied – in gently accented Japanese – that she was well, thank you, and would continue climbing.

I saw no shops as I climbed, no sign of industry, apart from a blue tarpaulin on which fish had been laid out to dry.

The hotel at the top of the hill was mostly dark, save for a few lamps burning on the porch. A wooden balcony to one side was built out over a steep drop to afford the best views of the sea. A sign in five languages informed the visitor that the hotel accepted credit cards, but not cheques. Wi-Fi was available for an extra charge in the lobby. The front door was locked, but I rang the bell and a woman with a pinched face, eyes wide, lids rolled too far back to reveal the whites of her eyes, pinching at forehead and cheeks, answered within a minute.

Byron stood behind me, silent, waiting, and I wondered if she felt the same tug of sympathy I did for the woman who opened the gate. Plastic surgery gone wrong, features twisted into something strange, a smile on lips that perhaps hurt to smile. Number of cosmetic surgery procedures performed in South Korea in 2009: 365,000. Number of procedures performed in Brazil 2013: 2,141,257. In the USA: 3,996,631. Most common surgical procedures globally: breast augmentation and liposuction. Most common surgical procedure in Korea: double eyelid surgery. An operation to make eyelids look less "Asian".

Could you be perfect, I wondered, without being white?

£9.99 for 125ml of "royal skin whitening cream". Apply liberally. Gently lightens and tones.

"We give you best room, Ms Smithi," the woman behind the counter said, bobbing in excitement at the sight of a customer in this autumnal time. And then yet more, more, how her delight soared when Byron walked through her door.

"This your friend?"

I turned to look at Byron, and she for the very first time came up to me, stood not a metre away and replied in a flat, southern English accent, just like Gauguin, "We've only just met, but I think we're going to be friends."

"Yes," I replied, and my breath was fast, my heart so fast, I felt the beat of the blood in the side of my throat. "Good friends."

They gave her the room next to mine. Our balconies adjoined. I stood, watching the sea break against volcanic rock, listening to the call of seabirds as they tracked a boat heavy with fish across the waters. The wind, first cool, grew cold, and I let it settle through my skin, slowing my heart, my blood, my breath, until at last Byron came out of her room, and stood on the balcony next to mine, divided by a low fence of woven twigs and a couple of potted plants.

At last she said, "I didn't see you come into the hotel."

Already, our encounter forgotten.

"Or on the ferry," she added.

She fears me; an interesting and not unwelcome development. Byron14 prides herself, perhaps, on her powers of observation, and yet here I am, appearing as if by magic, and that is astonishing, and she is afraid.

I cannot stay in this hotel long; if we are the only guests, the owners are going to be perpetually surprised when they see that I have a key.

"Cup of coffee?" I suggest. "Something to eat?"

"I was thinking I might go for a walk around the mountain. Having come this far."

In no rush: an assertion of her power. She knows I'm not going anywhere.

"That sounds nice. I'll see you when you get back."

She does not go for a walk around the mountain. If she could remember telling me her intentions, she probably would have acted on them. I go running along the beach. The shore is shingle, that turns into sand beneath a shield of hanging trees. I find that I am tired after only a few minutes, and return up the hill to the hotel.

I write a time, a place – the hotel restaurant, hastily cleaned for its unexpected guests – and slip it under her bedroom door.

Shower.

Change.

Plan, backup plan, backup for the backup. Stick too rigidly to a plan, and you may drown in it, but fail to plan ahead, and you will drown for certain.

I wondered where Luca Evard was, and if he thought about me at all.

Chapter 56

The Korean national dish is kimchi.

When travelling, it is important to have an open mind. It permits you to engage in conversation with a stranger, to compliment your host, engage in discourse and find some limited perspective.

I say this as one who tried kimchi with an open mind, and thought it was disgusting. Perhaps, aficionados say, I have not tried the best kinds.

Basic ingredient: cabbage, though cucumber or scallion may be used. Season with brine, chilli, ginger, radish, shrimp sauce, fish sauce, etc. Bury in an earthenware pot, perhaps with a dash of fermented shrimp to help the process, and leave underground for a few months, until the dish is nicely mulched. The first Korean in space, Yi So-yeon, was sent to the stars with some of the most expensive kimchi known to man, after it was specially treated to remove the most harmful bacteria and decrease the odour. Who wants to spend six months in a space station reeking of Grandmother's finest fermented vegetables?

Byron14 was already downstairs, at a table by a wide window that looked towards the sea. We were the only two in the restaurant. As I sat, our hostess put kimchi on the table with the menus, just to get us into the spirit of the meal.

Quiet, a while. The clouds across the sea were turning false-night dark, cutting off the sun, blocking out the sky. The smaller ships were heading to port, the larger freighters seemingly stationary on the horizon, until you looked again, and found they were gone. The light of the restaurant reflected our faces back to us against the glass. I hoped Byron had been to the toilet before she left – I would need her uninterrupted attention.

At last she said, looking at me

(for the first time)

(this time)

"Do you have Perfection?"

I put the USB stick on the table between us.

A flicker in her eyes, a slight pulling in of her breath – surprise? Excitement? Perhaps both.

"That's it?" she asked, eyeing the USB stick.

"That's it."

Her eyes lingered a moment longer than perhaps she wished, then rose to look at me, an active effort, conscious will. Intelligence in every part of her, intelligent enough perhaps to play dumb, to smile and nod at the stupidity of others, no pretence now, she was happy for me to be afraid.

"All this run-around, and you give it to me over dinner?"

"I thought I'd let you pay for the meal."

Byron speaks, soft voice, clipped English accent. "I confess myself perplexed. Why this journey? Why such hassle?"

"I needed to speak to you alone, face-to-face, in an isolated environment away from danger."

"Why?"

"Meeting on my terms gives me control of the situation."

"There are ways to exert control without taking risks."

"Words are complicated. I needed to meet you."

"Well then," she said at last. "Here I am. Was it worth it?"

I tapped the table top, the length of my index finger brushing against the USB stick. "You tell me."

Silence between us. Busy, fluent silence. Impressions made, images found. I let her look, met her eyes, defiance, me, my gaze, let her stare and draw every conclusion she can, it is nothing, it is only now.

A storm building out to sea, no thunder, no lightning, just the wind and the waves, a blotting out of the light.

At last she said, "I didn't see you on the ferry."

"No. You didn't."

"I didn't see you at the port."

"No. Not there either. I have questions."

She half raised her shoulders, chin coming down. "All right then: ask."

I said, "Who is Gauguin?"

A smile in the corner of her mouth, her eyes turn towards the sea, then to the ceiling, then return to me, taking her time. "He used to work for the government."

"And now?"

"Now he works for the Pereyra family."

"Why?"

"Better pension."

"An answer that means something, please."

"Guilt, mostly, I think. We used to be lovers."

So flat, so simple, so easy, a lie? A truth? A truth that sounds like a lie?

She went on, finger running round the edge of the plate of kimchi, not eating. "Rafe and Filipa believe that Matheus Pereyra was murdered. Gauguin feels the same way; more, he feels he should have been able to prevent it. He feels remorse at having failed to do so."

"Was he murdered?"

"The coroner gave an open verdict. There were ambiguities in the toxicology report."

"Does Gauguin think you killed Matheus?"

"Yes."

"Did you?"

She drew in her lips for a second, then puffed them out, smiled, looked at me without remorse or joy, said, "Yes."

She knows what she will give, she knows what she will take.

"Why?"

"Numerous reasons; do you care?"

"Gauguin connected me to you. If he hadn't, I don't think he would have cared. You landed me in the middle of your mess."

"That's not entirely true."

"Isn't it?"

"No," she mused, assembling her thoughts gently, voice light. "Of course not. You chose to steal the Chrysalis from Dubai. You chose to do so in the middle of Rafe's most important public event, in front of the eyes of the world. You chose to humiliate him, damage the prospects of Perfection in the UAE. You made your own bed and slept in it, and myself and Gauguin were merely drawn by the snoring."

"I just wanted the diamonds."

"Did you? There were other ways to steal them that didn't involve humiliating Rafe."

"I wanted ..." My words trailed off. I turned to watch the clouds darkening over the sea, a long way off, the horizon vanishing where sea became shadowed sky.

Byron adjusted her chopsticks, waited. In the East, never leave your chopsticks in a bowl of rice when you finish eating; to do so is an offering for the dead. Other traditions: four is an unlucky number, 四, sì, it has the sound of death, 死, also always remember that ... that ... fuck it. Whatever.

She waited for me to grow uncomfortable, waited for my thoughts to run amok, control gone, words and denials spinning uselessly through the part of my brain where discipline should have been. Waited a little moment longer, then said, her eyes indicating the USB stick between us, "I assume this isn't the only copy."

"No. Why did you kill Matheus?"

"I'm not sure this is that conversation."

"It is, believe me."

She sucked in breath, then let the words all out, controlled and practised. "Perhaps because he was responsible for the deaths of many thousands of people. Not by killing them himself, of course. Matheus was much more than a media mogul; he invested in politics, lobbied extensively, commanded campaigns. This is nothing out of the ordinary; he was a man with money and an ideology. Ideology colours truth. When a paper was produced suggesting, for example, that eating lemongrass was as effective a cure for cancer as chemotherapy, he ordered his editors to run the story. Naturally, the study was written by a crackpot and was instantly dismissed, but he gave it a voice. A policeman gunned down a child, cop called heroic at Pereyra's command, the child slandered as a thief, irredeemable aged thirteen. The cop was white, the boy was black; it's a common story. An electoral campaign based on hating the foreigner, the poor, the unknown, every lie of course destroyed by experts – but Matheus Pereyra did not print the views of the experts, but rather . . . printed the screaming. Always, the world screaming, loudly, screaming.

"Back then I was still working for the government, and one day I got a phone call saying Matheus was going to run a story about an MP's ex-wife. The MP was being tried for corruption – he had cooked the books, sold £1.3 billion of public assets to a bunch of his mates for £400 million, taking a pleasant £150 million commission in the process. His mates were old uni pals; pals of Matheus too. But he'd also been beating his wife, and one day she had enough, packed up all his records, proof of what he'd done, and went to the police.

"We put her in witness protection, new name, new identity. Matheus found her. The headline was 'The Face of Treachery', followed by a four-page exposé, painting her as a drug addict, adulteress, liar. Photos of her, where she lived, her kids. I told them the story was embargoed, court order. Don't run it; you will compromise an ongoing investigation. I went to the top, to Matheus himself. And he just looked at me and said, 'Get over it, bitch.'"

She repeated his words distantly, a thing half recalled, made inhuman with too much contemplation.

"The corruption case collapsed, of course, and the MP stood again in a safe seat, and won; and the day after he got the kids back, his wife took an overdose. Didn't die – these things are difficult to get right. We took Matheus to court for compromising an ongoing case. He lost, ordered to pay a fine of £75,000. He laughed, when he heard that. 'Get over it, bitch,' he said and of course he was right. He would do what he wanted, and that was that, and the most you could do was get over it. Words screamed loud enough: 'The prime minister lied', 'It caused heart disease', 'The immigrant murdered his landlady'. All those lives destroyed, the suffocation of debate, the raising up of noise over content, the simplification, objectification, the brutal destruction of thought that he committed against all mankind. The dead who refused to take the medicine because lemongrass would work, the guns that were fired because he's an extremist who took our job, the women branded sluts, whores, *bad mothers*, the ones who got away with it because they knew which hands to shake – and you wonder why someone would want him to die?"

I nodded at nothing much, thought of Luca Evard, tried, without much conviction: "This is the modern world – there are resources, means to find justice . . . "

"Such as."

"Truth."

"Meaningless, if you cannot make it heard."

"The law."

"Not if you don't have money to pay for it."

"History is full of battles being won by the oppressed against the great."

"Is it? Cite me a meaningful victory. When the Bhopal disaster hit, over three thousand people died and half a million people were injured or disabled. The outcome? Seven ex-employees of the chemical company were sentenced to two years in prison each and a fine of $2,000. The parent company was fined $450 million and is now the third-largest producer of batteries in the world. Deepwater Horizon, eleven dead and nearly five million barrels of crude oil spilt into the sea. BP fined $4.5 billion. BP profit in 2013: $23.7 billion. Would you like more personal numbers? Inter-racial hatred, discrimination on grounds of religion, gender; reportage on climate change, on scientific development, on medical breakthrough, versus reports on immigration numbers, violent crime and celebrity personality, shall we break down the truth, the bitter, unloved, bloody-nosed truth? Tell me, in a world where wealth is power, and power is the only freedom, what would desperate men not do to be heard?"

"Civil rights, sexual emancipation, freedom of speech, the abolition of slavery—"

"Economic necessities. In 1789 the French rebelled and found an emperor. The Americans found freedom from the British and enslaved the Africans. The Arab Spring bloomed and the military and the jihadists seized power. The internet gave us all the power of speech, and what did we discover? That victory goes to he who shouts the loudest, and that reason does not sell. Have you never heard priests proclaim that the meek will inherit the earth and wondered if the kings of old didn't smile to hear it? Your reward comes after death. Nirvana. The wheel of life turns and we are elevated from animals to women, from women to men, from men to kings, from kings to gods, from gods to . . . perfection. And what is perfection now? Not crucifixion, not poverty endured patiently on the mountaintop. No – the perfect life is to have an annual salary of £120,000, an Aston Martin, a £1.6-million-pound home, a wife, two children and at least two foreign holidays a year. Perfection is an idol built upon oppression. Perfection is the heaven that kept the masses suppressed; the promise of a future life that quells rebellion. Perfection is the self-hatred an overweight woman feels when she sees a slim model on TV; perfection is the resentment the well-paid man experiences when he beholds a miserable millionaire. Perfection kills. Perfection destroys the soul."

Silence.

She had not raised her voice. These words had been spoken a hundred times before, though perhaps only to herself. Across the sea the sun was down, reflection from its passage bouncing off the water and the underside of the clouds, black and gold. Our hostess, seeing an opportunity to strike, darted between us with a cry of "You ready order?"

Byron played it safe, ordered vegetarian, cabbage and noodles, broth and egg. I picked a plate at random and smiled faintly as our menus were collected, glasses taken away. Neither she nor I were drinking tonight.

Silence.

"Get rich," she said at last. "Get thin. Get medicines. Get a car. Get married. Get perfect."

"Sometimes it's hard to know what your life is worth."

A flicker in the corner of her mouth, contempt, perhaps? She is still unknown to me. That's fine; I'll follow her to the ends of the earth, meet her a hundred times until I know her.

"'Worth' is a concept almost as dangerous as 'perfect'," she said. "'Worthy', to be—"

"Important. Honourable. Having merit or value. Possessing qualities that merit recognition and attention."

"And are we not worthy?" she asked, rolling the end of one ceramic chopstick back and forth between the thumb and index finger of her right hand. "Are our lives devoid of merit? Are we not generous to our friends, kind to strangers, skilled in our areas of expertise, reliable with rent, gentle with children, quick to phone an ambulance when we see a man hit by a car, thoughtful in word and deed? Do we not have worth enough? Are we not already perfect? Perfectly ourselves? Perfect in being who we are?"

"I have no one to measure that quality against."

"Do you believe in God?"

"No."

"Do you have eyes, judgement?"

"And I see the world, but I have no one else's eyes to measure my own vision against."

"Of course you do. You have the words of friends and strangers. You have discourse and reason. You have critical thought, which may be trained to the highest degree. In short, you do not *need* the world to tell you what to be. Especially if the world tells you that you are never good enough."

"I am a thief," I said, and for the first time since . . . I was not sure how long . . . the words were not proud. Almost . . . angry, perhaps.

Again, a little shrug: these things don't matter to her. "Were we living in a different time, perhaps ballads would be sung to your honour. In this day and age, 0.7 per cent of the world owns 48 per cent of its wealth. Is thief such an indictment?"

"Yes," I snapped, surprised at my own vehemence. "If I stole for a cause, perhaps; if I stole for anything that mattered . . . "

"It is worthy to live," she corrected, "when the alternative is to die. Life is precious."

"But Matheus Pereyra died."

"And his children built Perfection – life is complicated. It defies mathematical ordering or the scales of justice."

I leant forward on the table, twining my fingers, resting my chin on the arch of my hands. "Why not kill Filipa?" I asked. "She built Perfection."

"Better to kill Rafe – he turned it from a science project into something he could sell. Filipa has always been a frightened infant; she thought she could program people to be smarter, kinder, braver, because these are all the things she is not. Rafe saw her work and transformed it into an algorithm that makes rich people richer, poor people poorer; that divides the 'them' from the 'us' and profits from the self-doubt of humanity. He made the 106."

"There have always been elites. Three quarters of the UK cabinet are millionaires. Winning a seat in the US Congress costs anywhere in the region of ten million US dollars. The 106 is nothing new."

"But the treatments are."

My breath stuck in my throat. She saw it, saw me fight not to show it, saw me lose, smiled at my effort. I realise that I am afraid – very much afraid – of Byron14. "Tell me about them."

"What have you observed?"

"You have everything Filipa ever created for Perfection here," I replied, tapping the USB stick. "The code of the app, the names of people who used it, the science behind the treatments – and at cut-price too. Tell me what I want to know."

A sigh, overplayed, she leant back in her chair. This is one of the many things she is willing to give for free, a little truth, perhaps, to smooth over all the lies. "The treatments were created by Filipa Pereyra. An awkward child punished for being awkward which of course made her more awkward. She has learned a degree of skill in covering it now, but it is only an . . . algorithm, shall we say. A routine learned by the numbers, as she tries to compute her way through life. I would say that she is very lonely."

I think she is.

(You are a stranger to me. Is it you?)

(How excited she had been to meet me, that last time.)

"Go on," I breathed.

"She studied the mind. Her family let her; no point involving the sister in affairs of business, that was all going to the brother – but her research grew expensive, difficult. They didn't fully comprehend what she was working on, not until she went bankrupt, too much of her own funding poured into the effort. This was some . . . two, three years after her father died? Rafe bailed her out, but he is a businessman more than a brother. The price was her research. She accepted, of course. Didn't matter to her who owned her work, so long as she could keep going. The treatments began as an experiment to help children with severe speech impediments. I believe there is something to do with electrodes – it's all very technical."

Deep brain stimulation. Use of an electric probe to induce weak electric current, causing activity in otherwise unstimulated parts of the brain. A largely untried tool, though some promising developments in treatment of depression, schizophrenia, stroke – further research required.

(Where had I read that? In Tokyo, in the hotel, researching Filipa. "All thought is feedback," she said. "Repetition of a thought strengthens neural paths." A simple sentence, easy to say in a hurry, assured not to cause offence, and within it, the building-blocks of consciousness.)

Byron, less interested in the how than the what. "The results were of limited interest to Rafe, of course. He could sell them for a bit, but they weren't something he could advertise in the papers. Then his sister told him what the ultimate aim of her research was, and of course, he became far more interested."

"And what was the ultimate aim?" I asked, sensing the answer already, tired by the suspicion, about to become certainty.

"To make everyone better. All people. Perfection is just a lifestyle tool. Positive activities are rewarded, negative punished – nothing new. The treatments are the next step. You take an ordinary human mind, with all its flaws and fears, and impose upon it a . . . " a pause, a smile, Byron chuckling over the word, no humour in her laugh, " . . . a 'better' pattern. From doubt – confidence. From terror – bravery. Anxiety becomes ambition; humility becomes assurance. The treatments edit out the patterns of human behaviour which are considered imperfect, character flaws you might say, and replace it with a model of humanity that is . . . shall we say – and I think here we should – shall we say 'perfect'? The perfect man. The perfect woman. In and of itself, an appealing idea, perhaps. Filipa was in love with it – not with the concept of perfection, but with the very simple notion that she could make people better. When she began, she could give a voice back to the speechless, help people suffering from depression to find a level from which they could begin to rebuild. She programmed away phobias, helped the shy woman speak in front of a crowd of her peers, all with science. Easier to do science, for Filipa, than human things, I think. Then Rafe took her product, and redefined the end goals. No longer was success the overcoming of extreme anxiety – treatments were to be offered to the 106, to help this new elite become something more. Rafe asked himself what behaviours it would be … *sexy* to reinforce. What it was that his buyers might want to become. He found perfection. A perfection defined by the magazines and the TV soaps, by movie stars and captains of industry. Perfectly charming. Perfectly refined. Perfectly confident. Perfectly ambitious. Perfectly a monster – would you go so far?"

Parker, smiling at me in Tokyo. Refusing to help when I was burning in Istanbul.

"Yes," I said. "I think I would."

"Filipa has created a device to make everyone perfect, and the same. Perfection sells Nirvana in an electromagnet."

Nirodha and *magga*, freedom from *samsara*, the end of the Buddhist eightfold path.

"Perhaps it is a kind of heaven," I mused. "Perhaps the 106, when they are perfect, are also free."

"Perhaps they are," she replied, rolling the chopsticks between her fingers. "Free from doubt, anxiety, guilt, compassion, empathy, and all that it brings. It will only be a matter of time before the treatments are rolled out to more than just the 106 Club. They are a good test sample; volunteers, monitored through Perfection. But Rafe sees the profit in it, and I have no doubt it will sell. Can you imagine a world in which everyone has treatments? Can you imagine a planet covered in happy, smiling, perfect clones?"

"Yes. I think I can."

"And are you not appalled?" she mused, laying the chopsticks down on the edge of her mat, over-played surprise on her face. "It is obscene."

"Many things are obscene – what makes this your battle?"

"Ah, I see – may I not simply have a cause? Environmentalists protest against climate change, and yet Arctic meltwaters haven't hurt their puppies yet."

"You won't tell?"

"Will you tell me why you stole the Chrysalis diamonds?"

"I wanted to fuck up some spoilt rich people. I wanted them scared and humiliated. My friend – she wasn't my friend – had Perfection, and was very alone, and I didn't spot it, and she died, and they didn't give a fuck and I thought . . . fuck them. It was a momentary lapse in my professionalism."

"It sounds like a cause to me."

"It wasn't; it simply wasn't. You won't tell me?"

Byron picked at a piece of kimchi with the end of her chopsticks and didn't answer.

I sat back in my chair, arms folded. The USB was between us, and for a moment I considered walking out, throwing it into the sea, see if that wiped the smile from her face.

Neither of us moved. At last I said, indicating the stick with my chin, "What will you do with the information on this?"

"Imagine."

"No. I have spent a lot of time imagining. Sometimes fantasies need to stop."

"I will sabotage Perfection, destroy it from within. I will show humanity that it is obscene, and no one will forget."

I flinched, and she saw the motion, didn't understand it, a flicker of a frown. I licked my lips, looked down and to the side, asked the floor, "Will people die?"

"Perhaps." The USB stick between us, the base-code of Nirvana, heaven without doubt, a world without fear. Her head, tilted slightly to one side, eyebrows raised. "Is that a problem?"

"Perhaps. I think . . . yes."

"To destroy Perfection, I must destroy Rafe's ability to sell it. To prevent people seeking treatments of their own accord, the damage must be significant."

"There are ways to achieve that which don't involve corpses."

"Perhaps you're right. Perhaps not."

Silence. I opened my mouth to say this is obscene, all of it, laughable, obscene, unworthy, we, unworthy, we ourselves unworthy, to judge, to be, to speak, a killer and a thief, ridiculous, of course, simply ridiculous.

No words came.

Instead, our hostess. Ceramic bowls full of broth and noodle, cabbage and strips of fried tripe, fish balls and, of course, more kimchi, to burn the taste away.

Byron was good with chopsticks. Held the bowl up with both hands to blow steam away from the surface. Slurped down soup, no need for spoons.

I said, "Can you replicate the treatments?"

"If this contains all of Tokyo's data? Yes."

"Can you strip out Rafe's programming?"

"Why?"

"There are parts of Filipa's design that deserve to survive. You said it began as speech therapy, as a treatment for depression . . ."

"Once you start attempting to reprogram the human brain from without, there's no stopping it," she retorted, harder and sharper than I think she'd meant.

"Hasn't that always been the argument against all science? Gene therapy, retrovirals, plant modification, atomic energy . . ."

"From which we have the potential to cure cancer, crops that can sustain a human population in the billions, drug-resistant bacteria and the nuclear bomb," she snapped. "I am no Luddite, but if the history of humanity has taught us anything it is that we are children, and this is not a toy we should use."

"I think you're wrong," I replied. "I think there is something within Filipa's treatments that could help me. I agree with you on practically everything you've said – I agree that they are obscene, and what they have become is vile. But the fundamental technology, as Filipa intended it, is neither good nor bad, merely a tool. I think it will help me become something I haven't been for a very long time, and I need to know if you have the ability to unpack that information, or if I need to go back to Filipa to get what I need."

Surprise, whole and true, a flash across her face. My voice had risen, our hostess was staring from across the room. Byron put the bowl down, chopsticks to one side, took a moment to gather her thoughts, at last breathed, "Do you want treatments?"

I let out a breath that had been cramping somewhere at the bottom of my stomach, and said, "Yes."

"In the name of God, *why*?" Horror, indignation, incomprehension, of me, of herself. Could she think she had begun to know me and now discovered that she had been so wrong?

"Because people forget me," I replied. "And I've been lonely for too long. And it was fine. I was doing fine. I had my . . . my rules. Run, count, walk, speak, knowledge, always, knowing things, filling up that place where . . . where there should be other things, things like . . . like work or friends or . . . but I was fine. I was doing fine. Because that's what had to be done, it was . . . and then I saw Parker. The one and only Parker of New York, remembered the words, remembered writing them, reading them – didn't remember him. He's had treatments, though. And I remember him now."

Byron, pressing her chopsticks flat together, then lifting both her hands and gently interlacing the fingers, a conscious act, a physical reminder to herself to be something, or not to be something else. Neuro-linguistic programming; a rubber band around the wrist. Swish and I am something else, swish and I am calm. She was calm; she was calmness.

Swish swish. Whatever I do, in this moment, I am terrified.

Slowly, comprehending/not comprehending, eyebrows down, lips tight: Byron, considering.

To consider: to turn over in one's mind. To think carefully.

> Consider the lilies of the field whose bloom is brief
> We are as they
> Like them we fade away
> As doth a leaf

Does knowledge hold back tears? "Consider", poem, Christina Rossetti, b.1830, d.1894, does knowledge drown out the place where fantasy should be, imagination, dreams of friends and love? Does breath fill the void where I should have humanity, grown and nurtured by human experience, experience of humans? Am I nothing more than this?

(Google search: perfect woman. Lips like celebrity x, hair like celebrity y, husband, car, house, diamond ring, young, white, child, maybe two – there was a time when I wanted to be perfect, nothing stood in my way because there was no one around me, behind me, with me, only myself, only my will, Nietzsche, will to power, Christianity, the triumph of weakness, words always words and thoughts and words and shut up shut up shut up!!)

Then she said, "To be forgotten is to be free, you know that, don't you?"

Easy, an easy thing, a tiny part of a greater argument, I heard the words and my hands hit the table so hard and fast that soup sloshed over the side of her bowl, cutlery tinkled, she jumped and I screamed, "*I have never been free!*"

My voice, loud enough to make the hostess duck, loud enough to frighten all other noise, so that the silence, when now it came, had the room to itself, deafening.

I am my breath. I am my ragged, gasping breath. I am rage. I am my tears – when did they come? I am injustice. I am damnation. I am here, I am real, remember me, remember this, how could anyone forget? How can you look on my red eyes and my blotched face, hear my voice, and forget me? Are you even human? Am I?

At last, she said, and she was kind, "All right."

I am my fingers gripping the table.

I am the table.

Body of plastic and metal.

I am cold.

I am the sky growing dark outside.

I am the washing sea.

Tears are merely salt water and warmth on my face; nothing more. Chemicals. Mucin, lysozyme, lactoferrin, lacritin, glucose, urea, sodium, potassium, that's all tears are. A biological mechanism for the cleansing of the eye. Curious fact: tears of emotion have a slightly different chemical composition than basal or reflexive tears.

I am knowledge.

And again, Byron says, and there is so much kindness in her voice, an old woman smiling at me across the table, resisting the temptation, perhaps, to put her hand in mine, "All right."

I made her write down the terms of our bargain.

Why: having delivered the base code of Perfection, Byron14 to give to Why, as soon as available, access to and knowledge of treatments such as may make her memorable.

Signed by both.

Neither of us offered up thoughts on what would happen in the face of betrayal. It would have been rude.

I took a photo of the napkin on which our deal was struck; so did she. Then I made her take a photo of me, my face, holding the napkin beneath it. She asked why; I said to remember.

She didn't ask why again.

We ate dinner, and she told me a joke she'd heard once from a Russian oligarch about fish. It was long, and surprisingly dirty.

I felt the salty lines on my skin where tears had dried, but they were someone else's tears. I was only my voice. I told her the one about the patriarch, the rabbi and the mullah.

She laughed, hearty and true, and when the bill came paid without asking, and looked out at the now-dark sea and said, "How shall we keep in contact?"

"I will send you a message with my instructions. You keep the napkin – a reminder of your commitments."

"I am not likely to forget."

"No," I replied, without rancour. "You will forget. But I'll help you remember."

"We have a deal, though I don't understand your terms."

We shook hands. There were thin calluses, reinforced and softened by repetition, on the bends of her right hand. I wondered if she had children, and imagined that if she did, they must love her very much.

"You are an extraordinary woman, Why," she mused. "Strange as it has been, I am glad to have made your acquaintance."

"My name is Hope," I replied. "You'll have the opportunity to make my acquaintance again."

I waited for our hostess to clear away the dishes, put my napkin on the table by the USB stick, smiled politely, and was gone.

Chapter 57

Things that I miss about being remembered:

- Friendship
- Love
- Company
- Truth
- Understanding
- Perspective

Things it is impossible to do alone:

- Build a monument
- Kiss
- Get references
- Play poker
- Talk through problems with a friend

A question: is it worth letting Filipa stick electrodes in my skull, erasing every aspect of who I am and what I believe in, if it permits me to be remembered?

I lie awake in the night, and have no idea.

Chapter 58

The ferry back to Mokpo.

Byron was on it, sitting in the same spot again, eyebrows drawn, fists tight balls in her lap. Had she slept last night? There were dark rims round her eyes, perhaps she'd been kept awake by the sound of the sea.

I passed her a couple of times, and she looked surprised every time, marvelling that her powers of observation had let her down.

I smiled once, frowned once, ignored her the third time, returned to my seat with a bottle of flat fizzy water, took a sip, returned to watching the sea.

Climbing off the ferry in Mokpo, knees loose after the sea, Byron briefly looked concerned, but shook her head and walked briskly into town, no need to consult a map.

I followed her to the station. She saw me several times, but as each time was the first time, she made nothing of it. She bought three tickets to three different destinations, boarded the first train, then got off as the doors were about to close; I stumbled foolishly after her, she saw me, my cover totally blown, but again, fine, she would forget.

She boarded the second train, a slower service that crawled through flat countryside and low, perfectly round hills towards Daegu. I sat a few seats away, discovered that my chair could turn one hundred and eighty degrees, giggled at this revelation, soon grew bored. In Daegu she took a room in a motel, and I took the room next to hers, and that night, when she went to find something to eat, I broke in and went through everything she owned, which was:

- Five pairs of pants, black
- Seven pairs of socks, grey

- Two bras, black
- Two shirts, one white, one grey, linen and cotton
- Two pairs of jeans, blue
- Three passports – one British, one French, one Canadian, in three names
- One combat knife, ceramic
- One toothbrush
- One tube of toothpaste
- One bottle of eyedrops
- One pair of reading glasses, flexible metal, powerful lens in the left, marginally weaker lens in the right, creating two different worlds as I peered through them
- One traveller's guide to Korea
- One copy of the international edition of *Die Welt*, five days old
- One bottle of sleeping pills, unopened
- One laptop, password protected

A single hair had been stuck down with saliva over the laptop lid. I removed it, popped the laptop's internal shell, inserted a tiny flash drive I'd purchased from a dealer in Seoul. I sealed the computer again, licked the hair to return it to its place, and photographed everything in sight.

Neither the Tokyo USB stick nor the napkin on which we'd written our bargain was anywhere to be found.

In a café across the street from Gyesan cathedral, a low building of red brick and fluted arches, I drank cheap coffee and gnawed on the tough, crackling curl of chicken legs served in a plastic bag, and contacted Byron14 again.

```
whatwherewhy: To remind you of our
bargain. You will give me access to all
your research into treatments. You will
help me develop a protocol for myself.
```

Byron14: So I see from a napkin in my possession. I see it has my signature – though I do not remember signing it.

whatwherewhy: I trust you on this.

Byron14: Strange that trust should live amongst thieves.

whatwherewhy: You have an honest face.

Byron14: You have seen it? I would be fascinated to see yours.

whatwherewhy: I am the woman in the photo on your phone.

Byron14: I do not remember taking it.

whatwherewhy: But the photo is there. Contact me when you are ready to honour your side of the bargain.

Byron14: Are you following me, whatwherewhy?

whatwherewhy: No.

I logged off.

I sought company in Daegu, but the best I could come up with was a production of *Turandot* at the Daegu Opera House. The audience in the stalls wore black tie and silk; the Chinese princess was played by an Albanian, the Persian prince by a Korean, the desperate woman who dies for love by an Argentinian. As Liu stabbed herself to death for the sake of the man who wanted to marry the princess who was torturing her, a woman in the third row from the front screamed in horror, and I wondered what personal tragedy had driven her to such a big reaction to a bad plot. At the end of every act the leads came in front of the curtain to curtsey and bow, and when the final curtain fell the sopranos held bunches of flowers passed to them by a stagehand, and the audience stood to cheer.

I achieved only ten minutes of conversation with an old lady with flawless English who'd learned it, she informed me, from her time as secretary to an American general who'd stayed in Korea after the civil war.

"Then all we wanted was unity," she sighed, "now people don't think we are the same species as our Northern sisters, let alone the same country. We all say we hope the regime will collapse, but when it does, who will tell the people of the North not to rise up and kill us all? Perhaps things are best left as they are."

"Do you believe that?"

She twisted her lips, tilted her tiny, bird-like neck forward and up, considering the matter. "I think it's complicated. I don't know anyone who tries to work out problems for people by numbers, except generals and prime ministers. I don't think there's good mathematics for what war does to people."

I wanted to ask her more, but the bell rang and the interval ended, and at the end of the opera, the prince kissed the princess and I looked away, unable to stomach it.

In the morning, I woke to find Byron gone. The hotel hadn't called her a cab, they had no idea where she was going, but there were only so many places she could be. I caught a taxi to the station, looked for her desperately, did not find her, cursed my arrogance in thinking I could track her, went to the nearest internet café, turned on my laptop and sat down to wait.

Four and a half hours of waiting, and when at last Byron came online I laughed with relief. The tracker I'd lodged into the internal hardware of her machine took a little while to pinpoint her, zooming steadily in on the map, but at last put her in a hotel in Gyeonju. By the time I reached the hotel, she was out I knew not where, but I stole the master door key from reception and slipped into her room, and all was at it should be, socks folded, a shirt drying by the sink, TV off, a single mattress rolled out across the wooden floor, sleeping bag open and ready for use. I couldn't find her laptop, but checking my own I registered her in a café a few streets away, and went to watch her eating dumplings with one hand, attention all on the screen and her work. My USB stick was lodged in the laptop's side, data being copied, transferred, digested. It was enough – for now, enough.

The next morning I was up at 5 a.m., and at 6 a.m. I heard her alarm go off. I sat a few tables away at breakfast, followed her into the streets, caught the train to Bulguk-Dong, watched as she surveyed the empty roads and quiet white hotels leading up to the temple on its hill. A town for tourists, hotels offering services in Korean, Japanese, Chinese, Russian, English, French, German, Spanish. A single supermarket for the few residents who remained, a tourist office, round with a sloping roof, a woman inside who handed Byron a leaflet and said, "It's very long way for you to come."

A car park, half full, a yellow dirt path heading uphill through the trees. I followed Byron fifteen paces behind, climbing towards the temple hidden on its hill, Bulgaska, ministry-designated *Korea Historic and Scenic Site No. 1*, do not forget to see visitor centre (newly opened) and grotto (sacred, hidden amongst the hills). Buddhist swastika carved into ancient timbers; autumnal red-leaved trees hanging over still ponds where ancient orange carp swim, watched by a curious grey kitten that senses supper.

There were no other humans on the winding climb to the grotto, just she and I, walking. A stone bench on the left, after a mile or so; a symbol of a boddhisattva carved into the cliff, a river running swiftly, trees loose in the breeze.

A pair of Korean tourists, descending the other way, all backpack and big camera, smiled at Byron as they passed, nodding their greeting. They smiled again at me, eyes bright, watchful, and continued on their way. I listened to their footsteps in the leaf and gravel behind me, a regular pattering of stones running downhill from their passage, and had walked another three or four yards before it occurred to me that their footsteps had stopped. I looked back over my shoulder, and there they were, staring up at me, still smiling their polite, interested smiles. I moved away, saw Byron ahead, her back to me, still, eyes down. I kept walking, then stopped. She turned, phone in her hand. My picture was on the screen.

"Oh," I said, as she examined the photo, my face, comparing it to me, me to it. "Hello again," I added, glancing over my shoulder – the tourists perhaps not tourists at all now, a definite something in the way they moved, the way they watched.

"Hello, Why," said Byron.

A flicker of doubt, a moment where my stomach caught, but my voice was steady. "Hello, Byron."

"Can I ask how many times we've met?"

"Only once, properly."

"In Dadohaehaesang?"

"Yes. We had dinner."

"I thought we must have. The bill seemed more than one person could eat, though I remembered eating alone."

The two tourists, definitely not tourists, close now, an arm's reach behind me, not exactly aggressive, neither about to go away.

"Any other times?" she enquired.

"We spoke on the phone in Mokpo."

"Did we? I received a text message telling me to get on a ferry, but you weren't there."

"I was."

"And on the ferry back?"

"Yes."

"And on the train?"

"Yes – all the way."

"You're following me?"

"Of course."

"How?"

"Not very successfully, at this moment, but that'll probably pass."

"As in . . . how do I not remember you?"

"I have a condition."

"What manner of condition?"

"Wherever I go, people forget me."

"You mean . . ."

"I mean," I explained simply, "people forget me."

A slow nodding, a time to think. Then, without looking away from my face, she reached into her pocket, and pulled out another mobile phone. Softly, "I recorded our dinner conversation. I have every word. I'm recording this now."

Wind through the trees, the swastika carved into the path, symbol for lucky or auspicious object in Hinduism and Buddhism, symbol of death in Europe and the West.

I looked from Byron to the not-tourists, and back again. I said, "Close your eyes. Count to sixty."

She hesitated, then closed her eyes. I closed mine too, felt the wind on the back of my neck, the slope of the path beneath my feet, time running by, and I didn't need numbers, didn't need to think, the time came and I was still.

Heard a little intake of breath, hard and scared, opened my eyes, saw Byron looking at me, her phone held knuckle-tight in her hand, hair ruffled by the breeze, mouth open, eyes tight.

Silence a while. Byron nodded with her chin, and one of the tourists took my rucksack from my back, and I didn't fight her. She riffled through its contents, checked my phone, found nothing, patted me down, thorough, hands down my arms, my chest, my legs, feeling round my ankles, nothing of interest, looked through my wallet, passport, ticket stub from the train. No weapons were produced, but we were four strangers on a path through the woods, and I didn't know what the tourists carried beneath their bright blue anoraks.

All the while, Byron watched. Fascinated now, unable to hide it, enthralled, until she blurted, "How do I forget you?" The tightness in her face was more than curiosity, more than a flush of success. It was almost erotic in its intensity.

I shrugged. "Just happens."

"Please." Contempt, insult, what an answer.

"If I knew, I wouldn't have followed you."

"*I'm* involved?"

"The treatments that Filipa developed made the only one of my kind I have ever met memorable. It erased his kindness, his intelligence and his soul, but I can remember him. That gives me two choices – I can go to Filipa and beg that she repeats the process on me, minus the eradication of my heart and mind – or I can give the information to you, with the understanding that you will one day do for me what I cannot do alone – make me memorable. As you cannot remember this bargain apart from the physical evidence it leaves behind, I'm here, following. Why did you record our conversation?" I asked.

An easy answer, sharp and true. "Because I'm getting old. My memory is excellent, but a nuance may make itself apparent in the second or third listening."

"And how did you recognise me?"

"I have your photo."

"That's . . . never usually enough."

"I stared at it for hours, but no matter how hard I looked, I couldn't remember you. So I remembered words. I created mnemonics to capture your description, and remembered the process of remembering. Gender, height, age, hair, eye colour, clothes – just words, useless without a face but, here, enough perhaps. Enough that if I led you to an empty path there could be no doubt. You don't use a machine?" Incredulous, trying to fathom it out.

"No."

"Have you drugged me?"

"No. You saw me," I replied. "Then you forgot."

"*How?!*"

"I said: it just happens."

"That isn't possible."

Her eyes moved to the two tourists who stood behind me. "Do you remember me closing my eyes? Do you remember this woman standing here?" she demanded.

"Yes, ma'am," said the woman, and, "Yes, ma'am," said the man, their voices softly accented, a hint of American perhaps in their English.

"They had a physical contact with me," I explained. "Their eyes were open, I did not fade in their short-term memory. People only forget when the conversation stops. You'll forget this moment too, even though you have your recordings."

She nodded, slowly. Questions came, questions went, none seeming suitable. For a minute, now for two, we stood. Now two minutes are three, now three are four, and I realise that Byron is counting. She is counting backwards slowly from sixty, and then from sixty again, using the rhythm of the numbers to settle her mind, to suppress a torrent of hypotheticals, of might and maybe, of impossible and probable, proven and inexplicable, boiling her thoughts down to just this moment, and the thing that must happen. The revelation brought a single gasp of laughter to the top of my throat, which I swallowed down before it could break, and so we waited.

Sixty, and sixty more. Then, as if time were nothing, and the wind had not blown and the present had not become the past, she looked up and said simply, "If I ask you to come with me, will you?"

"Probably not."

"I won't hurt you."

"You might not remember that promise."

"Please: come with me."

"No. Sooner or later you'll need to sleep, and when you sleep, you'll forget."

"I remembered our conversations online."

"I leave a memorable footprint. You will remember reading words I've written – it's just my face and my actions that vanish."

"So I will forget this conversation, but if you transcribed it and emailed it to me, I'd remember it?"

"You'd remember the transcription; it's a different thing."

"You want treatments."

"Yes."

"Then as you say, you have a choice – either go to Filipa and let her wipe your soul, or stay with me."

Seas eroded the land. Volcanoes rose from the centre of the earth, molten basalt turned to stone, ash fell, the world turned. The moon waxed and waned, waxed and waned, slowed in its orbit, drifted into space. The sun grew fat and red, the graves of the dead turned to fossilised stone.

I said, "I'm hungry. Do you know if there's anywhere round here that does sandwiches?"

Chapter 59

Her helpers had managed to get a four-wheel drive up the muddy tracks to a small courtyard behind the grotto on the top of the hill. From the side of the road you could almost see the sea, a line of greyer grey where the sky stopped. The forest swayed below, the clouds rushed above, heading east in a hurry, trailing loose hairs as they ran.

The inside of the car smelt of chemicals and hire companies. On the back of every seat was my photo, pinned up large, and a note in the same stiff hand which read: *She is _why.*

The driver, a man in a baseball cap and owl sunglasses, was waiting, a cigarette burning between two yellow-stained fingers, a Manchester United T-shirt billowing around his skinny chest. He threw the butt away as we approached, nodded wordlessly and swung into his seat. I huddled in the back, between Byron and the woman, and said nothing.

We drove in silence, until the driver's phone rang and he answered irritably, holding it in place under his chin. His mother, checking that he was all right. Yes he was, of course he was, he was always all right. Well, she'd heard . . . Mother, I'm working . . . Oh well yes dear but I just wanted to tell you . . .

The driver hung up. We drove in silence, Byron never taking her eyes from me.

At one point, the man in the front turned away, and grew enthralled by the passing of the forest around us, and when he looked back, he gasped to see me, and his colleague's eyes flashed to his face and he mumbled in Korean, something about truth and memory – I couldn't decipher more.

Then the woman's eyes narrowed, and she looked away, and perhaps intended only to look away for a minute at most, but forgot that she was deliberately diverting her attention, so looked back five minutes later, and caught her breath, and held onto the handle above the door as she stared at me, in case she might bounce out of her seat.

Then she crossed herself.

Census, 2005, South Korea: Buddhism 22 per cent. Protestantism and Roman Catholicism combined: 28 per cent. Flaws in the survey, however: no one was asked if they practised Confucianism, or honoured their ancestors, or sought the guidance of shamans. In this corner of the world, it was perfectly normal to pray to both Jesus and Kuanyin, manifestations, perhaps, of the same entity, expressed in different manners.

I glanced over at Byron, unsmiling, who said nothing. She would not take her eyes from me, not permit herself to break awareness of my presence.

At a motorway service station, we stopped for burgers. There weren't sandwiches to be found, and the burgers were hot halfway-houses between McDonald's and *bibimbap*, but it was food. Byron ate in silence as we pulled away, and only when she'd finished every corner and I was licking the last of the pickle sauce from my fingers did she say, "How do you live?"

"I steal," I replied. "I am a very good thief."

That seemed to be all the questions she had.

*

Some fifteen miles short of Daegu we stopped in a small town of 1960s concrete blocks, clinging to the terraced side of a mountain. A small building of beige-washed walls and pink-tiled roof overlooked a tumbling mountain stream that rushed over shallow smooth stones. A black and white cat regarded us from on top of the wall, while beneath it, a lethargic dog, grey with no collar, opened one watery eye to consider first us, then the cat, then us again, and finding nothing interesting, went back to sleep.

The driver was the first out of the car, and embarked instantly on a cigarette, hauling in long breaths as he leant back against his bonnet. The man and woman emerged slowly, neither willing to take their eyes off me for more than a few moments. I followed, the cold air pushing out some of the sickness in my stomach. Calm. I am the cold; I am my empty face.

Byron gestured me inside; I followed.

A corridor lined with reed mats where we could leave our shoes. A collection of slippers of various sizes, decorated in bright plastic beads. A staircase going upwards to unknown rooms; a picture of the Dalai Lama on one wall, smiling as he signed a book with a felt-tip pen. A door to a living room which was also a kitchen; cushions on the floor, a flat-screen TV against one wall, a gas fire, a collection of books in Korean and English. A travel guide to the local area.

A traveller's house, furnished for brief stays.

Byron gestured me to a cushion, sat opposite, folding her legs awkwardly, a bone clicking in a joint at her hip. The woman gave her a phone, which was switched to record and put between us. The man set up a digital camera on a tripod.

"Here is our situation, Why," she said at last. "One of us will remain with you at all times. Every conversation will be filmed. May we offer you tea?"

"That'd be nice."

"I don't want you to feel in any way uncomfortable."

"Might be a losing battle, that one."

"I need to understand what you are."

"I'm a thief."

"I need to understand *how* you are."

I shrugged. "Good luck."

A kettle put on a stove. Three matching cups pulled from a cupboard; a question, green tea or red?

Green tea for Byron; red for me, thank you. Make it strong, milk if you have it.

The woman's nose wrinkled at the idea, but she found some UHU, sniffed it, dribbled in the barest slap, didn't stir.

We drank in silence, Byron and I, her eyes never leaving me.

I said, "You know that if I walk away, you'll never find me."

"You're here, aren't you? Have you ever been . . . forgive the word, but it's the only one which will do . . . studied?"

"Doctors don't remember who I am."

"I have connections."

"I'm not a lab rat."

"Then you are not serious in your ambition to be remembered," she replied simply. "If that is the case then you are correct – you can leave and we will almost certainly never find you. But you will never find me either, that I can promise."

So saying, she stood, still watching.

"You'll need to sleep," I said. "You'll forget when you do."

"I know what I want from this," was her answer. "Do you?"

She left, and I remained.

A moment in the night.

I sat, cross-legged, in front of the camera.

The man watched me, and I watched him watching.

Byron, asleep upstairs.

The woman, asleep on the other side of the room.

Taking turns, shifts to remember.

Each time they woke, they were surprised to see me, but always they left themselves notes – *she is _why, you are set to guard her, do not forget.*

Every three hours they swapped to a different video camera, just pointed at me, recording.

At two in the morning, the man dozed off.

I watched his head roll gently down, the lights still on, the camera still running, and waited for a little line of spit to gather in the lower corner of his mouth, ready to drop. In the darkness outside, I could hear the far-off sound of the motorway, and the nearer rushing of the river. I stood up, turned the camera off, poured myself another cup of tea, took the mug outside and went to consider the starlight.

Chapter 60

Remembering Reina bint Badr al Mustakfi.

A question perpetually looping itself through my mind: should I have known? Should I have seen her pain, was there anything I could have done to help her?

Obvious answers: of course not. Don't be bloody daft.

Even if you could have done anything, she wouldn't have remembered. You speak words of kindness, you tell her it'll be all right, that she is beautiful, wonderful, perfect as she already is, and maybe she smiles, and maybe she laughs, and maybe for a moment she forgets Leena on her couch, and Perfection on her phone . . .

the power to succeed is inside you!

. . . and then she turns away, and your words are dust in the wind, and nothing you do means a damn, and she dies.

Walking through Tokyo streets, remembering the words of a long-dead emperor-philosopher. Marcus Aurelius, AD 121–180, author of the *Meditations*. Quoth said emperor: *It is not death a man should fear, but he should fear never beginning to live.*

And also: *You have power over your mind, not outside events. Realise this, and you will find strength.*

Amongst his less well documented declarations was a determination to obliterate the Iazyges in Germania. Genocide of Rome's enemies was a reasonable military tool; history's never as simple as it is in the movies.

How did I end up here?

十九八七六五四三二一 I think at some point I must have made some choices, though it feels like they were far away

하나 둘 셋 넷 다섯 여섯 일곱 여덟 아홉 열 fairer perhaps to say that some choices were made around me and I acted in a manner which could be seen to be

impulsive reckless petty spiteful vindictive crusade stupid angry lonely jihad

full of struggle.

Ju kyu hachi shichi roku go fuck it.

Fuck it.

I close my eyes and see, always and again, my mum crossing the desert, only now she turns to look at me as I walk in her shadow, and smiles and says, Why so angry, petal?

Fucked up, Mum. Totally fucking fucked up.

How so?

Thought I'd live. Thought I'd be discipline, life, living, the machine, everything I am, all of this, living and breathing and beating the world, beating this fucking forgetting, fuck the world, fuck memory, I thought I'd be a sun goddess, a pilgrim, crusader, thought I was . . .

. . . I thought I was in control.

Aren't you? she asks, pausing to drink from a flask hidden beneath her robes. (Must be water: I dream it is whisky.)

Don't think so. Made choices. Did things, went places; left a footprint on the sand. Didn't control me. Stole the fucking diamonds in a fit of pique. Went after Perfection because it pissed me off. Looked at Reina and didn't see. Came to Korea and got made. Not in control. Can't stop myself. Can't see myself. Don't know where I've come from or where I'm going. Just now – that's all I've got. If I close my eyes, do you think I'll forget my own face?

Now you're being daft, tutted Mum. And not only daft, you're tying yourself in knots in a thoroughly unhelpful way.

Mum?

Yes?

What if all of this is my fault? What if I'm forgotten . . . and it's something I did? A man looks at my photo on the other side of the world, and he sees my face, I'm not invisible, but then he looks up, and he's forgotten me. People fill in the gaps, find a way to meet me without being afraid, but it's all lies, all of it, my parents forgot me, you forgot me, the world forgot and what if it's me, what if it's my fault?

The power is within you!!

Beneath the starlight of the Korean night, with the sand of the desert beneath her bare feet, my mum laughed.

So what? she asked. You going to shout at the sun for shining and the wind for blowing? You gonna curse the sea for rolling with the tide, the fire for being hot? Hope Arden, I thought I taught you better than that. Now pull your socks up, and get on.

I thought about answering, but didn't want to, so opened my eyes again to see the now, the night, feel the cold and hear the quiet, and sat a while longer, and thought about nothing at all.

I am Hope.

I am a thief.

I am a machine.

I am living.

I am unworthy.

I am righteous.

I am none of these.

No words can contain me.

In the morning, when Byron came down, I was still there.

"Okay," she mused, long and slow, seeing me sitting on a rickety plastic chair outside her door. "I had a letter from myself on my bedside table saying we'd found you, but I didn't think it'd be true."

"You met me yesterday," I explained as she rubbed her hands against the still-heavy morning cold. "It's all on tape."

"My letter said you were unsure if you would stay or go."

I shrugged. "Your assistants fell asleep. I thought about going, and decided to stay."

"That's . . . good. That's very good. Did you tell me yesterday what kind of tea you drink?"

"Builder's, with milk."

"Am I going to forget that by the time I get indoors?"

"Yes – unless you're recording this, and remember to play it back."

"You must get terrible service in restaurants."

"I like buffets," I replied, detaching myself from my seat and heading for the door. "Also those sushi bars with the conveyer belts."

Chapter 61

They gave me a new passport.

A lift to the airport.

At every step, Byron, recording, someone, recording.

Byron had a notebook, maintained in impeccable handwriting. On every page a new line of thought was developed in perfect cursive script, black ink from a silver fountain pen.

"One of my little indulgences," she explained, rolling it between her fingers.

I flicked through the book, following the passage of her thoughts as we sat in the car heading for Incheon International Airport.

> Is _why following me?
> How did _why get this number?

Why am I on this ferry?
How did I decide to come to this hotel?

"All this before we had dinner?" I asked her.

"Yes. It was the hotel that alarmed me. I remembered walking up the hill with a great sense of purpose, checking in with purpose, but when the door closed on my bedroom I realised that I had no idea why I'd chosen to go there, to that place, that room. There was no message on my phone, my computer, nothing to justify these decisions, this time or place."

"I'm impressed – most people make something up."

"When one lives alone, one must develop strict critical processes."

I didn't meet her eye, looked back at the notebook. "And then you got my invite for dinner."

"Yes."

I turned the page, and there it was, notes entering sudden emphatic capital letters, terror seeping through the script.

WHY HAVE I RECORDED 59 MINS OF A CONVERSATION I DO NOT REMEMBER HAVING?

"I thought you'd just move on," I sighed. "Most people do."

"And you would come looking for your payments – your treatments – later?"

"That was the plan."

Byron nodded, took the notebook back from me, carefully wrote:

Why believes that the treatments can make her memorable.

"That is right, isn't it?" she mused, glancing up at me. "Have I asked that already? Every time I speak to you, I'm worried that I'm repeating myself."

"Everyone repeats themselves," I said. "I don't mind."

*

A plane to San Francisco. We sat together, but at some point, even Byron slept, and so did I. When we woke, she stared at her napkin in surprise. On it she'd written,

> You are travelling to America with Why. She is the woman sitting next to you. Her name is Hope.

"Is your name Hope?" she asked.

"Yes."

"We have of course had this conversation a dozen times."

"Fewer than you'd think, but I'm sure there are more to come."

"Astonishing. I can remember that I am travelling with someone I forget, but I can't remember it's you."

"People remember things about themselves, and you've been writing down the important things. That's how you remember why you're travelling. You forget me, my face. It's impressive that your methods let you remember as much as you do."

"You are astonishing," she breathed, and her hand reached up, and brushed my cheek, feeling the reality of my skin, a mother soothing a child perhaps. Or perhaps another thought – a master comforting a much-loved pet. "You are incredible."

We were separated at customs, but Byron held her phone tight, followed the photograph and the note which read, *You will meet this woman in baggage reclaim. Do not leave without her.*

She had difficulty seeing me in the crowd, so I approached her.

"Incredible," she breathed. "It's as if you are invisible, one moment to the next. You exist only in this moment, and then your face is eaten by memory."

"Shall we go?" I replied.

San Francisco. Once Spanish, then Mexican, then for a brief period its own little state, before finally integrating with the USA. It was a city flanked by other cities flanked by the sea.

Most of the city had been destroyed in 1906 by the earthquake, but that still made what remained a historical treasure in American eyes, and the taxi driver as he carried us across the bridge to Oakland lamented that the little house he owned down in San Ramon – he couldn't afford San Francisco prices – had been built in the ancient times of 1949.

"Isn't that a good thing?" I asked, as blue waters rolled beneath us.

"Ma'am," he retorted, "it's a nightmare. Local ordnance says if you own a house built before the 50s, you gotta keep it in its historical modality."

"What does that mean?"

"It means you gotta strip all the paint back to what it used to be back when the house was first built, to make it conform to the historical aesthetic. Well, we did that – and it cost a damn fortune, I mean, it's there's like one guy who can do it and he's got the market in a bind – and you know what colour the place was in 1949?"

"No, I don't."

"Baby peach. Can you fucking believe it? I was in the Marines for eight years, I teach baseball on Sundays, kids they look up to me, like, an example, and every night I go home to this house and baby fucking peach, damn me."

I nodded and smiled.

"I don't know much about politics," he mused, "but when I saw what colour the house was meant to be, that's when I knew the country's gone crazy."

We stayed in a hotel in Oakland, looking down towards the water from the top of the hill. Cypress trees swayed gently around the empty swimming pool, leaves brown and stiff. The owner's wife, dressed in bikini and sunglasses, spread herself across the recliner by the dirty tiles and said, "Sweetie, I'm sorry, but there's a drought on at the moment." A pair of children, seven and five apiece, looked up miserably from the edge of the place where water should be. "It's Ruthie's birthday today, but she's sulking because the party's at her gran's house this evening, and she wanted her friends to come here, but they couldn't come here, could they Ruthie, not while Mama and Papa are working."

So saying, she returned to her sprawl across the lounger, a reflective foil sheet resting below her chin to bounce light up her carefully pruned nostrils.

Her husband, all moustache and capillary-shattered red nose, said, "Twin or two singles?"

"Twin," said Byron quickly. "If you wouldn't mind."

"You two related?"

"Hope here is such a dear," replied Byron, putting one arm across my shoulders. "I don't know what I'd do without her."

In the face of the old woman's smiling ambiguity, what was a man to do except smile back, and hand her the keys?

Byron said, "If I take a shower—"

"You'll forget me, but I'll still be here."

"I'm beginning to find that quite an exciting prospect. I could learn to enjoy being perpetually surprised to discover your presence."

I smiled and said nothing, and she left the door to the bathroom slightly ajar as she went to wash, as if that might make a difference.

A few minutes of local news was all I could stomach.

"I don't need Washington to tell me what my children should learn, I don't need the fat-cats in DC to spend my money, to tell me what's right and wrong for my family, what I carry in my back pocket, like a knife or a gun, how to look after my health! It's my life, what the hell are they doing interfering in it?"

"Ma'am, can I ask, do you believe in abortion?"

"I believe that every life is sacred."

"Do you believe that the government has the right to legislate on what a woman can do with her body?"

"Now hold on there because you're doing a thing here, you're doing a thing . . . "

"Ma'am, I'm just trying—"

"... and I'm talking to you honestly, I'm having an honest debate about things that matter and you're trying to make it something it's not ..."

"... should women choose—"

"This government has spent my money on teaching children I've never even met about stuff I don't even know about ..."

I changed channels, flicking through an array of cop dramas and soaps, until stumbling on a current-affairs/gadget programme in which two men and a cosmetically gleaming woman went through the technological toys of the day and of course, but of course, there was,

"... Perfection – now, Clarice, you've been trying this, haven't you?"

"Well, Jerry, yes, yes I have, and it's been absolutely sensational! Not only do I feel positive about leading a more goal-orientated existence, really trying to achieve who I want to be, but the rewards it gives for consistent effort are just fantastic. It's not just a reinvention of a lifestyle app, it's a reinvention of me ..."

I turned the TV off and lay, face-down, on the single bed. The duvet cover was thin, layers above, layers below, ready for a hot, sunny California day, a cold California night when the breeze from the sea and the chill from the mountains combined. An embroidered sampler above the bed read "There's No Place Like Home". A copy of the Bible lay beneath the green-glass lamp on the bedside table. Someone had left a receipt for barbecued ribs and a bottle of Coca-Cola in it. *Hear diligently my speech, and my declaration with your ears. Behold now, I have ordered my cause; I know I shall be justified.*

I stood in front of the bedroom mirror, studied my face, my eyes, ran my fingers over my skin, stared at my reflection, and wondered why I could remember it.

Why was I here?

The sound of water stopped in the bathroom.

I counted packets of sugar standing up in the jar by the kettle.

Buttons on the TV remote.

Lights appearing in the city as the sun went down.

Byron gasped as she saw me, drew her towels tight, shook her head, said, "Wait," went into the bathroom, came back out in a dressing gown, added, "Maybe we should have got singles."

"Nervous of being caught walking around naked?" I suggested.

"Dignity and old age are difficult to reconcile, especially when you forget the company you're keeping."

"You wanted a twin so you could watch me," I sighed. "You're afraid that when you can't see me, I'm not real."

She didn't answer, and I turned away from the mirror, and lay down to sleep.

Chapter 62

I woke, to find Byron sitting on the end of my bed. Her notebook was open, new writings, new questions and recollections, filling the pages. The napkin on which I'd scrawled my terms was in her hand. The reflected light of sunrise came in off the bay below, California dreaming, perfect climate, orange trees and vineyards, wealth and water – but perhaps that was the past. Before the drought and historical modality and the world gone mad.

Again, briefly, that look in her eyes, almost sensual, her fingers flicking out, brushing my face, fascinated. "When I woke this morning I thought I came here alone, because I wanted to visit Berkeley."

"What's in Berkeley?"

"The beginnings of my team. My objective is still to dismantle Perfection, to re-write treatments, but to do that . . . there are some promising candidates on campus."

"You were just going to recruit them? Walk up and say

'Hi, I want to destroy Perfection from the inside out – you game?'"

"Of course not – charitable fronts, corporate appointments, layers within layers, I'm not new to this." She dismissed the question with a flick of one hand, butterfly-light flapping through the air. "When I turned on the bedside light, I saw you, and remembered writing about you, but even that's barely enough. It is extraordinary, how the mind creates a story to fill in the place where you should be; simply extraordinary."

Suddenly uncomfortable; I pulled the sheets higher around my chin, and she said, "I'll . . . find breakfast. Give you a little privacy."

She wrote in her notebook: *The woman who joins you for breakfast is called Hope. She is the one you cannot remember.*

This done, she let herself go, finger lodged in the page of the book, eyes fixed on it, in case the ink dissolved.

For a week, nothing happened. Byron went about her business. She visited Berkeley. She talked with people in quiet corners of cafés. She spent a lot of time on her laptop. She read the newspapers. She waited for phone calls, which she always took outside.

"I am thinking about you," she mused, "but plans were in motion before I knew of your condition."

"How will you destroy Perfection?" I asked, when she came home one night from a meeting with a person she would not name. "What will you do to it?"

In answer, she opened a file on her laptop. A document from my USB stick, stolen from Perfection. Names running down the screen, thousands, tens of thousands, hundreds of thousands – men and women from every corner of the world. Next to them, date of birth, home address, net worth, annual income, annual expenditure, credit score, current score on Perfection, and drop-down menus to bring up more data. Last two months of movement, according to the GPS logs from their mobile phones. Next of kin, friends, family, with links to Facebook pages and little yellow flags for any of those who were also on Perfection. Calories consumed, purchases made on the credit card, restaurants visited, illicit lovers contacted in the dead of night, last three films purchased through the internet on-demand service, most visited websites, last fifty text messages sent, last one hundred emails, shoe size, trouser size . . .

"Enough," I said, as she picked through the lives on the laptop. "Enough. What does Prometheus do with all this information?"

"Sell it, of course. What do you think?"

"And what will you do with it?" I asked.

Her lips thinned. "This list contains the names of everyone who's currently using Perfection. I do not have time to go to each one individually and show them the truth, so I shall create a spectacle."

"What kind of spectacle?"

"That depends," she mused, "on how the next few months go."

I poked again, and again, the next morning, the next evening, breakfast and supper, but one day she said, "I seem to have written down that you're worried about what I'm going to do with Perfection, now you've stolen it for me. Are you worried?"

"No," I lied, face flushing hugely, pulse suddenly fast and high in my skull. "Not at all."

She nodded, and made a note in her notebook, and I didn't ask again.

Terror. Horror. Maybe . . .

. . . ecstasy?

Is this what it feels like to be remembered?

Is this – this moment in which Byron challenges me on a thing I have said or done, a thing she can, in her own kind of way, *remember* me doing – is this what *consequence* feels like?

I race a trolley car up a hill, and for a moment think I might actually win.

Then Byron said, "I've been thinking about your condition. I've had a few ideas."

And all things changed.

A private clinic in a private hospital – were there any other kinds in America, I wondered? Private medicine brought bad coffee, a receptionist who greeted you with a cry of "Hey hi there!" and a waiting time of ten minutes.

The doctor, thin grey hair combed over a spotted scalp, incredibly long fingers curling to manicured, glossy nails, leather shoes and a bright blue stethoscope slung about his neck, greeted us like we were old friends come to visit, and ushered us into the room.

Byron did the talking. fMRI, bloods, spinal fluids, DNA, thyroid function, eye exam – the extent of tests she wanted performed on me was long and, in several cases, painful.

"This is how you'll be remembered," she explained, as they helped me onto the rolling platform of the MRI machine. "We'll find out how you work."

Inside the machine, they played soothing music through oversized headphones. I closed my eyes against the tightness of the walls, remembered a cupboard in Istanbul as the fire started, the cold of the waters in Hong Kong when I jumped. Despite myself, my breath came faster, and I squeezed my eyes tighter and counted the muscles in each of the toes on my foot, capillaries in my fingers, clicks in the machine, the thunk-thunk-thunk of magnets moving. I counted flickering, dancing points behind my eyelids and, when the motion of lights in the darkness became too jumbled and difficult to track, I counted my breath again, and found that it was steady, and I was calm.

The doctor, when they pulled me from the tube, was briefly – but only briefly – surprised to see me. He had remembered putting a patient inside, for of course he'd just spent the last forty minutes examining my brain – but in that time my face had blurred, and he managed just about to bite back on a surprised "Oh, you're British?" when I spoke.

On her list, Byron crossed off the word "fMRI".

Spinal fluid.

Knees to chest.

Tighter.

Chin down.

Spine curved, distended, a good word, distended; expanded, dilated – the French protuberant from the Latin *protuberare*, to swell, bulge out

the needle hurts like crap when it goes in

the pain is my body

just a body thing

they leave it in for a while, letting the spinal fluid drip, drip, drip out from between the vertebrae into a little plastic cup.

Byron watches, and I watch back, and her face shows nothing at all.

In the evening, Byron went to more meetings for her other work, her real work, Perfection, always Perfection.

"Are you going to follow me?" she asked. "I have it in my notes that you like to follow me."

"Not tonight," I replied, curling up on the hotel bed.

She nodded, without conviction, and left me alone.

A walk around Fort Mason as the sun went down. Here it was almost possible to imagine that you were in a European city: low rise-apartment blocks painted pale pastels, cyclists weaving between the cars, ginkgo trees ready to drop their foul-smelling fruit, chestnut trees heavy with prickly seeds, children dodging the cracks in the pavement. A woman was raising money for an animal shelter.

"Every year we receive over two thousand animals from the

bay area alone!" she exclaimed, shaking her tin under my nose. "That's dogs that have been beaten by their owners, cats thrown out of a moving car, pets that have been tortured and starved and left for dead; traumatised, vulnerable animals whose only sin was to trust people. We do what we can for them, but there are some that are just so badly hurt, psychologically as well as physically, that they have to be put down. But this year, with your donation, we can get the euthanasia rate down to just 1 per cent. That's thousands of beautiful, loyal, loving creatures given a second chance, a second home!"

"Why do people treat their pets badly?" I asked.

She shook her head. "Honey, I've asked myself that for years, and every time I think I come close to an answer, I realise it's just another sad story for a sad individual. Truth is, I can never understand what'd make a person hurt a thing that loves it, that just wants to be cared for, and I hope I never do understand it neither. You wanna meet Sally?"

Sally, a brown dog with scars fading across her ribs, backside and neck, stared up from behind her mistress's legs with huge, wet eyes, and, at the offering of my hand, came forward to nuzzle and press her skinny body against mine.

"Her owner was a lawyer down in Forest Hill. That man can argue the balls off a city judge but when he got home, he just raged out against Sally. She had pee problems, you see, and a guy like that I guess he didn't realise that you can't argue a dog into obeying, you gotta use love, you gotta be patient, you gotta help her understand for herself. One day he just went at her with a kitchen knife, left her bleeding fifteen blocks away, but she found her way home, and the city found her dying in his front yard. We ain't supposed to get too attached to the animals that come into the shelter, but Sally – I couldn't say no."

Sally stared up at me, tail beating out an expectant rhythm on the ground, and I wondered if animals remembered me in a way humans did not, if perhaps their brains were wired differently. Should I tell Byron? Would she then cut open a dog's brain, as well as mine, to see how it ticked?

I gave the woman twenty bucks and squatted for a while on the path while Sally put her paws in my hands, and licked my fingers, and wondered if I could stay there for ever, and couldn't, and kept on walking.

EEG. Inject radioactive materials, watch them flow through my body. I pissed blue for a week.

A doctor spluttered, "Oh, goodness, I hadn't ... Well, no of course I had, so sorry, my mind must have wandered ..."

A nurse said: "You're new here, aren't you?!"

A professor of neurochemistry exclaimed, "No, I was alone, then you came into the room, there wasn't anyone here, I would have remembered ..."

A student of cognitive science mused, "We don't have a model. We don't just not have a model, we don't even have a box to try and put the model in, we don't know where to begin with this sorta thing ..."

A patient sitting two chairs down from me as I waited in the hall sighed, "I was on twelve thousand points yesterday but today it's down to eleven thousand and I don't know why. Do you think I lose points for radiotherapy?"

Byron declared, "We're making progress, I promise you, I know it doesn't feel that way, but Filipa's research, the treatments, your brain, we'll find out how she did it, we'll find out how to make you memorable ..."

She was repeating herself, of course. Everyone always repeats themselves, when I'm around.

A night in ... some place. The Mission, probably. Tacos. I was tired, a little drunk, the streetlight burning, chilli on my lips, a pleasant pain, a pain that reminded me of the blood running through my body, count my pulse, de-dum, de-dum, de-dum ...

I run, and having run, I run further, Golden Gate Park, why am I here? I didn't intend to find it but I remember this spot, my feet found their way on their own, tarmac between the trees, the wrong shoes for running but I run anyway, in the day this is the perfect place to visit, an incredible place: the Japanese tea garden, archery range, bison enclosure, tulip garden, ducks on the pond, the AIDS memorial grove

I run.

Until my feet will run no more, and then I walk until I can find a cab, and realise I have forgotten the address of the hotel, and laugh.

And then, one not very special night, I go to the bathroom at 3:30 a.m., and when I return I hear Byron move in the bed, and in the dark, the click of the safety catch coming off a gun.

I am still, and so is she.

There is no past, there is no future, there is only now.

This moment.

I say, "It's me. It's Hope."

Silence in the dark. Then sheets moving, quilt being pushed aside. A click as the light comes on; I flinch away. Byron has a gun, don't know where she hid it, she holds it in her left hand, looks at me, the light filling all the lines on her face, hard in its sudden intensity.

I am this moment.

I say, "Look at your notes. Listen to your recordings."

She looks at the bedside table. A note has been written on it in her own hand.

YOU ARE TRAVELLING WITH _WHY. YOU CANNOT REMEMBER HER. YOU ARE SHARING A ROOM WITH HER.

Next to that, my picture. Slowly, she put the gun down, and picked the photo up, held it before her, between the two of us, my face recorded, looking slowly one to the other. A nod, a thought, a laying of the photograph down.

Without a word, she flicked the safety back on the gun, turned the bedside lamp off, and rolled over to sleep.

Chapter 63

Memories, sleepless in the dark.

Sometimes business is slow, a job is hard, and I need an easy fix for money.

Often, I choose casinos.

Card counting isn't so tough, once you know the rules. There are no laws against it; in Vegas they'll ask you to move on, in Macau they'll break your fingers, in Abuja or Mong La they'll break a lot more than that. Maths makes it easy for the house to spot, a statistical flare on their systems. Under such circumstances, the best course of action is to win quick and leave, walk round the block, and return to a different table, ready to bet on the next winning hand.

Playing blackjack in a casino in New Orleans, the man said, "Are you card counting?" smiling as he spoke, his voice low, his eyes fixed on mine, the dealer swapping shoes, attention elsewhere.

I ran my fingers along the growing stacks of counters and said, "Why do you ask?"

"You're winning at a higher statistical rate than is normal for the game."

"You work for the casino?"

He shook his head. "Teach high-school math. Here for a wedding. I lost five hundred dollars in twenty minutes and promised myself that was enough. Then I saw you, and I thought . . . are you counting?"

"No law against it."

"No law; no. I hope you don't think me too forward . . . ?"

His body, already half turned away. I caught his arm, pulled him back to my side. If he went, he would forget. "No," I said. "No. Stay. Watch."

Later, in the lift, his hand brushed my arm, and for a moment he looked as if he might kiss me, before his eyes darted away. I took his hand, and when we were in my room he said, "Jesus, how'd you get yourself such a fancy place to sleep?"

"Put big money behind the counter in the casino. This place likes to keep its fishes hooked."

"But you're winning," he replied. "Surely they can see that you're winning?"

"The computers can see," I said. "But computers can't act, and everyone else forgets."

When he went to the bathroom, I stayed outside the door, singing. "When I dance they call me Macarena! They all want me, they can't have me, so they all come and dance beside me!"

The sound of my voice kept the recollection of me fresh in his mind, and when he emerged he was laughing, and said, "You're like no one I've ever met before."

He was nervous when I pulled him onto the bed, and gentle. After, when he looked like he might fall asleep, I talked, and he stayed awake, blinking bewildered at nothing much, so I kept talking, and found that I couldn't stop, that the words wouldn't stop, until finally at 4:30 a.m. I was still speaking and he was fast asleep.

I got a blanket, and placed it over him.

I pulled on my running shoes and top, and went out into the streets, past the shuttered restaurants and through the drifting litter, beneath the sodium streetlights and round the broad boulevards where the young trees were beginning to grow again, and when I returned, he'd left the room, perhaps having woken and remembered nothing, and I showered and lay awake on my bed that smelt of him, and didn't sleep until dawn.

The next night I watched him on the blackjack table, trying to count cards. Some basic understanding of the things I had said to him perhaps lingered, even if I was gone. I find extraordinary hope in this thought – no, more than that: I find salvation, divinity in it.

When he lost, I sat beside him and said, "Hi. I've been watching you play. You'll want to try something a little different."

"Who are you?" he asked.

"I used to teach math in high school."
"Hey – that's what I do."
"I'm here for a wedding."
"Me too!"
I smiled and said, "What a coincidence."
That night, we went to his bedroom, and as he lay in my arms he said, "Jesus, I don't usually do this, I'm not that kinda guy," and was asleep within minutes. I snuck out a few hours later, so that he wouldn't be afraid when he woke to find a stranger in his bed.

Chapter 64

Byron, one day, as we ate breakfast quietly in a room lined with images of warring Indians, proud cowboys, slaughtered buffalo, looked up and said, "Yesterday, walking up the hill, I found myself stopping to look at every woman I saw."
I shrugged, said nothing.
"It is disconcerting, not trusting your own memory," she mused, cutlery resting lightly on the edge of her barely touched plate. "It is . . . more than disconcerting."
Again, a shrug, a bite of toast.
She watched me, coffee growing cold. Around the walls, the native peoples of America died, and buffalo skeletons lined the dusty fields. Thoughts, to pass the silence: an estimated sixty million buffalo roamed America in the 1400s; by 1890 that number was down to 750.
"You are incredible," Byron breathed at last, and I looked up, and saw her eyes shining.
"You've said that several times."
"Have I?"
"Yes."

"That's . . . also alarming. Alarming, I mean, that your condition not only prevents me from recalling you, but prevents me from recalling our interactions. If there was only one part of that equation, I could almost bear it, but both . . . Perhaps we should examine my brain? See if there is some part of me that is altered in your presence? Perhaps . . . damaged. Do you spend much time with anyone? Have you had a chance to observe the effects?"

Luca Evard, his fingers tangled in mine, a night in Hong Kong.

"No," I replied. "I haven't."

"To someone in my profession, your condition is miraculous. If we could bottle your forgettability and sell it . . . But no, don't worry. I am no laissez-faire capitalist, this is not Dr Moreau's island. Though perhaps you considered the possibility?"

"That you might chop me into bits to see how I ticked? Yes; I considered it."

A little note with her silver pen, tiny on the paper, as if ticking off a point. "And didn't run?"

"I took the risk. If I'm so remarkable, why help me?"

"I am interested, fascinated, of course. To make you memorable, we must understand how you are forgotten."

"It's irrelevant to Perfection, though?"

"Perhaps. But I am increasingly discovering that cognitive science flourishes on unusual conditions, shall we say. People who have suffered brain injuries are most beloved of neuroscientists, because in their lack of function, meaning may be ascribed to the region of the brain which is damaged. If, for example, we were to find that there was something in your brain which did not work, or worked too much . . ."

"You think it'd be that easy? A magic switch and boom, everyone can be forgotten or remembered?"

"No," she mused, slow and gentle. "No, I very much doubt it. But in answer to your first question, your unique condition may be of some interest in terms of unravelling how Filipa's treatments work. They made your friend memorable . . . "

"My friend is dead," I snapped, harder than I'd meant. "Parker died, and only Perfect Parker is left."

A half nod, an acknowledgement that she didn't have time to quibble. "But Perfect Parker is memorable, and Filipa's treatments achieved that. That in itself is interesting. Although you are technically correct: your presence here is a distraction from the main purpose. And yet a distraction that I am utterly absorbed in."

I waited, and found that I was holding my cutlery hard enough to hurt, bones straining against skin, muscles tight, breath held. I let it all go, all at once, and she saw it, and her eyes brightened and she exclaimed, "Phenomenal. You – yourself. Not just your condition, but you, the mind inside the memory, you are phenomenal. To have lived. To have survived. More – to have flourished! To have become who you are, to have stolen Perfection. You want to be remembered, and I have sworn to help, but you must understand that it could be the most appalling destruction of a beautiful thing, your forgettability has made you into something incredible."

"The treatments . . . "

"We'll find a way," she added, fast, a half nod of her head at nothing much. "All this, the tests, the scans, we'll find the part of you that is different, the part that makes people forget, and if we can de-activate it, I give you my word that we shall. That's what you want, ultimately, isn't it?"

"And in finding it . . . ?"

"Yes. Of course. Yes," she replied with a twist of her fingers through empty air. "If we can de-activate it, we can also activate it in others."

A moment, a pause as I tried to understand. An idea, almost too terrible to name. "You . . . want to be forgotten?" I stammered.

She didn't answer.

"It's a curse," I snapped, pushing against her silence. "It's a fucking death sentence."

Silence.

"If you tell me that you want what I have, then I'll walk away tonight."

Silence. Her fingers ran along the edge of the table, then folded, a deliberate act, into her lap. She looked up, met my eye, her lower lip uncurling from inside her mouth, a false smile. "I live alone in a place where no one ever comes. I work alone. I walk by the sea, I go to the shops and hide my face. I dodge cameras, travel by false passport, make no friends, have no need of company. My work is all that matters. I would give my life to see it done."

"And what is your work?"

"Freedom. I think it is freedom."

"What does that mean?" I asked, unable to meet her eyes, head aching from tequila, a night I could barely recall. "What does it *mean*?"

She shrugged. "I think … it is a crusade. A jihad. To struggle—"

"I know the meaning of jihad."

"Well then. To struggle in the cause of freedom of thought. The first battle being, of course, to show that thought, in this world, at this time, is not free."

"Is that why you're going after Perfection?"

"Yes."

"Is that why you keep me around? Because you think … I'm free?"

Silence, a while. Then, "Yes. I think you are the only free woman I have ever met."

I sat, shaking, and didn't have any words.

Like a child, all I could do was get up, and walk away.

Chapter 65

Tests.

More tests.

Three weeks in and out of labs and hospitals in California.

Scans, chemicals, swabs, injections.

I tried talking to Byron, but couldn't get anything from her. She couldn't remember building a relationship with me, and so she couldn't trust. So we idled along in quiet, business-like efficiency, ticking points off her list while she watched and re-watched recordings of our talks, annotated and updated observations and thoughts. Some thin impressions began to form in her mind, but they were, as she said, like memories of watching a play. She saw Romeo die and Juliet swoon, but it was not her lips the poison kissed, her heart that broke. She was a witness to events that contained her, not party.

On the fourth week we spent together, she slipped away for a few hours to have an fMRI on her own brain, looking for long-term damage caused by my presence. I didn't think she'd find any, and the next day she was back at the breakfast table, as calm and composed as anything. Science, I suspected, wasn't giving her the answers she was looking for.

On the fifth week, the doctors gave me LSD.

It wasn't called LSD, but the effects were roughly the same. They plugged me into a dozen electrodes and sat me back in a comfortable chair, and for the first time in my life, I tasted blue, and smelt the sound of Byron's voice, and dreamed while waking of what dreams would come, and swallowed time, swallowed the past and the future both, swallowed all the oxygen from the air and was absolutely fine until I found that I was having a panic attack and couldn't breathe, sobbing for breath, unable to stop crying, gasping, heaving, a pain in my chest which I knew was going to kill me, going to die for this, for Byron, for Perfection, until the doctor gave me something to calm me down and when

I woke, Byron simply said, "We still couldn't remember you, I'm afraid."

I watched footage recorded of the event later. The trip had lasted, for my money, less than ten minutes, but on the tape three hours go by in which doctors, nurses and students at the clinic all enter and leave, enter and leave, and each time Byron asks, "Have you seen this patient before?" and they all shake their heads, every one of them, and exit with an apologetic smile.

"Maybe a different mechanism," suggested Byron as she drove us back to the hotel. "Maybe something electrical."

She snuck out early that night, while she thought I was sleeping off the day's medicine, for another one of her backstreet meetings with contacts and servants. I wondered where she got her money from, if she was worth robbing, thought about following her, decided against it.

"Perhaps something else?" she said, the day a doctor suggested electroconvulsive therapy, but she was watching me from the corner of her eye, waiting to see how far I'd go.

Misnomers: electroshock therapy. Made famous by *One Flew Over the Cuckoo's Nest* as punishment, patients reduced to drooling slabs. Some risk; not much. Commonly administered bilaterally, with currents somewhere in the 800 milliamp range, an ECT machine pulls less electrical juice than a PC, and carries roughly the same risks to a patient as a general anaesthetic. However, relapses occur frequently, often six months or so after initial treatment, and there are concerns as to long-term memory loss and damage to cognition that may result from what is essentially an unknown mechanism for inducing a grand mal seizure.

"Unless you want to try . . . ?" Byron continued, softly, watching me, waiting to see where my thoughts fell.

Was it worth it? Six months of being remembered, maybe more, for the price of a bit of my memory, the ability to use a spoon? Six months of strangers being friends, of acquaintances knowing my name, six months of being loved, of being held, of being known?

It was worth it, of course, but when they showed me the room where it would happen, little more than a dentist's studio, a chair, oxygen mask, needles, a machine, and told me the statistics – 100,000 people in the USA have this every year, nothing to be afraid of – I remembered Gracie, my baby sister, measles aged four, the seizures when her fever hit 42°, holding my hand, Force be with you always – and I ran from the room and had to stand outside in the corridor, counting the dots on the green and white speckled tiles beneath my feet, while Byron stood with one hand on my shoulder and said, "It's okay. We'll find another way."

On the sixth week, they tried transcranial magnetic stimulation. The two researchers who administered it said, "Count up to ten."

One, two, four, five, seven, eight . . .

"I can't seem to say . . ." I said, and couldn't find what it was I was missing.

They chuckled. "Yeah," they exclaimed. "We know!"

There seemed no medical purpose in electromagnetically altering the part of my brain that could count to ten, but they enjoyed the exercise and I felt no pain as they ran their wand across the top of my skull, variously triggering the taste of fizzy orange juice, the memory of a concert I'd attended in Rome, the sound of the sea, the inability to recite the alphabet and at one point, a mild giggling fit that continued for a minute after they'd turned the wand off.

What they couldn't do, it appeared, was make me memorable, and the next day when we went back they held the wand over my skull again and said, "Count up to ten!" and found it exactly as funny as it had been the day before.

At night, Byron said, "Have you considered electroconvulsive shock therapy?"

We were eating barbecued ribs, pulling meat off bone, discarding the sucked grey remnants into a big bowl between us, like Vikings at a feast.

"You asked me that yesterday," I said.

"I'm sorry – I didn't realise."

"We went to the hospital."

"No, I was meeting a— Ah, but you were there too, of course. Apologies."

The next morning she said, "Have you considered electroconvulsive shock therapy?"

I said, "I've gotta pee," and when I came back she said, "Have you considered electroconvulsive shock therapy?" and I looked first at her, then at her phone recording our conversation, and said, "Yes. But no."

She made a note, and didn't ask again.

The day they sat me down to discuss deep brain simulation, I realised that I had stopped listening within a matter of minutes. I smiled and nodded and stared at nothing much, and when Byron said, "Do you want to have this conversation another time?" I smiled, stood up from my chair and walked away without a word.

One day I fell asleep in the MRI chamber. Didn't think it was possible, but it happened.

And three days after that, I dozed off while they were trying more transcranial stimulation, but that was normal, they said.

And when I woke, I had a splitting headache, which ibuprofen didn't even dent.

Chapter 66

On the sixty-second day, she said, "I have something exciting to show you."

She'd hired a car, an apartment too, got herself a US driver's licence – good forgery, nice photo, adapted from a dead woman in Baltimore – and she took me to a clinic in Daly City. Straight bright streets surrounded by matching straight pastel-coloured homes. Two floors high, sloped grey roofs, same cars, same flags, same bins, same plants, same shops, a suburb built at a time when suburbs seemed like a good idea, a place for the comfortably old who couldn't do better and the up-and-coming young who hoped to achieve more. It was an incongruous place for Byron to have set up shop, but there, between a nursery school and a motorbike-repair shop, was an unmarked single-storey white building which had once been a dentist's clinic, and which was now the property of Hydroponic Fertilizers Ltd., *Water Is Our Future*, a shell company whose shell was so fragile a sea anemone could have brushed it away.

"I used to love creating companies," mused Byron as we tramped up the path to the locked and bolted front door. "My proudest achievement was a pumpkin-pie company in Israel. Did so well I often thought I'd retire and do it for real."

The office was shuttered, almost entirely empty, the furniture of its previous owner moved out and never replaced. A coffee-coloured stain on one wall had been crudely covered over with an ancient picture of Ronald Reagan. A burn in the carpet had been less effectively protected with a three-legged wooden chair laid casually, yet eye-drawingly, over it. If Byron cared about these cosmetic difficulties, she didn't show it, but led me on past a pile of empty cardboard and plastic boxes, into a back room where a dentist's chair had been set up and converted to a newer, not-at-all hydroponic purpose.

I looked at it, she looked at me, and I counted backwards from ten before saying, "Where did you get it?"

"A broker in Mexico. It works; I'm sure of that."

A dentist's chair, for sure, but the apparatus around it was not for pulling teeth. I circled it once, twice, three times, and concluded that it was in every way which counted the same set-up as I had seen in Tokyo. The same machines for tinkering with your brain, the same devices for altering the way your mind worked, a mask for eyes, a sensor to lay on your tongue, earbuds and microphones, monitors and needles. In a back room in Daly City, Byron had set up her own treatments for Perfection.

I counted backwards from ten again, then stopped and said, "Isn't stealing it a risk?"

"Huge. Potentially catastrophic."

"You took precautions?"

"Numerous. Gauguin will be scouring North Carolina for me as we speak."

"Will it work?"

"I have every reason to think so. The mechanical parts aren't so complicated; the data you stole was the difficult part."

Calm in her voice, pride as well, curiosity, waiting to see what I'd do. "Can I use it?" I asked.

"Not yet."

"Why not?"

"We're still at the early stages of unpicking Filipa's programming. At this stage, the treatments we give you, even modified, risk re-writing your brain."

"You make it sound simple."

Her left hand rested lightly on the back of the chair; with her right she picked up the goggles hanging loose by its side, turned them over in her fingers. "Visual stimulation. Auditory. An electrode on the tongue; another in the back of your neck. Sedatives and stimulants pumped in roughly equal measure into your blood. Preliminary treatments are little more than medically enhanced hypnosis. Images of the perfect you, flashed up while pleasurable sensations are stimulated. Images of imperfection, correlated with the taste of bile; that sort of thing. Nothing extraordinary. Only on your eighth or ninth treatment do they drill a needle-sized hole in the back of your skull, and insert the electrodes. They don't leave them in for very long; a few hours at most, and you are only conscious for part of the procedure. Deep brain stimulation; a brain pacemaker, it used to be used for Parkinson's, chronic pain, but Filipa is more sophisticated than that. Perfection helps them map your mind, you see. Every time you use it, every purchase you make, every decision, every reward claimed and action performed, gives them a little more data for when the time comes for your treatments, so they know which part of your brain to keep, and which to burn. That is the other purpose of Perfection; that is why you need a million points before they give you treatments. Data gathering, for both marketing, and to target the results." Her head tilted to one side, watching me for a reaction, finding none. "We only know this because of you," she added gently. "Before you, we were guessing."

"We?" I asked.

"I have a lot of people working on the problem."

"How do you fund it all?"

"I steal," she replied simply. "Like you, I am an exceptionally good thief, although I mostly steal through stock markets, which doesn't even count as theft."

Her hand, resting on the back of the chair, like the proud owner of a prize horse, wondering whether now is the time to sell.

Then she said, "Do you still want treatments?"

"I want to be remembered."

"But do you still want treatments?"

I don't remember what I said in reply.

Headaches.

A doctor who'd seen me eleven times already said, "Ah, you're new here!"

Yes, I'm new here. I'm always new here.

Blood drawn; how much blood did I have left to take?

Brains, brains scanned, students brought in, introduced,

Hello, you're new here, still new, still always new, always and for ever just like yesterday, like tomorrow, goodbye, hello; hello, goodbye.

Byron woke from a nightmare, cold and shaking, saw me in the dark across from her, reached for her gun, froze, lips moving, struggling to find recollection. I saw her eyes white in the gloom, heard the rumble of a fat lorry passing by outside, waited, heard her breath slow, saw her lower her head back onto the pillow, close her eyes, go back to sleep, and I did not sleep.

I did not sleep.

On the sixty-eighth day of my association, I broke my own rule, and followed her, discreetly, to a meeting. It was the perfect evening for it, fog rising off the bay, a thin drizzle of rain obscuring the lights high in the hills, winter coming. I carried an umbrella, hid my face behind a scarf, wore a new, shop-stolen coat that I could discard on the way home. I followed her to the edge of Berkeley, watched her walk through the mist to the front door of a detached, two-storey white-timbered house with an American flag flying on the porch and a bright pink plastic rocking horse abandoned by the path, and when she looked back over her shoulder before knocking, I hid behind a car and counted to ten before peeking round to see who answered.

The man was in his fifties, olive skin and pepper hair, a checked shirt and grey jogging bottoms, a pair of slippers each with a rabbit face and a pair of floppy ears on the front. He shook Byron's hand quickly, and led her inside.

I looked up his address when I got home. Agustin Carrazza, retired MIT professor, quietly shuffled into obscurity when it was suggested he'd had a few too many links with questionable experiments, of which the highlight had to be a 1978 case in which the water supply for a small town in Missouri was laced with a mild hallucinogenic, resulting in two days of confusion and chaos, three deaths, six pet deaths including one iguana, two car crashes, ninety-four injuries of varying degrees, the slaughter of two hundred and seventeen dairy cows and a statistically significant jump in the birth rate nine months later.

When asked in interview in 1998 if he'd ever been part of unethical or illegal experiments, his reply was classically Nixonian: "If the government says it's ethical, then that's good enough for me."

That night I bought a couple of sleeping pills from a pharmacy that advertised itself with the picture of two grinning, Stetson-wearing snakes coiled round a crucifix, and slipped one into Byron's water when she went to sleep.

One hundred and fifty snores later, I rolled out of bed, took her notebook from her bedside table, turned on the torch at the back of my phone and sat, like a child, under the duvet covers to read.

Her name is Hope, said the first page. You will forget her.

Pages of notes. Reflections and musings, scrawls in the corner –

Scared of ECT? Possible sister? Northern English accent sometimes. Reluctant to talk about family. Drinks tea with milk. Runs, average 10k per day. Steals habitually. Unaware of own habit? Stole pair of running shoes, bar of chocolate, apple, bottle of brown sauce, multitool and knife (hidden, taped under bed – weapon?).

Late home tonight.

Did I pull a gun on her? In my dream I woke, and held a gun against an intruder, but there was no one there, and I went back to sleep, but in the morning my gun had moved. Why?

Smell of alcohol on her shirt this morning.

Today I like her.

Today she is uneasy.

Today she is calm.

Today she is funny.

Today I felt pity for her.

Today she spoke of honour.

Today she stole a new mobile phone, hidden behind bathroom cistern. (Must move hotel; see what she does with change.)

Too many recordings, too many videos, not enough time to track. Will record all notes here, attempt to compile.

She does not trust me.

She is frightened.

She hasn't heard the screaming.

She will not accept ECT; do not ask her again.

She is beginning to suspect that these tests will not cure her condition.

And fairly soon:

Is she following me?

Is she the she I think she is? Performance, a face in the camera, voice on the tape, what is she when there is nothing digital to recall her? What might she do? Who is she when I cannot remember her?

After nearly sixty pages of notes, the writing transformed into a language I couldn't recognise. Alpha-numeric, characters and symbols, numbers and dashes. I took a stab at deciphering it, but it resisted monoalphabetic frequency analysis, and I didn't have time or expertise to break it down into anything more complicated. Still Byron's handwriting, but a code, and my head hurt, and I was tired, so I photographed the pages and put the notebook back, and re-sealed the hair she'd left stuck over its pages, and tried to go back to sleep.

On the seventieth day, she said, "Have you been following me?"

"No."

"I shouted at a woman in the street today who I thought was you."

"I'm sorry. It wasn't me."

"I know. When I went back the other way, she was crying down the phone, and I remembered her face."

I shrugged.

"I mean to say . . . if I say anything, I think I should apologise now."

"You haven't said anything that bothers me," I replied, and that same evening she said, "Have you been following me?" and I said no, and we had the conversation again, but this time she didn't manage not to look afraid.

That night I stole a book on cryptography, and by the white light of the bathroom, studied while she slept.

On the seventy-first day, alone in an internet café in Bayview, I started an email to Luca Evard. I wrote it five times, and on the sixth attempt, deleted the draft and went for a run instead. That evening, as Byron held her secret twice-weekly meeting with a group of underemployed postgrad Berkeley computer-science students who were busy breaking Perfection down into its component parts, I caught a cab into the hills of San Rafael, and with two hundred stolen bucks walked into the China Creek Casino. I counted cards, made no effort to hide my methods. CCTV cameras watched, but no one came. I was a stranger who bet lucky

now

and now

and now

all past patterns forgotten.

At five thousand US dollars, I was ready to go home, when I saw the 106 Club. They were secluded from the rest of the casino by a sliding glass partition, playing high-stakes games in a function room where clean water rolled down the inside of the walls and champagne bubbled from a fountain ensconced in a bed of ice. I considered walking away, didn't. I stole a drunk woman's mobile phone, used the invite recorded in pixel form on its memory to get me through the doors of the club.

The lights were a moonlight blue, the games were poker and roulette. They played terribly. Ridiculous bets, $7,000, $10,000, and why? Because you're worth it, baby, hey, baby, you just say the word. $15,000 lost on a ridiculous turn of the cards, hit, she said, though she had seventeen in her hand and the dealer couldn't be carrying more than fifteen at a shot, and the dealer hit and as her money was taken, she laughed, screamed with laughter and said, "I wish my ex was here to see this!"

A man came up to me said, "You don't seem happy."

"I'm not sure I enjoy watching money being squandered."

"It's just money," he replied. "It's just paper."

"It's time," I said, sharper than I'd meant. "It's the means to purchase time. It's the cost of a new bed in a hospital, a solar panel on a roof; it's a year's salary for a tailor in Dhaka, it's the price of a fishing boat, the cost of an education, it's not money. It's what it could have been."

The man stared at me, physically pulling his head back on his neck, like a bird recoiling from a potential predator, and he was beautiful, and he'd had treatments – of course he'd had treatments, look at him, charisma, confidence, the sense of his own worth, worth, to be worthy – of a quality that is commendable, admirable, respected, and he said,

"Wow, that is so deep."

He meant it, of course.

"You're really real," he added breathily. "Say something else."

I decided he wasn't worth punching, and walked away.

Chapter 67

I buried $5,000 in a plastic bag beneath a cypress tree up the hill from Marin City. Would I need it? Didn't know. Never hurts to have a backup plan.

When I returned to the apartment, the sun was rising and Byron was awake, her skin as grey as the morning sky, and I doubted she'd slept. As I stepped through the door, she rose to her feet, fast, opened her mouth, stopped herself, and for a moment, the two of us faced each other, my picture in her right hand, her lips sealing tight.

I counted back from ten slowly, and when I reached one, so did she, and she said, "Did you follow me yesterday?"

"No," I replied.

"I saw . . . women. A woman. Women. Who I thought . . . "

"Matched the words that are my description?"

"Yes."

"Wasn't me."

"How can I know that? How can I ever *know*?"

There it was. Fear in her eyes. A woman who lived alone, who has nothing but her thoughts and this instant. Terror of the thing that sits on the shoulder of all lonely travellers in the night. Am I mad? Am I mad and I don't know it?

You – are you real?

Are you real, stranger I cannot remember?

Is this real, this moment, are you, am I, is this, is any . . . ?

There's a gun on the table next to Byron's bed, and she is so scared, so, so frightened.

"It's okay," I said. "It's okay. Listen to your recordings. Remember my name."

She licked her lips, and said, "The sword out-weareth the sheath,"

and the next day there wasn't any jam at breakfast, and I had a headache.

On the seventy-third day, I realised I'd been counting the days wrong.

Not seventy-three days, not ten weeks, not three months since I'd come to San Francisco with Byron. Not at all. A storm rolled up the bay, and rain ran down the hills, and as the overcast urban yellow of the sky gave way to unrelenting, sea-soaked black, I found the ticket stub from the flight from Seoul, and the date didn't make any sense, and I checked it against the date on the newspaper, and I'd got it wrong, I'd counted something wrong, not seventy-three days, but eighty-nine, eighty-nine days in America.

So I went upstairs and started to speak to Byron, but Byron said, "The soul wears out the breast,"

and there was jam at breakfast, but it was seedless, which I've never understood the point of at all.

Chapter 68

A day in a

café

diner?

Call it a diner.

Booths.

Counter.

Coffee machine.

Bacon.

Syrup.

Waitress in a funny frilly white apron and a green jacket with her name embroidered in gold. Rainbow.

At first I thought it was a brand name, or a style decision, but then she said, "Hi, my name's Rainbow, what can I get you today?" and

how did I come to be in this place?

Road outside, four lanes of traffic going this way, four lanes of traffic going that. A thin line of scraggly scrub in the middle. A pavement just wide enough for a wheezing mother and a narrow pram, for the poor people to walk on

because even the poorest of the poor have to drive; this is America,

General Motors, Ford, Nicola Tesla, DC/AC, the victory of the highway, the death of the trains, I had read something . . .

A plate put in front of me, bacon, tomato, sausage, potato, toast, strong black coffee I didn't order this, did I?

"Do you want something more?"

An empty plate.

Someone has eaten my food, when I blinked, and now the plate is empty and I said, "No," because I was full, really full, properly, properly full and my head ached and it was

now

which was two hours later than

then

which had been a now

which was dead.

And a woman whose parents had decided to call her Rainbow said, "More coffee, honey?"

And I replied, "Though the night was made for loving, And the day returns too soon, Yet we'll go no more a-roving, By the light of the moon."

She said, "Oh isn't that just so cute . . . "

but a man stood on my foot and I said, "Fuck off!" and he just made a face at me and kept on walking.

And I was hungry again, but I kept on running, just running, and in the morning Byron said, "Shall we try another today?"

and I can't remember what I said in reply.

Chapter 69

A

place.

A

time.

I am

this time.

This place and my head

is killing me.

These are the words I have written on the palm of my hand, big black letters.

My head is killing me.

When did I write these words?

I look around and it is

darkness.

This now, this present tense, this instant, this second, it will be for ever now as soon as I realise it, not a memory, not a thing embedded in the past, but the eternal revelation, an understanding that time does not diminish, an impact that distance cannot lessen and it is

now.

Now.

Now.

That I realise I have been forgetting.

Fairness: a correction.

I think I have known for a while.

A gap between knowing a thing, and comprehending it. Between perception and belief.

Undoubtedly time has been lost, but hours fly by every day on inactivity

office routine

commuting

dawdling, doodling

staring off into space

cleaning

cooking

washing

sleeping

the list is endless, *okashi* as the scholar said, delightful, delightful, a delightful little list

delightful clap our hands together oh how droll

you're so real, so quaint, so cute so

fuckfuckfuckfuckfuckfuckfuckfuckfuckfuckfuckfuckfuckfuck-

fuckfuckfuckfuckfuckfuckfuckfuckfuckfuckfuckfuckfuckfuckfuck-fuckfuckfuckfuckfuckfuckfuckfuckfuckfuckfuckfuckfuckfuck

I run.

I run, until at last I find a taxi, and that taxi takes me to a tree, and from under the tree I retrieve $5,000 and with it I buy a room in a motel just off Route 101, El Camino Real, the Royal Road, once used by Spanish monks to connect missions and pueblos, now the road from California in the south to the Canadian border in the north, running along the West Coast for more than a thousand miles

fuckfuckfuckfuckfuckfuckfuckfuckfuckfuckfuckfuckfuckfuckfuck-fuckfuckfuckfuckfuckfuckfuckfuckfuckfuckfuckfuckfuckfuckfuck-fuckfuckfuckfuckfuckfuckfuckfuckfuckfuckfuckfucketyfucketyfuck-etyfuckfuck

The owner of the motel, looking me over once, says carefully, "Cash first."

I give him cash.

"You got ID?"

I do not have ID.

"You in trouble?"

I am not in trouble. He hears my British accent and wavers. Casual discrimination is all very well and good, but I'm a foreign woman, who knows what problems I might bring?

I put more cash on the table, and he says no more on the subject, except, "We only clean towels on Tuesdays."

In my room, I discover my feet are blistered. Most are new; some are old. How far have I run? There's a mobile phone in my pocket, but I've already pulled out the SIM card, damned if I'm making that mistake now.

I have a bath, examine my entire body, needle marks in my arms, in my ankles, my wrist, my neck, no memory of when they happened. I explore the top of my scalp with a mirror, feeling my way through the hairs like a gorilla seeking lice, and yes, there, and here also at the back, slight bumps where needles have gone in, someone has been injecting things into my brain and I thought I was so clever, so clever and in control, so fucking fuckety fuck fuck fucking clever FUCK

I look through the photos saved on my mobile phone, find the pictures of Byron's coded diary, and go to work.

Chapter 70

Snatches of other people's lives, in a motel off Route 101.

A family of three in one room next door. He's a salesman, she serves fries at the drive-through. He says, Babe, babe, I promise, next week, next week I promise . . .

She says, You said that last week, and the week before that, and the week before that.

Honey, honey, I know, but I can do it, I can get the money together . . .

You always say that, she sobs, you always say the same thing.

They row into the small hours of the night, and I lie awake, listening through the cardboard wall.

A man in a cowboy hat on the TV, skinny as a stick, strong as a stone, moustache quivering on his top lip, sideburns to the jaw.

"Let's talk reason; let's make a little sense. Crime is committed by the blacks, that's math, that's statistics. So if the police want to use racial profiling I say, yeah, yeah that's right, because they're just using a truth we all know to help keep us safe."

"The FBI say that nearly 70 per cent of crime in the USA is committed by whites."

"No, I think you'll find—"

" . . . but there is a higher percentage of blacks imprisoned for the same crimes . . . "

"I'm not racist, this is me, having a debate, I'm not racist, you call me racist and I'll take you to court . . ."

Types of code: Caesar shift, monoalphabetic, polyalphabetic, single-key encryption, one-time pad, book code, prime number encryption, SSL, etc.

Of all the ciphers it seemed likely that Byron was using, the most obvious was polyalphabetic with a code word. Slow to write, slow to read, but speed could be acquired with practice and, if the code word were known, a computer could break it in a matter of seconds.

Without the code word, frequency analysis would take time, but Byron had written a great deal of material and, usefully, hadn't bothered to break her words down into five- or six-letter groups, but left all the grammar and spacing in, as thus: bwuwm xi sw ehtjaur pjcfv xdlmcknbn sfvcey adbam.

There is no problem human ingenuity cannot solve.

I looked for repetition of word patterns: "xi" "sw" – It? Is? On? If? "imd" "wix" – The? She? Her? I looked for repetitions of four-letter words, seeking the word "Hope", and in the end instead found a repetition of the same three-letter word, uxl, and decided it was Why. Crossing "Why" with "uxl" on an alphabetic square gave the letters "edo". Another three-letter combination, glq, I tried crossing with "the" and found the letters "fre". On the ancient PC in the foyer of the motel, I typed in a sample sentence from Byron's diary with the keyword "freedom", and watched the plaintext appear in an instant.

What I do is unethical, it said, *and in the service of humanity.*

"It's two bucks an hour for the PC," said the manager, mop over his shoulder, bucket in hand.

I left ten dollars under the keyboard, and kept on typing.

America doesn't have enough public libraries. I end up using the printer at the local fixit store, which also doubles as a seller of beer, milk, toiletries, stuffed animals and guns. It's a dollar a page, but who cares, the decrypted reams of Byron's diary fall from the machine into my hands.

Alone in the motel, surrounded by paper, the news on low, the couple next door fighting, fighting, always fighting.

I can't do this anymore, he screams, I can't do it! I was meant to be a banker!

"There are cities in England now, whole cities, which are Islamic, where they have Sharia law," explained an expert on the news, and the anchor looked shocked, aghast, how could this happen, how could Islam have spread so far?

"There are good Muslims, of course, but the faith itself, the religion . . ."

Change the channel.

My actions are monstrous, and I will not seek a moral justification. History is my guide, Byron wrote. Oliver Cromwell killed a king; the French revolution was led by terror. The serfs were freed and democracy was born; Lenin waged civil war and the Allies fire-bombed Dresden. History is full of vile acts and strange consequence.

I am afraid of Why. Hope – her name is Hope, but I remember her as Why. And why is that? I recall conversations carried out with a figure called Why, her gift, it seems, does not extend to computers, I have data which remembers her, where I cannot. Nor is it fair to say I am afraid of HER – I cannot remember her to be afraid. I am afraid of the concept of her. Of the woman I cannot remember. But that is foolish. My imagination runs wild with the question of the past and the possibilities of the future, but only now, only when I perceive her, is the question real. She is made real by perception, this world is made real by perception of now, of this instant, and that is all that I can permit to matter.

She is free, and does not know it. She is a god, looking at the world from outside the world. Her gift is beautiful. What I am doing to her is vile, but it is both of her own asking, and necessary. The basic structure has been superficially successful. If we can implant the trigger in Why, then we can implant it anywhere.

She is sublime; she is enlightenment.

I slept heavily one night, but my diary had not been disturbed, and you said you lost the phone I gave you.

In my nightmare, you are everyone, and I am alone in the world as you laugh at me.

Hope?

The word written, plaintext, embedded so far into the notebooks that I almost missed it.

Hope? If you read this – perhaps you have already – know that you wanted treatments. You agreed to all of it. I have stripped Filipa's programming from the system. You will not desire to be beautiful, you will not be made ambitious, a drone, a doll, a perfect woman, I will not kill your soul. But every day you sit in that chair, we come closer to understanding Filipa's work, and your mind.

And then, encoded, immediately after,

No More A-Roving.

Terror, alone in the night. I locked myself into my motel room, sat down with a new mobile phone, counted backwards from one hundred, cross-legged on the end of the bed, and looked up the words of the poem, "We'll Go No More A-Roving", by Lord Gordon Byron, 1788–1824.

So we'll go no more a-roving
So late into the night,
Though the heart be still as loving,
And the moon be still as bright.

For the sword outwears its sheath,
And the soul wears out the breast,
And the heart must pause to breathe,
And love itself have a rest.

Though the night was made for loving,
And the day returns too soon,
Yet we'll go no more a-roving
By the light of the moon.

I read the words, and finished the words, and nothing happened, though my heart was racing fast, so fast, not even breath, not even counting my breath could slow it. I put my phone down, went into the bathroom, washed my face, my hands, cold water, stared at my own reflection in the mirror, found it ragged and grey, stood up straighter, defiant, proud, glared my face into submission, looked down at my phone and saw that washing had taken nearly two and a half hours.

Shaking on the bathroom floor.

fuckfuckfuckfuckfuckGETUPfuckfuckfuckGETUPNOW-fuckfuckfucketyfuckfucketyfuckfuck

The desert.

The train.

And what is worthy, and what is justice, and what are words, at the end of the day?

Fucking get to your fucking feet, Hope Arden. Fucking get this done!

I crawled back to the end of the bed, drank a sip of water, I am warrior, I am runner, I am professional, I am discipline, I am freedom, fuck you all, searched for the poem on YouTube.

Various people had done readings; I chose one by a woman who'd recorded it for her son as part of a family festival on Skye.

"We'll go no more a-roving," she said, and her voice was

untrained but her meaning was clear. "For the sword outwears its sheath, and the soul wears out the breast,"

and I was sitting on the floor by the TV, and had been crying, though I didn't know why.

Hours, lost in a second.

I listened to the poem again, and this time I held a rubber band around my wrist, and snapped it hard, burning against my skin, and the reader said, "The soul wears out the breast . . ."

I was on the balcony outside my motel room, watching Route 101 rush by beyond the pines, and my wrist was red and raw, and only thirty minutes had passed.

Again.

Again.

I pinched my skin hard enough to cry out with the pain, and she said, "The soul wears out . . ."

and I was on the floor, gasping for breath, and I'd clearly turned the TV on, but that was okay, because only fifteen minutes had gone by and on the screen a man said, "So two hundred bucks and we've turned that into six hundred and that's skill, my man, that's expertise, that's us rising to the occasion when the pressure's on . . ."

Again.

Again again again until it'd done, again, getting this thing out of my head again again again!!

I listen to the recording and now

on the bed, silent, eyes open, lying flat on my back, I'm at forty-three counts of my breath and appear to be counting downwards from one hundred, who knows where the last fifty-seven breaths have gone?

Again, the soul wears out the breast and

reading the Bible, calmly now, calmer, though the impression of my nails in the palm of my left hand has raised a hard red lump, and there is bruising around the tops of both my arms where, perhaps, I clung too tightly to myself but again

the heart must pause to breathe

and the sun is rising, beautiful California day, not grey, not like home, not a sunrise of mists and shredding clouds, but goddess-golden, a thing to worship, Amaterasu, Bast, Bridgit, driving out the dark.

Again

I sing along to the words, tuneless, dancing round the room, "The soul wears out the breast oh yeahhhh!"

and stumble, but do not fall, dizzy, head aching, head killing me but fuck that, fuck this, screw you all, I am Hope, I am Why, I am a thief, I am forgotten, I am me, I am fucking me and this is now, this now I dance and I sing again again again

Again!

"The sword outwears its sheath . . . "

Barely a stumble this time, barely a gasp, I press myself to the wall for a moment, wait for the moment to pass, then turn and turn again, dancing on the spot, wild, limbs flailing, breath shaking, knees bending, the sword outwears its sheath and I am dancing, dancing, dancing, my body is stone, I am dancing stone again!

" . . . the soul wears out the breast, and the heart must pause to breathe and love itself have a rest HEY MACARENA! The soul wears out the breast *hey Macarena*!" Words replacing words, fuck this dancing fuck this the soul the breast replace repeat repeat until it's done *Macarena*! "The heart must pause to breathe and love itself fuck you fuck you fuck you fuck you fuck fuck fuck *Macarena*!"

A hammering on the door, dawn light through the sheer polyester curtain. "What the fuck is going on?" screams the manager of the motel and then, when I answer the door, gleaming with sweat, laughing, shaking, wheezing, "Who the fuck are you?!"

"I'm Hope!" I exclaimed, holding back a shriek of laughter. "I am Hope!!"

Chapter 71

A question for the floor, asked by the man waiting for the bus back into San Francisco: "How do you know if you're mad?"

He's maybe in his early thirties, but with a hunted innocence in his eyes that makes him seem much younger. He clings to a single sky-blue suitcase, and wears a grey sweater with a hood, and torn shoes, and says earnestly that he used to study philosophy, but the philosophers missed the point, that it wasn't about the rules, it was about the absences, the places where the rules broke down, that was the truth of it, the truth of the universe.

"We all pretend we're not mad," he whispered, "but that's because we're afraid!"

A question I mulled over on the bus, clutching my meagre travel bag close, my clothes dirty, hair wild, face set. How do you know you're not mad?

How many lives had I touched, who now considered themselves insane? My parents, slowly forgetting their own child, papering over the wallpaper in my bedroom, something they'd always meant to do. People I'd stolen from, the police in the interview room – she walked right up to you, she spoke to you, how can you not remember her face? Princess Leena in Dubai. Gauguin, who'd held a knife on me; people I'd robbed and people I'd bought. A passport forger on a boat in the Sea of Marmara, a girl playing video games in Tokyo, a lover drunk on the bed of the one-hour hotel. Men whose bodies I'd pressed close to mine, Parker in New York, a maths teacher who'd wondered if I counted cards, company, warmth, association, companionship – discipline.

Am I mad?

I have discipline to protect me. The discipline of thoughts questioned, of company sought, another pair of eyes, a different outlook on the world, they are my discipline, humanity is my discipline, Luca Evard is . . .

. . . a lapse in judgement.

I know that, have always known that, see it very clearly now. Not discipline. Anti-discipline. A burst of irrational obsession which, having nothing long-term to measure the term against, I called love. How I needed him now. How he must hate me, if he remembered anything about who I was.

I counted, until only counting remained.

Chapter 72

Byron was not at the apartment; of course.

She'd left an envelope taped to the wall by the door, the word HOPE written on it in large letters.

Dear Hope,

It would appear that either you have vanished, or I have ceased recording our interactions. If the former, I do not know why you have departed, though I can speculate. If the latter, then you should know that fear of not knowing who you are or why I am no longer recording our relationship has prompted my departure. If I have left you, then I hope I clarified beforehand that you have been receiving treatments. Not the full schedule as embarked on by Filipa and Rafe; not Perfection. But an experimental set of techniques designed to map and alter your brain chemistry. You have requested this; you may also not be fully aware of it, as the process is still being developed.

If you have left me, then it is possible that a side-effect of this process has driven you away. If so I hope you will believe me when I say that I mean you no harm, and would be honoured to continue to work with you to understand your condition, and wish in time we may collaborate again.

Much of what is in this letter you may know, or may not

know, or may know more, or think you know more, or may simply not care. I can perceive you only through my records, and they are insubstantial. I see from my notes that you once said you needed to meet me face to face to know me. I share this sentiment, but unlike you I cannot build up a picture of you from these encounters. Thus who you are is a blank to me, and I cannot trust a blank. I do not say this with rancour. Yet my mission is essential and discretion is paramount, and so here we are.

Know I wish you well and safe, and implore you to avoid all use of treatments save by those protocols that you and I have modified together. Your life and soul are too precious to be destroyed by Perfection.

yours sincerely,

Byron

There was a USB stick in the bottom of the envelope. I took it to my hotel, plugged it into the computer, put headphones on, listened to the audio file within.

Nothing surprising; my stomach tightened at the sound but I did not flinch, did not run, did not move.

"The sword outwears its sheath," said Byron's voice, steady and resigned. "The soul wears out the breast. Trust me. I am your only hope. You will come to me."

She said this last several times, then repeated the poem, and I listened, unmoved, and felt okay. Hey Macarena.

I went to Daly City, to the empty office up its little concrete path, Hydroponic Fertilizers Ltd., *Water Is Our Future.* The sign was still there, but the office was empty. I broke in through the back door, wandered past the place where Byron's chair had sat, a place of needles and drugs and . . .

. . . other things I had forgotten.

Did I feel horror?

I ran my hand over walls, under the window sills, and didn't. Thought perhaps I should, tried to force myself to feel queasy or angry at what had happened, felt nothing. I looked for anything, something, a sign, and found everything bleach-clean, empty, gone.

I looked up Hydroponic Fertilizers Ltd., but the company had vanished as quickly as it was created, the records blank. I knocked on the houses next door, asked if they'd seen anyone leave, lorries or faces, but they'd seen nothing, except for one old woman with insomnia, who'd been woken at 3 a.m. by a white van pulling away, and thought it was thieves, but no, you didn't get thieves round here, not where everyone was so nice.

In the end, I fell back on a stake-out.

For two weeks, I sat outside the house of Agustin Carrazza, the ex-MIT professor of dubious ethical practices whom Byron had visited during those long, long weeks of experiments. I watched him come, watched him go, followed him to meetings and dinners, and hid, not from him, but from CCTV cameras and mobile phones, hiding from the machine, for the machine never forgets.

Discipline; all things, discipline.

If he was working with Byron, he showed no sign of it, until one Wednesday afternoon, when he drove to a lab with no name, in an industrial estate off Route 24, where bright young things in slacks rushed out to meet him and shake his hand, before leading him inside to admire their operation, their well-guarded, locked-door operation. And when the lab was dark, I broke in, and found the self-same chair and the same needles and the same drugs and the same everything, electrical, brain-altering everything that had been in Byron's little office in Daly City, and unwashed coffee cups and cutlery left in the sink, and a glass full of green washing-up liquid that was beginning to crystallise from neglect, and a Giants calendar, because everyone here supported the same team, and a password-protected PC that didn't yield to anything obvious – password1, 123456, Giants001, etc. – and in a yellow biohazard bin, needles caked with freshly dried blood, waiting to be taken away and incinerated.

Three more days of staking out the building gave me the names and identities of everyone working in the outfit. A couple of grad students, a pair of researchers who should have known better, a trio of undergrads from Berkeley in it for the credit on their CVs. I approached them all, chatted in the canteen, brushed up against them in the library, and within a few days could have greeted any of them warmly and asked after their pet cat/lizard/spider/fish by name.

At the heart of the group was Meredith Earwood. Two years into a psychology major, with a minor in English literature, she was the lab rat in the treatment chair, her blood on the needles in the biohazard bin. Her hair was dyed, crafted and sprayed, five dollars for every snip of the scissors; her teeth were perfect little moons in her mouth, her home West Virginia, her ambition to be a counsellor to the famous in LA, her CV adorned with pageants won, her stomach a display of stone-carved muscle, her place on the top of the cheerleading team assured, she somersaulted and backflipped her way to popularity and fame but it wasn't enough, not enough, never enough.

I opened a conversation with her outside the library with an easy route in: do you have Perfection?

Of course she did, she'd got to 543,000 points back home, no one in her town had achieved so much but then, surprising, unexpected, "But I don't use that bullshit any more."

I raised my eyebrows, sat down on the edge of a wall beside her, held my student bag close, purchased three hours ago from the campus shop and rubbed down against bricks until it looked suitably used, and said, "What do you mean you don't use it?"

"Perfection is an elitist tool of social division," she explained with the absolute confidence of a second-year humanities student destined to rule the universe. "It's almost impossible for the poor to achieve more than a few hundred thousand points, and the only way you can achieve a million is by accumulating both the material goods, and the material values of the extremely rich and privileged. You know how the company behind Perfection decided what 'perfect' was?"

No, no I didn't, how did they . . . ?

"The internet. They took Google, Amazon, Bing, Yahoo, Twitter, Facebook, Weibo – all the algorithms, all the data, and mined it for what 'perfect' meant. Figured the cloud mind would know, because people always know best, all the people, data and numbers on the web and you know what they got?"

No, what did they . . . ?

"George Clooney and Angelina Jolie, that's what. They got movie stars and models. Rich boys and pretty girls. They got fashion and fast cars, Caribbean holidays, blue skies, clean waters, organic socks and vegan diets. They got fairytales – fantasies – a social construct of 'perfect' that's unobtainable, that's been pumped out by TV and films and magazines to make us buy, buy buy buy more stuff more advertising buy buy buy buy a house buy a car buy new shoes buy perfection – and they programmed it into their algorithm as the definition of what we should all be. I mean shit, that's nothing new, Hollywood's been doing it for years, Perfection's just riding that wave. Perfection is whatever the marketing men say it is, and we bought it."

"So you stopped?"

"Sure."

"But—" I caught myself before the words "you are having treatments" could pass my lips, half closed my eyes, put my head on one side, looking for a better way in.

"But I'm beautiful?" she offered, into my silence.

Not quite where I was going, but . . .

"I choose to look good," she exclaimed, highlighting every word with a stab of her finger. "The world admires me, and I like being admired. I know it's bullshit, but it's easy, it helps me get where I want to be, and I want to be at the top."

I counted bricks in the pavement, held my bag tighter, the weight of books that weren't even mine – must have stolen them from somewhere – pulling me down. "Did you hear about treatments?" I murmured.

She looked up, sharp, then smiled, hiding the knives in her eyes. "Sure."

"The 106, they say . . . "

"Sure, I heard that."

"I hear they make you perfect."

She didn't reply, and that night, I followed her to the lab, and watched through a hole I'd drilled in the walls three days before, fibre-optic camera pushed through the gap, as she sat in the chair, didn't flinch when they gave her the injections, smiled when they put the goggles over her eyes. A man in blue plastic overalls – who I'd never seen before – parted the hairs around the crown of her head, pushed a needle, four inches long, a round sort of antennae at the top, into her skull, all the way. Her heart rate didn't rise, her breathing was steady, O_2 99, BP 122/81. They put headphones on her, a metal node on her tongue, a tube up her nose. They waited. Machines ran and someone made coffee, and they waited.

Thirty-six minutes later, they disconnected her, a little bit at a time, and nothing had changed, but when she opened her eyes the man in blue overalls said, "A simple child that draws its breath, and feels life in every limb, what should it know of death?"

And she smiled, in no apparent pain, and answered, "I met a little cottage girl, she was eight years old, she said; her hair was thick with many a curl that clustered round her head."

They gave her a lift home, after the procedure, and she waved at them from the door of her house, and the next day got a 78 in her paper on cognition and culture, which was a ridiculously high mark, and went to English beaming, until her lecturer said,

"The little maid would have her will, and said, 'Nay we are seven!'"

At which point Meredith turned, still smiling serenely, and, with the corner of her expensive grey laptop, smashed the brains out of the student sitting by her side.

Chapter 73

An ambulance on the left, the police car on the right.

Meredith screamed for a very, very long time when they dragged her off the boy she was trying to kill. She screamed until they sedated her, and lay, handcuffed, in the seat of the ambulance, its gurney already occupied with the man whose brains now showed visible and pink between the broken bones of his cranium. I stood in the crowd of onlookers, some silent, some crying, more attempting to take photos, until a furious anthropology professor roared, "If I see a single photograph of that poor boy anywhere, anywhere at all, I will bounce you! I will bounce you so hard you'll wish you were a fucking tennis ball!!"

The professor was fifty-five at a pinch, diminutive, bespectacled and an expert in the meaning of meaning, whatever that meant. She had the lungs of an opera singer and the fury of a pitbull, and the crowd dispersed before her wrath, and so did I.

At night, I returned to the labs where Meredith had been treated, and found them empty, gone; just the smell of bleach.

I went back to the house of Agustin Carrazza, and he too was vanished, departed in a hurry, lights off, no one home.

I locked myself in a motel room, piled cushions around the doors and walls, and listened once again to the sound of Byron's voice, turned up full, as she proclaimed, "For the sword outwears its sheath, and the soul wears out the breast, and the heart must pause to breathe, and love itself have a rest . . . "

Hey Macarena!

This time, the urge to vomit came entirely from me, from the experiences I, myself, had found, and not from any implant in my mind.

Then I put on recordings of every Wordsworth and Lord Byron poem I could find, and lay back on the bed to listen to them all, and had no adverse response to either, and kept the clock in my line of sight to ensure I lost no time.

After six hours of poetical digestion, I put my running shoes on, and went to visit Meredith in the hospital.

They had her in a private room, handcuffed to the bed. A sleepy man in a blue cap sat watch outside, empty paper coffee cups crushed on the chair beside him, a packet of tortilla chips nearly finished, a nicotine stain around his fingers. I stole a nurse's badge from a woman in oncology, scrubs from a surgical ante-theatre, and a clipboard off the end of a bed. I tied my hair back, smiled at the policeman by the door, who didn't bother to check my badge as he let me in.

Meredith was dozing the fitful sleep of a woman unlikely to sleep well again. I sat down beside her, woke her gently, my hand on hers, and at her start said, soft, East-Coast American, "It's all right. I wanted to check on how you were doing."

"Is he dead?" she asked. "Did I kill him?"

"No."

"Christ! Christ oh God Christ . . . "

Relief, I thought, in her face, but there was too much anxiety to let the relief last long. "Meredith," I said, "the doctor needs to know if you're on any other medical protocols. Have you been having any sort of treatment for other conditions?"

"Treatments? No."

"There are needle marks in your arm."

"Oh . . . yeah, sure . . . I gave blood, or something."

"There's more needle marks than that."

"I . . . I'm not having any treatments."

Either a damn good liar, or she can't remember. "Do you remember an industrial estate out towards Walnut Creek? People in overalls, a reclining chair?"

"No. I don't. Why, is there . . . did I do something? I mean . . . did I . . . is there . . . "

Words trail off. She has no idea.

The girl has no idea at all.

"No," I breathed, pushing the dishevelled hair back from her blotched face. "It wasn't you – not you at all."

I let myself out, and didn't smile at the cop on my way to the exit.

Chapter 74

A question, the only one that matters: where is Byron?

Perhaps also another: *why* do I need to know? She said "you will come to me" and I am looking for her, is this just a compulsion? Has she embedded something in my brain, needles and antennae and . . .

. . . but no. First things first, I get a full medical, all in one day, fast so the doctors can't forget mid-test. Nothing embedded, no chips, no wires, no nothing, today is not the day I start wearing a tin-foil hat.

Discipline: if you cannot trust in yourself, trust in others. If you cannot trust in others, trust in the scientific method. Everything else is conjecture and doubt, dogma, fantasy and fear. I will not be afraid. I will *not* be mad.

I looked for Byron, and Byron was gone.

Vanished from America, vanished from the darknet, simply . . . vanished.

I searched the 106, I searched laboratories and lecture halls, scoured the airports and the border posts, rummaged through the internet, digging for her, luring her out, and nothing.

She had vanished more effectively than I'd ever imagined, and people could remember her, and she was still gone. Maybe she was right; maybe that was a kind of freedom.

Finding nothing, on a whim, I rode the Greyhound bus to Salt Lake City. The bus wasn't like the old movies; it was air conditioned, comfortable, a coach with a toilet at the back. "Hi there!" exclaimed the driver over the intercom, as we headed north. "There's Wi-Fi for your entertainment, magazines for your pleasure, lights above your chairs for reading and a toilet for an experience you won't ever forget!"

Salt Lake City: founded by Mormons, sustained by skiing and industrial banks. A puddle of straight lines beneath snow-capped peaks. I had a very good hot dog while choosing my next destination – so good I went back for seconds and the woman serving exclaimed, "Honey, you oughtta eat more and fatten up, else you won't never survive the winter!"

I squirted more ketchup into the bun, tipped an extra two dollars, and caught the bus at 3 a.m. down Interstate 80, heading east, towards nowhere much.

Chapter 75

Names on the road. Evanston, Rock Springs, Rawlins, Laramie, Cheyenne, Ft Collins. Places where founding fathers planted a flag, where the railwaymen came with spades and dynamite, where old tribes fought and died, driven ever further west towards the mountains and the seas. Why am I here? Why am I travelling?

Travelling from, travelling to. It seems like the thing a pilgrim does. It feels like a kind of prayer.

A slow shift in the landscape, the beginning of names tied up with a different kind of history. Lexington, Kearney, Grand Island, Lincoln, Omaha. A decaying industrial heartland. Denver. Ft Morgan. Sterling. Ogallala. The chimneys are dry and dusty, the gates are locked, move with the times or be crushed. Insurance salesmen, dealers in second-hand cars, TV crews, pundits and merchants of opinion and vanity, come east, come east; there's a ten-minute rest stop in Des Moines, thirty minutes in Walcott if you need to pee, toilet stinks but what of it, someone else will clean up the mess, litter in the road, tomorrow's problem, today is today is today, what next?

Chicago. I sat by Lake Michigan, still as settled silk, and wondered if the first Europeans to come here had thought they were seas, oceans, and that Japan lay beyond.

I rode the L, marvelled that it could be so slow, crawl so close to the towers in the Loop, craned my neck to see a little piece of sky. I ate pizza by Wrigley Park and cheered for the Cubs, though they were destined to lose. I found a man who liked to rumba, thought, why not, why the hell not, and rumbaed with him all the way to his flat, which smelt of habanero and kidney beans, and it was only fucking, nothing else, and he didn't ask if he'd see me again and I wasn't interested in anything more, and I caught the bus the next morning towards South Bend, Toledo, Cleveland and New York.

And in New York, I looked across at the statue of Liberty, and I cried.

Seven-day-old clothes, the smell of pepper and sex on my skin, I hadn't run for days, my legs were dead from the bus, my mind saw only the passing of the world outside, not me, not me at all, discipline, gone, breath, gone, counting, gone, knowledge, truth, thief, all . . .

Nothing.

Where had I come from? Where was I going?

From nowhere, to nowhere.

The past was just a present that had been, the future was a present yet to come, and only now remained, and I stood by the sea, recovering my land-legs from the road, and wept.

Chapter 76

The strangest thing.

A funny feeling.

I bought a French passport off a guy in the Bronx, a proper professional, his ID on the darknet an alpha-numerical tangle that expired the instant he had cash in hand. He'd done a good job too, right down to stamping it with an entry visa from the Canadian border, a couple from Turkey and one from India. I complimented him on his efforts, and he shrugged, great rippling basketball shoulders, and said when he was working it was like nothing bothered him, yeah.

I went to Fifth Avenue to find something fashionable to steal, but nothing leapt to mind, and that night I went to a casino off Eighth and West 36th and counted cards and lost a little but won more, and at one point a security guard stood behind me, and counted cards with me, but someone dropped a cocktail and started screaming at the man who'd bumped into her, and that briefly diverted the guard's attention, and when he turned back, he'd forgotten what he was doing there.

Standing at JFK waiting for the plane, I saw a woman with a beautiful silver bracelet set with amber, and I went to steal it, and then stopped myself, and didn't, and sat back down, and when a few minutes later she saw me, and I smiled, she smiled back, and her day was fine.

The cashier phoned her manager when I paid for my flight to London entirely in cash, but I showed her the paperwork from the casino and explained that I'd got lucky, but never had a bank account in the USA.

"You know you can't take all that currency across customs, don't you?" said her manager, and that was okay, I replied, I had a friend in the British embassy who was going to handle it for me. Then I sat in the toilet and counted out $9,990 from my stash, put the rest ($2,681.55) in a brown envelope and dropped it into the donations box for "Bioliving New York – for a greener city for all our children". They stopped me at customs, and counted out my cash.

"Sweet," said the lady who helped me re-pack my bag. "Ten bucks short of all the paperwork."

"I had luck in the casino," I explained with my best comedy-French accent. "Going to start again, a new life. You can only take what you carry."

"Swell," she exclaimed. "I always wanted a clean break, but you know, who doesn't?"

I flew economy class, half watched a couple of films. A man in a grey suit fidgeted all the way to London, flinching at every bump of turbulence. Sometimes he looked at me and saw someone new, but he didn't care. His fear would have wiped away all details of this journey, even if I weren't his companion for the long journey home.

Home.

London.

Hotels, B&Bs, places I know, the river, the winter sun setting behind the London Eye, dog walking on Hampstead Heath, kites flying, is this home?

I took the train to Manchester. Straight streets between stiff, industrial architecture. Short cathedral tucked in between a shopping mall and roaring traffic. Museum dedicated to football, galleries from warehouses, town hall snaked round with trams, stone columns, red brick, not enough trees, crossing the canals at the lock gates, clinging to the black iron handles as you edge, one foot at a time to the other side. The screech of the railway line, the cyclists ready to pedal through the Pennines, is this home?

I ate chips in Albert Square while a steel-drum band played, went to the pub for a quiet pint, put a quid into the fruit machine, lost, and caught the train from Piccadilly to Derby as the sun went down.

*

Derby.

Is this my home, is this a thing that matters, a place that has some meaning? More than flagstones and concrete, bricks and tar?

I took a hotel room near the station, an ExpressPremier-ExclusiveSomething, room the size of a cupboard, sheets superglued to the surface of the bed, everything too hot, curtains too thick, night too dark, pipes creaking, slept like a stone.

Walking through the streets I hadn't walked through for I didn't know how long. Shops I had hung out in as a kid – CDs, DVDs, three for a tenner, four for fifteen quid, bargain, if you liked what they had. Phone shop, accessories; cases with owls on, hair extensions, toe rings, the tattoo parlour we'd never quite managed to go into as kids, despite bragging.

Is this home?

I walked, slow, taking my time, a tourist again, and let my feet carry me, a long slow journey, past my old school – the voices of my teachers, You're not very academic, are you? – if you could see me now. The library where I took shelter those first few weeks, the taekwondo club gone, hatha yoga now, a baby-friendly session on Fridays. My parents' house. A light on in the living room, but no one there. But wait, wait a little, watch, and someone comes in, an old man, a man grown old, who's decided that dammit, if old is what he is then you just watch him, he'll do the whole business, the whiskers, the cardigan, the slippers, the corduroy trousers – my dad has waited his whole life to wear corduroy trousers, and now that he's old no one will stop him, you'll see. He watches the TV, a medical documentary of some kind, something about food, good foods, bad foods, fatty foods, skinny foods, foods for your liver, food for your brain.

Dad's face is neutral, quiet, serene. I study it, enthralled. Hard now, almost impossible, to imagine him chasing crooks. Did this harmless old codger grapple people to the ground, look into the eyes of bad men who knew nasty secrets, tear the truth out of them one lie at a time? Or has he always been here, in this moment, drinking tea and watching TV, and if I return again in another now, will he still be here, frozen for ever?

The door to the living room opens; Mum comes in. Her hair is bright white, cut down to the surface of her skull, and age has made her face something extraordinary. Each part of it needs an atlas to describe; her chin is many chins, still small and sharp but etched with muscle and line, layered one upon the other. Her cheeks are contoured bone and silky rivers of skin, her eyebrows waggle against great parallels of thought on her forehead, her mouth is encased in smile lines and pout lines and scowl lines and worry lines and laughter lines and there is no part of her which is not in some way written over with stories.

She says something to Dad, and Dad moves up, and she sits next to him and he puts one arm around her, not taking his eyes from the TV, and she sits with her knees tucked up, feet hanging off the edge of the sofa, a child-like posture she always chided me for, the indignity, hypocrite!

She dips her digestive biscuit into his mug – this always annoyed him, get your own tea, he'd say, but no, she doesn't drink tea with milk, what's the point of that, as George Orwell said, if you want milk and sugar in a cup then just put milk and sugar in a cup, why waste the tea? But milk and sugar in a cup don't taste so good when absorbed into biscuit and so you see, she dunks her biscuits in his mug. He's given up arguing. I watch them together, and they are happy. Still in love. Doing just fine.

A moment, a temptation. The Stasi used to be challenged by their instructors – "In five minutes I want to see you standing on the balcony of that building having tea with its owner" and in they went, bluffing their way into a stranger's house, onto the balcony to discuss . . . whatever lie they were telling to get there.

I could do it. My mum was no slouch, but she was a hearty law-abiding citizen and if I come from the water company or the surveyor's office, she'd let me in, of course she would, and I nod and hum at things only I could perceive with my excellent training, and she'd offer me a cuppa tea and trust me all the more because I was a woman, who looked, perhaps, a little bit like her little girl Grace...

... oh and how old is your daughter, Mrs Arden?

... all grown-up now. She had some difficulties as a child, but she's doing so well now, so well, she's our little delight, our perfect wonder. Never wanted another child, she was always so beautiful ...

And perhaps in the course of my inspection, I would go upstairs to examine insulation in the roof ("I can do you more insulation, better, part of the council's drive to have more energy-efficient housing ... ") and there would be my old bedroom, a guest room now, or maybe a study, a place for Mum to sit in as she sorted out the taxes, she certainly wouldn't let Dad do them, no head for numbers, doesn't keep any receipts, disastrous, and I'd say,

You've certainly got a lovely home, Mrs Arden.

A bit big for us now Grace has gone, but then it has such memories ...

And if I were memorable, this would be the moment in which we bonded. The moment in which I told her that growing up, I too had a little sister who was ill, but who was doing so much better now, and whose favourite film was *Star Wars* and whose favourite colour was blue, who didn't know how to lie and she would say,

"You could be talking about my Gracie!"

and we'd have another cup of tea – "Are you sure I'm not keeping you from something?"

and I would say no, no, my last appointment of the day, if it's not an imposition ...

And she'd take my number and I'd take hers because you see, I'm interested in all the things she's interested in too, angry at the lack of affordable social housing, angry at so many good, cheap homes being torn down and replaced with bad, expensive ones, angry at the language of prejudice and bigotry in our politics, angry at the press, the media – but hopeful for the future, for a youth raised more aware than we were, a coming generation that will do better than the one before and she will say . . .

"Hope is a beautiful name; if I'd ever had another child, I would have called her Hope."

And I would say, "My mother once walked across the desert."

And she would say, quiet now, not wanting to make a thing of it, not wanting to force a connection, implausible, amazing, wonderful, "I once walked a very long way as well. When I first started walking, I was very afraid. In the desert there is always the sound of movement, a busy silence of sand falling beneath your feet. When you are alone, even the quiet is full of monsters."

Then she would love me, and I would love her, and we would be the best of friends and she would smile whenever she opened the door to me, and give me a hug and introduce me to Dad and say, "This is Hope, and she is wonderful!" and we would spend Christmas together and go walking in the hills and I'd help them with their errands and go on holiday and . . .

if I were memorable.

And considering this, two thoughts come to mind, seeping in with the quiet as I watch my parents' house from across the street.

1 If I had Perfection, and the treatments had worked, I would be memorable.
2 If I were perfect, I could never be my mum's friend.

Settling cold, growing dark. Watching them watching.

They are . . .

in their own, unspectacular way, to which no ballads are written or songs sung, in a domestic, daily, life-being-lived way,

. . . happy.

I walk away.

Chapter 77

There is a place, on the edge of Nottingham: a grand old house with a view of the Trent, fields that flood often in winter, oak trees shedding curling leather leaves, a dog playing in the grounds, the residents, sometimes happy, sometimes sad, sometimes in that strange place that does not conform to your meagre emotional understanding, but living – for all this – living.

A walk up the path on a blustery day, my umbrella turns inside-out, is pressed down hard by the wind from the east. Trousers soaked up to the knee with water and mud, where did you park the your car demands the receptionist, I didn't, I reply, I took the bus and this is an outrageous notion but who is she to argue?

I sign in as me, as Hope Arden, just this once, in just this place, and climb the stairs to the second floor, while a woman, fifty, head on one hand, fingers clenched tight, descends on a stairlift on the other side, and smiles as we pass each other in the middle.

An old house, but the corridors have been converted to medical dullness and I count the doors, the steps, the windows and the cracks in the wall until I reach her room, and knock twice and let myself in and as I do,

Gracie, my baby sister, looks up from her chair by the window, and her face bursts into a smile and she says, "Hope!"

Chapter 78

I find that I am . . .

. . . changing.

Things I steal for:

- Survival. I have, in recent months, attempted a few legitimate jobs, but it is hard – so hard. I have a profile on a website, with a picture of myself smiling to camera; I'll clean your house, trim the garden hedge, fetch shopping, wash your car, walk your dog, deliver your parcel, repair your bike. Sometimes people contact me, sometimes they don't, and sometimes I steal so that I don't starve, to keep a roof over my head, and I will not feel remorse for living. I will not.
- Information. Byron14, where are you? Steal police database, steal ID of a man with contacts, steal knowledge, steal CCTV footage, steal a server, steal a network, steal whatever it takes to find her. Byron14 – what are you doing now?
- Justice. I live by my own code. I am a god, my eyes clear because no one sees me. I am the enlightened one. I am a criminal and a hypocrite. I am a pilgrim, struggling in jihad. I am obscene. I am wrong. I am righteousness.

The day I stole £65,000 from a defence lawyer in Doncaster whose speciality was getting people-smugglers off, I felt ... proud. Not the ecstatic pride of a job well done, not the glee of Dubai, not the adrenaline rush of diamonds in my hand. The pride of ... myself. Of who it was I was becoming. Not just thief. Thief who was also me.

I stole his money and cleaned it through fifteen different accounts, breaking it apart and rebuilding, scattering it through the internet before at last re-coalescing it into a hundred different cashpoints across the north-east, sending lump sums of £200–800 to the home where Gracie lived, a charitable donation, a promise of more to come.

The manager of the home, a needy, nervous lady, was at first excited, then frightened, then angry about these sudden donations. They presented that most dreadful of problems for anyone settled into a cushy position – *change.* With cash coming in, it was now possible to *alter* things, to have better food at dinner, or think about putting new thermostats into the rooms, or fix the leaking roof in the southern corner, or maybe save the money to buy a van for the house so they didn't always have to hire when they went on trips, or to get another night-nurse for the patients who needed twenty-four-hour care or . . . or . . .

"We can't spend it! It might stop!" she exclaimed after nearly £6,000 had arrived over the course of four months of gentle donating. The next week I donated £1,000, to make a point, and the manager shrieked in despair, her hands quivering like flytraps in a gale, "*Who is doing this to me?!*" and by a unanimous vote of the governor's board that following week, the problem was removed from her power and work began immediately to install more handles in the corridor and bathroom areas for patients who would otherwise struggle to walk or use the toilets unsupervised.

The week they gave my sister a new wheelchair, lighter than the old, narrower around the hips and with footrests that locked in position, I wheeled her round the garden hollering, "You shake my nerves you rattle my brain! Goodness gracious great balls of fire!"

After a while, the NHS declared that it was unfair for the home to have such a generous private donor without spreading the goodness around, and I did see their point, so continued donations gently on the side even as funds were siphoned off to other projects around the trust, and as the money dribbled away, began to look for someone else who seemed a worthy

worthy, how strange this new use of *worthy*

target of my nefarious expertise.

And then, eleven months after I'd lost her in California, Byron was back.

Chapter 79

Perhaps nothing.

A three-hundred-word article, thrown in as trivia, less important than what celebrity did what to whom, or which prime minister's wife was snubbed at what event, or whether immigrants were causing a strain on the bus services of Tyneside.

But it caught my eye, and I looked a little closer, and it was Byron.

A report from a book launch in Nîmes, a swanky affair, celebrities and the unsung wealthy elite gathered to hear their spiritual guru, Marie Lefevre, spirit-healer and mystic, launching her latest title: *Soul of Love, Spirit of Truth*, a book demonstrating that the path to great business and romantic success was through knowing your past lives.

I looked at a picture of Lefevre, and she was beautiful, stunning, perfect. The perfect man on her arm, the perfect smile, the perfect life. And I looked at pictures of the people gathered at the event, and they too were beautiful, rich and full of big ideas about time and space and their own position within, and I envied them, and wanted to be that beautiful and confident and memorable too, but then I saw the after-pictures, and even the beautiful bled, it seemed, and even the beautiful needed seventeen stitches to their faces and necks before the doctors would let them go.

Their attacker was Louise Dundas, an exceptionally beautiful, exceptionally lovely member of the gathering, who, listening to Marie Lefevre read one of her favourite bits of poetry, had suddenly, inexplicably and without warning attacked her fellow guests.

No – not just attacked, whispered the social media, hastily censured. The girl went *insane*.

In a statement issued by a somewhat shell-shocked Marie Lefevre after:

"We deeply regret the actions of one member of the gathering at today's launch. Sometimes people who do not know themselves do extraordinary and violent things; the path to truth can be frightening and we are very sad to hear of how many of our loyal readers were injured in this event. We will of course co-operate fully with the investigation and wish peace, love and the eternal light to everyone caught up in these tragic happenings."

Flicking through the photos from that night, the blood and the chaos, the out-of-focus shots as people fled for their lives, one man bleeding out as the insane girl bit deep enough to puncture the veins in his wrist, I saw terror and horror and chaos and

Byron.

Right at the very, very back, Byron, her face half turned away, moving like the crowd for the exit

there she was

Byron.

A copy of Marie Lefevre's book under her arm, her head down, a pearl necklace at her throat, a few mere pixels against the chaos of the screen but it was her, it was

Byron.

A question for the survivors of the event.

What was happening before Louise Dundas went insane?

An answer, unanimously rendered: Marie Lefevre was reading a poem.

Question: what poem?

The answer, less unanimous through poetical ignorance. Eventually enough came together to pick the answer from the chaos, and it was this:

> She walks in beauty, like the night
> Of cloudless climes and starry skies;
> And all that's best of dark and bright
> Meet in her aspect and her eyes:
> Thus mellow'd to that tender light
> Which heaven to gaudy day denies.

"She Walks in Beauty" by Lord Byron, 1813

I found Louise Dundas' Facebook profile, trawled through its contents – photos of her on a yacht, with friends at a club, hugging her dog, trying new shoes, grinning hugely to camera as she stands beneath the departures board of Heathrow airport, a straw hat with corks on set at a rakish angle over her head. A catalogue of a life lived high, full of acronyms, OMG, LOL, WTF!

And there, of course, there, three months ago, the post I was looking for.

OMG so excited starting treatments today!!!

From that post onwards, the acronyms declined, as did the photos of her being silly. More and more she became what the treatments wanted her to be – beautiful, confident, unobtainable, untouchable, perfect.

Going to Marie Lefevre's exclusive party tonight, she wrote, the day of the attack. *Very excited to hear her speak – so inspiring, so truthful and giving.*

That evening, I went to my sister's room – you're new here, aren't you? – said the receptionist as I signed my name, and I kissed Gracie on the forehead and said I had to go, I'd be back soon, and she tutted and replied,

"You must keep your promises."

"I promise," I murmured. "I'll be back as soon as I can."

I sat in silence on the train to Manchester.

Chapter 80

Plane Manchester–Paris, train Paris–Nîmes.

TGV, sleek and grey, winter in France, the snow falling silent outside the window, low valleys in the north, flat plains in the south at the foot of the Alps, the mountains distant against the gathering darkness.

I ate a croque-monsieur, hugely overpriced, and resurrected my rusty French reading *Le Monde* and listening to the radio on a set of headphones. I hadn't had time to prepare, so stole a couple of wallets in the Gare de Lyon, keeping the cash and discarding the rest; stole a mobile phone, bought a new SIM from the *tabac* at Nîmes station.

This is not unworthy.

I am a woman with a cause, to struggle righteously, great struggles, worker struggles, racial struggles, gender struggles, rights and battles and marches and

this is not unworthy.

I steal to live, I live for a cause.

I am a sublime thief.

Impressions of Nîmes:

Unflashy but pretty, a little Paris for the south without the burden of being Paris. Medieval heritage prized over its Roman one. Fantastic chocolate shops, hugely overpriced. The smell of perfume, the sizzle of meat on the grill, children demanding the latest toy, the newest pretty fluffy thing, their gloves sewn together on long strings, a cold winter coming.

The University Hospital, a megalith, a city within a city, bow down before the French medical system all ye who enter here, a monument to 1960s brutality, you had better be very ill indeed when you step within.

This is the place where survivors of the attack at Lefevre's book launch would have been taken. I tie back my hair, pull my coat tight around my chest, and head inside.

Easy to find the room of Louise Dundas; it's the only room with a police guard outside. I steal scrubs, ID badge – hospitals like this are big enough that there's always something that fits the bill – smile at the policeman, he asks me what I'm doing, I say, "Checking fluids," and he hears something medical, so waves me through.

Louise Dundas lies, as Meredith did, handcuffed to the bed,

asleep. Her heart rate is 72 BMP, her BP is 118/79, she is as fit and healthy as you would expect of any woman who had Perfection, who could afford her own personal trainer and to-your-door delivery algorithmically constructed vegan diet plan. A girl, maybe twenty-four, twenty-five, who simply went insane at a poetry reading and attacked seven other guests before she was restrained, as Byron watched.

No sign of Byron now, of course, but that is to be expected. No sign, alas, of Dundas' phone or personal belongings, blood-splattered as they would be. Taken away by the police. I gently try to wake the girl, but she's fast out. I wonder if any drugs will be of use, but the door is opened before I can go far in my quest, and in come a man and a woman, she someone unknown, he . . .

. . . a face I know very well indeed.

"Good evening, ma'am," his French is perfect, of course, newsreader-flat, "how is Mme Dundas?"

A moment in which I stumble on my lines, but it's all right, it's okay, he's a stranger in a police-guarded room, though curiously the cop is gone from his chair outside; I'm allowed a moment to count quickly backwards from five and say,

"Sedated, but her stats are good. You are . . . ?"

"My name is Mr Blanc," he replied, offering me his hand, which of course, I shook, for why wouldn't I, I'm a nurse, he's a polite stranger enquiring after a patient's health, of course I shook it, hygienically iffy though it is.

"You are not a relative?"

"No – we work for the insurance company."

He doesn't say which insurance company, and doesn't offer ID. The woman is already moving round the bed, examining the girl's face, her nails, her hands, her fingers. I nod and smile, making quickly for the exit, then hesitate by the door. And why not? I stop, I turn, I smile at Mr Blanc and say, "Is it Perfection?"

The woman looks up fast, an answer far more expressive than Mr Blanc's slow smile, half turn of his head, gentle shuffle of his feet to bring his body, a little bit at a time, into full alignment that he might look at me. "Why would you say that, Mme . . . ?"

"Jouda. Mme Jouda."

"What about Perfection, Mme Jouda?"

"Do you work for it? I know Mme Dundas used it," I said with a shrug, a slight tilt of my head, nothing to be concerned about. "I know she received treatments."

"And how do you know that?"

"She said as much, before she was sedated."

"Did she? Did she say so?"

The woman, frozen like a wading bird, uncertain if death circles above, or food swims below. Do you feed and die, your back exposed to the enemy, or stand still and starve?

The man who calls himself Mr Blanc has gone by a few other names before: mugurski71, Matisse, Gauguin, a fixit man for Rafe Pereyra-Conroy, ex-spy, sometime lover of Byron14, of course it makes sense for him to come here. He would be looking for Byron too.

He watches me, and I watch back. I don't mind making an impression.

Does he remember me?

No, but like Byron perhaps he has words filed away in the back of his mind, mantras, repeated actions and hazy concepts which declare, *there is a woman you cannot remember, these are her qualities . . .*

If this were a hospital in Iceland, or rural Russia, he would absolutely be asking those questions now, wondering how a woman of my description came to be in this place. But this is Nîmes, and the French have a colonial history as long and ignoble as the British, and the south is full exiles who crossed the waters from Algeria in the 1960s, of travellers from the west coast of Africa, of women with my hair and my skin who are French to their very bones.

So he watches, and I watch back, and at last he smiles and says, "Has she had an MRI?"

"Not as far as I know."

"A psychiatrist . . ."

"Is scheduled to see her."

"I would like my own psychiatrist to attend." He hands me a business card, M Blanc, no company listed but a telephone number.

"You have your paperwork?" I suggest. "The P77, your proof of policy; you'll need to take it to reception."

No idea if these bits of paper are real, but he has no idea either. "Of course," he replies. "The hospital is aware of my visit. Mme Dundas is being moved, at the family's request, to a different facility."

"I wasn't informed."

"You'll find all the paperwork ready."

"She's still in a . . ."

"All the paperwork," he repeated, the smile still fixed to his face. "The ambulance will be here soon."

I matched his smile with my own. He was Gauguin, a servant of Perfection, he will smile all the way to the apocalypse. I rolled his business card between my fingers, and went to find a motorbike to steal.

Modern technology makes it both easier and harder to steal cars. Harder, because electric locks and digital codes now all too often require higher levels of technology to beat. Easier, because digital codes and electric locks, once beaten, make it easier to do everything clean, a press of a button, a flick of a switch and hello those open doors, those warm, running engines. There is nothing human ingenuity cannot make which human ingenuity cannot break.

In the South of France, however, the Italian fashion for little farting bikes, barely a scooter with an engine, was still in vogue. Three minutes with a screwdriver did the job, and I was waiting outside by my stolen vehicle when the private ambulance arrived to take Louise Dundas away.

They didn't wake her, but wheeled her out flat on a gurney, up the ramp into the van. Gauguin and the woman walked a few steps behind; the woman signed papers for the accompanying medic, Gauguin watched the street, saw me, noted me, looked on by, forgot. He was no Byron. I saw no sign of Louise's family.

Following the ambulance through the night-time streets of Nîmes. I didn't have a helmet. The air was freezing cold through my coat, my toes growing numb. I'd learned to ride a bike in a ten-hour intensive course (is there any other kind?) in Florida, but it had been a while, and every bump rattled up through my tailbone. Tailbone: connected to the sacral nerve. Kneebone: medial plantar nerve, lateral plantar nerve. Hit the knee in the right spot, it stimulates the plantar nerve, triggering the famous knee-jerk reaction. Elbow: ulnar nerve, possibly referred to as the funny bone for its link to the humerus; perhaps because of the sensations induced when struck.

Knowledge trickled through my mind, and I found it was simply . . . knowledge.

Not words to calm, not thoughts to focus, not fuck-you knowledge, not knowledge-as-freedom, knowledge-as-pride, knowledge-as-the-place-where-a-soul-should-be, just . . .

thought.

Where are we?

Straight French roads built on top of their Roman ancestors, trees rising up and curling in, the branches battered to a curve describing the size and shape of the highest and widest lorry to venture down these roads, a tunnel of leaf that cuts out the moonlight, the glow of the main road far away, the ambulance stops suddenly, hard, and I drive by, too close to stop without making a scene. A hundred yards, stop, turn off my headlights, wait, look back to see why the vehicle stopped – but it was for an owl in the road, a curiously stupid animal that sits in their path, blinking, wondering why this machine won't get out of its way. The passenger door opens, and Gauguin climbs out. He walks towards the creature on the tarmac, kneels down a foot from it, reaches out slow, so very slow, his face caught in the headlights of the ambulance, kindness written on it – but the bird flies away before he can touch it, and a moment more he remains kneeling, before getting back into the vehicle, driving on.

I let them pass me, and know I will have been noticed, and count to twenty to let them forget, before switching my headlights on, and following.

Chapter 81

A place which had once been a school, in a hamlet which had once been a village. A small river rolled down from the mountains of the Massif Central, decelerating and widening out as it plummeted towards the sea. A bridge spanned it at its highest point, and on the bridge were wrought-iron streetlamps decked with flowers, and within each hanging basket of winter-whites and purples, a speaker had been hidden which played, even at one in the morning, childish folk songs sprinkled with happy messages from the mayor.

The shop shutters were down, the hotel overlooking the river was shut up for the season, the graffiti on the wall of the bank said, "*nous sommes morts*". At the top of the hill, a gothic Victorian mansion was nearly all boarded up, a vampire's dream of spiked towers, cracked weather vanes. High walls surrounded sprawling, overgrown gardens, all black slate tiles and red curved bricks. On the gate hung an *à vendre* sign, eaten away by rain and time. Gauguin hadn't bothered to remove it, figuring perhaps that no one would come – that no one ever came – but a man in a grey hat opened the gate as the ambulance approached, closed it behind them, and snapped the padlock into place.

Some lights were on behind the chipboard-covered windows. I circled the place a few times, once on bike, twice on foot, looking for cameras and signs of life, but only the lights in the eastern wing were on, and there was no sign of anyone patrolling.

I went over the wall by an old, leafless fig tree, slipping down the grey bark to a muddy floor of mulch on the other side. Irritating to have to do the work without proper preparation or the usual tools of the trade, but exciting too. A breathless speed in my lungs, a racing in my heart, I counted my steps, I counted the pulse in my neck, forced it to slow, stood still for a moment beneath the shade of the trees, my back to the wall, and let the cold and the darkness fill me, bringing my body back under control.

Pieces of the life of the mansion, watched for an hour and a half from the darkness of the grounds.

- A man in a white tunic, a panel crossed over his chest and pinned tight, like a chef, or a pharmacist, sits outside for a while to smoke a cigarette and stare up at the cloud-scudding sky.
- A woman in a grey suit and pink trainers steps out to speak down a mobile phone. She is comforting, consoling, promising to be home soon, yeah, babe, I know, I know, yeah. She speaks English, not French, an Essex accent, and her eyes are sharp even in the gloom.
- Two voices are briefly raised behind a chipboard window, arguing in French, it's not, unacceptable, no, the tests, you said, unacceptable, *unacceptable*! A third voice hushes them, shush, not now, not the place . . .
- The ambulance which came with Louise Dundas, having deposited her, drives away.
- A woman in blue, alone, and shaking. Not with cold, or fatigue, but a deeper vibration that comes from within. She raises her head to look at the morning stars, then pulls out her phone, thumbs it on, her face illuminated grey by the light from its screen, and calls a number on speed dial. "*Salut*," she whispers. "I know it's late – I'm sorry. I just wanted . . . yes. No, it's fine, it's . . . yes. No, I know. I know you do. I love you too. I just . . . wanted to hear your voice. Yes. No, go back to . . . love you. I love you. I'll see you soon."

This conversation done, she hangs up, and sits shaking a little while longer.

A scream, sudden and furious, high enough to make the crows burst from their nests, shrill enough to drown out the quiet tinkling of the town's relentless, chirpy folk music. It is 1950s horror movie, B-movie intense, but it is real, full of saliva and blood, veins bursting against the skin, eyes bulging, tongue rolling, it is the scream of someone who perhaps wants to die, or kill, or both. It doesn't stop – it doesn't stop, she keeps on screaming, barely pausing to pull in breath, who would have thought that human lungs had such power in them? (A human baby's cry can reach 122dB. 120dB is the threshold of human pain, 130dB is a machine gun being fired, 150dB a jet plane, *focus*!)

The scream dies. There are voices murmuring, wondering. I am against the walls of the mansion now, looking for a hole in the chipboard to peer through.

A door opens to my right, a figure emerges, fast, a man already on a mobile phone, speaking Spanish; no, no it's not – no, another – well, yes, of course he can but – ugh!

His words dissolve into an animal sound, he throws his hands in the air, turns the mobile off, looks for a moment tempted to throw it hard against the wall, to smash a thing for the joy of smashing, but no, it's an expensive handset, £320 if he got it new (and of course he did), so for a moment, venality trumps the raging bull, and he storms back inside, leaving the door open for a woman to step out instead, Gauguin at her side.

He holds coffee in a plastic cup, and so does she, though neither drink. The steam blows off the surface of the liquid and the two stand there, staring at nothing much, before at last he says, "I have to tell him something."

The woman, thick black tights, knee-length grey skirt, her hair pulled back into a bun, no rings on her fingers or jewels at her throat, nods at nothing much, and I know her too, remember her name, her smile, sharing noodles in Tokyo, is it you?

Is it you, Filipa Pereyra-Conroy? Is it you?

"Until we know how far—"

She stops him with a nod, eyes fixed on nothing much.

"I'll make the call," he says, but is slow to go, hesitating, doesn't want to leave her alone.

"Go," she replies, seeing his doubt. "Go."

Gauguin goes, and only Filipa remains.

I watch her a while, from the shadows, and for a while that is all there is between us. Thought without words, silence without meaning, we stand and the stars turn and this moment is for ever, she and I, and I'm okay with that.

Then she turns without warning, and sees me, and jumps, spilling hot coffee over her hand, and gasps at the pain and steps back, face opening in surprise, then tightening in fear, before opening out again in curiosity. I step forward, hands empty, and say, "Filipa?"

A moment, as coffee drips off her hand, in which she stares into my face and tries to solve me. She takes in my eyes, my lips, my neck, my shoulders, my coat, my arms, my wrists – and sees silver, a Möbius strip rolling for ever into its own geometrical form, and recognises that, both the thing itself, and the meaning of the item, imbued long before I came along to wipe her memory clean.

A realisation.

A revelation, she is brilliant, after all, Filipa is nothing if not brilliant.

"Is it you?" she whispers. "*Is it you?*"

"You won't remember me, we met in . . ."

"You're the one people forget, you're . . ."

She stopped, mid-sentence, turned to look over her shoulder, suddenly aware of the time, the place. Then marched towards me, grabbed me by the sleeve, pulled me away from the door, away from the light. "Is it you?" she breathed again, wonder written on every part of her. "Did you come here for me?"

Not the reaction I'd been expecting. There is something about her tonight that has always been there, a headlong wildness, a speed of words and brightness of eye, but larger, hovering on that tipping point between brilliance and something else entirely.

"Filipa," I whispered, "I stole Perfection."

"I know! I know you did! Rafe was *furious*. He doesn't believe you exist, but I've seen the footage, I know everything – why did you steal it? Was I part of your plan, did I say something to you?"

There wasn't any rancour in her voice, merely curiosity, a woman trying to puzzle out a thing she has no great emotional connection to. "I stole it for ... money," I lied. "And no, you were not part of my plan. I enjoyed your company."

"Did you? I thought perhaps I had enjoyed yours too, I seemed very happy in the footage they showed me, and I remembered the night with warmth and assumed that an emotional memory might not have been erased even if the visual pathway was severed, and that therefore maybe you were good."

No malice, no fear, what the hell is wrong with her? I grabbed her by the tops of her arms, held her tight, looked into her eyes. "Filipa," I hissed, "you told me that Perfection was the end of the world."

"Did I? Was I drunk? Rafe doesn't let me drink, but sometimes ..."

"You weren't drunk."

"No, I can't imagine I was. It is, of course. It is the end of the world. And now you've made it worse. Although thinking about it, I think maybe it's a necessary step, the correct plan, a good response to the situation ..."

"What's happened? What's happening to Louise Dundas?"

Her head, bird-like, tilting a touch to the side. "Don't you know?"

"No, I don't. I saw a woman in America, Meredith Earwood ..."

A flicker of a frown, a biting of her bottom lip. "I don't know her."

"She went nuts, the treatments ..."

"You know it's my fault?" she interrupted lightly. "Although the science is only what people make of it really, split the atom and get the bomb, save the planet, kill the planet, save people, kill people, it's all the same really fundamentally unless human thought makes it something else . . ."

She was babbling, her eyes drifting away to somewhere I couldn't see, my fingers tight in her flesh, trying to hold her in this place. "Filipa," I whispered, "I can help. What the hell is going on here?"

"Do you want to see? Will the people inside forget you? Will they forget that I was with you?" A tiny giggle at a sudden, happy idea. "Rafe would be so mad!"

"Are there security cameras?"

"No."

"Then yes; everyone will forget."

"Good. Good good!"

She grabbed my hand, fingers brushing past the bracelet she'd given me, all those months ago, dragging me towards the door. "Come, come!" she clucked. "Come, come come!" and pulled me into the house.

Walls, painted over boiled pea green. Creaking floorboards covered with speckled linoleum. High ceilings, a brass chandelier hanging uneasily to one side in the central hall. Coats thrown across a dresser by the door, no hooks to hang on. Staff: young, mostly, a few middle-aged executives, turning to stare as Filipa pulled me down the hall.

"This is my friend," she barked at one man who stood in our way. "She's an expert."

A turn of the corridor, a gurney left outside a door. This place was once full of the chattering of the French upper classes, or the quiet silence of wealthy wives left to pine while their men slipped off to more interesting climes and hotter beds. Perhaps in the Second World War it was occupied by German soldiers, the family told to make do or get gone; or no, maybe not, not this far south, perhaps it was a hotbed of quiet resistance, of little gatherings on a Sunday where men and women spoke in hushed voices of their fathers' guns still hidden under the floorboards.

How it had come to be a medical facility, quietly transformed in the dead of night, I didn't know, but that was what it was, a large room, perhaps a place that had once been for dancing, now transformed, six beds across the wall, five of them occupied. They were beautiful, even asleep, even with pipes in their veins and electrodes in their skulls, even with goggles over their eyes and nodes taped to their lolling tongues, obviously they were beautiful, in a surgical kind of way. Five slumbering beauties, three men and two women, Louise Dundas in the bed nearest the window, eyes shut, her hair spread out behind her across the white pillow, a sleeping princess.

Two nurses and a doctor overseeing them, surprised to see me, but deferential to Filipa who said, "Can we have the room, please?"

Filipa Pereyra-Conroy, for all that she is not her brother, is still a member of her clan. They gave her the room. "Filipa . . ." I tried again.

"They are all perfect," she explained, taking in the sleeping figures with a sweep of her hand. "Germany, Spain, two from France, one from Italy. Nine in America, eight in China, four in India, one in Indonesia, three in Australia, Rafe said fix it, it's your machines, you fix it, make it better, just like that, boof, like the atom was split in a month, like the apple just fell from the tree splat like—"

"Filipa . . ."

"He shouted at me. Usually he laughs, doesn't shout. Did you do it? You stole the base code; with the code you could do this, of course – I'm not angry. I wouldn't have done it that way, I never would have dared, but if it works? If Rafe pulls the treatments then that's a good thing, that's how it should . . . is it you?"

She didn't meet my eye as she asked, kept her back straight, head turned towards the sleeping figures. Bravery: courage, valour, daring, prowess, audacity, nerve, spirit, mettle, pluck.

Takes bravery not to look at a woman who you're afraid of as you accuse her of murder, and in her way – yes – Filipa is scared of me too.

I took her hand, gently, and she looked at the floor. "I didn't do this," I said. "I stole Perfection for someone else."

Her eyes, rising quickly, a woman on a mission. "Who?"

"She called herself Byron."

"Byron? Ah, yes, of course – the woman who murdered our father." She nodded at nothing much. "Matisse told me about her."

"Matisse . . . "

"His real name is John, did you know that? But he does all this spy-stuff. I thought he had to be wrong about Byron, it was all too silly for words, but . . . " A half shake of her head, a different thought for another time. "And the poetry, yes? They all heard something which triggered the change, the treatments you see, an evolution from basic NLP, but better, much better. Thought is association, you anchor a concept – beauty – repeat, repeat, repeat until it becomes true, you can be beauty, you are beauty, beauty beauty beauty beauty—" I gripped her hand tight, and she stopped as quickly as she'd begun, head turning up, then down again, rolling around her neck like a thing beyond her control.

We stood a little while in silence, staring at the sleepers.

Then, very quietly: "Perfection's been hacked, you see. I knelt at Rafe's feet, told him to stop, begged, but he wouldn't. It's worth too much money. Panic if it's pulled, he said, just put the bodies away some place and fix it on the quiet, fix it! Loss of customer confidence. Small-scale incidence, a statistical blip, individual cases rather than a product issue. Not just Perfection, but the data gathered from Perfection, the marketing of course, access to phone, email, search terms, location data, eating habits, shopping, travel, ambitions, aspirations – he sells it for a fortune, in-app product placement, the hair, the clothes, the holidays, the shoes, the magazines, the make-up. He told me to go back to the lab and fix it. Go and tinker, he said. Go tinker with your toys. For a while I thought that I'd done it, that it was my fault. I thought my treatments were doing this," a hand, taking in the room, head down again, now she is ashamed, "but I looked again and there was a hack. Two months ago, something else put into the treatments, hidden in the beauty beauty beauty beauty beauty. Hard to find; hard to fix. I think it sends people mad."

Fact. Here is the problem, there is the truth.

You are beauty you are beauty you are beauty ...

Repetition making a thing the truth.

You are beauty you are beauty you are beauty ...

Can't repeat your way out of five sleeping bodies in a house in France. I am sane I am sane I am sane I am sane ...

Silence a while between us.

I said at last, "I stole it. I didn't ... do this." My words, dead even before they were spoken.

"That's okay." She shrugged. "I think what you're doing makes sense."

"You do?"

"Of course. Perfection destroys the human soul. You know I used to help kids with brain damage find their voice? That was before Rafe made me a monster."

"You're not ... "

"I killed humanity," she corrected, light as a feather, before I could speak. "I gave people the tool to suck out everything that was flawed, ugly and bitter, and it turns out that all that is left is a piece of marketing. Of course I blame Rafe too – he chose the parameters, he decided that Perfection was an advertiser's dream. If your Byron could kill Rafe, perhaps it would stop, but I doubt it. I think she probably knows that. I think maybe that's why this makes more sense."

"Can you fix it?" I asked. "Can you make them ... better?"

Her eyes flickered fast to me, surprised. "Why on earth would I want to do that?" she breathed.

Her hand fell from my fingers. I took a step back, Filipa now meeting my eye, clear and defiant. "My work," she explained, steady, calm, "needs to be destroyed. It is an absolutely necessity. I'm grateful to you, for stealing Perfection. It gives me hope that one day all of this will be over."

I looked to the sleepers in their beds, five men and women

who had heard some words and gone insane, looked back at Filipa, saw something that could be madness in the corner of her eye, turned to the door, to walk – to run – far away. She said, "Matisse is determined to find you, almost as much as he wants to find Byron. He wants to show that you're real. If he finds you – if Rafe finds you – I think you may end up on the dissection table. Please be careful."

I stopped, fingers on the doorhandle. "Don't you want to know how I work too?"

"Yes. Of course I do. But you're human, whole and true, and whether your condition is artificial or naturally induced, it is . . . extraordinary. In Tokyo I gave you my bracelet. I have no memories of you, but I can conjecture based upon the data that is given. Sometimes there is cognition without words; a reading of a situation that cannot be rationalised by the artificial merits of logic. Words complicate things, sometimes. Numbers are simpler, but only black and white. Thought is . . . constrained, and we never really see it. But with you, I saw myself smile. I – I sometimes make myself smile, because it's what people expect, smile smile smile for the camera smiling all the time because it's what . . . but with you it seemed real. I think, for a few hours, you may have been my friend. And even if you weren't, you are still human, still extraordinary in being human, and human is a species which is currently under threat."

I opened my mouth to answer, didn't have any words, stood in front of her like a mannequin, locked in her stare.

Then she said, "Luca Evard has been looking for you."

The words slipped out so easy, so simple, that they caught me entirely off-guard. She saw it, the slight leaning back onto my heels, the flexing of my fingers at his name, and struggled for a moment to understand. "He was sacked from Interpol," she added. "Matisse employed him instead."

"Why?"

"He told his bosses that a thief he was tracking had the ability to be forgotten. He thinks he may have slept with you. Did he?"

"Are you recording this?" I replied.

"No – but that's not fair, that means you want to tell me something you know I'll forget, that . . . but then I'll forget all of this, so go on. One of us may as well have a meaningful experience tonight."

"I slept with him."

"Really? Why?"

"He . . . he's the only man I've ever met who's been interested in me."

"I'm sure that's not true," she tutted, turning back to the patients, a dismissal again of a silly idea, and Filipa is a woman who has no time for silly ideas. "You're so beautiful."

"Filipa . . . " The words broke on my lips before they could get out, I ran my tongue round the inside of my mouth, tried to find them again. "Filipa. Your treatments could make me memorable."

Surprise; then just as quickly, rejection, a fast shaking of her head. "Oh no no no no. That's not right at all."

"I met someone, like me, a man from New York, only I remembered him and he was perfect—"

"Absolutely not. Your condition – chemicals, perhaps, some sort of inhibitor; or electrical, a device, a . . . a field, yes, perhaps some sort of field generated, must be artificial in that case in which case you choose, but treatments? No, not at all. They don't do anything . . . *surgical*."

"You're a scientist; I'm telling you what I saw."

"Don't be—" she began, then stopped herself, pulling back. "Is this why you stole Perfection?"

"Part of it, yes. But the treatments changed Parker, they made him . . . I thought maybe the treatments without Perfection . . . "

"It's just a series of ideas, that's all they really are. Chemically enhanced, electrically aided, but still only thoughts. If I could remember you, I could study you, I could make recordings, we could . . . you don't want that?"

Seeing something on my face, which I couldn't hide. "Byron studied me."

"And what did she find?"

"I don't know. She said she'd make me memorable, but there was . . . there was a poem she'd say, the soul wears out the breast, and the heart must pause to breathe and love itself . . ." I stumbled over the words, dragged down breath, *Hey Macarena!*

"Programming." Filipa spat the word, utterly unimpressed. "Crude concept. Advertisers programme us, see image of perfume bottle, think of beautiful women. See picture of running shoes, think of sex sex sex sex always sex, of course, low-level manipulation, but the treatments – deeper, much deeper. Hard to control consequences, stupid hangover from foolish notions of hypnosis, not at all what it's about, not how it works, ignorance, naivety. There are approximately eighty-five billion neurons in the brain, and we can image it beautifully, very beautifully, but imaging isn't comprehension, isn't power, it just makes scientists feel good!"

She spun on the spot, throwing her hands into the air, an academic faced with poor processes, a woman whose life, whose every breath had taken her to the place she thought she wanted to be, only to discover on arrival that it was nothing like she'd imagined. Silence between us. My fingers traced the curve of the Möbius strip around my wrist, rolling over and under, over and under.

Filipa's shoulders dropped, her eyes turned back towards the floor. "I wanted," she began, and stopped. Then again, "I wanted to be . . . silly now, of course."

"Perfect?" I suggested.

"No! Not that – never that! I just wanted to . . . I wanted to make a difference. I wanted to like who I am." Again, stopping, head turned to one side, picking at her own memory, shutting down lines of enquiry. "Do you like who you are?" she asked, eyes fixed on something far away, out of sight.

"I . . . don't know. For a while I thought . . . [words get complicated, I try to find a way through them and] . . . I thought I wasn't worthy."

"Worthy? Of what?"

"Of anything. That my life was without worth. I went from

place to place, took what I wanted, did what I felt like, pretended to be whoever I wanted to be, and it was . . . good, as good as things can be when you're . . . but it was without meaning. Or without worth. An unworthy life. Worthy as in honourable. Upright. A life of merit. To myself. To others."

"And now?"

I thought about it, straightening my back, hands tight at my sides. "Byron called me enlightened. She thought that if the world forgot me, I was outside the world. Free from its chains, my life shaped only by myself, my soul a thing entirely of my making, not made by . . . by the screaming. By the world screaming at me to be something I'm not. I think she was wrong, I think she's wrong about a lot of things. But also . . . not as wrong as words or numbers might make her."

She nodded, at what I wasn't sure. "I have not led a worthy life," she said at last. "I have come to terms with nothing."

"That's not—"

"It's true," she replied simply. "As a child I was a disappointment to my father, then to my brother, and finally to myself. I have been consistently informed that I am a genius, and brilliant – not by people who matter to me, of course, but still by enough people so that the words have acquired a certain baggage – and with my brilliance I have constructed tools to perpetrate the end of the world. Is that too much, is that wrong? Devastation, destruction, damnation, death. But it is foolish to let anyone say 'genius' outside a cartoon. I have perpetrated a device that obliterates the minds of all who use it, making them little more than internet memes, walking marketing boards, human placards selling us the sex, the clothes, the cars and the holidays that the markets demand. The 106 Club is a hangout for clones – physically and mentally – the surgeon's scalpel, my treatments. I have no doubt that they are happy. Self-doubt, insecurity, neediness, emotional fragility – these are not traits of perfect people. Have you spoken to anyone in the 106? They can respond to any situation with a two-dollar retort from a self-help book at a pinch. Is your father dead? He's gone to a better place. Have you lost your job? Stay strong – if you believe in yourself, you'll find a way. Husband left you, taking the kids? You can fight this one, and with the strength you have inside and the love of your children, you can win. The world is boiled down to aphorisms and fairytales. I watched them, my brother's programmers, trawling the web. 'How to deal with anxiety: remove anxious foods from your diet. Eat strawberries.' Perfect people always have a solution to a problem, you see. But what do you do when words fail? Truth: sometimes a murderer cannot be found. Truth: sometimes your children are taken and you are left behind. Truth: poverty is a prison. Truth: disease and age come to us all. These are so terrifying, we program them out of the human brain. Treatments make everyone who has them happy, and happiness is always sexy, isn't it? Happy happy sexy happy beautiful sexy sex happy beautiful happy sex—"

Tears on her face, something wild in her voice. A thousand times she has looked at her own reflection in the mirror, and said these words to herself, a thousand times she has tried to pick them apart, to tell herself no, no, it's not like that, see, see, there's a silver lining after all. And again: she has failed. Only truth remained.

I shuffled towards her, uncertain, stopped, hands useless at my sides. What did the perfect people of this world do when they saw tears?

How To Comfort Someone: 4 Steps:

1. Place a hand on their shoulder.
2. Be compassionate and understanding. Even if you think they have done something wrong, do not blame them.
3. Think of yourself, if you were in their place. Remind them that you will always be there for them.
4. Before you leave, ask them if there is anything else they need to talk about. Maintain eye contact.

I placed my hand on her shoulder, and she flinched.

I held her head tight, her hair in my fingers, and she wrapped her arms around my middle and cried for a while, and I said nothing, and she just cried.

After a while, her tears slowed, but she didn't let go. Snot and salt seeped through my shirt, and I held her, and that was fine.

"When I dance," I hummed, swaying a little as I held her, "they call me Macarena. They all want me, they can't have me, so they all come and dance beside me."

Her fingers clung in the small of my back, and still she didn't let go, but let me sing, my feet stepped and so did hers, though she didn't raise her head, "Hey Macarena!"

I spun her gently, and she let herself be spun, face red and swollen, a smile somewhere behind her tears.

"I see why I liked you," she sniffed, wiping her face with her sleeve.

"We could help each other."

"Could we?"

"I know Byron. I saw her photo at the party in Nîmes, that's why I came here. I know who she is, what she does."

"Can you find her?"

"I can try."

"Matisse couldn't."

"She's hiding from him, not from me."

"And what if she's right?"

"To hide?"

"To destroy Perfection. What if thought is not free? What if memory is a prison, society a lie? Sometimes I look around and all I hear is screaming, screaming, screaming – what if you are the enlightened one?" She was smiling as she asked this, but the smile was empty.

I dug my heels into the floor, found I had no words, and so gestured at the sleeping patients in the five white beds, an explanation more fluent than any I could find.

"My brother won't take Perfection off the market," she breathed. "It's too valuable. But if Byron hacks it . . . "

"People have died," I replied. "Perhaps Perfection is monstrous, perhaps the treatments are . . . but I'm a thief, we can find another way."

"When you are gone I won't remember you."

I took the bracelet off, pressed it into her hand. "You trust me. I can help you."

Her fingers closed over it, then with her other hand she grabbed my now bare wrist, and pulling me close murmured, "There's another club, more than the 106. For the ones who went all the way, finished all the treatments, the most perfect people on the planet. Two million points – $2x10^6$. 'The Perfect Million'. I told him to stop but he . . . Go to Venice. Matisse can help you, he's already afraid, he thinks Byron might . . . and I think she might too, I think . . . also Luca Evard, speak to Luca, tell them what you know, I know you are forgotten, but you can send pictures, messages, things which remain. I know they're . . . but they're good men too. Will you?"

"I will."

"You promise."

"Promise."

She smiled now, her body loose with sudden release, squeezed my arm tight, then let go, stepped back, pulled the bracelet over her wrist. "I wish I could remember this," she said. "I wish I could remember everything we said together."

"Treatments make me memorable," I replied. "Maybe when this is done, when it's—"

"Maybe," she answered, a little too fast, hard, cutting off the idea. "Maybe."

She seemed to have nothing more to say. I looked round the room, at the sleeping patients, perfect even in sleep, blood still under Louise Dundas' fingernails, still in the roots of her hair, Filipa standing in the middle, small and cold. I felt the place on my wrist where her bracelet had been, a sudden bareness, and I smiled at her, and she smiled back, a weak and imperfect gesture, and I turned, and walked away.

Chapter 82

Train, Nîmes–Venice. At Marseilles I bought an armful of local newspapers and a new mobile phone, and spent the rest of the journey to Nice scanning headlines and poring over the internet. I had supper in a restaurant over a little river that ran down to the sea, where once I'd eaten with a beautiful timber merchant from Turin to the sound of little green frogs hiccupping beneath our feet, whose car I stole after he refused to pay the bill.

The train from Ventimiglia to Genoa hugged the sea to the right, the Alps to the left. Hard to work, surrounded by such sights, hard to stay focused when cliffs plunged into cobalt-blue water and towns crawled up towards snowy peaks. By the time the train turned towards the dull industrial flatlands of Milan, I was exhausted from gaping, and at Milan station, a monument to Fascist architecture and imperial ambition, all huge ceilings and marble floors, I broke my journey to have a triangle of pizza in a greasy piece of paper.

"Fold it!" exclaimed the man who served me my dish. "Don't peck at it like a little bird, you wrap it over and eat it properly, like a woman!"

I stared at this indignant chef, tomato sauce down his apron, and for a moment tottered between a tourist's enthusiasm for local ways, and a traveller's resentment of intrusion. He had a silly watch which he wore beneath his blue latex gloves, and had left his mobile phone balanced unwisely by the till. I didn't need either, but the temptation to inconvenience him, the satisfaction of knowing he was robbed and I was gone, bristled against my brain but no

No.

Not today.

The lagoon was dark and disturbed, when I crossed it. The lights of Mestre behind, chimneys and cranes, empty warehouses and slumbering ships. Ahead, Venezia, a tourist paradise, spires and towers, canals and over-priced dinners. Wonder of the world, step from the station and immediately behold the Grand Canal. Walk through a city where cars never go, stones worn smooth by hundreds of years of passing pedestrians, smell the sometimes less than fragrant aroma of the lagoon, swat the mosquitoes, stand in San Marco's square and feel the ghosts of the traders and the whores, soldiers and assassins, the shadows of doges dressed all in gold, and lesser men who whispered in corners. Pigeons fly away from a child who delights in chasing them; a group of tourists photograph themselves with a camera held on a telescopic stick, the doge's palace behind, hawkers selling Manchester United and Barcelona T-shirts crossing in and out of the frame. The gondoliers don't bother to market their services; anyone foolish enough to pay so much for a slow ride through the canals of Venice (opera singer optional extra) will come to them of their own accord. Gondoliers have survived plague and fire, conquest and decay; they'll survive tourism too.

I tried a couple of hotels, and despite the tourists, found a room easily enough. The woman behind the counter looked askance at the cash I offered, but money is money, winter coming on, so all right, a small room up a tight stair, a floor that moans, a roof that slants, duck onto a little metal balcony that creaks alarmingly beneath your feet. I asked her directions to the nearest supermarket, and she looked sideways at me, despairing of this lone woman who paid cash and didn't indulge in the over-priced, under-interesting Venetian dining experience.

"Try Cannaregio," she tutted, and managed to stop herself before adding, *no eating in your room.*

In Cannaregio I found a supermarket, automatic door and bright green logos grudgingly wedged into a sixteenth-century guildsman's house. I picked up fruit, a couple of pairs of socks, a bar of chocolate, a loaf of bread, and as I went to pay, discovered that my wallet was empty, only a few coins left, and looked at the woman behind the till and said apologetically, "Sorry," and grabbed my goods and ran.

"Police, police!" she screamed, but no one followed and after a few streets I slowed to a walking pace, and wandered on quietly to the foot of a church – saint someone, raised up by someone in honour of something, in Venice these things began to blur – to eat my purloined goods.

I needed money, but the only casino in town was a poor venue for card counting. Ten euros to enter, low stakes, an atmosphere that suggested you should be grateful to be here, the oldest casino in Europe – perhaps.

I tried picking a couple of pockets in the crowded, twisting streets around San Marco, but had only pulled two wallets before a rival team, a boy and a girl, barely teenagers, made a bad pass in a nearby alley and someone called out thief, thief, thief, and the police came running, damn amateurs getting in my way.

I crossed the waters to the Lido instead, newer, cars and yachts, resort hotels, beaches in summer, a place for the wealthy who have surfeited on too much Renaissance art, too many Titians, bodies bursting with muscles, sheets of white and blue slung across breasts and penises, strategically blown there by a modest breeze.

I robbed the first hotel I came to, a grand monolith of white walls and rectangular windows. Stole a master key from a boy in the foyer, stole cash and a few clothes from the luxury suites on the top floor.

Worthy: to do the most righteous thing available to you, under a difficult set of circumstances.

I considered whether these words rang true, as I returned across the waters to Venice.

Chapter 83

Preparation.

A new computer, new clothes, new internet connection, new

download of Tor through the Wi-Fi of San Servolo, a good place to work, a little university campus for people looking for three months of art history, or two months of intensive Italian in the city of wonders, easy to blend in, buy yourself a coffee, sit in the café and surf the web.

Tor: The Onion Router. It has its flaws.

Arguments for increased government surveillance of the internet:

1. To curtail bomb-making manuals, terrorism, pornography, drug dealing and crime.
2. Trolls, bullies and hackers. To a feminist blogger: "I'm going to rape you till you bleed your home address is ███████████." Hate crime: "Fucking black bitches only good for being slaves." It's just the 1 per cent, say the apologists. Toughen up. (Fuck you, comes the answer. Fuck you for being too fucking cowardly to take responsibility for the society you live in. Fuck you for not giving a damn.)
3. If you have nothing to hide, why does it matter?

Arguments against:
The online privacy laws in the USA state that any email left for more than six months on a server owned by a third party, becomes obsolete, allowing that company (Hotmail, Gmail, etc.) to do whatever the hell it pleases with that data. Personal emails you have written to friends, lovers, colleagues now enter the public domain.

I love you. I want your skin against mine, your tongue in my mouth, your hands on my

I'm sending the money today, here are the details

My fucking sister is fucking getting on my tits again, fat bitch

Do I care that Google knows my religion, if I'm divorced or pregnant, that Facebook uses my face in an ad campaign? When I challenge my government; when I attack a media mogul, when I question a belief that others take for granted, do I care that my family history, finances and home address can be found immediately by my foes? Of course I don't: I have nothing to hide.

Do I care that the only way to be free from the fear of surveillance is to be absolutely harmless? To conform to a sociological norm, and never say anything that is personal, or real, or half thought through, or challenging?

I ordered another espresso, and waited for Tor to load.

A new address from which to contact an old friend.

I chose Zenobia1862, and sent my message to the most plausible corner of Prometheus' infrastructure.

```
I am _why. I am the woman that the man
called Gauguin, also Matisse, forgets. I
wish to discuss Byron14.
  Yours sincerely,
  _why
```

It took them nearly three days to reply, but I kept myself busy. I ran through the city, learning the streets, the bridges, the dead ends and the waterways. Learning where to hide and where to steal. Finding my way into police-radio frequencies, counting the rich and the beautiful, the vulnerable and the criminal as they mingled beneath the palazzos and inside the hot, wine-soaked bars.

I looked for the 206, the elite of all elites, and it was easy to find, the glamour sheets and the gossip rags already buzzing, the Perfect Party, Perfect Millions they called it, and look, wasn't it exciting, *he* was going and *she* was going, and didn't *his* fiancée look *beautiful*, she'd clearly beaten the cellulose. And *she'd* be there and so would *she* even though *she'd* once slept with *his* brother and *she'd* called *her* a slut but that was another time, they loved each other really, you see, and she'd lost so much weight since getting Perfection did you see her exclusive hot beach holiday pics?

"You don't want to be photographed, don't make an exhibition of yourself," said one paparazzi I gave a bottle of whisky to as he sat outside a grand hotel on the Grand Canal, cameras slung around his neck.

"What about people who want to make an exhibition of themselves in private?" I asked, and he shrugged.

"They're rich, they're famous, they gotta deal with the stuff that comes with it."

The next day I went back, and there he was again, a little bit tipsy by 11 a.m., and I gave him another bottle of whisky and he said, "Hotel Madellena, that's where it's at, they've got royalty coming, all the rich princes and their pretty girls, you know how it is, pussy, hot pussy, all of them."

I smiled politely, and thought about stealing his camera, throwing it into the canal, but no, that would be unworthy, must remember, even though it would be kinda righteous.

I counted my steps away from him, and by thirty paces the urge to steal had passed, and I laughed as I began to run again, heading back into the city.

When I returned to my hotel, Gauguin had replied to my message, with Luca Evard cced in for good measure.

Chapter 84

Meeting spies.

I paid a prostitute whose working name was Portia ("Like … Porthos?" I hazarded, and she glared and said, "Like Shakespeare, idiot") four hundred euros to sit with a mobile phone outside a café on the Riva degli Schiavoni, drinking thick black coffee and huddling in a fur-lined coat. The weather was turning cold; a bare spit of snow fell upon the rooftop and melted again, but for four hundred euros Portia wasn't going anywhere, and for a further two hundred neither was my water taxi, the driver sat with his feet up on the dashboard, a cigarette drooping from the corner of his mouth, a book about giving up everything to become an alpaca farmer open on his lap.

I sat at the back of the cab as the wake from the passing buses tossed us from side to side, and watched the café through a pair of binoculars. First to arrive were three security goons, two men and a woman. When they were settled, Gauguin approached on foot from the direction of the Arsenal, sensibly dressed in rubber boots and a waxy brown anorak. Luca Evard walked half a step behind him, thick black jacket and dull green jeans, an offence to fashion even at five hundred yards, head down, eyes up, a hint of bald spot becoming a definite declaration on his shining skull, panda rings around his sleepless eyes.

They arrived at the café, consulting their phones, images of my face saved within, and as they looked I dialled Portia, and said, "Those two."

Portia harrumphed, a busy woman having her time wasted, stood up, marched to Gauguin, and thrust the phone towards him screen first, arm locked and straight, and said, "It's for you."

Gauguin thanked her cordially, took the phone. She marched away, all buttock and thigh, haughty chin and Shakespearean pride.

"Who am I speaking to?" Gauguin enquired, English, polite, clipped.

"My name is Why," I replied, watching him turn, turn, through my binoculars. "I want to talk about Byron14."

A shuffle on the spot, Luca Evard behind, Luca wants the phone, glances at his own, at my face on it, stares at the crowd, sees no one he knows, looks down. A thing which might be anger; a thing he does not want the world to see in his eye.

I look away too, and it's obviously shame, pure and true.

"I thought we would—"

"Meet personally? You have a habit of knives and guns, Mr Gauguin."

"Do I?"

"You've watched the CCTV? Tokyo, Oman? Might not have footage of Istanbul, but seriously – knives. I assume you're recording this?"

"I am now."

"Good: that will save me having to repeat myself. I think that Byron has hacked Perfection, altering the treatments given to the 106. Louise Dundas was one of several people to have violent reactions to trigger words, probably poetry, probably by Byron or Wordsworth. You know this. What you don't know is that the process began in Berkeley eleven months ago. Look for a student called Meredith Earwood, look for Agustin Carrazza, ex-MIT professor. On the phone in your hand you'll find the addresses of facilities used in the San Francisco area by Byron to conduct her research. I haven't been able to find her from this information, but you have more resources. There are also photographs of her journal, and the codeword to read it. I have a complete inventory of the goods she travelled with, including three separate passports which you may be able to do something with."

"This is all—" he began, but I ploughed through the banality.

"I need you to stop the 206 event you currently have planned for the Hotel Madellena the week after next. Shut it down. Keep the app going if you like, but cancel all treatments and identify everyone in the last eleven months who may have received them."

"Why?"

"Because the treatments will make them fucking insane murderers whenever they hear a bit of fucking poetry, are you stupid or just annoying? Because Byron wants to destroy Perfection, and what's a spy with a grudge gonna do?"

"What do you think she is going to do?" he asked, easy and calm, a tourist enjoying a pleasant chat in a pleasing city.

"You're launching the 206. The world's press is going to be watching. If I were Byron, and I had a room full of people who'd received treatments – my treatments – I'd make them tear each other to pieces."

A little pause, a slow intake of breath.

"She'll do it," I added, when his silence stretched. "Louise Dundas was a test and it worked beautifully. Filipa can see it – so can I. You put members of the 206 in front of the cameras, and Byron will turn it into a bloodbath."

"Do you have any proof?"

"Nope."

"But you seem very confident."

"Met her. Lived with her. She's got a cause. Fuck it, you'd think that having members of the 106 going insane and trying to kill people with their teeth would do it, but no, Rafe's got his principles, like the fucking idiot that he is. So here we are, Gauguin, you and me, blowing smoke in the fog."

A long quiet, interrupted by a police boat swooshing by, a little too close, the cops grinning at the cabbie as my boat swayed from side to side.

"Why are you helping us?" Gauguin asked at last.

"Byron is killing people. I gave her the means. That makes it, in its way, my fault. I'm not entirely without . . . honour."

"I find that difficult to believe."

Honour: honesty, fairness, high respect, worth, merit, rank, high esteem, fame, glory. Integrity in one's beliefs and actions.

Idiom: there is no honour amongst thieves.

I said, "In Istanbul you found you had the diamonds I stole in Dubai. You also had my passports, which you used to destroy most of the life that I had built. I don't know what fantasy you used to justify having these things, but you took them with you when you left. Can you remember what you did next?"

"I . . . we went to the airport and—"

"What did you do before going to the airport?"

"I was attacked . . . "

"And?"

"You attacked me?"

"Yes. To escape the knives, if you're wondering."

"How did you . . . "

"I hid. In the warehouse."

"But we . . . " His voice trailed off. "We burned it. We burned the warehouse down." Cold in his voice, cold on the waters, the growl of a bus as it rumbled by, grey skies overhead wanting to snow. "You were still inside."

"Yes. You forgot."

"That fast? In Tokyo, I remember coming too late to prevent your robbery. You'd left traps, explosives, tear gas, but you were gone. But I've seen camera footage that shows I came on time."

"In Tokyo I could have killed you. Do you remember what I said?"

"No. But I remember trying to remember. I wrote a word, over and over again until I remembered the act of writing it. Your name is Hope."

"And only by what you remember can you judge me."

"No," he snapped, sharp, turning where he stood, scanning the street. "By the consequences of your actions," glancing back at his phone again, trying to force the image of my face into his memory, "we can judge you by those."

"Can you? Do you have that right?"

I thought I heard a smile; hard to tell through binoculars. "Maybe," he mused, softer. "You stole Perfection; you are a thief."

"And now I am making good. Tell Rafe that if I was Byron, I would look at the 206 Club and I would rejoice to know that here, at last, is a chance to paint a picture soaked in blood. Tell him to pull the treatments; tell him to cancel the event."

"And if he won't listen?"

"Then you must ask yourself what you consider right, what is worthy."

Turning, turning, he was still turning, and now he stopped, and looked straight at me, and looked at his phone, and looked again across the water, a tiny figure without the binoculars, no way he could clearly see me, but then, "Are you on the water?"

"Yes."

"I think I can see you."

"Yep. Guess so."

Luca, following Gauguin's stare, has also found me. He pulls a little sight from his pocket, a ×10 magnification telescope, no longer than his extended middle finger, and for a moment, he looks at me, and I look at him, our faces obscured by optics.

"Did Byron tell you why she is doing this?" murmured Gauguin, watching still.

"Yes. She said that Perfection was obscene."

"Do you agree?"

"Totally. Perfection is derived by a consensus of society. Perfect – to perfectly fit the mould. Fuck that shit. My code, my honour, my . . . righteousness. I will help you bring down Byron, and I will find my own solution to my own problems, and maybe Perfection is obscene, the end of the world, and maybe it isn't, but I'll decide my own way, for my own reasons."

"I'm not sure if that's the sentiment of a hero or a sociopath."

"Judge me by my actions," I replied with a shrug, "if that's all you've got going for you."

"Hotel Madellena . . ." he began, a note of caution in his voice.

"Shut it down."

"I may not be able to."

"Then Byron will come. She will destroy everything."

"Perhaps I want her to try; perhaps the 206 can serve as bait?"

"She's smarter than you, don't try and make this into a stupid bloody trap, Jesus that'd be dumb. Cancel the event. Stop the treatments. I'm helping you now; I don't have to be co-operative."

"You're threatening me?"

"My code, my honour, my deeds, my actions," I snapped. "Filipa said that Perfection was the end of the world, and she was right. Sociopath or hero, I just don't care."

I hung up, and threw my phone into the lagoon before he could call back.

Chapter 85

I gave Gauguin everything I'd promised. Meredith Earwood, Agustin Carrazza, Berkeley, the hydroponic clinic, photographs of her passports, snapped from a hotel room in Korea, copies of her journal written in San Francisco. He replied through the darknet, politely thanking me for my information. He even activated his old name: mugurski71, and I replied as _why, all things returning to where we had begun, back to Dubai, back to Reina, the summer sun and a bunch of stolen diamonds. It all seemed a long way away, now.

The occasional question comes in from Gauguin. Describe Byron's current appearance. Describe her eating habits. Does she exercise? How was her Spanish? Did she express any views on politics or popular culture? Did she admit to the murder of Matheus Pereyra-Conroy? Did she say anything about me?

She spoke with regret, I replied, *but I don't think it went as far as remorse.*

Gauguin asked nothing more.

Talk to us, said mugurski71 one day. *Come in and talk to us in person. Let us record you. You won't be harmed.*

Memories of Tokyo, Luca Evard, you won't be harmed.

A present tense, a memory that is like the present tense, he said before, you won't be harmed, and now he says it again, and Gauguin is mugurski71 again and I am _why, time has changed nothing, regret changes nothing, hope changes nothing there is only now, and now, and now, this moment, this decision as I say

no.

Running through Venice, past the Hotel Madellena. Every day I buy the loyalties of a housekeeper by the name of Yanna, slipping her a hundred euros in exchange for an answer to the question – is the 206 Club coming here?

"Oh yes," she says, "it's all such a fuss."

The glamour mags, excited, celebrity this, sensational that, is she pregnant, is he having an affair, the 206 coming to strut their perfect, beautiful stuff, so wonderful, we could all be like that one day . . .

`Why is this still happening?!` I demand.

`There is no proof that Byron will be there`, Gauguin replies.

`If I could email you a fucking nosebleed you pillock!!`

Five days before the party, Rafe Pereyra-Conroy arrived, a beautiful woman I had never seen before on his arm, all legs and hair and teeth and dress. His sister walked behind.

Filipa looked . . . something in how she stood, perhaps. Something in how she dressed. Lace panelling across her back, down to the coccyx, all suggestive of other things. I'd never spotted before how slim she was, not skinny, but slim, a word which meant better things. If you cared about words.

`I am forgettable!` I screamed down the data highways and the network links, the secret cables and waiting satellites, roaring it over the darknet at Gauguin.

`I will call the police, tell them there's a bomb. I will rob every journalist blind, I will put poison into your party treats, I will destroy it before it ever has a chance to begin, I will stop this thing if you don't stop it now!!`

`Mr Pereyra-Conroy has decided to go ahead with the event`, replied Gauguin, `he does not feel the risk is significant.`

The risk is significant, you coward! You idiot, she will destroy everything and people will die!!

Mr Pereyra-Conroy feels that even if Byron were to attack the 206, this is an opportunity to catch his father's killer. We are monitoring trains, cars, boats – there are only so many ways in and off this island, if Byron comes near the venue she will . . .

She is smarter than you all. You are walking to your own damnation and she will destroy you!

I'm sorry, _ why. The event will proceed, and if Byron comes, we will apprehend her.

I threw the laptop across the room with a gasp of rage, and sat on the bed, shaking, sweating. Where is your knowledge now, thief, where is your stillness, where your honour, your worth, your code, you nothing, forgettable nothing, having a temper tantrum in your room, little girl, cross that desert. The desert will eat you whole, hey, hey hey, hey Macarena!

Need a friend to talk to, need Luca, need Filipa, need to clear my head, go for a run, go to a bar and pick up a guy, tell him everything, and he'll nod and smile and say, "Wow, that's so deep" and we'll fuck and he'll forget and it'll be fine, it won't mean anything but it'll be good, it'll be great, it'll be me, my power, me, in control, me, using the world to steal, to speak, to live, to survive to live fuck you, fuck you all!

On the balcony, shaking with rage, tears in my eyes.

A boat on the small canal outside, struggling to find a place to park. It's going to rain soon, smell of it on the air, the cobbles are slippery, difficult to run.

I am the rain.

I am the cold.

I am my breath.

I pick my laptop up from the floor. It's still working, hanging on in there, sorry about the sulk. I look up "need a friend".

Need a friend? Choose your option:

1 Talk NOW to a therapist, $50 for the hour online (pay as you go).
2 Talk NOW to a stranger (free!) and find your way through your problems through our online chat.
3 Talk NOW to our online community (free!) and post your questions, anxieties and stories in our online subscription-based community forum.
   - I try to talk, but no one listens.
   - I just want to be judged for who I am.
   - No one ever seems interested.

I went to close the laptop, but before I did, another message, from mugurski71.

This is Luca, it said. *This is my number.*

Chapter 86

Venice in the rain. The tourists flee, the canals hiss like an angry goose, towers vanish into blurred-out grey, veils of water slipping off the bridges. Hawkers, hair glued to their faces, wheel their tarpaulin-covered wares through narrow metal doors in the basements of undecorated houses given over to the storage of a thousand papier-mâché masks.

Hard to use an umbrella, too many others competing to get

through the narrow spaces; those shops that were smart enough to stock brollies now cash in, thirty euros a go. Better off with an anorak, head down, concentrating on placing your feet one before another, the sun gone, dizzying, north-south-east-west, Calle del Magazen, Calle Arco, Calle de la Pietà, Calle Crosera, turn left, turn right and you're back at the Grand Canal though you could have sworn you were heading in the opposite direction.

I held a new mobile phone in my hand, only Luca Evard's number saved, and walked.

Come to Accademia, I texted, breaking the lock into the tower of Chiesa di San Vidal as the message sent. He came to Accademia, arriving twenty minutes later, hatless, water dripping off the end of his nose.

I watched him from the tower and texted, *Campo Sant'Angelo.*

He received the message, looked around, started walking, hands buried in his pockets, a thin attempt at staying warm, towards Campo Sant'Angelo, passing me by, unseen in my perch. A baroque quartet was warming up as I descended the tower, cat-gut strings and horse-hair bows. A lone vendor was left in Campo Santa Stefano selling masks: the Bauta (good for eating in); the Columbina; the plague doctor and the Moretta, Arlecchino, Harlequin and Pantalone; the Volto, the most famous of the Venetian masks, stark white face around which colour bursts, gold and silver, bright greens and polished bronze, have I told you about

focus

Focus.

I passed him at Sant'Angelo, moved a few streets on, took refuge in a café selling pancakes filled with fruit and melted chocolate, ordered one and, as I waited, texted, *Campo Manin.*

A few moments later, he went by, elbowing his way through the crowd, and I let him pass, and looked for followers, obvious signs of protection or security, and didn't see any.

Rialto, I said and followed fifty yards behind him, hood over my head, eating my pancake from its paper bag, stopping in doorways only twice, as he looked back.

He walked to the middle of Rialto and stopped at the peak of the stairs, looking down to both ends of the bridge. Rialto Bridge, completed 1591, not the first bridge on the site, at least four wooden predecessors collapsed beforehand and ruin was predicted for the final evolution but here it is hulking above the waters

here we are

hulk: the main part of an object i.e. ship which is no longer used. One that is bulky or unwieldy; to move ponderously; to loom

together at last

hulk: big green monster with stretchy pants and rage issues and here

now

Can't put it off, could just go, walk away, but he texted me, he contacted *me*, I am in his awareness he will remember that I didn't show or will he?

Will he not in fact remember that he went to Rialto Bridge and perhaps we met and perhaps we spoke and perhaps it was wonderful and he forgot so really I could go now, and maybe his fantasy will be better than the reality what did anyone expect and

he turned, standing at the top of the bridge, and saw me, and recognised me.

Not, perhaps, me.

Words that described me. Black is the colour of my true love's hair, her lips are like some roses fair . . .

If he didn't guess who I was before, he knows now, I am staring at him and can't look away, and he sees the truth of it, and doesn't move, and neither do I, both deciding perhaps if we're gonna bolt

a moveable bar or rod

a part of the lock

a sudden dash

flight

escape

desertion

a length of woven goods from the loom

woven goods, 疋, a bolt of cloth, measure word, Chinese uses measure words whenever counting, most commonly 个 also 位 分本台 shitty shit what the fuck am I doing here

I can't move, feet frozen in place, so he comes down to me.

"Hello," says Luca Evard. "You must be Hope."

Chapter 87

A café near Hotel Madellena.

He's already paying by the time I notice.

No, I say, no, I'll get it.

Too late, he's bought the drinks, but thank you. He has never had a thief offer to buy him a cup of coffee before.

We sit. Checked red and white tablecloth. Luca put a packet of brown sugar in his coffee, stirred, anti-clockwise, four times, tapped the spoon twice, held the cup by its little handle, sipped, almost slurped, head rolling back, put the cup down, the liquid drained.

I watched all this, as a supplicant might watch a priest, then looked slowly from the prophetic grains of coffee left behind in the cup to Luca's more eloquent face.

"Hello," I said.

"Hello."

Silence a while.

Then at last, "I have a Dictaphone."

"That's fine."

"Good. I'm . . . good."

He laid the recorder on the table, digital, a single red light to show that you were winning, a USB portal at the back.

Silence.

At last, a laugh, a shake of his head. "I am being a bad policeman," he said, "but now that we're here, I'm really not sure what I want to say."

I shrugged, and then to fill the silence chose bad words. "I heard you left Interpol."

His head rose like a dog starting at the sound of a gun, and his bottom lip curled in and out before saying, quiet, "Sacked. Not left. Though the time was coming, I suppose."

"Was it me?"

"Yes. You were part of it."

"I'm sorry."

"Are you?"

"Yes. I didn't mean . . . sorry."

Confusion; now that we're here, nothing is what he imagined. Then leaning forward, hands palm-down on the table, pushing into it as if the world might drop away beneath him, holding on for dear life. "Did I ever arrest you?"

"Yes, once, in Vienna."

He slapped the table top hard, leant back in his chair, shaking his head. "I knew it! All the notes, the paperwork, your fingerprints! We had it all but no one could remember – I thought it was a clerical error but the error was so big, it was all so neat, so perfect, in the end we let it go because thinking about how it had happened was more awkward than ignoring it, I told them, I said that we . . . how did I do it? How did I catch you?"

"You pretended to be a potential buyer."

"I tried that several times, but it never . . . "

"It did. In Vienna I fell for it."

"And how did you . . . ?" He gestured feebly, looking for a word.

"You left me alone in the interview room. I waited for a while, then demanded to be released. Since the duty officer couldn't remember who I was, he assumed I was what I claimed to be and let me go. Like you said, it's sometimes more awkward to deal with a thing than to pretend it doesn't exist."

"So you just walked out of there."

"Yeah."

He let out of a puff of breath, a smile on his face, an injured man vindicated at last, justice, your honour, justice to the wronged.

"And any other time? Did I catch you in Brazil, or Oman?"

"No, I'm afraid not."

"What about Hong Kong? The file, the information I received . . ."

"Yes, that was me."

"*Why?*" The question burns, he shakes with the releasing of it, so many years, and now, the Dictaphone between us, his fingers white where they press into the table top.

I shrugged. "My buyer betrayed me, tried to have me killed. It seemed like a kind of . . . justice, I guess. And I wanted you to come to Hong Kong. I wanted you to be near me, You seemed like a good man. Sounds daft now." A half truth, a half sentence, stopping myself short, frightened of everything the truth might mean, the truth of me, I am Hope, I am thief, I am stalker, I am the stranger you can't remember kissing.

He leant back in his chair, fingers clinging now to the edge of the table, a climber just holding on. "In Hong Kong . . . no," he stopped himself. "That's not the order of things. A year ago I was contacted by the man you call Gauguin. He'd pulled some strings, seen the Vienna file, matched fingerprints he had from Dubai to your file. He said, 'Look, you have her fingerprints, the paperwork from her arrest, you arrested this woman and now you can't remember her.' He was very persuasive. And I thought back through your crimes, and I thought back to São Paulo, Hong Kong, places where I'd followed you and where things had seemed . . . strange. In Hong Kong there was a night when I woke and there was lipstick on my neck. I hadn't . . . but there it was and I thought . . . it was madness of course, but I checked the CCTV, saw . . . and there you were. I had to put your photo on the computer screen, tape it on to compare your face, but I knew, because I couldn't remember you. We went into the elevator together. You were limping, I assume . . ."

"I'd been shot on Hung Hom Pier, yes. Said it was an accident at work."

"And I believed that?"

"I don't think you were expecting a thief to say hello. I'd approached you in São Paulo, I knew—"

"What did you do in São Paulo?" Incredulity, rage, beginning to rise, but he's keeping it under control, just, pulling back the tempest.

"Nothing. We had a drink."

"We had a *drink*?" The fingers of one hand grip white against the table, then jerk up, as if stung, hang for a second in the air between us, and for a moment I don't know if he's going to hit me or not.

Then there it is, the copper's sigh, getting control of himself, pulling it all back together, jaw tight, eyes narrow.

"We had a drink," I repeated. "I pretended to be a policewoman from the local service. It was just a drink."

"Why?"

"You were . . ."

"Investigating? A *good man*?" The words came out edged with bile, and he heard it, and half closed his eyes again, and when they opened again he was calm, flat, listening, a cop on the job.

The café turned, the door opened, the door closed, cold air drifting in from outside. A woman laughed at the counter, the checkout till pinged shut, we sat in silence.

Then I said, fast and flat, surprised to hear myself speak, "In the short term, these deeds are yours, as well as mine." His eyebrows flickered, fingers tight, but he said nothing. "You met me. Spoke to me. Formed an impression. Your short-term memory can hold me long enough. You made a judgement. Would you like me if you knew who I was? Probably not, you have long-term impressions that a short-term experience cannot trump. But for a second, forget that. Meet me now, for the very first time. In this moment, who do you see? Create a picture of me second by second, no past, no future, no care, no responsibility. *You* do that; I do not do it for you. I can position myself in a certain way, say certain things, but in the end, the choice is yours. You chose this. In Hong Kong—"

"We went up in the elevator together," he interrupted, stopping words he didn't want to hear.

I shrugged, let him finish.

"And six hours and twenty-eight minutes later, you got into the elevator on my floor, and took it to yours."

Silence.

"Would it make a difference if I told you?" I asked, chin resting on the netted top of my hands. "Everything I can tell you is just words, and you'd have no way of knowing if it was true. Only trust, or rejection, or something doubtful in between. Your choice."

Silence a while. Then: "I am a good man." He said it so softly, I wondered if he knew he had spoken at all. Then he looked up, and a little louder, "I am a good man. I don't forget the people I've slept with; that's not who I am."

"And here we are. Is that why you wanted to meet? To ask all of this?"

"Yes."

"Why did you think I'd come?"

"Because of Hong Kong. Because I think you're obsessive and lonely."

I shrugged.

"Do you want pity? A thief is a thief."

"How would you live, in my shoes?" I replied. "It's tough drawing housing benefit when no one down the Jobcentre remembers you. You'd think that stuff would be automated, but hell no, government can't have slackers, slackers have to be assessed, interviewed, catalogued. Tough getting catalogued, when people forget to file the report. Try getting flatmates, doing an interview, getting treated by a doctor, finding friends – what would you have done?"

"Isn't it your fault, that you're forgotten? Isn't it something you choose?"

My turn to consider hitting him. I contemplated the idea with cool detachment, and found it surprisingly easy to let it go. "No. I never chose any of this."

"You chose to steal Perfection."

"Yes."

"You chose to manipulate me. To . . . to . . ."

His voice trailed off. He rolled his teaspoon between his fingers, one way, then the other; reached a decision, and turned the Dictaphone off. Put it in his jacket pocket.

"We slept together in Hong Kong," he said at last.

"Yes."

"And in Brazil?"

"No."

"What about here?"

"No."

"Do you want to?" Not an invitation; a simple question.

"Are you sure you don't want to keep recording?" I replied.

A shaking of his head. "I don't want to remember this."

"If you don't remember it, it doesn't mean anything."

"It'll mean something to you."

"Is that enough?"

"I don't know. I am what you could call a coward. You say that you are a thief, you say it like it's . . . it's something of what you are. I say that I was a policeman, a career man. They knew my name at the local deli, I was in the community choir, a would-be family man. I was many things that made me who I thought I was, and now I am not. All of that was taken away, and I followed you. You pulled on my strings and I followed, and I lost my job and I would have done it again to catch you, you became . . . finding you became a part of who I am, just like the rest of it. You were . . . my obsession. Does that excite you? Are you aroused by that, to know that I needed you, needed to catch you, just as you needed someone to fuck?"

Anger, rising, though his voice hid it, his face tightening, compressing with the effort of keeping it in.

"No," I replied quietly. "It doesn't excite me anymore."

"I think I am a coward. If you walked away now, I would forget you, and then I could enjoy being seduced. It would be a pleasant short-term interruption to a long-term malaise. I might hate myself afterwards, finding that the reality of my actions does not conform to who it is I like to believe myself to be; and then I would forget, and wouldn't hate myself after all. An easy option, yes? The coward's way out. The man you stalked was an illusion. You created him from your own loneliness, fabricated someone you needed in your life. It's all pathetically obvious, really. As Matisse says, you are infinitely more interesting to a scientist than to a shrink. Does this horrify you? I wanted to turn the recorder off so I couldn't hear myself say this, I would hate myself for these words too, you see, not good, not courteous, not who it is I think I would like to be, but of course, with you, I can say whatever I want now and forget, I won't remember myself calling you bitch, whore, fucked-up little infant, child, slut, thief. It feels incredible to have those words out, it's like – I am ashamed and frightened and excited and this must be how you feel, how it feels to be a criminal! Christ it's like . . . cunt! Fucking bitch, I hope you tear your fucking eyes out. Eat razors, piss fire, remember and shed your tears alone in the night, die alone, this is wonderful! Saying this is . . . fuck you, fuck my fucking life!" His hands, locked on the edge of the table, knuckle-white, eyes red, tears pooling in the bottom, blinking them away, hands not moving to wipe the salt as it rolled down his cheeks. "I am a failure, so fuck you, whoever you are, fuck the truth!" He lunged across the table, one hand wrapping around my throat. I grabbed a fork instinctively, ready to drive into his eye, his neck, any easy target – but his hand didn't squeeze, just pressed there, ready to dig, his body arched up and forward in an awkward L, leaning on the elbow of his left arm for support, the tears flowing free.

Faces turned in the shop; someone screamed, someone else said, call the police.

He was frozen there, and I held the fork in my hand and wondered if I needed to hurt him, and the tears rolled and his lips moved and he said nothing and did nothing and finally, slowly, let go. He let go, and sank back into his chair, and held himself, wrapping his arms around his chest, and wept in silence.

A while, we stayed there.

The café watched us, and when we did not move, they turned away.

Quiet, a while, save for Luca's tears.

Quiet.

I put the fork back down on the table. Said, "You are a good man."

Only the sound of tears, of little ragged breaths from a rag-doll man.

"Funny, the things we do when we think no one will remember," I mused. "Tempting, sometimes, just to punch a stranger in the street, just to see what it feels like. Is it like the movies? Or to sleep with the guy you really, really shouldn't, but hell, go on, today, just today. Or to steal something from a shop. A packet of crisps, a chocolate bar, nothing big, nothing that anyone will mind, really, but just . . . go on. Break the rules. Just a little bit. Just today. Most of the time, people stop themselves. They stop because they think they'll be caught, or because they're afraid. Or because their conscience kicks in and whispers, if you break this rule, you'll be breaking the trust on which society runs. You're not scared of going to prison – I mean, maybe you are, but more likely you're scared of a world in which anyone could just attack you as you walked by. Or in which your property wasn't your own, and the only thing that mattered was might and power and the will to act. Goodness is a concept as loose as any value imposed by man throughout the ages. Good: correct or proper. Of high quality. Agreeable. Pleasant. Virtuous, commendable. He's a good'un, that'un. Fighting a good war. Good: good wives, good daughters, good housekeepers, good women in their place. Good: burning witches. Good: catching thieves, putting that druggie away behind bars, blowing yourself up in the name of . . . whatever. Allah or Jesus, Vishnu or Jehovah, everyone's got their thing. And everyone, no matter who, at some point, hears the call, *go on, go on, go on, say it, do it, hit it, smash it, go on!* And usually they stop themselves, or if they do not, they remember their actions later, and are ashamed."

I reached over, into his jacket, pulled the Dictaphone out. Turned it on. Put it between us. Sat back in my chair. He watched it, holding his breath, stifling the sound of tears.

"Two commandments," I mused. "Know thyself, and know everyone else. Having no one else to know me, having no one to catch me or lift me up, tell me I'm right or wrong, having no one to define the limits of me, I have to define myself, otherwise I am nothing, just a . . . liquid that dissolves. Know yourself. But finding definition without all the . . . the daily things that give you shape – Mum, Dad, friend, sister, lover, work, hobby, job, home, travel – without the limits of place or society, I could define myself as anything. I am breath. I am mercy. I am the sea. I am knowledge. I am beauty. I am perfection. I am . . . anything at all. What am I, then? I look at the world and it seems like a distant thing seen through the window of a speeding train. A glimpse of a field where a woman sows, a child waving from the platform, a man fixing his car by the side of the road, I move and the world passes by, untouchable. But in the act of seeing, in the act of moving, I gather memories and they become me. Others do not remember me, so only I remain. You try to remember me by words, and you only remember the words, not me. I become formless. I don't know what my destination is, but I keep on travelling, surrounded by other people's stories, absorbing them, and in their way, though they are not me, they become me. I am just . . . travelling. Nothing more. I am me. I used to think there was no goodness in men, not really – just laws and fears. But you are a good man, Luca Evard. You are a good man."

So saying, I stood up, turned off the Dictaphone, pushed it towards him, left a tip on the table, and walked away.

Chapter 88

Running.

A bad sport, really. Terrible on the knees – they say running is free, the cheapest sport there is, but good shoes cost a lot these days

the ancient peoples of Australia going walkabout, a rite of passage into manhood, barefoot, following the songlines, they didn't need expensive shoes

what did Pheidippides wear when he ran to Marathon?

I run from

I run to

I run to be free

freedom from thought

Luca Evard's hand wraps round my throat, and he weeps, and he forgets, and I carry the memory of what he did where he does not and that's

fine

another part of the journey.

His journey, but I'll take it for him, just this once. I'll make the pilgrimage he doesn't have the courage to take.

Look out across the lagoon.

Count my heartbeats

and stop.

Find that I do not need to count. Not any more.

Chapter 89

A monk sat on a pillar in Indonesia.

What are you doing up there? I asked.

I am a man on a pillar, he replied. I sit on the pillar to be closer to God.

How do you eat?

Every day I drop my basket down, and it is filled with food by devoted followers, and then I eat it.

How do you shit?

Should you be asking that?

I'm just curious.

I drop my pants and I shit over the side.

How do you sleep?

I balance carefully, and tie myself on. These days I find I need less and less sleep, though.

Why are you up there?

I said: to get closer to God.

What for?

To find a path to spiritual truths.

Why?

So I may go to heaven.

But down here there are people suffering and dying. Forests burn and the seas rise, why aren't you helping?

I am. I am showing them the way. You should come and live on top of a pillar sometime soon, you know. Material matters only tie you to this life, and this life is suffering. How much better life would be if we all sat on top of pillars.

How much better life would be if we all helped each other build pillars together?

Exactly! Now you get it!

What about books? I asked, for I was going through a learning stage. Books are material objects. If I own books, am I suffering?

If you desire them, yes, they limit you!

But they contain the knowledge of the world. Who knows: one day someone may write a book about you.

I hope they don't! They would be much better off sitting on top of a pillar.

I thought about this statement, then said, Drop your basket down to me, and I'll give you some food.

No meat, he said, as he lowered the blue plastic bag. No fizzy drinks either.

I received the lowered bag, then reached up and cut the rope that held it, took the bag and began to walk away.

Hey! he shouted after me. What are you doing?

I'm not really sure, I called back. But I think it might be something good.

Pilgrimage: to journey to a sacred place.

Pilgrim: a traveller or wanderer, a stranger in a foreign place.

Crusaders: pilgrims with swords who attempted to conquer the Middle East.

Hajj: the journey to Mecca, one of the five pillars of Islam. Shahadah, Salat, Zakat, Sawm, Hajj.

Pleasant, perhaps, to say that I am a pilgrim, but looking at it, counting the swirl of white as the devout move round the sacred stone in Mecca, watching the fans scream at the movie premiere, listening to the old men sitting on their benches by the sea who report that everything changes, and that's okay . . .

fuck me who isn't a fucking pilgrim anyway?

I run, and my run takes me to the Hotel Madellena, and I think I see Byron out of the corner of my eye, climbing out of a river taxi, but when I look back, she is gone.

Chapter 90

Countdown to Armageddon.

Hard to make a convincing bomb threat when you're forgettable. My first two attempts to convince the Venice police that I was a madwoman determined to blow apart the Hotel Madellena did nothing. Perhaps the person who took my call forgot the details by the time he'd rushed to inform a superior. Perhaps they get more crank calls than I realised. I wrote instead, a good, memorable typed message. Included detailed descriptions of the device I was building, and said, this is real, this is fucking real. If the 206 come here, I'll kill them all.

They didn't reply, and when I went to inspect the hotel the next morning, I saw no sign anyone was taking it seriously.

Gauguin was there, of course.

A message through the darknet:

Please desist in these antics. The event will proceed whether you wish it to or no. We will catch Byron if she comes.

Would that I had the time to weep.

I photographed the housekeepers and waitresses at the hotel; cut out the glam mag pictures of the fabulous and the perfect already arriving in the city. I picked the pocket of one of the security men, and found my photo in laminated plastic, and a piece of paper listing words to describe me, a commandment to memorise, if not my face, then at least the act of attempting to learn it.

On the back was an old grainy photo of Byron. She'll probably wear a wig, said the notes. And glasses. And maybe prosthetics. And different clothes. And she'll be older. If she comes at all. If she isn't working by proxies. Other than that: she'll be easy to spot, right?

I kept it to remind me of my purpose, and went about my business.

Three test passes at the hotel, in the four days leading up to the party.

Pass 1: as a potential guest, decked out in all the finery I can steal, adorned with the personal information of Awele Magalhaes, swiped from her mobile phone. Awele used to work in marketing, but she married a rich coal magnate three years ago and quit her job for a life of parties, very time-consuming; got Perfection two and a half years ago, got perfect four months back, loves the treatments, loves how they make her feel, they feel like . . . Oh, they just make me feel like *me*.

My identity passed without a hitch, and I explored the hotel, bustling in my white not-quite-fur coat, head held high, shoes impractical for running in. An ornate metal staircase in the main foyer, that divided a few steps up to curve out then in like the petals of a tulip. A landing above, decked out with an imitation of something famous of St Sebastian killed by arrows. Below: a bank of authentic 1600s elevators, lined with silver- and black-backed mirrors, at once inviting and discouraging reflection and self-contemplation. The top floor accessible only with a security key (stolen from the head of housekeeping), the basement leading directly out onto a private quay where punters could board their taxis.

I rode the lift to the top, and was not one step out of the elevator before I was confronted by security men, not here, ma'am, this floor is reserved.

I made an educated punt, exclaimed, "I'm here to see Mr

Pereyra-Conroy," and sure enough, this was the floor privately reserved for Rafe and his entourage but how did I even get access to it without a key?

"He's not here, ma'am," began one and I huffed and puffed and pressed the button for the floor below and as the lift doors closed, they barely had time to be confused before they began to forget.

The floor below was decked out in more black carpets, silver doors, the soft breeze of heating against the humid cold outside, cables along the ceilings and floors, newly put in. I looked through every open door with imperious confidence, noted TV cameras and men in black, women with tripods and notebooks, suites of rooms being set up with lightning-bright white lights for the interviews with the great, the famous, the fabulous and the rich. How much do you love being perfect? Oh, so much, it's just the greatest feeling in the world!

A ballroom, being prepped. A low ceiling that rose rapidly away from the front door towards a dome of glass and steel, a Victorian extension to an older building, arches of black steel all around embedded in the walls as if someone had wanted to build a greenhouse, then given up halfway through and gone for a church instead. Hard to see the glamour in people gaffer-taping velvet drapes and hammering in steel platforms for the band. Tools across the floor, cables along the ceiling, but a few days and it would all be suitably

perfect

for its guests

Perfect: without blemish.

A security man spotted me, and this time he had the presence of mind to reach into his pocket where a little laminated photo lay, and so I turned, and fled, down the tulip steps and past the waiting guests, through the streets of Venice in my silly shoes, a snowball in a stolen dress.

Pass 2: as technician. Much easier costume. Black jeans, black T-shirt, leather belt, multitool, roll of gaffer tape. Access: universal. Security: utterly uninterested. I explored from the very top to the very bottom of the hotel, through the service corridors and behind the stairs. I photographed main power inlets, server hubs, stole a few more keys, lifted a couple of mobile phones, swanned around uninterrupted for nearly two hours until at last, sated on information, I packed up my goodies into a plastic bag, and let myself out by the service door.

A thought: if it's this easy for me, I wonder how easy it is for Byron?

Pass 3: one day left, and I thought as I entered in my housekeeper's blue that I saw . . . but no, easy to imagine these things, Byron couldn't stay hidden from sight, not from all of Gauguin's men, not from me, she's good but not that good. The mind is a fallible, dodgy contraption to have to rely on, and yet not, complexity, complexity in the simple words that cascade meaning, that *focus*

made it forty minutes as a housekeeper before someone who should be in the know saw me, and didn't know me at all and said, "Hey! Who the hell are you?"

Good thing about the housekeeper's costume: excellent soft shoes. He was a senior management type, all hard leather and tight black laces. I outran him without breaking a sweat.

Chapter 91

So here it is.

The end of the line.

Or the beginning, depending how you look at it.

Hin und zerück – there and back.

The train reaches the end of the tracks, and I get off, and one day I may get on again, and return home, and the journey will be different and the same, just like me.

Night-time in Venice. I settle for a middle-ground costume, smart but unflashy black cocktail dress. Slip sleeping pills into the drink of a photographer with a friendly face, steal her cameras and ID, and catch the river bus to a party.

Things that are ridiculous about even the least ridiculous of events:

- Selective blindness. A guest at a big party must choose not to perceive the service staff around them. Waiters and waitresses, security men, duty managers, cooks, musicians, technicians, all melt into the background. This night is yours, it is about you and your friends, and the intrusion of strange, prying eyes, of eyes that are not of your world – best ignored, not a living thing at all.
- Canapés. Ridiculous. Mango from Sri Lanka, caviar from Russia, stripes of banana leaf flown in from Kerala, Thai rice, Norwegian salmon, Australian wine, Chinese squid. A small empire has risen and will fall in the name of a piece of food no bigger than the circle formed between my pinched thumb and index finger, cost: $17 a bite.
- Music. Not too good, not too bad. Mozart is fiddly, Beethoven a little too passionate. The Russians have good tunes, but sometimes stir too many emotions, the British tend to pathos. Something middle ground. Something we can all admire, but which no one bothers to listen to, because the beauty is in the listening, in the growing complexity, the unfolding of a story, and no one at a party has time for that.
- Speeches. Welcome everyone, we are honoured you can come to [x]. I was talking to [name] about what was expected of me tonight and he said [insert joke]. No, but seriously, tonight is all about [subject] and of course about you, and in honour of this we have some amazing events lined up, including [x] and [y] and not to forget [z].

Would that I could forget speeches as fast as they forget me.

- Champagne fountains: a waste of good booze.
- Ice sculptures, gently melting into stone bowls.
- Headpieces: in the 1700s, how many women died when their great wigs and beehive heads got caught in the flaming wax of the chandeliers? These days the only threats to some of the hair on display were low doors, the insides of cars, and the inability of anyone with that hairdo to nod.

Snap, snap, take the photo, are you looking at me? And freeze and smile, teeth bright, smile aches, you are your smile and click beautiful photo, thank you, thank you so much . . .

A film star arrives and she's signed a sponsorship deal with a jeweller in the USA. Value of the diamonds around her neck: approx. $7.5 million. In the old days I would have cared about that, but not tonight. Not tonight.

I turn and photograph, click click, darling, you look beautiful. There's CCTV everywhere, but you'd have to look for me to find me, you'd have to remember what you're looking for, to know to look. Another photo, another turn, wasn't *he* in that, wasn't *she* in something else, and here comes Rafe, applause at the door, oh Rafe you are wonderful (click click) tell us how you did it (click click), he smiles and shakes the hands of the perfect people around him and says, "I never lost faith in myself."

I did, I think, click click, turn turn. I went forward, I went back, I crossed the desert and found myself wanting, stood on the railway tracks and discovered I was scared of trains, scared of travelling, travelled anyway, left it all behind, lost everything again, until only I remained.

Rafe – what are you wearing? Gucci. Ah: of course! Of course Gucci, and your watch by . . . ?

Gauguin behind him. His eyes settle on me for a moment, and instantly, he reaches into his pocket. Poor Gauguin, are you worried about your own responses? You see a woman in a crowd and now you think, "Is it her?" The anxiety must be killing you. But you still carry my photo so I turn away, let the people eat me up, you'll forget you saw me, though you'll worry about it, this photo in your hand, did you get it out for me? Probably. Probably you did. Fat lot of use that is for you now.

Where is Byron?

Turn, click click. No sign of Luca, no sign of Byron.

Where is she?

The 206 are here, the elite of all elites, two hundred and six of them, the most beautiful of the beautiful, click click, she whose skin burns gold ("I went for a face glow … the doctor burned me … have you any idea …?"), he whose smile is silver (tooth whitening: apply carbamide peroxide, breaks down in the mouth to hydrogen peroxide (used to dye hair) and urea (usually excreted via urine). In olden times, wealthy men and women would rub their teeth with charcoal to create the impression of tooth rot, demonstrating that they had access to expensive goods such as sugar)

click click

I am knowledge

I am me

click click

the world turns and I am still

Look upwards, and there, anatomy of a ballroom, go! To the left, on balcony one, photographers and cameras interviewing the select beauties of the 206, a man in there now, a golfer, I think, one wrist folded over the other so you can better see his watch (sponsorship, nothing flashy, and look, you get to tell the time!)

in the middle, balcony two, an acrobat warming up, a string quartet in full swing, twiddly dum twiddly dee, jazz later of course, when they dance, the 206 all know how to dance

to the right, separated off by red curtains, a control area, I remember it from pass two, a place of amplifiers and dimmer racks, cables and electrical outlets, not very 1600s having 63A three-phase power in your ancient stone walls, not very in keeping with the Venetian aesthetic, so hide it, turn down the lights and I look, tilt my camera upwards to hide my face click

and think perhaps I see the curtain twitch.

How would I do it, if I were Byron? How would I be here?

Not for the first time, I feel a great deal of admiration for her, a memorable, incredible spy.

I turn to go, following my instincts, nice, professional instincts,

and there is Filipa.

Of course.

Standing in the door.

Someone takes her coat and she smiles and instantly

it is easy to see

there is something wrong with her smile.

Filipa? My voice. Not my voice. My voice is strong and self-assured. A weaker voice, a voice of a child. Filipa?

She looked at me, from the top of two short stone steps that led down into the hall, as the great and the beautiful flowed round her, and smiled, a wide, friendly smile on white teeth and said, "I'm so sorry, I think . . . ?" She let her voice trail off. She thinks we might have met, but perhaps . . . ? Just remind me, the name . . . ? "My name is Hope," I said. "You gave me your bracelet . . ." I look to her wrist, but the Möbius strip is gone, replaced by something bangle-like, white gold, flecked with rubies.

"Of course! Hope! So sorry, how silly of me, such a pleasure!"

She swept down the stairs, caught one arm in mine, pulled me with her, exclaimed, "With all the cameras for a moment I thought you were someone else, how have you been?"

Her words, high and easy, a flute singing its love-song. "I'm fine. I'm . . . why are you here?"

"Why wouldn't I be here? My brother's big event, and not just that, so important, don't you think? A real chance to speak to the aspirations of everyone, to make a difference. I'm very proud of everything we've achieved, but there's always so much more to do."

Her walk pulled us towards the centre of the room, towards the champagne fountain, thin clouds of vapour rolling off the ice sculpture, an image of Aphrodite clinging longingly to the neck of long-speared Ares, her nose beginning to melt, melting into his arms, in the style of . . . of someone . . .

"Filipa," I said, grasping her arm tight in mine, "Byron's here."

She looked up quickly, her smile not faltering, held the gaze a second, then brightly exclaimed, "In spirit, or in person?"

A joke. Making it a joke.

I held her tighter, until my fingers began to hurt, a frown flickering across her face, moving to disentangle her arm, but I just gripped harder and hissed, "What have they done to you?"

"Done to me?" she replied. "Nothing at all! Do you mind, you're hurting my arm?"

"Filipa, who am I?"

"You're Hope; you said."

"And when did we last meet?"

"I . . . well, you know, I meet so many people."

"Nîmes, the hospital, the people in the beds, Perfection, the treatments . . . "

"Ah, yes, that's all been resolved."

I gripped her hard enough to make her gasp, my fingers burrowing into her skin. "*What the fuck have they done to you?*"

Already knowing the answer.

"Let – go!"

She dragged her arm free from mine, staggered back, a scene, we were now the centre of a scene, people turning to look, security men turning to look, couldn't have that, needed to move, dammit dammit dammit!

I cradled my cameras close to my chest, and ran.

What now?

Sit in the women's toilets and cry?

When you are lonely, it's hard to get a little emotional perspective. Like a child, every cut hurts deeper, every wound bleeds from your very heart. Bruising has not knocked strength into me. Society never taught me how to hide.

Fuck this.

No more fucking crying.

No more counting, I am my feet!

I am my feet in their black boots as I move through the hotel, I am justice, I am vengeance, fuck you world if you think you can do this to me, fuck you if you think I don't know how to fight back, if you think I'll just roll over and die, my dad looked murderers in the eye, my sister would swing a light sabre through evil's fucking head, and I

Hey Macarena!

Will be all that I am.

Now!

Up the stairs to the control room, duck under the red cordon separating it from me. No security guards on this stair – surprising, there had been two days ago, when I was a technician, but now, gone, abandoned, wonder why (don't really), up to a wooden door, built for a smaller species in an older time. The lock was old, too cumbersome to pick, but I forced it with a kitchen knife and let myself in.

A balcony, the size of my childhood bedroom. Low stone ceiling, a hint of a stone flower blooming above the door, a shadow of ancient red bricks plastered over by a man in straw sandals and a floppy hat, back in the days of smallpox. A red curtain, shielding it from the ballroom, a narrow slit down the middle where you might peep out to see the beautiful people with their perfect lives, watch and be amazed, dancing, dancing, dancing.

A bottle of pepper spray in my camera bag, which the security guard had dismissed as a roll of film (ridiculous; we are in a digital age, go back to school, fool!). I looked around, but Byron wasn't there, of course she wasn't. Gauguin knows she's coming, security is tight (but I got in), she wouldn't be able to get past the door (yet here I am and where was security?), probably already been caught in fact (hey Macarena!) and

I begin to relax.

A quick inventory of the room.

Amplifiers; changing displays indicating the peak sound being pumped through the system from the string quartet

radio racks, currently muted, for when speeches begin

sloppy – hubs for the security men's radio system too, should definitely be guarded, peculiar that they're not

dimmer racks and cables, great fat red ends, fat copper in black tubes, it's fine, it's fine, it's

two photos, pinned to the wall

I'm so eager for everything to be fine, I almost miss them.

A woman, her face turned down and to the side, as if caught in a lie. The sun behind her, filling her curling dark hair with reddish cobwebs. Another, she looks direct to camera, but doesn't seem to see it, attention focused on something else, and that was San Francisco, I recognise the internet café behind – had Byron followed me, or was the photo from another, more trusting time?

The woman, asleep in a chair. Or at least, probably asleep, hopefully asleep, two electrodes pushed through her skull, a pair of goggles round her neck, ready to be worn. A sensor taped to her tongue, she looks like the dead, all that technology, none that I can remember

Hey Macarena!

none that I choose to remember, perhaps

she is me.

And beneath the photos, messages, written in a familiar hand, stuck up on Post-it notes.

SHE IS REAL
SHE IS_WHY
SHE WILL COME

Movement behind me, and at once I turned, raising the pepper spray, cameras swinging around my neck, bruising my belly as they bounced.

The knife bumped on a camera, but then slipped on by, carried by the momentum of the woman who used it. As it passed between the floating ribs on my right side, it was bigger than all the world. She held me up as I began to fall, one hand across my back, the other still supporting me by the knife stuck through my body.

"Is it you?" she asked. "Is it you?"

Not as much blood as I'd thought – not yet – not with the knife still in me, a plug blocking the flow. I looked up into Byron's face, and she'd chosen a very different path from mine. She'd shaved her head, glued a skullcap on, then a wig of black hair. She wore a grey dress, high-collared and swathed with a black shawl, pinned with a butterfly brooch. A security pass bounced around her neck, declaring her to be press, and a long Italian name that blurred as I tried to focus on it. She wore a green wristband to give her all-area access and – here I would have laughed, if the blood wasn't seeping from my body – had glued on an extra piece of latex to the bridge of her nose, changing it into a Roman beak, and now she reached into her mouth and removed two little pieces of sponge, deflating her cheeks to their natural dimensions, and discarding them, held my hand tight again and inspected the place where the knife was stuck in my chest.

"It is you," she breathed, but I couldn't answer, and she pulled off her shawl and wrapped it tight around the wound, pressing down hard, though I wasn't at the point where I could process pain. "I wondered if you would come."

I tried to speak.

Nothing came out. Just back-of-the-throat noises, like an engine trying to start, no oil in the system, a pipe broken somewhere, nasty stain on the tarmac, someone will have to clean that.

"Stay down," she said, "stay hidden. This will be over soon."

Her right hand, red with my blood, brushed the side of my face. Maternal. Caring, perhaps. A kind of love.

But she had business to be doing, and I screamed for Gauguin (no sound came) and I screamed for Luca (who didn't hear) and I screamed stop it, stop it, for God's sake stop it and nothing stopped and I made no sound.

She turned her back on me. Walked to a little mixing desk, knobs and faders, buttons and dials, a microphone plugged in for announcements and emergencies. Turned it on. Pulled down the sound of music, though the buzz of conversation in the ballroom below didn't falter. Cleared her throat.

> And the widows of Ashur are loud in their wail,
> And the idols are broke in the temple of Baal.
> And the might of the Gentile, unsmote by the sword,
> Hath melted like snow in the glance of the Lord.

So saying, she put the microphone down, and I found that I was shaking to hear her speak, and the silence was busy in the hall below as the killing began.

Chapter 92

For a moment, I'd hoped I was wrong, and that Byron would not come to Venice.

Fat chance of that.

How do you stop a madman in the street?

How do you contain a lone wolf?

Byron speaks, and the world goes mad, and she presses her shawl into my wound and whispers, "I'll find you," and is gone.

Bleeding out.

(Dying.)

Facts and figures, to pass the time.

In the USA nearly one in five boys and one in eleven high-school girls were reported to have received an attention deficit disorder diagnosis: 6.5 million children

of those, 3.5 million on medication

(Someone screaming below, shush now)

Said the Scientologists of psychiatrists: "[they commit] extortion, mayhem and murder."

Quoth the Anderson Report, conducted by the state of Victoria into the Church of Scientology: "Scientology is evil, its techniques evil, its practice a serious threat to the community, medically, morally and socially."

(Blood heading towards the edge of the balcony – funny that, implies a slope, flowing not pooling; subsidence?)

Oxygen use in the body: liver 20.4 per cent, brain 18.4 per cent, heart 11.6 per cent.

Liver functions: breakdown of insulin, breakdown of toxins, conversion of ammonia to urea, production of coagulation factors, protein metabolism, lipid metabolism, amino acid synthesis, platelet regulation, production of growth factors, storage of vitamins, production of albumin, production of . . . production of . . .

(something smashing, the music has stopped and so has the conversation but funny, would have expected more really)

Diabetes: suspected long before its formal identification and discovery by the usual suspects of historical medicine, from Galen through to Avicenna. 1910 Sir Edward Albert Sharpey-Schafer isolates insulin

(crawling. Very slow, pushing a fingertip at a time towards the balcony ignore the pain ignore the knife, don't touch the knife the knife is what's keeping you alive, keeping the blood from spilling everywhere crawling)

Elliott Joslin publishes the first texts on treatment
however not before some interesting experiments on dogs
remove the pancreas observe the effects
which dogs live
which dogs die
how
why

(crawling, a smear of blood behind me, my clothes glued to my back, silent below now, too silent, even the sobbing has stopped)

Frederick Banting, Charles Best, J. J. R. Macleod, James

Collip, purification of insulin for use in humans, only two of them got the Nobel Prize though must have caused a stir back at the office

(crawling, try to lift my left arm but no, blood-thrumming, eye-bursting, body-popping agony, to lift my left arm is to move muscles around the knife, to move muscles around the knife is to die, I know that now, I will die here in this place with a knife in my chest and here comes the pain, it comes it comes)

Three main causes of death from injury: shock, pain, blood loss

(Concentrate!)

Shock: low blood perfusion to tissues. Clammy skin, high heart rate, pale skin, confusion, loss of consciousness, for best diagnosis measure heart rate divided by systolic . . . systolic blood pressure for an answer of

treatments raise legs

(I can't)

essential that what blood is flowing goes to the major organs, cardiac arrest, respiratory arrest

(my right hand can reach the curtain, twitch it aside)

Shock: cold shock response e.g. from falling through ice. Vasoconstriction owing to extreme cold. Heart has to work harder to pump blood – heart fails.

(I reach, but can't seem to move it enough to see the world beyond. Pull harder scream no sound pull harder scream in my eyes my eyes are screaming I am my eyes screaming my hand screaming my voice screaming my)

the curtain falls.

Tangled for a moment in its embrace. The curtain falls and I look, turning my head slowly to the side, peeking down between the balustrades of the balcony.

I am pain, and that is fine.

Shock: acute stress reaction – numbing, amnesia, dissociative awareness, depersonalisation, muteness.

I am witness to these events.

I am my eyes, screaming.

I witness:

A woman, dressed in gold, crouched over the body of her dancing partner, twisting the shattered stem of her champagne glass deeper, deeper into his throat. He's dead already, but she's fascinated by the play of glass and blood, the brightness of the ruby drops on her skin. They complement her dress; perhaps someone can do a design based on this moment?

A man, his tuxedo turned red, a caviar knife embedded in his leg, but he doesn't mind, dragging another man by the throat across the room. He gets to the door, and is confused by it, and lets go of the man in his grasp, but the body is dead and he's still bewildered, so he goes back the way he's come, stepping over the eyeless waitress who lies by the door, and sees if he can find enlightenment in another place.

Enlightenment: the final spiritual state; an absence of suffering or desire.

A woman, who sits on her haunches next to the man whose head now hangs by a string. There's blood around her mouth, and blood on her teeth, but she's satisfied for now, just rocking gently back and forth, I think I saw her in a movie once, I think she played an unhappy wife in a drama about American suburbia

(my blood drips off the edge of the balcony)

(it will not be noticed)

A man whose ear has been ripped from his face but that's okay, that's not the problem, bangs his head gently against the wall

rocks on his heels

backwards

forwards

bang

backwards

forwards

bang

A woman more beautiful than moonlight, confused, sees the dead and the dying, sees someone she thinks she knows, impaled on the melting ice sculpture in the centre of the room. He died there after he drowned a man in ice cubes, and look, his victim now lies beneath him, still face-down, gently preserved in champagne. The woman rises. Walks across the room. Pulls the white silk scarf from the throat of the man in the ice, then walks the other way, looking for a way to hang herself with the three or four others who also chose that route.

A girl strangled with pearls.

A man, his gold pen jammed into his spine.

There wasn't much in the way of screaming. As the 206 began to slaughter each other to the sound of Byron's voice, they were so busy killing that they didn't really care about being killed. It was only the imperfect ones, the technicians and the waiters, the photographers and the press, who screamed as they died.

Rafe Pereyra-Conroy died screaming, I suspect, beaten to death with his own microphone just before he was going to speak. Who would have thought that such a little thing could be used to break so many bones?

His murderer sits behind him now, cross-legged on the floor, chewing her nails.

Filipa's eyes roam the room, meet mine, but she doesn't appear to see me. Doesn't appear to see much at all, any more.

The cameras in the paparazzi's box keep on rolling. YouTube awaits.

I am witness.

I close my eyes.

Chapter 93

I was cold for a while, now I'm warm.

I have a feeling that this is not a good sign, but fuck, who cares anymore?

Words from . . . somewhere.

Kafka, Franz, b. 1883, d. 1924, unknown in his lifetime,

famous after death. "One of the first signs of understanding is the wish to die."

Or other side-splitting japes: "My guiding principal is this: guilt is never to be doubted."

But then again: "Youth is happy because it has the ability to see beauty. Anyone who keeps the ability to see beauty never grows old."

1924 was a leap year.

Lenin dies.

The Ottoman Empire gives way to the Turkish state.

The Immigration Act in the USA paves the way to racial discrimination against Asian communities, and will later be cited by the Japanese as proof of American colonial imperialism.

Nellie Taylor Rose is elected first female governor in the USA.

Edwin Hubble declares that Andromeda (previously believed to be a nebula) is a galaxy, and that the Milky Way is merely one of millions of billions of galaxies spinning through the universe.

Approximately eighty-six billion neurons in the human brain. Approximately three hundred billion stars in the Milky Way. Approximately two hundred billion galaxies in the universe, assuming infinity to be an unhelpful term. Approximately 7×10^{27} atoms in the human body.

I am . . .

here.

Chess: after three moves on a board, there are over nine million different possible positions that can be achieved in the following game. In a forty-move game, there are more possible positions than the number of electrons in the observable universe.

I am

awake.

My eyes.

Slowly.

No more screaming.

The screams went into my mind, but that's okay, there's plenty of room, and much weight of knowledge that I may cast down upon them, if they grow too loud. I am knowledge, you see. I find it is less harmful than many of the other things I could be.

My eyes are quiet, and so am I.

I open them, and I see.

Hospital.

Kinda unexpected, really.

All hospitals look the same.

Blue curtains separate the beds. A bedstand next to me, a jug of water and a plastic cup. A drip of something mixed with something running into a cannula in my left hand, the clear tubing threaded through my hospital gown. In the bed opposite mine, an old woman is awake and scowling, rolled onto one side, her feet bulging beneath the tight anti-thrombosis socks that contort her pale, spotted flesh. Hard to imagine her face, with its jowls and furrowed thick black brows, looking anything other than angry, but perhaps I do her a disservice. Perhaps everyone is angry in this place, with the grey winter light coming through the window at the end of the bed. Perhaps the doctors are rude.

A TV on in the booth besides me. Italian reality TV, something about seducing a rich man, a paradise island, a disastrous dinner – whatever. Waiting a while.

Traditionally this moment, this wakening, is when the doctors come and say, "How are you, are you in much pain, can you remember your name?" and I reply no, no I can't, oh God what year is it who am I who am I who am I . . . ?

Not so much.

A nurse pads by, sees I'm awake, smiles brightly and perhaps assumes that I've been awake a while, and someone else has already said hello. I smile back. She's forgotten me by the time she's gone, but that's okay, there are a lot of patients on this ward, it's easy to forget. A miracle really that I wasn't left in the ambulance, an extraordinary thing to be here at all.

Wait a while.

Easy to be forgotten to death in the medical system, but it's okay, there's paperwork, NHS targets (do they have those in Italy?), no patient to be left in A&E for more than four hours, just keep on rolling rolling rolling

the woman across the aisle from me turns onto her other side. She'd forgotten I was there, and is unimpressed at the sight of me. In her free time, she shouts at children, I decide. They make too much noise. They're always smiling and happy and running and free and it's for their own good that their dreams are crushed asap.

A senior doctor arrives, three juniors in his wake.

How are you feeling? he asks, hands in pockets, casual, relaxed, a flicker in the corner of his eye as he tries to work out if he's ever seen me before. He's seen tens of thousands of patients in his career, and forgotten most of them, but they all know he remembers them by name and cares deeply for their condition. That's how good he is. His badge says his name is Dino, but I find that hard to believe.

I've been better, I admit. I think I was stabbed.

Ah! The horror at the hotel, yes of course! The senior doctor smiles, the juniors recoil, suddenly a little alarmed at being near me for, sure, I was stabbed but is there not a danger that I might have stabbed someone else too?

Well then yes, let's have a look . . . could be worse, could be worse, nice clean dressing, looking good, missed the lung I see that's good, antibiotics of course we'll have a nurse come take some readings

(the nurse does not come)

no name, whispers a junior

Dr Dino is relieved – he hasn't forgotten my name, he never knew it, perhaps he doesn't have to go on a mind-boosting fish-oil diet after all.

What's your name?

Faye, I decide. Faye Cavarero. Where is this?

You're in the Ospedale dell'Angelo, in Mestre. The Paolo was overwhelmed by the scale of the medical emergency, and the paramedics were able to stop the bleeding on the scene, so you were evacuated here. You were a guest? A note of caution in his voice.

No: a photographer.

Instant relief. Oh, a photographer! I imagine the police will want to see your pictures.

I imagine they will.

Do you need counselling? he suggests carefully. There's a chaplain, someone to talk to, I can have someone sent up.

Sure, why not.

Of course! Minions! (The juniors stand to attention.) Alert psychiatric services!

They depart.

No one comes.

No name on my chart.

No name on the board above my bed.

Doctors do not bother to write these things down, they have people for that. I call a nurse over, more water, please, she takes my stats while she's there, writes it down, says, there's no name.

My name is Faye Cavarero.

Ah, like the philosopher, yes!

Yes, just like the philosopher.

It's a good name, a strong name. You'll be strong!

When dinner came, I asked for toast, but they forgot my order, so sorry, I go to get it now, forgot again, and I went without.

That settles it: I cannot stay here for ever. I will starve to death if I do.

Nurse! screams the woman in the bed opposite mine. My head hurts! Bitch – give me more painkillers! Bitch, why won't you do it my head hurts it hurts it hurts it hurts!

Her words deteriorate to a low groaning, an animal sound from deep within, a low mewl that the nurses cannot silence.

Please give her painkillers, sighs the woman in the bed next to hers. Please: just anything to make her stop.

*

When the lights are turned out, the woman is still moaning, and I am out of water, and no one comes.

Chapter 94

On the second day, in the dead of night, I put my left foot on the ground.

In the depths of space, nebulas coalesced to stars, hydrogen fusion commencing at the core, light and heat bursting across the universe.

Put my right foot on the ground.

In the darkest places of the oceans, thermal vents cracked, spilling fire into the dark, and species of bacteria, amoeba, protozoa and tiny, wriggling organisms that could barely be called living, save that they respired and moved and reproduced and decayed, flocked to this eruption of heat, and fed on its energy, and evolved into something new.

I stood up.

Almost immediately, I fell, catching myself on the side of the bed, the pain in my side numbed by stitches and drugs, head spinning, knees strong but head weak, stars in my eyes, oceans in my brain.

Sat back down.

Counted to sixty.

Put my left foot on the ground.

Counted to thirty.

Put my right foot on the ground.

Counted for thirty more.

Held onto the metal stand on which had been suspended various sacks of antibiotics and saline drips, blood and all the goodies chemistry could supply. Used it as a crutch.

Took a step.

Counted to twenty.

Took another.

Lessons from being a runner, lessons from life. Divide the problem into parts. Not: today I shall run a marathon. Today I shall run to the end of the park and back. Tomorrow I shall run to the shops. Now I shall say something kind to a person I hate. Tomorrow I will study compassion and learn French.

Today I shall walk to the bathroom, replete with hooks, handles, straps, fold-away chairs and lift-up seats for every conceivable scenario.

Today I shall lock the door.

Take a piss.

Drink water from the tap; blessed water, drink water until I hurt, I AM THE QUEEN OF THE UNIVERSE!

Shuffle through the gloom of the night-shift hospital.

The nurse, catching up on paperwork at the desk, is confused by me, but I'm not her problem, and I seem to be walking slow but well, goes back to her paperwork.

Sleeping wards, half-sleeping patients.

Beep beep beep, a monitor has detected something wrong, waking the entire room, who squeeze their eyes tight shut and lie very still, in the hope that by ignoring the sound of the machine beep beep beep it will go away, just go away!

A spill of light from a bed where a woman has given up on sleep, put her headphones on, pulled the TV screen on its artificial arm close and now watches last year's movies, a surgical drain filling slowly with fluid down one side of the bed, a five-litre bag gently swelling with urine on the other, the tube strapped to the inside of her thigh.

I am my feet
stepping
stepping
stepping.

A moment to recover breath. I sit in the big brown chair next to a woman on an oxygen feed, her eyes shut, her curly hair pushed up high across the pillow behind her head, her hands folded one over the other and back straight, like a pious funerary statue in an ancient church. She slept, and when I could breathe a little better I opened up the small cupboard by her bed, pulled out the green bag of patient belongings, and stole her jeans and a shirt and a fifty euro note. Left her the credit cards and the rest of the cash, apologised silently and bundled these goods into my robe.

Hobbling back to my bed.

Gender-segregated wards, no point going into the men's unit, a nurse by the door saw me and smiled, might make a fuss, will forget. A junior doctor, badge round her neck, asked me if I was all right. I said yes; had just needed to pee. Did I need a hand getting back to bed? No. I'd be fine, really.

The woman with the headache was asleep at last in the bed opposite mine when I returned. I stole her smartphone – just for a little while – and was surprised to see how many calls she had received, from people with familiar nicknames, text messages laden with love and care, to which she hadn't bothered to reply. With the volume turned all the way down, I sat in the chair beside my bed and ate plums and licked my lips and looked up Hotel Madellena.

It was easy to find. Not a news outlet in the world hadn't picked up on the story and run with it. Explanations abounded – environmental catastrophe being the most favoured – but mass hysteria, terrorism, a virus, and at last, and most pooh-poohed, brainwashing, were all suggested to explain the images that were being pumped out to the world, streamed across YouTube and Twitter, Instagram and Facebook.

Images not merely of the dead; images of the killing too.

Here: the CEO of a TV manufacturing company smashing his wife's head into the wall, and she wasn't resisting, resigned almost it seemed to her fate, dropping silently to the floor when his work was done. There: a weather woman calmly drinking the blood of the man whose throat she has just slashed with her nail file. She sits on her haunches, then looks up suddenly, startled, like a fox caught prowling by a wolf, sees the camera, doesn't perceive it as a threat, and slowly goes back to feasting.

Here: a TV pundit, famed for his comical yet racist views on immigrants, women and homosexuality, a man who specialised in dismissing people and ideas with the immortal argument "Well, they would say that, wouldn't they?", winner of last year's "sexiest man on entertainment TV" award, quite happily beating a waitress to death with a chair. The padded seat fell out after the first few strikes, but he carries on with the frame regardless, long after she stopped moving.

Facts and figures.

Of the three hundred and twenty-nine people caught up in the events at the Hotel Madellena, only ninety-eight were confirmed dead, with a further forty-two in critical condition. A surprisingly low number, really; but that that is the difficulty of trying to physically kill someone with your bare hands.

Of the remaining victims/suspects (the line was blurred), fifteen were in custody, one hundred and eleven were receiving treatment for various non-critical injuries and the remaining sixty-three had escaped unharmed and were being interviewed by the police, when not being interviewed by the media.

Quoth the head of reception: *They just went mad. They went mad. All of them: they just went mad.*

I looked for Rafe Pereyra-Conroy, and there was a picture of a body being taken to the morgue.

I looked for Filipa Pereyra-Conroy, and there was no information. Nothing. Not merely a media blackout, but a silence on the internet, a dead space where her name should have been, only Google cache recalling the faintest trace of articles that had been, stories which might once have carried her name.

That was interesting. That implied she was still alive.

A statement from Prometheus:

deep regrets

losses

profound condolences

full investigation

criminal acts

etc., etc., etc.

Words that had no meaning.

I looked away from the phone, and the woman who I'd stolen it from was awake, watching in silence.

I stood up.

Hobbled across to her bed.

Put it back where it had come from.

Went back to my own berth.

Climbed beneath the sheets.

Rolled over.

Closed my eyes.

She said nothing, and no one came.

Chapter 95

In the morning, Dr Dino came round around, saw my chart, said it was a disgrace, that I would be within my rights to cry neglect, and being so senior, people mustered at his command, and in the drama of the moment a cannula was removed, a dressing checked, while he stood glowering at all who obeyed before finally, the information now before him, declared that I was doing very well and I needed to speak to my insurance provider as soon as possible.

So saying, he left, and I interrogated one of his juniors, who had flawless English, about how to treat myself, once I was released from hospital.

"Don't worry," she said, "We'll give you all that information when discharged."

"Indulge me," I replied, "so I don't feel neglected."

She blanched at little at that, and answered all my questions without further complaint.

*

At midday, three policemen arrived, but they didn't go to my bed, but to the room next door, and I shuffled in my tight white socks into the ward to eavesdrop, standing with my back against the door while they talked to a woman, a fashion designer, who'd been at the Hotel Madellena when the world went mad, and had broken her leg falling down some stairs as she fled the scene.

No, she hadn't seen much.

Yes, it had been terrible.

No, she didn't know how it had started.

Yes, she'd help with enquiries, if she had to.

No, she just wanted to go home.

No, she wasn't one of the 206. She'd just been there to help a client with her clothes and make-up. She had a tie-in with Perfection. It worked well – she'd got some incredible clients, and made them beautiful.

That seemed to make the cops happy. I wondered what they'd have done if she had admitted to having Perfection herself.

In the early afternoon, Byron came.

She was dressed as an old woman, playing an old woman, shuffling in with the rest of the families come to visit their loved ones, leaning on a walking stick she didn't need, sporting a slouch she didn't have, holding a photo of my face, which she checked carefully, now, and now, and now.

She must have visited half a dozen wards before finding me, and on finding me, bent to check her photo again, smiling to herself like a dear old gran who's no bother to no one, a brilliant performer, a consummate liar, I had to admire her, and seeing my face in her hand, and then seeing my face staring at her from the bed, she smiled again, and hobbled to my side.

A few paces away, I raised my hand and said in Arabic, "If you come one step nearer, I will scream."

She replied in the same language, with a slight Syrian accent, "I'm not here to hurt you."

"You fucking stabbed me, you crazy mass-murdering bitch."

I wasn't shouting, wasn't even angry, the words came and they were true, and that was all there really was to it.

Others, looking at us. They'd forgotten me, but they'd remember her, the little old lady in the hospital speaking Arabic, though she looked about as Syrian as a broccoli. The recollection endangered her more than me, I realised, and I smiled and added, "Your limp is beautiful, but I can make you memorable."

"May I sit?" she asked.

"No."

"I called the ambulance for you, at the hotel. They wouldn't have found you otherwise."

"I don't believe you."

"I have photos – you were upstairs, behind a closed door, in a place where no one should have been. I'd paid off security; they weren't coming back. Beautiful, important people were dead or dying in the room below you. You would have bled out long before anyone saw you, if I hadn't made the call."

"Thanks, great, next time someone stabs me I hope they have the same instinct."

"I didn't want to hurt you."

"Fuck that."

"You were going to stop me. You understand I couldn't permit that to happen."

"Fat lot of good it did. Why are you here?"

"I wanted to find you, to make sure you were alive. I looked in the Paolo in Venice, but they were overflowing, so I came here. I wanted to apologise for having to injure you in the execution of my mission."

"I might scream," I replied. "I might just scream just to see what happens. See how long it takes Gauguin to come, you can have a competition, just the two of you. How fast can you get out of a straitjacket? How quickly can he pull a trigger?"

"My actions . . . " she began, a half step towards the bed.

I raised one hand again, stopping her, warning. "I swear," I hissed, "a scream to fucking burst your fucking ears."

She stopped, backed away, left hand turning gently, placating, palm towards me, fingers of her right still locked round her walking stick.

Quiet between us, for a while. In the bed opposite, the woman with the sour face was watching, fascinated. Ignorant of the language, perhaps, but our bodies spoke poems. I forced my features to settle into something neutral, felt my hands fold into my lap, the slow exhalation of breath which, another time, I might have counted as it passed. Not now.

At last she said, "In America—"

"You tried to brainwash me."

Surprise flickered over her face. "No."

"For the sword outwears its sheath, And the soul wears out the breast, And the heart must pause to breathe, And love itself have a rest." Something in her eye, a little exhalation, I kept going, because I could, Hey Macarena, all the boys wanna dance, Macarena Macarena. "Though the night was made for loving, And the day returns too soon, Yet we'll go no more a-roving by the light of the moon."

Hey.

Macarena.

Silence a while. Then: "You agreed to the treatments. In San Francisco, you agreed."

"How do you know that?"

"I wrote it down."

"Do you believe everything you write?"

"Do you trust everything you believe?" she replied.

Is it possible? Did I agree to treatments? It is, of course, possible. Of course it is.

"You tested your protocols on me?"

"We conducted some basic limit-testing. Not to make you violent. But to see what could be implanted. According to my records, you agreed to that as well. You said it was worth it. You said that if that was what it took to destroy Perfection, you were willing, and you didn't mind being remembered for it, so long as you were remembered."

Again, a lie?

I look back into the past, into the dead space I cannot remember, and I see . . .

. . . another Hope Arden, looking back.

A woman who hasn't yet sung the Macarena, a liar and a thief, the seducer of Luca Evard, a woman who survives, who counts and breathes and walks across the desert and the decisions she makes are

. . . questionable, at the best of times.

She fades from view, and only I remain.

"I'm not sure I believe you," I said at last. "But I don't think it really matters now, does it?"

"I behaved badly, at the end," she sighed. "I was becoming paranoid, my own memory loss in your presence, I was . . . fearful, I tested things, pushed at boundaries, I have notes which say—"

"You were fine," I corrected. "I stole your journal: you were fine. I don't mind telling you that now. It makes me happy to know you'll forget it."

Is this it?

Byron stands at the end of the bed, silent, watchful, not running, not attacking, not defending or denying, merely a woman in a time, in this moment.

Is this it?

Is this the end of my path, is this how my mum felt when she reached the edge of the desert, and looked towards the city and thought, that's not so much, is it?

Then she said, "I once set all the clocks ten minutes fast in my house. I was always running late for things, and so I set the clocks fast. For the first few weeks it worked well enough, and I'd just about make it to meetings on time. After a few months, I forgot that was what I'd done, and I was punctual for everything. Then one day a friend was round, and he said 'Your clock is ten minutes fast' and I remembered what I'd done, and suddenly I was late for everything again, because I knew – and could not forget – that all my clocks were fast, and in the end I had to set them back to the real time and just leave at an appropriate hour."

She stopped, as abruptly as she had begun, and silence settled again.

Then, again: "I thought I dreamed that there was a mouse dead in my bread, and one day I cut open a loaf of bread, and a mouse was inside, and I couldn't tell for a moment the difference between my dream and reality. Had I had this dream, or at the moment of finding the mouse had I invented this dream, making myself a prophet? Thought can travel through time, you see, memory reinvents itself, making the past something that always has been, now, in this second, now, for ever. You can't ever really trust your own memory, your own mind. Reality, time, the past, it's as fickle as a dream, when you look back on it."

Again, she stopped.

Again, silence.

"After I met you, I recorded myself for days, just alone in my cottage, just to see if what I remembered was what I actually did. But then I looked at the tapes and I realised the futility of my own actions, since I could tell myself that I remembered performing the acts I saw myself do, at the very instant I saw myself doing them. The mind tricks itself to certainty, I think. I think when you are alone, that is the only thing the mind can do."

Silence, again, a while.

"I'd be your friend again, if you'd let me," she said. "You and I. Juries are told to disregard the past, historians write their books as if the ancient world were unfolding now. Today Caesar rides to Gaul. Now Perfection dies in Venice. The past is a very loose concept at the best of times. Do you understand?"

Silence.

Is this it?

I cross the desert, I wait for the train, and at the end, the one person who waves from the platform, the mirage in the dust that turned out to be true, is her?

No. Not quite her. Old and bent, she is needing this, needing me, and she is so terribly, terribly alone.

One thing left: something I have to say.

"Filipa took the treatments."

I found myself unable to look directly at her, so focused instead on the wall behind her left shoulder, studying its infinitely flat quality of grey.

"Oh?"

Slight interest, no more.

"She killed her brother, I think."

Again: "Oh."

"I tried to stop you."

"I know. I saw you, watching. Knew it was you. Couldn't remember your face, but knew it had to be you. Wrote it down. Probably saw you more, forgot to write it. Can't remember now; that's all right."

"I would have killed you, if I'd had the chance."

"I'm sorry to hear that."

"I will destroy you, if I can. Are you recording this? Doesn't matter either way. Remember or forget, each has its cruelties. If I can, I will destroy you. It is . . . I want to say 'right'. I used to think I knew what right meant. Then I didn't know. Now I think I understand it again. Go away, Byron14. Go away and forget."

"You are . . . " she began.

"Miraculous?"

"Yes."

"You envy me?"

"Yes."

"You are wrong. You are wrong. Go away. By the time you've got to the door, you'll have forgotten that you saw me. By the time you come back round again, I'll be gone. Go away and forget, Byron. Go away."

She stood, frozen a while, leaning now on her stick for actual support, one shoulder higher than the other, brow locked low.

"Perfection is dead," she said at last. "We killed it."

"We killed a lot more than that," I replied, and, as she didn't seem to be moving, turned my head, looked away.

A movement at the end of my bed. I glanced down. She laid

the voice recorder on the sheets between my feet, the system still running, light on. She didn't smile, didn't meet my eye, but left it there and, with her old lady's limp, walked away.

Chapter 96

I discharged myself on the fourth day of my stay. They'd forgotten to feed me, forgotten to check my notes, forgotten to change my cannula, and after four days of the doctors being outraged at the state of things, and nothing changing, I left.

Stolen clothes, stolen money.

I could walk, but found myself aching all over, legs heavy as if from a marathon, though I'd covered barely a hundred yards.

I called a taxi, looked across at the flat nothingness of Mestre, beige houses behind beige walls, beige apartments looking out at shuttered stores. Northern Italy is beautiful, where the history remains, and industrial and drab where modern times have imposed.

At the station there were only so many places to go. I caught the train to Milan, where all those years ago I'd stolen diamonds from a man who believed in beauty, back to my favourite hotel, to the room next to the room where once I'd lain back on crisp sheets and dangled jewels between my fingers, giggling at my own brilliance.

Now I lay down again, same sheets, different universe, and closed my eyes and slept.

I watched the news. A newspaper in France was the first that dared to run with the story that the massacre at Hotel Madellena had been created by the use of Perfection. Prometheus threatened to sue the shit out of the offending journal, but the lawsuit quickly died away as other papers joined in, citing in great and exactly researched detail the nature of Perfection, the application of treatments.

Byron was behind the story, obviously, and as the scandal unfolded, pundits from every corner joined in.

- Privacy pundits: Perfection is the prime example of corporate intrusion into private lives.
- Fashion pundits: you can't put a price on individualism.
- Political pundits: it's so hard to defend against terrorism in this difficult age.
- Celebrity pundits: we've been targeted for being beautiful. Society has gone mad.
- Legal pundits: can there be charges against the survivors? Surely they are victims too (new legal code required, fee to be negotiated).
- Online pundits: guys, these stupid bitches had THEIR BRAINS re-written like fuck what the fuck do you fucking expect will fucking happen I'm perfect just the way I am, stupid!

I sat in the shower cubicle with a bottle of antiseptic, a bundle of bandages and cotton pads, a roll of surgical tape and all the painkillers I could find, and peeled the dressing away from the knife wound in my side.

Not nearly as bad as I'd thought it would be. I had expected to see a great gash, a vile, oozing thing – but maybe Byron hadn't intended to kill after all. The knife had gone in, and the knife had come out, and a dark puckering remained, stitched tight shut with self-dissolving thread, no more than an inch across. More spectacular was the bruising, the swelling, the purple-redness around, as the flesh in the vicinity of the perforation had tried to work out what this change in status meant, and was confused to discover it meant very little at all.

I re-dressed the wound, and looked up scientific papers on injury recovery programmes. Physiotherapy, antibiotics, timescales, dos and don'ts, and in a little blue notebook from the general store drew up a plan of action.

Discipline.

I will live.

On my sixth night in Milan, I went to a casino.

Card counting – a basic method:

- Assign cards within the deck a value i.e. cards 2–7 have a value of +1, 7–9 have no value, and 10–ace have a value of −1.
- As the low cards are played from the shoe, add value to the remaining deck i.e. if ten cards of a value of 2–7 are played in a row, the remaining deck has a value of +10. The higher the value of the deck, the higher the probability that better cards are about to be played. As the higher-valued cards are played, deduct points from the value of the deck i.e. once all aces have been played, you have deducted −4 points. A negative value deck is more likely to yield low cards.

Rules for getting away with it:

- Adjust bets. Bet high when the deck has a high value, low when it's running into the negative. Don't flee the table; that draws attention.
- Learn how to count cards *while doing other things*. Dealers can spot card counters; chatting to them will allay suspicion. Tipping generously may reduce the odds of being called out; dealers are human too.
- Consider how many cards are left to be played from the shoe. If you are running at a count of +10 and there are only a few hands left to be played, your odds of a big win are higher.
- Reset your count with a reshuffle. If the reshuffle appears unexpected, the dealer may be onto you.

That night I scored nearly €3,000 before they caught onto me, so I scooped up my winnings and went to the ladies' loo, and waited twenty minutes for them to forget, and played again to bring my total to €8,500 before my side began to ache and I called it a night.

Physiotherapy in a hotel room.

Different hotel, different room, hard to tell the difference.

Leg lifts.

Stretches.

Weights.

Arm lifts – slowly, at first, just in front, not to put too much pressure on the wound.

Frustrating, frustrating! I can run miles at a time, always in control, and here I am

lifting my arms to my shoulders like that's an achievement, like that means something so fucking

sit a while

and breathe.

Again.

To it again.

On my tenth day in Milan, and over two weeks after the massacre in Venice, I contacted Gauguin.

Chapter 97

Where now?

A place not nearly as impressive on reaching as getting there.

The train through the Alps takes you as far as Biasca, hugging the bottom of a dark forest, the tops of the mountains lost in the clouds. Cold, getting colder, window steaming up.

At Biasca it's a drive through winding roads, tiny villages, a phone on the side of the road in a yellow box, call if you see an avalanche. Mountains above, sun setting behind, my face in the window of the taxi as we curl through the mountains.

A village, clinging to a narrow road. The road itself is barely holding onto the edge of the mountain. Mushy snow falls. The taxi leaves me outside the one hotel. The hotel has seven rooms, all empty. The matron speaks perfect English; I'll give you the bridal suite, she says, you should have a hot bath.

The bridal suite is two rooms, a bedroom and a bathroom. The bath sits in the middle of the floor of the bathroom, a terrible waste of space, but I am fascinated by it; where do the pipes go?

You know, said the matron, I genuinely don't know.

Chapter 98

Gauguin's house was just out of town.

It clung to a sheer slope of black cliff, giving the impression of an inverted ziggurat. A garage on the ground floor was topped by a larger first floor above, topped by a yet larger second floor that pressed into the jagged stone of the mountain, crowned by a half balcony/bedroom at the top from which you could survey the valley in all its glory, peeking over conifers down to the yellow ribbon of road below.

Finding a front door required walking up a path to the second floor, where you had a choice between a small drawbridge into the house, or a staircase down to a gully and the warmth of a kitchen entrance.

The kitchen was unlocked; the driver waited outside.

I went in.

The place smelt of almonds. A log fire burned in a black stove.

Bundles of untouched dried herbs hung on the wall, like a prop, too perfect to ever be used in cooking. A knife block, each blade slotted into its respective hole; a kitchen sink scrubbed to mirror-brightness, a long workbench on which were laid out fresh eggs, fresh meats, fresh spinach and a bowl of walnuts, ready for eating. A kettle on the stove, steam coming from the spout.

A second home.

Obvious, easy, a burglar's eye instantly diagnoses it, a second – maybe a – third home, a skier's chalet, a place to come in winter, kept to standard by a housemaid, possessions rarely used, mugs never chipped, table never sullied, the whole thing now warmed to a welcoming, crispy homeliness that has no humanity about it, a place that is . . .

I smiled, and pulled the door shut behind me.

Perfect.

Of course.

The perfect place to meet Gauguin.

No fear – not any more.

Gauguin worked in the kitchen with sleeves flapping around his wrists, preparing an omelette – he looked up as I entered, and didn't know me, but knew who I had to be, and wasn't surprised, and I was not afraid.

"Hello," I said.

"Hello," he replied, pausing in his whisking of eggs in a bowl. "You must be Why."

"That's right."

"Thank you for coming."

"No worries."

A single nod, his eyebrows locked in a frown – not for me, I felt, not at my appearance, simply that a frown was where they'd settled some time ago and no orders had been yet received to the contrary. He resumed whisking, by hand, yellow juices flying round the edge of the bowl, threatening to burst over the lip. I sat down on a stool opposite him, watched a while, said, "The kettle's boiled."

"Yes – thank you, do you . . . ?"

"Where do you keep the tea?"

"There'll be some in a cupboard, somewhere. Can't say what it'll be like. We're in a coffee part of the world."

"I'll see what they've got."

I rooted through cupboards. Behind a jar of preserved dates and next to a tub of Swiss luxury white chocolate/cinnamon drink, I found breakfast tea. The handle of the kettle was pleasingly scalding. I poured water, set two mugs down between us.

"Thank you," he said.

A shrug; you're welcome.

He tapped the whisk out carefully on the side of the bowl, poured the mixture into a pan, put the pan on the stove, talked quietly, almost to himself, as he worked. "While you were looking for the tea, I listened to you moving, and remembered you were here, but didn't look, and forgot what you looked like," he mused. "I know of course that it's you, as you sit here before me, but had to reacquaint myself with your features again. I've said this before, haven't I?"

"It's nothing new."

"You must tell me if I repeat myself."

"I wouldn't make many friends if I did that."

"Do you have many friends?" I didn't answer. "Sorry – that was rude."

"Rude doesn't bother me."

"Do you mind if I . . . ?" He reached into his pocket, pulled out a mobile phone, laid it between us.

"Go ahead."

"Thank you."

A pause to turn his mobile phone on, set to record, leave it running between us.

As he cooked, he talked. "I have records," he said, "showing you tried to stop the 206 event in Venice. Emails, phone calls, letters – you were persistent."

"I was."

"I . . . regret my decisions in that regard, more than I can express."

"You weren't in charge."

"No, Mr Pereyra-Conroy was, but I had a responsibility to him, his guests and his company, and I failed."

"You couldn't have known Byron would get in."

"On the contrary, I was sure she would. She has always been hugely capable."

"How'd she do it?"

"She undermined my staff. I am not an island, Ms Why; I cannot be everywhere."

"Undermined your staff?" I repeated, blowing steam off the top of my mug.

"To be exact, Dr Pereyra did it for her."

"Filipa?"

"Gave Byron every detail of the security operation I was running, yes, down to the finest detail."

He opened the door to the stove, pushed the pan inside. I sat, frozen despite the warmth in the room. Gauguin turned, looked at me, again, new, again, first time seeing, now, taking in my face, smiled without feeling, sat down, wrapping his fingers round the mug on the table, looked grey, worn down.

"Where is Filipa now?" I asked.

"Upstairs, asleep."

"What kind of asleep?"

"Sedated. She is likely to face prosecution for the murder of her brother – the evidence against her is irrefutable. But the lawyers were able to argue that she was acting under a malign influence, her brain addled by the treatments. Their efforts have brought her a brief respite in which she may remain here, safe from the law, until such a time as some appropriate legal framework has been established. How she will afford lawyer's fees ... but we'll find a way."

"She helped Byron."

"Yes. I only found out after the fact, of course. She broke into her brother's computer, stole his login, accessed the company servers and stole everything Byron could possibly need to execute her plan."

"Why?"

"I think because she agreed with her. I think she had decided some time back that Perfection was vile, and that the treatments were the destruction of humanity. I think the day she went to Rafe and begged on her knees – and she was on her knees, I was there, I saw it all – for him to pull the product, the day he told her that she was nothing but a disappointment to him and their father – I think she realised that he would never see the danger, never give up on what Perfection offered him. Which was money and influence, of course, but also a world he wanted to live in – a world just like the movies. Rafe has never – was never – fond of the more messy realities of this life. I should have said something, but not my place, you see. I've . . . always known my place. So she went to Byron instead. She saw what Byron saw, that the only way to truly destroy Perfection wasn't to re-write the system, but to shatter the dream. She gave Byron everything she could possibly need to slaughter the 206, and, with the job done, she gave herself treatments."

A half tilt of his head, again, a little shaking, so sad, nothing to be done, his eyebrows tight, his gaze not quite meeting mine.

"I thought treatments took time," I murmured.

"Oh – they do. Months. Filipa gave herself the full course. She plugged herself into her own machines, and set them running. She stayed in for thirty-six hours. We found her still locked into the program. When we pulled her out, she wasn't there any more. Rafe was furious, he said she wasn't any use to him now, but she was still his sister and . . . " His voice trailed off. His Adam's apple rose and fell, eyes turned to one side, head tilted at an angle. "'At least she is presentable now.' That's what he said. I think that's when I stopped looking too. I think that's when I realised that I wasn't going to fight. Byron was coming to Venice; you knew it, and so did I, and I worked, I did, I worked so hard to stop it but . . . but I think I could have worked harder. Do you understand?"

"Yes. I think I do."

He stared into his mug, like one trying to read the fortune in his tea, the oven humming behind, the shadows turning outside.

"She spoke about you," he said at last. "She felt sure she'd seen you everywhere. Not just in Tokyo, she said. She felt like you were always there, in her life, whispering to her. She couldn't remember you, but in Nîmes she found her bracelet again, the one her mother had given her, and she said ... she said she thought you were a friend, perhaps the best she ever had, if only she could remember you. I think, by the end ... guilt does some curious things to a mind. She hasn't slept well for years. Sleeping now, though. For what it's worth. Were you in Nîmes?"

"Yes. I was. We met at the hospital."

"Did we? I don't—But of course I don't. Silly me."

A tiny push of his bottom lip, a kind of facial shrug, his hands welded to his cup of tea, which he did not drink.

At last I asked, "Will the company support her?"

"Probably not. The revelation that Perfection may have led to the massacre in Venice sent shares tumbling. The directors of several holdings moved to separate themselves from what they see as a sinking ship. Mergers are taking place. Takeovers, in others. The business will still stand, in some other form, owned by some other people. Bankers, no doubt. Faceless wealthy men from ... somewhere."

"You're still here," I pointed out.

"I failed her and her family," he murmured. "I owe ... penance."

Penance: a punishment undergone to redeem a sin. A feeling of regret for one's wrongdoings. A punishment or discipline imposed for crimes committed. Self-mortification as a token of repentance.

Silence a while, as the omelette set in the oven.

He said, "Why are you here?" and didn't meet my eye.

"To see Filipa."

"Why?"

"She ... would you understand what I mean if I told you that she is my friend?"

"I don't know. I can't imagine your world. Your life."

"I can help find Byron."

"She's gone; she's done what she wanted to."

"She came to see me in the hospital, in Mestre."

"What were you . . . ?" he began, then stopped. "You were in the hotel? You were hurt?"

"Byron stabbed me. She knew I'd come, and she . . . She won't kill me, I think. I can help you find her. I tried before, but didn't have your resources, and you didn't have my information. Now we have both."

Again, silence. Again, the passing of time. Tea cooled, shadows turned, mountains rose, mountains fell, and time passed.

"I find you strangely convincing, now I see you face to face, Why. Did I find you convincing before?"

"No."

"It's a peculiar thing, but I find emotion, when it comes to you, rather hard to engage with, since, not remembering who you are, I have little attachment to the matter. Instead of feelings, I find with you there are only facts. I don't think I can find Byron. Do you understand? I wanted to, for so many years, when she killed Matheus – we were together at the time, I thought I should have seen it coming, there should have been . . . but I didn't." A chuckle, a single shake of his shoulders, laughing off an idea that isn't funny. "Penance," he declared. "I should have stopped her, and I didn't, and she fled, and I spent years hunting her, years of my life to do . . . something. Something right, perhaps. I don't really know any more. And here we are."

I half closed my eyes, smelt expensive tea leaves and gently burning egg. Thought about Filipa Pereyra-Conroy, about the geometry of the Möbius strip, an expression of non-Euclidian . . . of Euclidian . . .

knowledge, there, but no use.

Not for this.

I opened my eyes, said, "Where is Filipa?"

Filipa sleeping on a bed.

She wears pale green pyjamas, silk, no pattern or obvious seams.

Lies on her side, her hair around her head, the blankets pulled up high.

I ask: did she leave anything, a note, a message, anything at all, before she took Perfection?

No, he replied. Nothing.

I ask: does she have her mother's bracelet? Silver, plain – a Möbius strip?

No, she hasn't got it here.

Do you know where it is?

No. When she . . . after the treatments, she didn't seem interested in it any more.

Filipa sleeping.

I think about waking her.

What will she say?

Nothing, I think, which matters any more.

Help me, I said.

I can't . . .

Help me.

I won't . . .

Help me. Goddamn you, you stupid fucking man, you waste of space, where's the guy who tracked a thief across the Middle East, where's mugurski71, where's Gauguin, where's the spy, the security man, the manipulator, the killer instinct, where's your hunger for revenge?

Byron beat me, he said. Byron won.

She stabbed me and left me bleeding on a Venetian floor, I replied. She stuck electrodes in my brain and tried to make me her machine. She used me and made me her doll but she did not fucking beat me, now pull yourself fucking together!

He stared at me through the laced fingers of his hand, and said, How many times have we had this conversation?

A hundred fucking times, I snapped, and you forgot them all, but every time I was right, and every time you joined me in the end. So before Prometheus is torn apart, before Filipa goes to jail, before the last cent and the last contact you have vanishes for ever, *help me.*

And I was shouting, but not at him.

And he said: what do you need?

Chapter 99

Gauguin has many shiny tools at his command.

A CCTV expert caught a glimpse of Byron as she boarded a train at St Lucia, three hours after the Hotel Madellena, then lost her somewhere in northern Italy, after she failed to disembark at any of the regular stops.

We think she jumped while the train was stalled at a red light, he explained. Gauguin mustered his troops, expanded the search: transport hubs, airports, railway stations, ferry ports. A woman thought she caught a glimpse of Byron passing through Lugano, but it was the back of her head, seen from a steep angle, and who could say, really, in the grand scheme of things? Who could say?

"Probably is her," mused Gauguin. "If only because we never see her again."

I stayed next to Gauguin, and he kept the recording running, swapping out mobile phones for USB recorders whenever batteries died, watching me, always watching, from the corner of his eye.

I said, "It's okay. Byron got paranoid after a while too."

"I'm not—" he began, then stopped.

"You fear who I am, when you forget me. You fear that I may say something, do something, and walk away, and when I come back, you won't remember. The recorders are your weapon, but what if they stop? What if they stop and I rob you blind, and you never know. I'd be afraid. That's okay."

He turned away, half closing his eyes, and said not a word.

*

A time must come when Gauguin forgets.

I stand over him while he writes in a large, capitalised hand, all his impressions of me. He uses a heavy silver fountain pen, black ink. It reminds me of something – the pen that Byron used to write with, recording her notes in America. Not merely an association – he is using its twin. I think about asking, then let it go.

He takes a photo of the two of us, standing together in the kitchen, the clock behind and no smiles on our faces. I resist the urge to stick two thumbs up for the camera, or do bunny ears behind his head, and as stars turn and the moon sets I return to my hotel in the town, two big boxes of paper slung one under either arm.

I do not sleep.

The life and times of Byron on the floor.

Everything Gauguin had, starting with a name.

Siobhan Maddox. How strange to think of her as something human. Siobhan Maddox, born in Edinburgh to a primary school teacher and an installer of window frames. Studied French and Russian at UCL, lived in Germany for three years, working by day as a nanny for the British Embassy, and by night raising both her German and Russian to native-level fluency. Had a brief and entirely amicable affair with an attaché, found a certain curiosity about the world of diplomacy, applied for SIS.

Said the recruiting officer, in the faded notes of her faded file: on paper there is no reason to accept this candidate. It is in person where you realise that she would be invaluable.

A series of photos. Byron staring sombrely at the camera. Byron, aged seventeen, with her mum and dad in Newington, arranged in a triangle on the doorstep to their house, proud owners the day her mum paid the mortgage off. Byron was skinny as a rake, hair nearly down to her waist, knee-high leather boots, leather mini-skirt, incongruous woolly jumper and knitted beret set back loosely on her head, a look in her eye of pride, and defiance. Her home; her family; come take it if you dare.

Documents, redacted. Swathes of black ink across operational details.

Beirut, Tehran, Moscow, St Petersburg, Dallas, Washington, Paris, Berlin.

An agent runner. At first, in accordance with the time, she was used to run mainly female assets. *A woman's touch*, wrote her director. *So much more comforting for the ladies.*

In time, male agents were added to her rota, and sometimes they were caught, and sometimes they died – a pilot hanged in Iraq, a weapons engineer who vanished into the Israeli Defence Forces and never re-emerged – but mostly they lived, and retired happy, their treason never known. One man's treason is another man's loyalty, after all.

Dates, more notes.

Considered for section head – passed over.

Considered for section head – passed over.

Considered for . . .

Will our male colleagues be able to accept a female head? wrote a director, considering her application for head of counter-intelligence. *I personally do not think so.*

These were those times, and so

. . . section head – passed over.

Later, when the photos changed to show a Byron with shorter hair, going grey at the roots, a face that was perfectly smooth across the forehead but beginning to crinkle tightly around the eyes and lips, a different concern was raised.

Ideological, it said. *Ideologically determined.*

Two words which, in another context, might have been grounds for instant elevation, but spies knew the dangers of having a view.

How quickly those words grew from merely a footnote to a problem.

Operational decisions compromised based on political views, wrote a disciplinary report. *Orders refused.*

And then, in Gauguin's hand on the side: *she let them die.*

There was no explanation for these words, the text to which

it referred gone, and perhaps Gauguin had never intended for anyone else to read these musings, but there it was, simple and true, at such a time in such a place, Byron had let someone die for a cause unknown, and in that word *let* was the problem – had she wished, she could have saved them all.

A quiet departure from government duties, an offer of a back-room job on an NGO, but no, thank you, she'll take her modest severance package and be on her merry way, farewell and goodbye, Official Secrets Act signed, ID badge burned, adios high office and hello the road less travelled.

Sioban Maddox left the world of espionage aged forty-six, and three years later Matheus Pereyra-Conroy was dead, and Byron was born.

Glimpses of Byron.

A shot of a woman buying coffee at the Gare du Nord, Paris.

A flash of a passport as it entered US customs via New Orleans.

A blip on a credit card in Lagos, the card cancelled the very next day.

A ping off a mobile phone in Shanghai.

And Gauguin? He left the world of shady men one week after Matheus Pereyra-Conroy died, to track down the woman he thought had killed him. There was a time, he said, when I imagined she would marry me. But I never mustered the courage to ask, and I think she grew bored with waiting.

Eight days after I met Gauguin at the house beneath the cliffs, we were no closer to finding Byron.

I phoned ahead, and when no car came to pick me up, I called a taxi and rode up to the house to meet him.

Not in the kitchen this time; a study, complete with portrait of Matheus Pereyra above a fireplace, painted by a man paid to like his subject, but who couldn't quite do it. A halfway image, where regal was tyrant, and smile was smirk, depending how you looked at it.

Gauguin, wearing thick rabbit-lined slippers and a green woollen cardigan, looked up as I walked in, took in my features for the very first time, said, "You must be Why. I didn't realise you'd be coming by."

"We spoke on the phone."

"I didn't write it down. My apologies."

I shrugged, sat on a padded sofa against a wall of unread, unloved, expensively bound leather books. "I've been thinking about Byron."

He put his pen aside, raised one hand to request patience, reached into a drawer, pulled out a notebook and a USB recorder, opened one, set the other running. I let him flick through his notes, gathering his thoughts, before he finally looked up and said, "You've read all the background material I have?"

"Yes."

"Have we discussed it?"

"Yes."

"Ah – good."

He made another note, then pushed the book carefully to one side and turned all the way round on his chair, back to the desk, recorder in his lap. "You were saying?"

Calm – so calm. A calmness made of the thin white sheet over a frozen lake, perfectly smooth until pressure is applied. This is the first time Gauguin has ever met me, but he sees a note saying it is not and so here is he, talking like an old friend, and calm – very, very calm.

"I think we're pursuing the wrong tack."

"Are we?"

"I think we should go after Agustin Carrazza."

"The MIT man?"

"Yep."

"All right; why?"

"I think he'll be easier to find. He's not Byron – he'll make mistakes."

"There's no reason to think he's still connected to her."

"And no reason to think therefore that we'd pursue him."

"Have we had this conversation before?" asked Gauguin. "Is this an old suggestion?"

"No. We discounted him because his work is done, and he went underground months ago. I think we should put him back into the equation. He's an academic, he'll contact family, friends, use the same mobile phone, be caught by cameras, at customs—"

"But will he contact Byron?"

"I think he will if pushed to it."

"A trap?"

"If you want to call it—"

The door opened. I stopped. Filipa stood in the gap, wearing a burgundy dressing gown and nothing on her feet. She blinked round the room, saw Gauguin, saw me, said, "Could you direct me towards the most convenient breakfast?"

Gauguin's eyes flickered to me, then back to her as he said, "Downstairs there is muesli."

Her upper lip curled. "Harsh on the digestion, I find. High in sugars too." Then her eyes settled on me again, and for a moment she contemplated my existence, trying to place me in this room, and finding no answer treated me to a dazzling smile and said instead, "I'm so sorry, I don't believe we've been introduced? I'm Filipa, and you . . . ?"

"My name is Hope."

"A beautiful name for a beautiful woman! You're not from round here; I can tell."

"No, I'm from England."

"England? Where in England?"

"Derby."

"Ah – wonderful; never been there myself, but always meant to."

I smiled, but could not out-smile her brightness. "Well," she said, a second before the silence grew awkward, "Hope, it's such a pleasure to meet you, I hope to see lots of you soon and we can talk all about England. But now I really must get some breakfast; I trust you don't mind my disgraceful hours and appearance, last night was a bit of a trial."

"I don't mind."

"You're a darling – we're going to be such good friends."

So saying, she beamed at me, beamed at Gauguin, turned, and walked away, closing the door behind her.

I looked at Gauguin, who looked away.

"Does she remember killing Rafe?" I asked.

"Yes."

"But she's—"

"She says she's going to sue whoever ruined the party, and that she'll need counselling. She used Perfection to find herself a suitable therapist – it can supply that sort of thing. She chose one in Paris, and received four thousand points when she booked a ten-week course. I had to cancel the booking – the police won't let her go, with matters as they are – but though she lost the points, she didn't say she was upset. Perfect people don't cry. Crying is ugly."

"You sympathise with Byron?" I mused. "With what Filipa did?"

"I . . . no. Byron is a murderer. Her cause – can we call it a cause? Cause is a righteous word, a word that implies . . . "

"Sufficient reason?"

"Sufficiency is lacking."

"Agustin Carrazza," I repeated firmly. "He likes to run."

Three days was all it took to find our missing professor.

His mistake was stunning in its stupidity; he'd logged into his music collection from a computer in Guatemala, having concluded, perhaps, that it was worth risking his location in order to reclaim several thousand dollars' worth of cloud-stored songs.

Gauguin flew to Guatemala the next day. I went on the same plane, but booked my own tickets. A hands-off approach, gentle and light.

He arrived at Agustin Carrazza's door at ten p.m. in the middle of a rainstorm, knocked three times, waited, knocked three times again.

"Coming, coming!" snarled the professor, and opening the

door, there he was, in a white vest and beige shorts, a pair of purple flip flops on his feet, hair and beard grown long.

Gauguin smiled. "May I come in?" he said.

He was in the house for twenty minutes, and two days later, he returned with company.

Luca Evard smiled as he looked through the kitchen window while Agustin made him coffee, and said, no, Interpol, the investigation has grown now, a possible link between Meredith Earwood and the attacks in Venice, you must have seen the news, you must have heard . . .

No, heard nothing, Agustin replied, nothing at all.

I listened through the microphone I'd planted in Agustin's kitchen light. I would have put more in his telephone, radiators, computers, back of the TV – but Gauguin had got there first, the whole house wired, so I made do.

Luca was persuasive and kind, gently laying out reports of associations between Agustin and Meredith Earwood, connections that were tentatively being proven, the advantages of co-operation, the opportunities of helping to crack this case. The professor was an expert, of course, an expert, it would be so useful to get his input . . . and why had he moved to Guatemala?

The people, snapped Agustin, harder than he'd meant, and in the silence that followed I imagined the patient expressions on both Gauguin's and Luca's face, the smiles of two men who know that their mark has made a mistake, that he's going to crack, but won't say anything, won't make a move, just waiting for him to unfold like an evening primrose, open up the petals of his truth and die in the light of day.

"Wonderful coffee, thank you," said Luca, as they walked away. "I do see why you love it here."

I watched at a distance as Luca and Gauguin walked back to their car, and followed on a stolen moped into the city. At a café hung with purple flowers, I sat two tables away and listened, as Gauguin said, "I believe I've been working with Why."

Luca didn't answer.

"Is that a problem?" asked Gauguin in the silence. "I wanted to tell you, but if it's a problem . . ."

"Not a problem," he replied, quickly. "Not a problem."

Gauguin stirred sugar into his coffee, and nodding at nothing much, looked up, and saw me. A slight start, a jerk in his body as he stared. Was I the woman under discussion? He reached for his pocket, instinctively, then stopped himself, put his hand back on the table.

Luca Evard flew back to Switzerland the next morning, and I let him go.

Things I am:

I am my legs as I run through the rain.

I am darkness, broken.

I am a shadow of a figure beneath the light.

I am disturbance to the dreaming mind of a man who lost his job today, and who tosses and turns in his broken sleep and wonders, what now, what now, what now, and thinks he hears a woman run by, and turns over, and forgets.

I am a figment of a woman's contemplation as she looks out of her kitchen window across the city, through the maze of telephone lines and jacked-up electrical cables that have been spun and threaded across the street like a spider's web on LSD

she looks and sees the lights of the city and for a moment thinks she can conceive of a world of infinite possibility, of infinite lives, of hearts as real as hers, thoughts as clear, beating, living, moving against that light

and she looks down

and sees me

and I wave

and she waves back, a moment of connection, two strangers who are, for a moment, the same

but I run on

and she forgets

but I do not.

I am memory; I am the sum of my memories.

I am the sum of my deeds.
I am thoughts for the future.
Compilations from the past.
I am this moment.
I am now.
At last I think I know what that means.

Three hours after Luca left Guatemala, Gauguin called me on a disposable mobile phone.

"Is this Why?" he asked.

"Yes."

"Agustin Carrazza just dialled a number in London. He's trying to reach Byron. The note says you'd want to know."

Gauguin explains.

Carrazza dials a phone in London, the phone is answered by an unknown male.

The phone is in a Wapping solicitor's office a few streets from the river. From there a young man in a white shirt with dog-head cufflinks writes down Carrazza's message, folds it into a perfect little square, takes the DLR to the Isle of Dogs, foot tunnel under the river, ambles to Greenwich Market, buys deep-fried gyoza at a stall, which he eats with his bare fingers, walks round the edge of the hill, the observatory at the top, and finally slips into a public telephone, one of very few still left in London.

Inserts coins.

Dials.

Says, "The better days of life were ours, the worst can be but mine."

If there is someone on the end of the line, they do not answer.

"Your cousin says hello from Trieste," he continues, and proceeds to read out Carrazza's message. When he is done, he hangs up the phone, puts his hands in his pockets, bends his head against the wind, and walks away.

Chapter 100

A phone in Greenwich.

Within three hours, Gauguin had everything he wanted on the phone, the number it dialled, the young man with canine cufflinks, the lot.

Said the guy with cufflinks: "Oh shit shit fuck shit I just answer the phone, man, like shit fuck that's all I fucking do. Please, it was just a job, an easy job, I didn't mean . . . "

Said Gauguin: "It's fine. You're fine. Now breathe. Okay? I want you to keep answering the phone, and tell me everything."

A phone on the floor of a living room in Morningside.

Just a phone, set in its cradle in the middle of the floor.

Outside: snow. Grey Edinburgh snow not quite cold enough to settle, not yet, not on the paving stones, but clumping on the cars, thicker in the shadows, cold in the room too, an apartment near the Observatory that hasn't been heated for months.

The landlady grumbled, "Well I rented it out nine months ago, and the rent all came in good, and if you just want to have a phone then who am I to complain, there were never any parties or loud noise or problems with the electricity bill!"

Gauguin looked at the landlady without words, and the landlady left.

"Is this it?" I asked.

"It forwarded the call from London – but we don't know where."

"Can't you . . . " A gesture, a flap of arms, come on, can't you . . . ?!

Gauguin looked away. "Somewhere in Scotland," he murmured.

I opened my mouth to say fuck you, fuck this, fucking fuck the fucking desert walking through the fucking desert riding the fucking train . . .

and stopped myself.

Waited for the silence to settle where I would usually have counted backwards from ten.

Walked away.

Chapter 101

Walking through Edinburgh, the last time I was here I stole Mary Stewart's belt buckle, mostly because I could, and held it to ransom until the Museum of Scotland very grudgingly paid a cut-price £12,000 for its safe return, very hush hush, very much against Lothian Police's advice.

The snow began to fall more heavily, and I walked. Up through Morningside, past shops selling alpaca yarn and baby boots, past the second-hand booksellers and hair-styling salons, £95 to have a trim, £130 if you want the full spa experience. Past the purveyors of nonsense and kitsch, the sellers of cupping and ear-wax treatments, the aromatherapists who can cure your irritable bowel syndrome, the yoga studios for beautiful people looking to find themselves through stretching, past the organic yoghurt shops and authentic dealers of finest tartan, made in the Philippines. For a minute, I could burn it all. Yoghurt is nice; yoga is good, but this isn't yoghurt, this is the organic yoghurt experience, eat it and be beautiful. Be beautiful. Be perfect.

I could burn the fucking city to the ground.

I walked until I reached Bruntsfield Links, the thickening snow driving back the last warmth of the day, beginning to settle on the grass, only one golfer left near the kirk, one last hold-out of Scottish sporting passion that even the settling dark cannot drive away.

I walked, the castle rising to my left and the taller, denser apartment blocks of Newington rising to my right, and realised after a while that I was counting my steps, and stopped, and stood in the middle of the street and screamed a wordless scream of frustration and rage, and people turned to look at me, and I screamed again then stopped, and felt a bit better, and kept on walking.

I had booked a room in the hotel where Gauguin was staying, and now I cancelled that booking.

"Filipa is being indicted tomorrow," he mumbled. "The money – it's all running out. People don't take my calls any more, and she's, I know she's not her, but she's . . . It's not much, but I should be there, for the end, I just should . . . " His voice trailed away. A shadow man, who'd spend his days chasing shadows and found no illumination from the process.

I moved to a hall of residence beneath the Crags.

Looked up at Arthur's Seat, thought about climbing it, thought about snow and ice, felt the sun go down, stayed in the warmth of my thin-carpeted, plywood-desked little student room, felt at home. This was better than a hotel; in term time, people lived here, worked here, had sex here, ate baked beans here, pinned posters to the wall, smeared toothpaste over the sink, grew squalid and settled. I could almost close my eyes, and pretend it was a kind of home.

I opened up a laptop, connected to the slow Wi-Fi, downloaded every note and every photo I'd ever taken of Byron's life all the time I'd known her, and started again.

Knowledge.

What should I do with this place inside me where experience – tears of joy, shrieks of laughter, the anxiety of work, the warmth of friends, the love of family, the expectations of the world – what should I do with that place which was never filled?

I put knowledge there.

And in knowledge, I find myself.

This sounds like an intellectual void where heart should be, but look and you may find . . .

The speeches of Martin Luther King Jr.

Let us not wallow in the valley of despair ... I say to you, my friends ... I have a dream that one day every valley shall be exalted, and every hill and mountain shall be made low, the rough places will be made plain, and the crooked places will be made straight.

The history of the Taj Mahal. Shah Jahan raised it in love of his wife.

Should guilty seek asylum here, like one pardoned, he becomes free from sin. The sight of this mansion creates sorrowing sighs; and the sun and the moon shed tears from their eyes.

The European Space Agency launched the Rosetta mission in March 2004, and ten years later it woke up after a journey of 6 billion kilometres to land a probe on a comet travelling at 15,000 km/h around the sun.

After killing hundreds of billions of people down the ages, smallpox was eradicated in 1980. Before Edward Jenner tested his first cowpox vaccine; before Lady Mary Wortley Montagu marvelled at the Ottoman physicians of the 1600s inoculating their children with the pus from a smallpox scab, a Buddhist nun up a mountain in China attempted her own inoculations, by grinding up smallpox scabs and blowing them up the noses of willing patients, becoming an anonymous mother of variolation.

"Reserve your right to think, for even to think wrongly is better than not to think at all." Hypatia of Alexandria – philosopher, mathematician, astronomer. Died while the great library burned.

Google search for feminism:

feminism is

→ *wrong*
→ *for everybody*
→ *bad*
→ *sexism*
→ *the radical notion*
→ *destroying America*

What is knowledge?

It is inspiration. It is a call to battle. It is a reminder that there is nothing which cannot be achieved. It is humanity in all its forms, in my heart.

Byron is in Scotland.

I am sure of it, and being sure, I trawl through every file, every note, everything I've ever had on her.

"I live alone in a place where no one ever comes. I work alone. I walk by the sea, I go to the shops and hide my face. I dodge cameras, travel by false passport, make no friends, have no need of company. My work is all that matters. I would give my life to see it done."

The bank account with which she rented a flat in Morningside was opened with cash and a false ID; the false ID came from the darknet, hard to trace, even the sellers don't know who they're selling to, so long as the price is right.

Files and dead ends, phone records going nowhere, paper trails ending with nothing, Gauguin sends me messages, where are you, are you there, we're leaving now, we're leaving. They're opening proceedings against Filipa on Tuesday, I have to be there. Will you come? Are you there? (Are you real?)

I watch the TV reports of the first hearings into the 206 in Milan. Filipa smiles for the cameras, seemingly oblivious to the fact that she is most suspected, and Gauguin is just on the edge of the frame, holding her hand as she climbs the steps to the courthouse. Where be your lawyers now, your PR machine and your men who hold doors ajar? All fleeing, all fled, as Prometheus dies.

A week, another, just reading, planning, searching, Byron, Byron, where are you?

A committee is set up in America; another in Brussels to investigate Perfection. Said the head of the US inquiry: "Not just America, but all the nations of the world suffered a loss when the victims of the 206 were so viciously attacked and slaughtered, and it is the duty of any freedom-loving nation to make inquiries into these events."

Said Fox News: "So, yeah, we think that Perfection is, maybe, reprogramming your brain."

(And ten minutes later: "Tonight we're asking the question: Is Islam fundamentally violent and incompatible with the American way of life?")

In the end, I settled on Byron's spectacles. I photographed them, when was this? Korea – the first time I broke into Byron's room, I photographed everything she had, but her glasses might be the best thing I have to go on.

I bought a map of Scotland from the student union shop, pinned it to my bedroom wall. Marked a dot for every single optician in the country. Not as many as I'd feared, really, not once you were north of Dundee. Couple of hundred at most.

Printed out Byron's picture, from several angles, over several years.

Printed out a blown-up picture of her glasses.

Printed onto thick paper wrapped in plastic a reasonable approximation of a Lothian Police warrant card, and then bought an antique badge that looked legal enough to stick to the inside of my wallet for flashing in a stranger's face. How many people knew what an actual warrant looked like?

Checked out of the hall of residence after a breakfast of baked beans, fried eggs, fried sausages, fried bacon, fried potatoes and a glass of cold milk, and with my one rucksack of worldly goods on my back went forth to find opticians.

Chapter 102

In Edinburgh, the poverty is carefully hidden, pushed out by gentrification to the tower blocks and estates, out of sight, out of mind, the cleansing of the streets, the bankrupt crawl of the tram towards Leith, the spreading of high-performance baby prams.

There are forty-two opticians to see, and only twenty-nine bother to look at my warrant card, ask the nature of my business. The rest just stare at the photo of the spectacles, the picture of the woman in my hand and say no, no no. Even if she came here, we don't stock those frames. That's fine: I didn't think it likely she'd get her eyes tested in Edinburgh, she spoke of a cottage, loneliness, the sea – but I will be thorough. I will eliminate all options.

In the fashionable shops, their shelves lined wall-to-wall with frames, a woman with legs that never end, a tiny body balanced on their high-heeled protuberances, shakes her head and says, "They're very last year, aren't they?" and means it, and looks askance when she sees the look on my face and adds, "Well, I mean, in terms of what we'd sell, yes?" and begins to flush, having been caught Speaking Stupid as a habit of her work.

In Leith, a man with deep, dark south Asian skin and a turban on his head tuts and says, "Ah, a missing woman. My mother vanished some years ago, but alas, we found her again."

At Edinburgh Airport there is a purveyor of glasses on the wrong side of customs. I buy a ticket to London, cross the border, go to the shop, find nothing, wave my police badge to exit the other way.

I steal a car from the long-term airport parking, and drive to Livingston, Bathgate, Armadale, Whitburn. The accents along the border, in Lindsay and Jedburgh, are thicker and harder to penetrate than in Edinburgh, as if, so close to England, these little Scottish villages have sworn to be more Scottish than the Scots, wearing their cultural identity like a sword and shield. Up yours, English!

In Jedburgh I have cream tea by a rolling stream carved through a snow-soaked valley. The butcher across the road has won "Best Haggis in Scotland" for nearly ten years running, bar the odd off-year when he was pushed into second place. The butcher wears a white apron, striped red and white sleeves and a little straw hat. When he comes in for his cuppa, the snow clings to the edge of the boater, and his nose is bright red.

In Hawick, I take refuge from the increasingly bad weather in a pub hotel, and tell the lady behind the counter about my journey through southern Scotland, following the course of a stream from the sea to Teviothead, where it finally shatters into the hills.

She pours mulled wine and says, "And what's this woman done, that you're looking for?"

"Wanted in connection with a murder inquiry."

"Really? But she looks harmless!"

"We think she helped kill those people in Venice."

"No – the 206?"

Everyone knows about the 206, even in Hawick, with its floral competitions and empty hanging baskets, waiting for the spring; its monument to the soldier-children who drove back English invaders, its betting shops and quietly churning textile mills, its pride in being itself – even here.

"You know, I think it's shocking what those people did to themselves," mused my landlady, as the smell of wood smoke drifted through the pub and a man with flaxen hair cursed two cherries at the fruit machine. "I mean, the things you hear – surgery, brain surgery too, living your life by what a machine tells you, buying what a machine tells you and for what? To be perfect? When did we stop learning to just love ourselves for who we are, that's what I want to know?"

I smiled over the rim of my hot cup, and wondered if this woman knew what it was to love yourself, to forgive yourself, to be at peace with yourself, or if these words too weren't merely the end product of another algorithm churning out words into the void. Love yourself, whispers Perfection, forgive yourself – here, have £5 off your first "love yourself" forgiveness session, two thousand points upon completion of the course . . .

In Newton Stewart I took a day to walk the local area, climbed into the forest, looked down on pine and scrubland, found a concrete obelisk raised up to the highest point, sat alone and ate jam and peanut butter sandwiches, met a dog walker on the way back down said, where have you come from?

Oh, about, about, he replied. I don't really think about where I walk any more.

The ferry to the Isle of Arran left from Ardrossan. The sea was sick and bucking, the skies grey, the wind howling, stranding me in Brodick for the night. I walked from one end of the town and back again in twenty minutes, found the B&B already booked up, slept in the back of my car, was woken at midnight by a seagull landing, its fat white body thumping hard against the metal roof. My breath shimmered in the air and in the morning the optician was closed anyway, so I drove round the island, and had fish and chips in Blackwaterfoot, and went to a perfumer and took the tour, listened to an explanation of all their works ("floral, fruity, woody, faecal odours, oh yes, I did say faecal, the low note catches the attention and then the higher scents keep it; ambergris is simply whale poo you know") said, thank you, very interesting, ate a duck egg for breakfast the next morning and went at last to the optician, who said no, never seen her before, sorry.

Rode the ferry back to Ardrossan, then over the waters again, to Campbeltown, and up that narrow spit of land towards the highlands and the north.

A month, two more stolen cars.

I stayed one night in a spa hotel on the edge of Loch Tay, because I stank, because I hadn't washed my clothes in weeks, because my eyes hurt and my back was sore. It cost more than I'd spent in the last four days of driving, but I ran along the northern edge of the loch, seven miles to the halfway point, then seven miles back, and sank into the sauna on my return and stretched out every bone until it cracked, and took my clothes down to the laundry room and sat in hotel-supplied pyjamas and a dressing gown watching them spin, spin, spin, and had blueberries for breakfast and talked with a husband and wife in their seventies, he an ex-neurosurgeon, she an ex-cardiac surgeon, who'd married in Glasgow after the Cuban Missile Crisis and now came up here once a year, every year, to walk the scrubland before the purple flowers grew.

"Some people call it bleak," she said, "but I think there is a kind of beauty in emptiness. It lets you remember that you're there, that you matter."

"Have you heard of the 206?" I asked, and the neurosurgeon tutted and said yes, such a tragic waste. Waste of lives. Waste of dreams. Waste of . . . everything, really.

"These days, we offer solutions for everything," she agreed. "Including things that don't really need fixing."

That morning, the snow fell harder, and they were delighted at this turn of events, and strapped on their best walking boots and went out, hand in hand, towards the edge of the lake.

I waved them off, and drove on towards Perth.

A month became two.

The press lost interest in the case of the 206, every detail chewed over, every image inflated and analysed.

"Disturbing scenes," said the report, "do not look if of a gentle disposition" and hello, yes please, here we are looking yum yum yum.

Filipa was confined to a mental institution, then almost immediately freed, then confined again. So were a few other survivors.

"It is clear that these individuals were not in their right mind, when they perpetrated these bloody acts," said a legal expert, drafted in from the University of Bologna. "The question seems clear – were it not that the 206 had *chosen* to have their brain chemistry altered. Does this choice render them culpable? This is what the lawyers will be arguing . . . "

A quick piece of mathematics.

Five lawyers to a legal team, £200 an hour, eight hours a day, five days a week, a year of trial – £2,080,000 per annum in legal costs, if you were lucky. Legend said the defence team for O. J. Simpson were on $20,000 a day.

Average monthly wage in:

- USA $3,263
- Turkey $1,731
- Kazahkstan $753
- India $295
- Pakistan $255

GDPs, according to the International Monetary Fund:

- Gambia: $850,000,000
- Djibouti: $1,457,000,000
- Apple Inc.: $182,795,000,000

Funds donated to combating the Ebola outbreak of 2014–15:

- United States: £466,000,000
- World Bank: £248,000,000
- African Development Bank: £91,000,000
- Germany: £81,000,000
- Gates Foundation: £31,000,000
- China: £20,000,000
- Mark Zuckerburg: £16,000,000

I turned on the radio.

"Hey Macarena!"

Drove on, into the night.

Chapter 103

On my third month driving through Scotland, and on my thirteenth stolen car, I caught the ferry from Ullapool to Stornaway, stood on the back deck and smelt spring, salt, petrol fumes and cheap beer, watched the land pull away behind the ship, felt the wind tear at my hair, and it was

good.

No anger, no frustration, merely the open sea.

In Stornoway (population 9,000; football teams Stornoway Athletic vs. Stornoway United, rivals to the crown) I walked the two hundred metres from the ferry port to the first optician, opened the door to the little jangling of a bell, pulled out my crumpled picture of Byron, her spectacles and my police badge and said, "I'm looking for . . ."

"Mrs MacAuley, aye!"

The optician, a cheerful man with white hairs around his chin and eyebrows that stuck out from his face like two grey umbrellas, sheltering his eyes from rain and sun, stared at me in my silence, eyes wide and face curious, a man not used to strangers, let alone Lothian Police so far from home.

The quiet stretched between us, a long, long while, until at last he blurted, "Are you dead or what?"

"Excuse me one moment," I said, and walked out of his shop.

I paced round the block, counted to one hundred, then marched back in and tried again, police badge in hand.

"Hello," I said. "I'm looking for Mrs MacAuley."

"Aye," he replied, staring again, friendly, curious, meeting me for the very first time. "She comes in here to get her prescription."

I held out my police badge. "I'm investigating identity fraud," I said. "We think Mrs MacAuley might have been a victim."

"You're a long way from home."

"The investigation is large. The thieves have been travelling far. Some of their victims may not even know they've been targeted, their details used in crimes."

"What manner of crimes?"

"Insurance scams, mostly."

"And you say she might be a victim? Why would anyone want to steal Mrs MacAuley's identity?" Not denial, not rejection of my premise – merely a man who spent a lot of time alone in a shop, talking to himself, now talking out loud, musing over a dilemma.

"Can you help me find her?" I asked. "Do you know where she lives?"

"Oh sure, I've got the address somewhere round here."

He opened up a screen on a computer, an ancient, chugging thing whose buffer, as you typed, struggled to form words.

"Here – it's a bit of a drive, you know where you're going?"

"I can find it."

"I wouldn't trust your phone, if that's what you're thinking. Don't have much of a signal out here."

"I've got a map," I replied, copying down the address. "I'll be fine."

"Good luck to you, then."

"Thank you."

And there: she was found.

Chapter 104

I drive as one in a dream.

I can't decide: is this land beautiful, or is it bleak? Is bleak beautiful?

Grey stone juts from the thin green grass, poking into a grey sky.

A withered tree, bent sideways by the wind, sweeps clawed fingertips of black twig out towards a tuft of brown, scratching grass that grows on nothingness.

Pylons runs along the brow of a shallow hill.

The water from a pond, or pool, or from a nameless protuberance of water that changes so often with the seasons that no one has bothered to name it, spills onto the road, flooding it to half the depth of my tyres. I drive through slowly, listening to the sloshing around my wheels, and pick up speed again on the other side, heading towards the beacon of an abandoned croft.

Flatness, greyness, emptiness. Sometimes the land rises sharply, then sinks almost as fast. Most of the time it is washed smooth by water, flecked with salt that has thrown itself inland like Poseidon's buckets.

Stones fallen from the hills, how did they get there? Sharp teeth of white, like a cathedral cracked by thunder, sitting growing yellow moss, from nowhere, of nowhere.

A cottage in the shape of a beehive, no road to its door, no power to it either, looking down towards a loch, the mouth of the bay where it hits the sea, brown with mud and sand.

Is this place beautiful?

Is it the end of the world?

As night falls, I take refuge in a farmhouse, the number given me by the woman who sold me a meat pie (what kind of meat? – no, forget I asked) from a van parked on the side of the road.

Do you get much custom? I asked.

People come to find me, she replied, as the radio blared behind her.

Do you know where I can stay tonight?

Try the MacKenzies, she replied. They've got a spare room.

The room was £10 for the night, and the lady of the farm gave me an extra blanket, "as you're probably not used to the cold".

A spider wove patiently in the corner of my room, so used to solitude that it couldn't process the presence of a human in its den. I ducked under the door of the bathroom, sat on the toilet and stared at a sampler on the wall which declared:

AND THESE SHALL GO AWAY INTO EVERLASTING PUNISHMENT: BUT THE RIGHTEOUS INTO LIFE ETERNAL.

I had no mobile phone signal, but they let me use their landline.

I made one phone call, brief and to the point, thanked them for their hospitality, and went to bed.

I woke with the sun, because my hostess did, marching up and down beneath my window quacking furiously at her ducks.

The ducks quacked, and she quacked back, and they swarmed around her as she threw down feed, declaring quackquack! Quackquackquack, singing along with their clamour. I went up to her and said, "Hello, I'm new here. Can I buy some breakfast?"

A lazy cat sat next to the stove in the kitchen, folded in the solitary rocking chair, one eye open, daring anyone to even attempt to depose it from this, the warmest part of its domain. I steered clear, but the woman scowled and it leapt away, sensing a battle lost before it was begun.

"Eat, damn you, eat!" she exclaimed, seeing me hesitate, and I ate homemade bread with homemade honey, collected from the hives before the bees died back for winter, and she put on the radio loud and did the washing-up and we did not talk, and I didn't see her husband.

At the end of this meal, as I headed towards the car, she asked, "Where are you heading?"

"To the bottom of the island."

"Holiday, is it?"

"No. Seeing a friend."

"Friend, is it?" she tutted. "Well, they do say."

What they said, and whether it was good, I didn't ask, but thanked her for the breakfast and turned the heater on inside my car, before getting in and driving away.

Grey sky becomes one.

Grass becomes one.

Abstract painting, colours melt together.

Motion with the paintbrush, they blur, right to left with travel, left to right with the wind off the sea.

Feet on pedals, hand on steering wheel, I never passed the test but I can drive, a survival skill, a discipline, my dad would be furious, breaking the law, a child of mine, but my mum would understand.

You do what you must, when you cross the desert, she says. The rituals you make, the devotions you perform, they are what binds you to yourself. If you do not have them, if you have not found them within you, you are nothing, and the desert is all.

I'm proud of you, says Mum from the passenger seat, smiling at the blurring sky. I'm proud of you, Hope Arden.

Thanks, Mum. Hey – Mum?

Yes, dear?

When you saw the edge of the desert, what did you feel?

Honestly? I felt sad to be leaving the desert behind. But I kept on walking anyway.

A cottage on the edge of the sea.

I parked at the top of a track, too thin to get a vehicle down. How did you get furniture into this house? I wondered, as I picked my way towards the sounds of the water breaking on a stony beach.

You carried it, I replied. You asked your friends down to help, and together you got it done.

Two storeys to a stone house, slate tiles on the roof, yellow-lichen rounded stones in the wall, tiny square window frames, eaten by salt, the glass within coming loose. A white front door. A ceramic cat was stuck to the wall above the knocker, ancient and malign. A few weeds grew between the bricks. Lace curtains hung in the windows. A light was on in a room upstairs. A manhole fifty yards away suggested that at some point recently, pipes and electricity had been run underground, away from the raging winter wind.

I knocked with an iron knocker that grinned beneath my fingers.

Knock knock.

Waited.

A light turned on in the hall, though it was daytime, morning, but the skies were thick enough to cast shadows that grew thicker indoors.

A shadow passed across the spilling glow around the wooden frame. A bolt was lifted, a chain slid back.

The door opened.

Byron peered at me from within a warm, wood-smoke glow and said, "Yes?" Her accent, Scottish, thickened by her time on the isle; her face, curious, open, unrecognising.

"Hello," I said. "My name is Hope."

A moment.

Memory.

She does not remember me, but she remembers perhaps

a mantra repeated: her name is Hope her name is Hope her name is Hope her name

remembering the act of trying to remember.

She looks at me, at my face, my bag, my travel-worn clothes, my overgrown hair that I haven't had time to weave into something self-contained, my stolen car parked up the way, and though she can't remember, she knows.

"Oh," she said. Then, "You'd better come in."

I stepped inside, and she closed the door behind me.

Chapter 105

She made tea. She left the teabag in hers, and barely dribbled any milk.

I sat at her kitchen table, watching her work, filling matching green mugs from a calcium-clad kettle, before setting the cups down on knitted round mats and taking a seat opposite me.

"Thanks," I said, and drank.

"You're welcome. I've got biscuits, if you . . . ?"

"I'm all right, thanks."

"If I'd known you were coming I'd have brushed up on my homework. As it is, I feel like I don't know anything about you."

No effort to disguise her accent, not any more. One leg folded over the other, one hand across the other, her body at an angle in the chair, turned towards me, but with room to rise, to move, to fight, if she needed to.

"My name's Hope," I repeated. "I'm a thief. We spent some time together in America."

"I know I spent time with someone I can't remember – I have months of notes and recordings in the loft. Did I stab you? There's a note saying I stabbed you."

"Yes, you did."

"I'm very sorry about that. I assume it was necessary?"

"I was about to stop you committing mass murder."

"Ah – right. How are you now?"

"I healed."

"I went looking for you in the hospitals. I remember that. Didn't find you though."

"You found me. You didn't keep the recording."

"Why not?"

"I think you didn't want to remember its content."

"Why, did I say something stupid?" A flicker of doubt, a sudden thought. "Did I tell you how to find me?"

"No, no, nothing like that. But you seemed to want something from me which I was unwilling to supply."

"You can't be cryptic, not about things like that."

"Are you recording this conversation?"

"No – like I said, you caught me by surprise."

"Then what does it matter? You won't remember."

"Then what does it matter," she replied, "if you tell?"

I drank another sip of tea.

Silence a while, save for the whistling of the wind from the sea, the promise of rain yet to come.

"Are you here to kill me, Hope?" she asked.

"No."

"Why are you here?"

I didn't answer.

"How did you find me?"

"Your glasses."

"My . . ."

"I went to every optician in Scotland."

"Seriously?"

"Seriously."

"How long did that take you?"

"A few months."

"Why Scotland?"

"Your history. The way you described your home. The telephone from Wapping, the signal came up here. Sometimes it's dangerous to cross international borders; stick to familiar territory. Had to eliminate possibilities."

"And someone remembered – no, of course they remembered. It's a dilemma, when you need to disappear. If you try to vanish in a large city, blend with a crowd, you increase your chances of being detected by technology. Cameras, cards, chip and pin – data is hard to avoid, these days. So you move somewhere remote, somewhere the cameras haven't come yet, and of course . . ."

"People remember."

"Yes."

"You said you envied me, once."

"I do. You can vanish without a trace, and avoid conflicts such as this."

"And personally? Do you envy me personally?"

She hesitated, sucking in her lower lip, rolling the mug of tea carefully between her fingers. Then, "Yes. In a way. I imagine that your condition leaves you free of certain considerations. You cannot plan – no, you can plan, but you cannot . . . agonise, shall we say, for the future, because you don't have one. Is that too harsh? Is that unfair?"

I shrugged; neither fair nor unfair, true nor false – carry on.

"Nor can you wallow in the mistakes of your past, because the only person who knows them is you. Those you have injured, whose lives you have destroyed – the ones who would seek vengeance or cry out for justice – they have forgotten you. You have done material harm, yes, but emotionally you are a blank. Your actions are a lightning strike, to them, an act of God, or chance, not a human thing, not an actively conspiring mind seeking their downfall."

Actus reus: guilty act.

Mens reus: guilty mind.

I commit a crime, and only I remember my guilt.

"You have a kind of freedom," she said. "Free from the eyes of the world; free from a kind of suffering. It is, in its way, enviable."

Silence a while.

I asked, "Is it hard? Do you find it hard?"

"What?"

"Answering to yourself."

"No," she replied, soft as the sea, steady as the stone. "Not any more."

"What you've done . . . "

"I find my conscience clear. You are forgotten, and no one comes for you. I am remembered, and here you are. And I am fine with that."

"I think I despise myself, some of the time," I said.

She shrugged: so what? Get over it.

"I look at my life, and find it full of failings."

Another half tilt of her head. Again: deal with it.

"I find that the only way I can survive is in the present tense. If I look at my past, I see loneliness. Loneliness and . . . and mistakes made of loneliness. If I look at my future, I see fear. Struggle. The possibility of much pain. And so I look only at now, at this present tense, and ask myself, what am I doing now? Who am I now? For a while this was my great discipline, now, and now, and now, who am I now, now I am professional, now I am calm, now I am exercising, now I am speaking to those who will forget. Now I am a self that I wish to be, now I am a picture of who I have to be, now. Now. Now.

"Then I met you and now I am all things, I think. Now I am

a woman who, in the past, did some shoddy things. Now I am a woman who, in the future, will do better, where I can. Now I am in this moment and I am just this. Just myself. Talking. Just talking, to you. You will forget and now will pass, time will consume your memory and with it, any reality that this moment may have existed but for now, here, we sit, you and I, and are entirely ourselves, speaking. Does this make sense?"

"Yes."

"All the time I was looking for you, I never asked myself what I'd do when I found you. Never. Refused to ask. It was a question for a different now, a different moment, I would not construct it from fantasy. You think I'm here to kill you?"

"It's a possibility," she mused.

"I'm not."

"Why are you here, Hope?"

"I wanted to see you."

"Why?"

"It seemed necessary."

"Again: why? If it's not vengeance you want then I don't see . . ." Her voice trailed off. I stared into my mug.

Silence.

Silence.

Silence.

Then, "All thought is association and feedback," she said.

I looked up, quickly, studying her face, but her eyes were in some other place, her mind contemplating a different path. "Loneliness is no more than a construction of ideas. I am lonely because I am not with people. I need to be with people to feel fulfilled. And in time you say: I am not with people, and yet I am fulfilled. I have my books, I have my walks, I have my routines, I have my thoughts, and though I am alone, I am not lonely. And in time you say: I have myself, my body and my mind, and people would intrude upon that, and I am lonely, and it is for the very, very best. It is a paradise. Do you know why I chose to be Byron?"

"No."

"He lived a while in an Armenian monastery. He was as sexy

a shagger as any of that lot, but for a while he chose . . . he wrote that there is a pleasure in the pathless woods, there is a rapture on the lonely shore. Do you know it?"

"There is a society where none intrudes,
By the deep sea, and music in its roar:
I love not man the less, but Nature more,
From these our interviews in which I steal
From all I may be, or have been before
To mingle with the universe and feel
What I can ne'er express, yet cannot all conceal."

She beamed. "You've read his stuff."

"I read up while looking for you. I thought it might help."

"And yet the opticians have it."

"All the way."

Her eyes returned now to me, her head turning slightly to the side. "You fear it, no? The dangers of being alone. Of having no one to help you find your path. No friend to say 'you went a bit too far', no lover to say 'you could be tender with your words', no? No boss to say 'work harder' and no shrink to say 'work less', no . . . no society, to tell you how to choose, or what to wear, no . . . no judgement, to help guide your own? You fear it?"

"Yes. I fear the fallibilities of my own reason."

"Of course – yes, the madness that comes from a thought process that's unchecked, from logic that is not logical, but isn't told so, of course, very wise."

"I impose disciplines upon myself, discourse, reason, knowledge . . . "

"To fill the place where society should be?"

"Yes. And to keep me sane. To help me see myself, as others might see."

"Through the eyes of law, reason, philosophy?"

"Yes. What do strangers see, when they see me? They almost never tell, not the truth, and so I seek to understand them, that I might understand myself."

"There's your fallacy," she interrupted, turning her body now so everything uncoiled, everything facing me. "There's your mistake. You have a gift, Hope, one of the greatest ever given. You are outside it all; you are free of it."

"Free of . . . "

"Of people. Of society. You have no need to conform, what's the point? No one will thank you for it, no one will remember you, and so you have the freedom to choose your own path, your own humanity, to be who *you* want to be, not some puppet shaped by the TV and the magazines, by the advertising men, by the latest definition of work or play, by ideas of sex, gender, by—"

"Perfection?"

"By perfection. You choose your own perfect. You choose to be who you are, and the world cannot shape you, unless you permit it. The world cannot move you, unless it is by your own welcoming in. You are free, Hope. You are more free than anyone living."

Silence a while. Then I said, "Is that why you killed them?" She leant back in her chair, disappointed, a huff of breath. "Is that why you wanted to destroy Perfection? To set people free?"

"We have sacrificed thought," she replied flatly, voice hard, eyes steady. "We live in a land of freedom, and the only freedoms we can choose are to spend, fuck and eat. The rest is taboo. Loner. Slut. Weirdo. Faggot. Whore. Bitch. Druggie. Scrounger. Ugly. Poor. Muslim. *Other.* Hate the other. Kill the other. Aspire, as us, to be together, to become better, to become . . . perfect. Perfection. A unified ideal. Perfection: flawless. Perfection: white, rich, male. Perfection: car, shoe, dress, smile. Perfection: the death of thought. I programed the 206 to kill each other. If I have the chance, I will gather together every member of the 106 I can find, and make them eat each other whole."

Her eyes, burning into mine, daring me, go on, speak.

I said, "I thought maybe . . . " And stopped. "I thought perhaps . . . " Stumbled on the words.

"Go on."

"I thought maybe there was another kind of story here. I thought perhaps you had seen things or done things or things had been done – but that's not it, is it? You destroyed Perfection because it needed to be destroyed. There's no personal tragedy or ancient oath to be fulfilled. You saw a thing that was vile, and you took up arms against it. I think I could admire that, if things had worked out different."

Silence.

The tea cooled in its cups, the wind blew off the sea.

Then, "I called Gauguin."

Silence.

"Last night," I added. "I told him everything."

Silence.

"Why?" Incomprehension – I had never seen such a thing in her before, incomprehension, incredulity, barely contained, her fingers white, the veins standing out in the soft folds of her neck, her body shaking with its own stiffness. "Why?"

"Because ... because ..." I sucked in breath. "Because while I agree with you in almost every possible respect, about everything – Perfection, loneliness, freedom, power, choice – practically everything – I think there has to be a place where it stops. I think there has to be a moment when you turn round and permit yourself to be defined by the world that surrounds you. I am free. I choose to honour the freedom of those who live around me. I choose to honour them. I think your freedom does not do that."

Silence.

Then she stood up, quickly, turned, poured the last of her tea into the sink, put the cup down on the side, turned, took a deep breath and exclaimed, in one fast burst:

> For the sword outwears its sheath,
> And the soul wears out the breast,
> And the heart must pause to breathe,
> And love itself have a rest.

She stopped, fingers shaking at her sides, hauling down air, as if those few words had sucked the oxygen from her lungs. I put my mug down, rose to my feet, my eyes never leaving hers, and replied softly, "Hey Macarena."

Silence.

She put her head on one side, looked to see if her words triggered anything more – obedience, perhaps, an openness to command – and when she saw no sign of it, she simply smiled and shook her head and said, "Shall we walk by the sea?"

I raised my eyebrows.

"It's very beautiful round here, I think. When the light is right – when you can see the stars. Sometimes it takes my breath away. Sometimes it's vile. It changes, moment to moment. Like . . ." She stopped, caught herself before her words ran away, smiled a shaking smile. "Like the present tense."

"Let's go for a walk," I said. "We've got time."

"I'll get my coat."

We walked.

She wore large pale brown boots and a thick dark green coat.

"Made in Stornoway – forget the hi-tech stuff, the Scots got all-weather gear five hundred years ago. Only other people who know what they're doing are the Scandinavians, and even they've gone in for polymer rubbish and polarised glasses these days."

I said nothing, and walked by her side, coat pulled tight around my chest, hands buried in my pockets. The sky grew heavier and flecks of freezing rain, desperate to be snow, began to fall, biting with fat white teeth where they struck exposed skin, pattering on my back. The sea below exhaled like a troll, rattling stones as the water was sucked back into the deep, breaking breath where it burst against the cliffs. I could see the beauty in it now, the dark-on-dark-on-dark without end. Far away, a tanker crawled between the island and the mainland, heading north, towards Kirkwall and Lerwick, the Arctic Circle and the oil wells, belching fire across the sea.

"Gauguin said he wanted to marry you," I said at last, raising my voice over the grasp of the wind.

She smiled. "He never asked."

"But he was going to?"

"He never asked," she repeated.

We kept walking, her cottage growing small and far away.

I said, "Are you going to run?"

"Run? From the Isle of Lewis, and John on his way? I suppose I could. There might be something to be done. But I doubt it. A refuge is a prison, by any other name."

"How long have you lived here?"

"About three years."

"How did you pay for everything? The equipment, the experts, the passports, the—"

"I stole," she explained simply. "It was necessary."

We kept walking.

Below, the sea dropped away beneath the cliff, the seagulls perched beneath our feet. The waves crashed and the clouds raced across the sky, running on to an unknown rendezvous. The long grass hissed and the short stones bumped, bumped back against the wind, a Morse code of currents disrupted and reformed, thump thump goes the sea, bump bump goes the earth, run run goes the sky and we, tiny figures in a vast and churning world, walk on.

We walked.

And for a moment, I was the sky.

I was the sea.

I was the grass, bending in the wind.

I was the cold.

I was Byron, walking by my side, and she stopped and turned to face the ocean, then raised her head to the sky, closed her eyes as rain flecked against her face, breathed the air deep through her nose, and counted backwards from ten.

I watched her count, and heard her say, with her eyes still closed, "If they find me, they will have a trial."

"They won't have much evidence – I imagine they'll kill you instead."

"Doesn't matter," she replied. "The press, the media, the internet – they'll make the noise, make the screaming, the screaming all the time, and the truth and my voice will be lost. The blaming and the noise, human things, they'll make it about human things, not the truth. How can anyone live with it? How can anyone live with so much screaming in their lives, all the time? Matheus Pereyra loved the screaming. I guess these days people love to feel themselves burn."

"Siobhan," I said, and hesitated, when she didn't move, didn't blink. "Byron," I corrected. "We can find a better way."

She opened her eyes, smiled at me, looked as if she would speak, hesitated, raised her head, looked up into the sky.

A sound, half lost behind the clouds. A whoomp whoomp whoomp against the roar of the sea.

A helicopter.

"Look," she said. "They're here."

"Byron . . ."

She raised one hand, silencing me, and smiling, turned her face to the ocean, and with a little puff of breath, ran for the sea.

She closed her eyes, just before she reached the edge of the cliff, and if she made any sound as she fell, the roaring waters ate it.

Chapter 106

A body between the rocks.

A police car, driven all the way down the isle.

An ambulance, two hours later.

I sat on the edge of the hill, and watched it all.

Gauguin came running, fell to his knees by the edge of the cliff, half wails stuttering in his throat, an old man in an inappropriately light coat, his head in his hands, weeping.

I watched, but he didn't seem to see me.

And when, in time, the policemen had forgotten and remembered my presence enough to grow confused, I picked up my bag, and walked away.

I walked north, along the edge of the sea.

I walked over grey stones and faded grasses.

I walked past the van that sold meat pies of uncertain provenance, to which the people came.

I walked with my eyes half closed against the rain.

I walked as the sun went down.

I walked when it rose again.

I walked inland until I could see the sea no more, then walked until I was at the water again, and sea was all I could behold, as far as the eye could see.

I walked.

And as I walked, I felt the desert beneath my feet, and the sun on my face even as it rained.

And I walked to the ferry, and I rode it across the water.

And I walked to the station, and I caught the train.

And I looked out of the windows of the train, and I saw the lives of others pass me by.

A man on a bicycle pedalling to work.

A pair of children in school caps, fighting over a bag of crisps.

A man fixing his truck by the side of the road.

A woman on her phone, standing in the middle of a bridge across a running brook, gesturing angry, sad, thwarted.

An old woman and her husband, their grandchild held between them, waving at the people moving by.

I bought a newspaper at some point, and read it from my seat by the window, and its headlines were . . .

full of screaming.

So I put it away.

And at Edinburgh Waverley, I bought a notebook from the stationery shop, and a bag of pens, and as the engine blared its victory over inertia and the train began to crawl south, back to England, back to the warm, back to Derby and my sister who waited, I began to write.

I wrote of the past.

Of the things that had brought me here.

Of being forgotten, and being remembered.

Of diamonds in Dubai, fires in Istanbul. Of walks through Tokyo, the mountains of Korea, the islands of the southern seas. Of America and the greyhound bus, of Filipa and Parker, Gauguin and Byron14.

I wrote, to make my memory true.

The past, living.

Now.

Here, in these words.

I wrote to make myself real.

And when at last my train reached Nottingham, I clambered from the station and ordered a cab, and when I arrived in the place where my sister lives she was sleepy, but recognised me as I came through the door, and she said, "Hope! You lied; you went away for ages."

I apologised, and showed her the presents I'd bought – films of adventure and derring-do, of good triumphant, of beauty winning out over evil, of heroes and villains, of . . .

an easier world.

And when she was asleep, I wrote some more, putting down the truth between the screaming.

Remember these, my words.

Now that I am home.

Now that I am, at last, myself.

Now that I am Hope.

Remember me.

COPYRIGHTS

"Hey Macarena", by Los Del Rio (1993); English language remix by Bayside Boys (1994). Arrangement and musical direction by Jesus Bola and Manuel Soler; remix produced and mixed by The Bayside Boys: Carlos A. de Yarza and Mike Triay based on the Fangoria River Fe-Mix; concept: Jammin Johnny Caride; English lyrics: Carlos A de Yarza. Copyright © Nova Ediciones Musicales Sa, Warner/Chappell Music Spain S.A., Universal MCA Music Publishing, Universal Music Publishing Mgb Spain S.A, BMG Music Publishing Spain S.A., Canciones Del Mundo S.A.

"Great Balls of Fire", performed by Jerry Lee Lewis (1957). Written by Jack Hammer, Otis Blackwell; produced by Jack Clement. Copyright © Mystical Light Music, Mijac Music, Chappell & Co. Inc., Donna Dijon Music Publications, Unichappell Music Inc.

"I Have a Dream" by the Rev. Martin Luther King Jr. at the "March on Washington", delivered 28 August 1963, at the Lincoln Memorial, Washington DC.

MEET THE AUTHOR

Photo © Siobhan Watts

CLAIRE NORTH is a pseudonym for Catherine Webb, a Carnegie Medal–nominated author whose first book was written when she was just fourteen years old. She went on to write several other novels in various genres, before publishing her first major work as Claire North, *The First Fifteen Lives of Harry August*, in 2014. It was a critically acclaimed success, receiving rave reviews and an Audie nomination, and was included in the *Washington Post*'s Best Books of the Year list. Her most recent novel, *Touch*, was also in the *Washington Post*'s Best Books of the Year in 2015.

INTERVIEW

What did you find the hardest part about writing this book?

Ugh, so much research. Soooo much research. Arguably the internet makes researching things easy—type a question, get an answer. But unfortunately the law still holds true which states that everything you read in the newspaper is true, except for the five percent you happen to know about. The internet is a minefield of nonsense, lies and misrepresentation and you probably spend more time cross-checking the internet than you would scanning footnotes in a book.

And the trivia! It's not just that Hope lives her entire life through the medium of knowledge, having no other tool for emotional expression—it's the fact that she lives her life through Google searches. Arguably this means that you can do a quick search and just copy out the result, but my God, it's depressing. Googling "perfect women" is one of the more demoralising things I've ever done. Learning about beauty routines and fashion and magazines and personalised detox get fit get beautiful wellness youness beauty programmes...I'd rather be reading about battles and chaos, I think, than have to spend another minute finding out what counts as inspirational in this modern age.

Also, as you so rashly asked, writing someone who can't really have human relationships does take a useful tool out of the scribbling arsenal.

"What, you're writing someone who people forget? Someone who can't have any meaningful long-term relationships?"

"Yes, I am!"

"But how can you have helpful expositionary conversations with engaging secondary characters who can express things the protagonists wouldn't through their intimate knowledge built up over long years of experience?"

"I don't know—I mean, you're just so useful for working through both narrative problems and providing a vessel for emotional expression..."

"Why yes, yes, I am..."

And so on. Other than that, however, it was dead fun to write.

As *SFX* said in their review of this novel, "globetrotting jewel thieves are never not cool." Is Hope the coolest character you're ever written?

Hum...probably not. Sorry. For a start, I'm not sure what "cool" is. At the moment, a "cool" heroic archetype seems to be super-intelligent gits who can build a rocket from their spit but don't have time for human qualities such as compassion, kindness or sympathy. Cool is a changing value, but whatever it is, I suspect that Hope ain't it. She's kinda screwed up. Joyfully so, but still, that girl's got some things she needs to get sorted in her head.

Also, if I was to pretend I knew what cool was, I'd suggest that all the blue electric sorcerers, sorta time-travelling adventurers, body-hopping ghosts, universe-saving devils, games-playing manipulators of vast world events, Victorian detective/inventors and health and safety conscious shamans I've written in the past are all probably noble competitors for being cooler, in their own different ways.

Whatever cool is...

Why "The Macarena"?

Heeeeeyyy...Macarena!!

Firstly, if you're going to realise that your brain is not your own and everything you thought you knew is potentially a lie, you may as well work this out through the medium of something comically trivial. But more importantly...

Heeeeeyyy... Macarena!!

Go on.

Sing it.

Sing it right now.

See that way you're bopping already? Even though no one actually knows the words and odds are they aren't any good even if you do know them? Does it matter? Hell no!

Heeeeyyyy... Macarena!

And that's your annoying head-buzzing song sorted for the day...mwhahahaha!

People allow the Perfection app to control every aspect of their lifestyle. What do you think the appeal is of social media platforms and apps, and how close are we to Perfection existing?

There are two parts to this.

Firstly, Perfection in the way in which it was written in the book doesn't really exist. In separate parts you could probably create it, from fitness trackers which monitor not merely how far you've walked but where you went and how you got there, through to calorie counters which demand to know what you've eaten and endless online retail suppliers who are algorithmically generating the next best buy for you, and you alone. The tools are there, the data is there and we already use it to a lesser or greater extent.

There's a tightrope to be walked between privacy and convenience. It is convenient, for example, that Google knows that I'm in London (and can tell me the weather tomorrow) and that I regularly take the train to Balham (so can warn me of disruptions to the Northern line). It is convenient that Amazon can see my past purchases and make recommendations for similar things I might enjoy (without giving me the freedom to easily browse and choose for myself) and handy that my supermarket knows to offer me discounts on yoghurt (as long as I buy a certain large quantity regularly). For all these conveniences, I sacrifice privacy—my search data, my purchasing and viewing history and my movements—and as a result who I am is sold so that the more I look at books about the history of Buddhist nuns in Japan, the more likely I am to start seeing ads for wimples every time I log into Facebook (which is also delighted to see that I was in Estonia in May, have I considered these excellent posts by promoted advertisers?)

Do you find it sinister that Outlook can read your emails?

Of course not—because there's no need for anyone to do so, right? Unless you're accused of a crime you didn't commit, maybe, in which case your internet provider will happily share the search history of bad YouTube videos you've watched (200+ hours of kittens, who'd have thunk it?) and emails in which you call your mother a smelly old woman and say how you're thinking of breaking it off with your boyfriend.

Are you concerned that, because the people who you follow on Twitter share your values, the world you see created through their stories will reflect only their values, and you will not be challenged, and the internet, as it learns who you are, will tailor the search results it gives you based on your studied character. And so your world will shrink and shrink again as the internet learns who you are, and goes out of its way to show you the most promoted, most liked, most *relevant* answers to your questions, rather than say, a balanced truth.

Do you find it sinister that your life is constantly bombarded with ads?

Maybe not.

But if those ads are continually pushing certain ideals of what your life should be—the clothes you should wear, the things you should eat, the diet fads, the fitness fads, the holidays, the body shape you should have, the partner you should find, the glasses you should buy, the kit that your life will not be complete without…

…Do you then find it sinister that no matter how inured you are to advertising, sooner or later you will get a picture of the world, tailored to you, which not only tells you how the world is but also how you should be?

This is the world we already live in.

Algorithmically counted, tracked and monitored to create a customised image of what we should buy—and we must *always* be buying—and how we should be.

Perfection as an app doesn't exist.

But the structure of the world which constantly tells us where to live, how to live, who to be, and both what and how much we should buy—that's there already. Pervasively woven into both our analogue and digital lives, pushing an idea of identity that is, yes, in its way "perfect" and is shaped by advertisers, fashion and marketeers, rather than by our individuality. Society is shaped by this; we are shaped by this.

Then there's the second part to this—which is that this is a thing we chose.

We *chose* to measure our lives by the yardstick of society, even when that society is shaped by ads, commerce and selling new things the latest way. All of us are seeking a way of valuing ourselves, a sense of self-worth. We find that value through the work we do—but we'll have bad days, and when we do we seek self-worth somewhere else. Women are pushed into going shopping as their comfort act whenever they feel down, which I find deeply offensive, really. We enjoy having a machine tell us that today, we were A* 99 Percent Top of the Class Awesome, for all those times that humans can't, and our own souls feel uneasy on the subject.

We also measure our physical self-worth by the images of male and female which are pushed to us. To be a proper woman is to be inhumanly skinny with ridiculously tiny hips and absurdly disproportioned breasts. It's to wear make-up all the time and have haircuts every five minutes. To be a proper man is to have bulky arms made from protein shakes and effortless self-confidence. It's incredibly easy to feel insecure about your physicality—I'm very much insecure in this regard, uneasy at the fact my body isn't shaped like other people's, that I still get acne aged thirty—and when there isn't a societal message of "Dude, you look like you and are perfect for who you are" but rather a constant pressure of "women look like this", of course we will find value and self-worth from buying beauty products, gym packages and the latest sports legging, as helpfully offered to us by the algorithms which have noticed that you're using your loyalty app down the gym three times a week instead of once a month and is happy to remind you at 8 a.m. that it's time to log into your squat-counter in order to fulfil your online internet-generated personalised fitness diet plan.

None of which is bad.

It is deeply, profoundly, beautifully human to try to measure our own value against the yardsticks of others.

Every time we say, "Yes, well, of course she's perfectly good at her job, but I'm just not sure she's got what it takes..." We both pass judgement on others, and on ourselves, for lo, here it is implied that we can do what she cannot, and we build ourselves up by the reduction of others.

Every time we exclaim, "She's so beautiful. How does she do that?" and try to learn her secrets—her expensive secrets—we too seek to build ourselves up by comparison with others.

And this is fine.

This is human.

To be uncertain and to struggle to find a sense of self in the minefield of society and what society values, it is wonderful and fair and good.

The terror creeps in when you ask this question: to what extent are the yardsticks I try to measure my self-worth mine, and to what extent am I measuring myself by the values that advertisers are imposing on my society?

Ask that, and then look again at the world around you and the images that are being pushed at you every day on every TV and cinema screen, internet browser, side of buses and every search result you receive, and maybe the time will come to get a little more leery about the world.

Which book do you wish you had written?

Lord of Light by Roger Zelazny. Except I don't, because if I had, Zelazny wouldn't have written it, and thus the universe would be a lesser place.

From body-jumping serial killers to time travel by reincarnation, many of your books feature exceptional people who can do exceptional things. In real life, what do you feel exceptional means?

This is an excellent question to be asking during the 2016 Olympics! You know those dudes running really fast and stuff—that doesn't look so hard, right? I mean I bet I could jump off a ten-meter platform and do like, twenty somersaults or stuff on the way down, yeah...? I can sometimes touch my toes and everything!

A sound engineer I know once helpfully summed up the Claire North books (excluding the Gameshouse) as the "people with problems trilogy." For the last few books, I've written people who are sorta incredible, in the sense that they have incredible problems. However! I've also tried to write people who are deeply human, caught up in their predicaments and trying to live in a very human way despite it. Harry August, who cannot die or escape the circle of his own life, spends most of his years just trying to keep his head down and stay warm until someone can invent central heating. Kepler, the body-hopping ghost, is almost obsessed with the trivialities of human life, trying to find some meaning and identity in all the little routines that people exist through. Hope, who no one can remember, tries to understand the world she cannot live in through knowledge, reading every book and magazines, learning about society through what it writes and says, since she can't experience it for herself.

In that sense, these characters *aren't* exceptional. They're in exceptional situations, but their response tends towards the deeply mundane. They crave tedium and normality, and their exceptional situations in a way allow them the greatest privilege of being able to see how beautiful "normal" seems.

With that in mind, I'm probably a big fan of the idea that what everyone describes as "normal" in the real world will probably have a degree of extraordinary in it, no matter what. The number of people you meet who describe themselves as "really boring"—the nurses treating children with cancer, the engineers working on satellite components, the teachers who are educating the next generations—the daily routine of everyday life tends towards an explanation of "Oh, I'm just a kung fu master and chartered accountant, nothing interesting, really."

Even where you think the job description is self-deprecatingly dull—"I stack shelves"—I have yet to meet anyone who doesn't have something within their soul that counts as incredible, made beautiful by the uniqueness of who they are and what they value. The dustbin man who helped save a stranger's life on a winter's morning because his kindness exceeded his fear; the publisher who plays bass guitar in a punk rock group for the love of the music and the joy it brings; the carpenter with a masters in neuroscience who, when not building boxes, worries about the way the brain works, because humanity is wondrous; the mum raising kids on £72 a week, who knows they will have a future which will be better than her past; the dad who teaches his kid a sense of wonder at the universe.

Don't get me wrong—people can be right pillocks, and just because someone has done something incredible doesn't mean they won't also be a twatface who can't boil an egg. And people can do incredibly cruel things, usually in the name of something they seem as good.

But if science fiction and fantasy loves writing extraordinary people, it is a two-fold love. It is firstly because all of us, no matter what, tend to dream of being a heroic prince who saves the day with our magic sword.

But it is also because sometimes being in an incredible

situation, cut off from the rest of the world by the strangeness of our predicament, can perhaps help us to get a perspective on just how wonderful the lives of others can be.

How did the character of Hope come to be? Is there anything of yourself in her?

So...are you sitting comfortably? There's a bit of a story to tell...

For years I didn't write female characters as the main lead in my books. I wrote a panoply of secondary female characters, most far more competent than the male protagonists, but I shied away from writing an actual heroine because, frankly, every time I tried I wrote gender statements rather than human beings, and because I was shit-scared of just writing a version of myself. Which is something I have no interest in doing—there are far more interesting lives and stories out there to be told than mine.

So! When I sat down to write Hope I did so with this determination that I wouldn't write me, and I wouldn't write a "strong female character"—three words which once had noble intentions, and which I fear have become warped by bullshit as the years go by.

However...

As well as writing novels, I work as a theatre technician. As I write these words, I am sat in a room where once, nearly a year ago, a cast of actors had their post-show party. The technicians weren't formally invited, not least because while the actors went away to get drunk, we were working flat out to strip the theatre back and get it ready for the next show. I was helping with this process, as I was the lighting designer on both plays.

About three hours after the cast went off to get drunk, one of the actors burst into the theatre where we were all working. "Where are the technicians?" she demanded.

We were under the stage, up ladders, on the fly floor, crossing the grid, lugging scenery in the dock, rigging on the bridges...

"Well, come at once!"

She wouldn't take no for an answer, and so we put our tools

down and trooped out of the theatre to where the cast was in full celebration. On our arrival a bell was rung, and silence descended so that the lead actress could give thanks to one and all.

First she thanked the cast for being so wonderful, the director for his brilliance...

...then she thanked the set designer, very briefly, and the stage manager, also briefly, and both received a bunch of flowers.

Then she thanked the dog, for this show had indeed had a dog in it, and the dog received a huge bunch of flowers and a bottle of champagne, and there was much applauding.

Then she turned to her peers and exclaimed, "You may not have noticed them much, but of course there were these funny little people in black running around behind the stage..."

(I glanced at the funny people in black, faces stained with sweat, muscles aching, who had built the set over many laborious, fourteen-hour-shift weeks, before turning up two hours before the cast to run their show, and leaving at the earliest one hour after the show ended, after emptying the blood buckets, putting the sweat-dripping costumes into the wash, resetting the 250 kilogram revolving set and cleaning up the torn remnants of raw shredded meat and thrown vegetable matter from the floor...)

"...these funny little people," she went on brightly, "who are just so important!"

"Not as important as us!" chimed in one actor to much merry guffawing.

"And we just wanted to thank them for whatever it is they do! The crew!"

They gave us a six pack of beer. There were eight of us working on the show, but thankfully I don't drink.

Their intentions, as is often the case, were good and noble—without fault.

Their execution, as again often happens, kinda suggested that here was a room of total numpties who hadn't fully clocked the scale of their own ignorance.

I tell you this story by way of a convoluted, nervy answer.

Is there something of me in Hope Arden, a woman who people don't notice, let alone don't remember? A woman who lives her life separated off from the general course of humanity, and in doing so finds comfort elsewhere?

Perhaps in a tiny, tiny way, there may be something of me that snuck through there…

What's next on your to-read list?

OH GOD I DON'T KNOW I just reorganised all my books because I got new bookshelves NEW BOOKSHELVES I TELL YOU it's the most exciting thing I can see all my books properly now…

…lovely lovely books…

…and while having new shelves is basically the second best thing ever after getting more books to put on them, it has thrown into sharp relief just how many awesome books there are still on my to-read list, and how many need to be re-read and just the choice…

…*THE CHOICE*…

It's all been a bit overwhelming.

Tell us a bit about what you're working on right now—what's next for Claire North?

So the next book out is called *The End of the Day* and tells the story of a man called Charlie. Charlie is a pretty ordinary dude. He's got a full-time job with a lot of travel, collects the air miles and sometimes, if he's lucky, gets to upgrade to premium economy class. He meets a lot of different people, has been to a lot of different places and always tries to sample the local cuisine.

He's also the Harbinger of Death, the one who goes before the Four Horsemen of the Apocalypse, sent sometimes as a warning, sometimes as a courtesy to those who have caught the eye of Death herself.

Generally speaking, his job is fine. As Harbinger he's busy

busy busy, but is usually on the road again before his boss turns up and spoils the party. Occasionally his job has downsides. People don't always react well to the news that Death is flying in by the 1409 from Atlanta, but Charlie is good enough at his work to know that this isn't a personal thing. In truth, he's probably more worried by the trials of trying to get visas for all the countries he visits, and the frustrations of getting a fugu chef to the Sahara desert for his occasionally whimsical boss, than he is about the end of the world. You just do the best you can with the job you've got, don't you...?

INTRODUCING

If you enjoyed
THE SUDDEN APPEARANCE OF HOPE,
look out for

THE END OF THE DAY

by Claire North

At the end of the day, Death visits everyone.
Right before that, Charlie does.

You might meet him in a hospital, in a war zone, or at the scene of a traffic accident.

Then again, you might meet him at the North Pole—he gets everywhere, our Charlie.

Would you shake him by the hand, take the gift he offers, or would you pay no attention to the words he says?

Sometimes he is sent as a courtesy, sometimes as a warning.
He never knows which.

Chapter 1

At the end, he sat in the hotel room and counted out the pills.

He did not do this with words, nor mathematics, nor did his hands move, nor could he especially blame anyone else.

It didn't occur to him that Death would come; not in the conscious way of things. Death was, Death is, Death shall be, Death is not, and all this was the truth, and he understood it perfectly, and for all those reasons, this ending was fine.

Tick tick tick.

The world turned and the clock ticked

tick tick tick

and as it ticked, he heard the countdown to Armageddon, and that was okay too. No point fighting it. The fight was what made everything worse.

He was fine.

He picked up the first pill, and felt a lot better about his career choices.

Chapter 2

At the beginning . . .

The Harbinger of Death poured another shot of whiskey into the glass, lifted the old lady's head from the dark blue wall of pillows on which she lay, put the drink to her lips and said, "Best I ever heard was in Colorado."

The woman drank, the sky rushed overhead, dragged towards another storm, another thrashing of the sea on basalt rock, another ripping-up of tree and bending of corrugated rooftop, the third of this month, unseasonal it was; unseasonal, but weren't all things these days?

She blinked when she had drunk enough, and the Harbinger returned the glass to the bedside table. "Colorado?" she wheezed at last. "I didn't think there was anything in Colorado."

"Very big. Very empty. Very beautiful."

"But they have music?"

"She was travelling."

"Get an audience?"

"No. But I stopped to listen. This was student days, there was this girl who … People won't be booking her for a high school prom any time soon, but I thought … it was something very special."

"All the old songs are dying out."

"Not all of them."

The woman smiled, the expression turning into a grimace of pain, words unspoken: just you look at me, sonny, just you think about what you said. "A girl who?"

"What? Oh, yes, I was, um … well, I hoped there'd be a relationship, and you know how these things sort of blur, and she thought it was one thing and I never really did say and then she was going out with someone else, but by then we'd booked the plane tickets and … look, I don't know if I should … I'm not sure I should talk about me."

"Why not?"

"Well, this is … " An awkward shrug, taking in the room.

"You think that because I'm dying, I should talk and you should listen?"

"If you want."

"You talk. I'm tired."

The Harbinger of Death hesitated, then tapped the edge of

the whiskey glass, held it to her lips again, let her drink, put it down. "Sorry," he murmured, when she'd swallowed, licked her lips dry. "I'm new to this."

"You're doing fine."

"Thank you. I was worried that it would be . . . What would you like to hear about? I'm interested in music. I thought maybe that when I travelled, I mean, for the work, I'd try and collect music, but not just CDs, I mean, all the music of all the places. I was told that was okay, that I was allowed to preserve . . . not preserve, that's not . . . Are you sure you wouldn't rather talk? When . . . when my boss comes . . . " Again his voice trailed off. He fumbled with the whiskey bottle, was surprised at how much had already been drunk.

"I know songs," she mused, as he struggled with the top. "But I don't think they're for you to sing. A woman once tried to preserve these things, said it would be a disaster if they died. I thought she was right. I thought that it mattered. Now . . . it's only a song. Only that."

He looked away, not exactly rebuked, but nonplussed by the moment, and her resolve. To cover the silence, he refilled her glass. The tumbler was thick, clean crystal, with a clouded band at the bottom where the base was ridged like a deadly flower – one of a set. He'd carried all four up the ancient flagstone road from Cusco, even though only two would ever be used, not knowing what he'd do with the remainder but feeling it was somehow wrong to part one from the other. He'd also carried the whiskey, stowed in the side of his pack, and the mule driver who'd showed him the way across the treeless road where sometimes still the pilgrims came dressed in Inca robes and carrying a blackened cross had said, "In these parts, we just make our own," and looked hungrily at the bottle.

The Harbinger of Death had answered, "It's for an old woman who is dying," and the mule driver had replied, ah, Old Mother Sakinai, yes yes, it was another thirty miles though, and you had to be careful not to miss the turning; it didn't look like a split in the path, but it was, no help if you get lost. The mule driver did not look at the bottle again.

They had camped in a stone hut shaped like a beehive, no mortar between the slabs of slate, a hole in the roof for the smoke from the fire to escape, and in the morning the Harbinger of Death had watched the sun burn away the mist from the valley and seen, very faintly in the dry stone-splotched grass, the tracings of shapes and forms where once patterns miles wide had been carved to honour the sun, the moon, the river and the sky. Sometimes, the man with the three surprisingly docile mules said, helicopters came up here, for medical emergencies or filming or something like that, but no cars, not in these parts. And why was the foreigner visiting Mama Sakinai, so far from the tarmacked road?

"I'm the Harbinger of Death," he replied. "I'm sort of like the one who goes before."

At this the mule driver frowned and sucked on his bottom lip and at last replied, "Surely you should be travelling on a feathered serpent, or at the very least in a four-by-four?"

"Apparently my employer likes to travel the way the living do. He says it's good manners to understand what comes before the end." Having said these words, he played them back in his mind and found they sounded a bit ridiculous. Unable to stop himself, he added, "To be honest, I've been doing the job for a week. But … that's what I was told. That's what the last Harbinger said."

The mule driver found he had very little to give in reply to this, and so on they walked, until the path divided – or rather, until a little spur of dark brown soil peeled away from the stones laid so many centuries ago by the dead peoples of the mountains, and the Harbinger of Death followed it, not quite certain if this was indeed a path used by people or merely the track of a wide and possibly hungry animal, down and down again into a valley where a tiny stream ran between white stones, and where a single house had been built the colour of the dry river bed, timber roof and straw on the porch, a black-eyed dog barking at him as he approached.

The Harbinger of Death stopped some ten feet from the

dog, crouched on his haunches, let it bark and dart around him, demanding who, what, why, another human, here, where no people came except once every two weeks Mama Sakinai's nephew, and once every three months the travelling district nurse with her heavy bags not heavy enough to cure its mistress.

"You'll want to learn how to deal with dogs," the last Harbinger had said as he shadowed her on her final trips. "Ask any postman."

Charlie had nodded earnestly, but in all honesty he wasn't bothered by dogs anyway. He liked most animals, and found that if he didn't make a fuss, most animals didn't seem to mind him. So finally, having grown bored of barking, the dog settled down, its chin on its paws, and the Harbinger waited a little while longer, and when all was settled save the whispering of the wind over the treeless ground and the trickling of the stream, he went to Mama Sakinai's door, knocked thrice and said, "Mama Sakinai? My name is Charlie, I'm the Harbinger of Death. I've brought some whiskey."

Chapter 3

In a land of forests . . .

. . . in a land of rain . . .

There had been an aptitude test.

Reading, writing, general knowledge.

- Q1 Rank these countries in order of population, from most populated to least.
- Q2 Who is the director of the United Nations?
- Q3 Name five countries that were previously British colonies in the period 1890–1945.

Q4 "Man is no more than the sum of his experience and his capacity to express these experiences to fellow man." Discuss. (500 words.)

And so on.

Charlie did better at it than he'd expected, not knowing what he should have studied in advance.

There weren't any other candidates in the room as he answered the questions. Most of the time it was a classroom for students learning to teach English as a foreign language. On one wall was a cartoon poster explaining how adverbs worked. An overhead projector had been left on, and whined irritatingly. He finished with twenty minutes to spare, and wondered if it would be rude to just walk out before the time was done.

There weren't any other candidates in the reception room for the psychiatrist either, as he sat, toes together, heels sticking out a little to the sides, waiting for his interview.

"Associations. I say a word, you say the first thing that comes to your mind."

"Really? Isn't that a little—"

"Home."

"Family?"

"Child."

"Happy."

"Sky."

"Blue."

"Sea."

"Blue."

"Travel."

"Adventure."

"Work."

"Interesting."

"Rest."

"Sleep."

"Dreams."

"Flying."

"Nightmares."
"Falling."
"Love."
"Music."
"People."
" . . . People. Sorry, that's just the first thing that . . . "
"Death."
"Life."
"Life."
"Living."

When he got the job, the first thing he did was phone his mum, who was very proud. It wasn't what she'd ever imagined him doing, of course, not really, but it came with a pension and a good starting salary, and if it made him happy . . .

The second thing he did was try and find his Unique Taxpayer Reference, as without it the office in Milton Keynes said they couldn't register him for PAYE at the appropriate tax level.

Chapter 4

And the world had turned.

. . . in a land of mountains . . .

. . . in the land of the vulture and the soaring eagle . . .

. . . the Harbinger of Death ordered another coffee from the café across the street from his Cusco hotel, and looked down at the black-eyed, black-eared dog that had followed him out of the mountains, and sighed and said, "It's not about what I want, honestly, but there's no way you're getting through customs."

The dog stared up at him, sitting stiff and patient on its haunches, no collar round its neck, ungroomed but well fed. It had followed him from Mama Sakinai's cabin without a sound, waited in the pouring rain outside the stone hut where he slept, until at last, guilt at its condition had made Charlie push open the wooden door to let it inside, where it had sat a few feet off from him without a whimper, to follow after him as he walked back down the ancient way to the city.

"Look," he had said, first in English, then in cautious Spanish, not knowing Mama Sakinai's favoured tongue. "Your mistress isn't dead." He'd stopped himself before adding "yet". Somehow the word felt unclean.

The dog had kept on following, and the next night, as they lay together by the ancient path, Charlie thought he heard a figure pass in the dark, bone feet on ancient stone, heading deeper into the mountains, following the paths carved by the dead, walked by the living. And he had shuddered, and rolled over tight, and the dog had pressed its warm body against his, and neither had slept until the moon was below the horizon.

The next day he'd come to Cusco, and wasted the best part of a day when he should have been sorting transportation trying to find a home for the persistent animal. He finally succeeded by chance, bequeathing it to a car repairman and his teenage daughter, she already dressed in mechanic's blues over her football shirt, face coated in grease, who at one look at the dog had exclaimed, "I got your ear!" and grabbed its ear, and it had pulled free, to which she had laughed, "I got your tail!" and grabbed its tail, and it had pulled that away, at which point she got its ear again, then tail, then ear, then tail, then . . .

. . . until the pair of them were rolling on the ground, panting with delight.

"Who did the animal belong to?" asked her somewhat more circumspect father, as he and the Harbinger of Death watched them play.

"An old woman in the mountains."

"Ah – she is dead?"

"Yes. She is dead. Old age took her."

"You were her family?"

"No. I was sent as a courtesy. She said that she was the last of her people, and spoke a language that no one else knows. My employer likes to show respect."

"I see!" Understanding bloomed in the mechanic's face. "You are an anthropologist!"

The Harbinger of Death nodded and smiled, briefly relieved, and filed that excuse in the back of his mind in case he needed it later.

"Your T-shirt," he said to the mechanic, as the girl laughed on the floor with her new best friend. "Local team?"

"Yes, just a small side, but we're doing all right. Runners-up in Region VIII national division last year."

"Where would I find the shirt?"

INTRODUCING

If you enjoyed
***THE SUDDEN APPEARANCE OF HOPE*,**
look out for

THE FIRST FIFTEEN LIVES OF HARRY AUGUST

by Claire North

Some stories cannot be told in just one lifetime.

Harry August is on his deathbed. Again.

No matter what he does or the decisions he makes, when death comes, Harry always returns to where he began, a child with all the knowledge of a life he has already lived a dozen times before. Nothing ever changes.

Until now.

As Harry nears the end of his eleventh life, a little girl appears at his bedside. "I nearly missed you, Doctor August," she says. "I need to send a message."

This is the story of what Harry does next, and what he did before, and how he tries to save a past he cannot change and a future he cannot allow.

Chapter 1

The second cataclysm began in my eleventh life, in 1996. I was dying my usual death, slipping away in a warm morphine haze, which she interrupted like an ice cube down my spine.

She was seven, I was seventy-eight. She had straight blonde hair worn in a long pigtail down her back, I had bright white hair, or at least the remnants of the same. I wore a hospital gown designed for sterile humility; she, bright-blue school uniform and a felt cap. She perched on the side of my bed, her feet dangling off it, and peered into my eyes. She examined the heart monitor plugged into my chest, observed where I'd disconnected the alarm, felt for my pulse, and said, "I nearly missed you, Dr August."

Her German was Berlin high, but she could have addressed me in any language of the world and still passed for respectable. She scratched at the back of her left leg, where her white knee-length socks had begun to itch from the rain outside. While scratching she said, "I need to send a message back through time. If time can be said to be important here. As you're conveniently dying, I ask you to relay it to the Clubs of your origin, as it has been passed down to me."

I tried to speak, but the words tumbled together on my tongue, and I said nothing.

"The world is ending," she said. "The message has come down from child to adult, child to adult, passed back down the generations from a thousand years forward in time. The world is ending and we cannot prevent it. So now it's up to you."

I found that Thai was the only language which wanted to pass my lips in any coherent form, and the only word which I seemed capable of forming was, why?

Not, I hasten to add, why was the world ending?

Why did it matter?

She smiled, and understood my meaning without needing it to be said. She leaned in close and murmured in my ear, "The world is ending, as it always must. But the end of the world is getting faster."

That was the beginning of the end.

Chapter 2

Let us begin at the beginning.

The Club, the cataclysm, my eleventh life and the deaths which followed – none peaceful – all are meaningless, a flash of violence that bursts and withers away, retribution without cause, until you understand where it all began.

My name is Harry August.

My father is Rory Edmond Hulne, my mother Elizabeth Leadmill, though I was not to know any of this until well until my third life.

I do not know whether to say that my father raped my mother or not. The law would have some difficulty in assessing the case; the jury could perhaps be swayed by a clever individual one way or the other. I am told that she did not scream, did not fight, didn't even say no when he came to her in the kitchen on the night of my conception, and in twenty-five inglorious minutes of passion – in that anger and jealousy and rage are passions of their kind – took revenge on his faithless wife by means of the kitchen girl. In this regard my mother was not forced, but then, as a girl of some twenty years old, living and working in my father's house, dependent for her future on his money and his family's goodwill, I would argue that she was given no chance to resist, coerced by her situation as much as by any blade held to the throat.

By the time my mother's pregnancy began to show, my father had returned to active duty in France, where he was to serve out the rest of the First World War as a largely undistinguished major in the Scots Guards. In a conflict where whole regiments could be wiped out in a single day, undistinguished was a rather enviable obtainment. It was therefore left to my paternal grandmother, Constance Hulne, to expel my mother from her home without a reference in the autumn of 1918. The man who was to become my adopted father – and yet a truer parent to me than any biological relation – took my mother to the local market on the back of his pony cart and left her there with some few shillings in her purse and a recommendation to seek the help of other distressed ladies of the county. A cousin, Alistair, who shared a mere one eighth of my mother's genetic material but whose surplus of wealth more than made up for a deficit of familial connections, gave my mother work on the floor of his Edinburgh paper mill; however, as she grew larger and increasingly unable to carry out her duties, she was quietly moved on by a junior official some three rungs away from the responsible party. In desperation, she wrote to my biological father, but the note was intercepted by my shrewd grandmother, who destroyed it before he could read my mother's plea, and so, on New Year's Eve 1918, my mother spent her last few pennies on the slow train from Edinburgh Waverley to Newcastle and, some ten miles north of Berwick-upon-Tweed, went into labour.

A trade unionist by the name of Douglas Crannich and his wife, Prudence, were the only two people present at my birth, in the ladies' washroom of the station. I am told that the stationmaster stood outside the door to prevent any innocent women coming inside, his hands clasped behind his back and his cap, crowned with snow, pulled down over his eyes in a manner I have always imagined as being rather hooded and malign. There were no doctors at the infirmary at this late hour and on this festive day, and the medic took over three hours to arrive. He came too late. The blood was already crystallising on the floor and Prudence Crannich was holding me in her arms at his arrival. My mother was dead. I have only the report of Douglas for the circumstances of her demise, but I believe she haemorrhaged out, and is buried in a grave marked "Lisa, d. 1 January 1919 – Angels Guide Her Into Light". Mrs Crannich, when the undertaker asked her what should be on the stone, realised that she had never known my mother's full name.

Some debate ensued about what to do with me, this suddenly orphaned child. I believe Mrs Crannich was sorely tempted to keep me for her own, but finances and practicality informed against this decision, as did Douglas Crannich's firm and literal interpretation of the law and rather more personal understanding of propriety. The child had a father, he exclaimed, and the father had a right to the child. This matter would have been rather moot, were it not that my mother was carrying about her person the address of my soon-to-be adopted father, Patrick August, presumably with the intention of enlisting his help in seeing my biological father, Rory Hulne. Enquiries were made as to whether this man, Patrick, could be my father, which caused quite a stir in the village as Patrick had been long married, childlessly, to my adopted mother, Harriet August, and a barren marriage in a border village, where the notion of the condom was regarded as taboo well into the 1970s, was always a topic of furious debate. The matter was so shocking that it very quickly made its way to the manor house itself, Hulne Hall, wherein resided my grandmother Constance, my two aunts Victoria and Alexandra, my cousin Clement, and Lydia, the unhappy wife of my father. I believe my grandmother immediately suspected whose child I was and the circumstances of my situation, but refused to take responsibility for me. It was Alexandra, my younger aunt, who showed a presence of mind and a compassion that the rest of her kin lacked, and seeing that suspicion would fairly quickly turn to her family once the truth of my dead mother's identity was revealed, approached Patrick and Harriet August with this offer – that if they were to adopt the child, and raise it as their own, the papers formally signed and witnessed by the Hulne family itself to quiet all rumours of an illegitimate affair, for no one carried authority like the inhabitants of Hulne Hall – then she would personally see to it that they received a monthly amount of money for their pains and to support the child, and that on his growing up she would ensure that his prospects were suitable – not excessive, mind, but neither the sorry situation of a bastard.

Patrick and Harriet debated a while, then accepted. I was raised as their child, as Harry August, and it wasn't until my second life that I began to understand where I was from, and what I was.

Chapter 3

It is said that there are three stages of life for those of us who live our lives in circles. These are rejection, exploration and acceptance.

As categories go, they are rather glib, and contain within them many different layers disguised behind these wider words. Rejection, for example, can be subdivided into various clichéd reactions, like so: suicide, despondency, madness, hysteria, isolation and self-destruction. I, like nearly all kalachakra, experienced most of these at some stage in my early lives, and their recollection lingers within me like a virus still twisted into my stomach wall.

For my part, the transition to acceptance was unremarkably difficult.

The first life I lived was undistinguished. Like all young men, I was called to fight in the Second World War, where I was a thoroughly undistinguished infantryman. Yet if my wartime contribution was meagre, my life after the conflict hardly added to a sense of significance. I returned to Hulne House after the war, to take over the position which had been held by Patrick, tending to the grounds around the estate. Like my adopted father, I had been raised to love the land, the smell of it after rain and the sudden fizzing in the air when all the seeds of the gorse spilt at once into the sky, and if I felt in any way isolated from the rest of society, it was merely as the absence of a brother might be to an only child. an idea of loneliness without the relevant experience to make it real.

When Patrick died, my position was formalised, though by then, the Hulnes' wealth was almost entirely extinguished through squander and inertia. In 1964 the property was bought by the National Trust, and I with it, and I spent the latter part of my years directing ramblers through the overgrown moors that surrounded the house, watching as the walls of the manor itself slowly sank deeper into the wet black mud.

I died in 1989 as the Berlin Wall fell, alone in a hospital in Newcastle, a divorcee with no children and a state pension who, even on his deathbed, believed himself to be the son of the long-departed Patrick and Harriet August, and who died eventually from the disease that has been the bane of my lives – multiple myelomas which spread throughout the body until the body itself simply ceases to function.

Naturally my reaction to being born again precisely where I had begun – in the women's restroom of Berwick-upon-Tweed station, on New Year's Day 1919, with all the memories of my life that had gone before, induced its own rather clichéd madness in me. As the full powers of my adult consciousness returned to my child's body, I fell first into a confusion, then an agony, then a doubt, then a despair, than a screaming, then a shrieking, and finally, aged seven years old, I was committed to St Margot's Asylum for Unfortunates, where I frankly believed myself to belong, and within six months of my confinement succeeded in throwing myself out of a window on the third floor.

Retrospectively, I realise that three floors are frequently not high enough to guarantee the quick, relatively painless death that such circumstances warrant, and I might easily have snapped every bone in my lower body and yet retained my consciousness intact. Thankfully, I landed on my head, and that was that.